David Elginbrod

George MacDonald

Table of Contents

Table of Contents

Table of Contents

David Elginbrod

George MacDonald

Kessinger Publishing reprints thousands of hard–to–find books!

Visit us at http://www.kessinger.net

David Elginbrod

And gladly wolde he lerne and gladly teche. CHAUCER. TO THE MEMORY OF LADY NOEL BYRON, THIS BOOK IS DEDICATED, WITH A LOVE STRONGER THAN DEATH.

BOOK I. TURRIEPUFFIT.

With him there was a Ploughman, was his brother. A trewé swinker, and a good was he, Living in peace and perfect charity. God loved he best with all his trewé heart, At allé timés, were it gain or smart, And then his neighébour right as himselve. CHAUCER.—Prologue to the Canterbury Tales.

CHAPTER I. THE FIR-WOOD.

Of all the flowers in the mead, Then love I roost these flowers white and rede, Such that men callen daisies in our town. I renne blithe As soon as ever the sun ginneth west, To see this flower, how it will go to rest, For fear of night, so hateth she darkness; Her cheer is plainly spread in the brightness Of the sunne, for there it will unclose.

3

David Elginbrod

CHAUCER—Prologue to the Legend of Good Women.

"Meg! whaur are ye gaein' that get, like a wull shuttle? Come in to the beuk."

Meg's mother stood at the cottage door, with arms akimbo and clouded brow, calling through the boles of a little forest of fir–trees after her daughter. One would naturally presume that the phrase she employed, comparing her daughter's motions to those of a shuttle that had "gane wull," or lost its way, implied that she was watching her as she threaded her way through the trees. But although she could not see her, the fir–wood was certainly the likeliest place for her daughter to be in; and the figure she employed was not in the least inapplicable to Meg's usual mode of wandering through the trees, that operation being commonly performed in the most erratic manner possible. It was the ordinary occupation of the first hour of almost every day of Margaret's life. As soon as she woke in the morning, the fir–wood drew her towards it, and she rose and went. Through its crowd of slender pillars, she strayed hither and thither, in an aimless manner, as if resignedly haunting the neighbourhood of something she had lost, or, hopefully, that of a treasure she expected one day to find.

It did not seem that she had heard her mother's call, for no response followed; and Janet Elginbrod returned into the cottage, where David of the same surname, who was already seated at the white deal table with "the beuk," or large family bible before him, straightway commenced reading a chapter in the usual routine from the Old Testament, the New being reserved for the evening devotions. The chapter was the fortieth of the prophet Isaiah; and as the voice of the reader re–uttered the words of old inspiration, one might have thought that it was the voice of the ancient prophet himself, pouring forth the expression of his own faith in his expostulations with the unbelief of his brethren. The chapter finished—it is none of the shortest, and Meg had not yet returned—the two knelt, and David prayed thus:

"O Thou who holdest the waters in the hollow of ae han', and carriest the lambs o' thy own making in thy bosom with the other han', it would be altogether unworthy o' thee, and o' thy Maijesty o' love, to require o' us that which thou knowest we cannot bring unto thee, until thou enrich us with that same. Therefore, like thine own bairns, we boo doon afore thee, an' pray that thou wouldst tak' thy wull o' us, thy holy an' perfect an' blessed wull o' us; for, O God, we are a' thine ain. An' for oor lassie, wha's oot amo' thy trees, an' wha' we dinna think forgets her Maker, though she may whiles forget her prayers, Lord, keep her a bonnie lassie in thy sicht, as white and clean in thy een as she is fair an' halesome in oors; an' oh! we thank thee, Father in heaven, for giein' her to us. An' noo, for a' oor wrang–duins an' ill–min'ins, for a' oor sins and trespasses o' mony sorts, dinna forget them. O God, till thou pits them a' richt, an' syne exerceese thy michty power e'en ower thine ain sel, an' clean forget them a'thegither; cast them ahint thy back, whaur e'en thine ain een shall ne'er see them again, that we may walk bold an' upricht afore thee for evermore, an' see the face o' Him wha was as muckle God in doin' thy biddin', as gin he had been ordering' a' thing Himsel. For his sake, Ahmen."

I hope my readers will not suppose that I give this as a specimen of Scotch prayers. I know better than that. David was an unusual man, and his prayers were unusual prayers. The present was a little more so in its style, from the fact that one of the subjects of it was absent, a circumstance that rarely happened. But the degree of difference was too small to be detected by any but those who were quite accustomed to his forms of thought and expression. How much of it Janet understood or sympathized with, it is difficult to say; for anything that could be called a thought rarely crossed the threshold of her utterance. On this occasion, the moment the prayer was ended, she rose from her knees, smoothed down her check apron, and went to the door; where, shading her eyes from the sun with her hand, she peered from under its penthouse into the fir–wood, and said in a voice softened apparently by the exercise in which she had taken a silent share,

"Whaur can the lassie be?"

And where was the lassie? In the fir–wood, to be sure, with the thousand shadows, and the sunlight through it all; for at this moment the light fell upon her far in its depths, and revealed her hastening towards the cottage in as straight a line as the trees would permit, now blotted out by a crossing shadow, and anon radiant in the sunlight, appearing and vanishing as she threaded the upright warp of the fir–wood. It was morning all around her; and one might see that it was morning within her too, as, emerging at last in the small open space around the cottage, Margaret—I cannot call her Meg, although her mother does—her father always called her "Maggy, my doo," Anglicé, dove—Margaret approached her mother with a bright healthful face, and the least possible expression of uneasiness on her fair forehead. She carried a book in her hand.

"What gars ye gang stravaguin' that get, Meg, whan ye ken weel eneuch ye sud a' been in to worship lang syne? An sae we maun hae worship our lanes for want o' you, ye hizzy!"

"I didna ken it was sae late, mither," replied Margaret, in a submissive tone, musical in spite of the rugged dialect into which the sounds were fashioned.

"Nae dout! Ye had yer brakfast, an' ye warna that hungry for the word. But here comes yer father, and ye'll no mend for his flytin', I'se promise."

"Hoots! lat the bairn alane, Janet, my woman. The word'll be mair to her afore lang."

"I wat she has a word o' her nain there. What beuk hae ye gotten there, Meg? Whaur got ye't?"

Had it not been for the handsome binding of the book in her daughter's hand, it would neither have caught the eye, nor roused the suspicions of Janet. David glanced at the book in his turn, and a faint expression of surprise, embodied chiefly in the opening of his eyelids a little wider than usual, crossed his face. But he only said with a smile:

"I didna ken that the tree o' knowledge, wi' sic fair fruit, grew in our wud, Maggy, my doo."

"Whaur gat ye the beuk?" reiterated Janet.

Margaret's face was by this time the colour of the crimson boards of the volume in her hand, but she replied at once:

"I got it frae Maister Sutherlan', I reckon."

Janet's first response was an inverted whistle; her next, another question:

"Maister Sutherlan'! wha's that o't?"

"Hoot, lass!" interposed David, "ye ken weel aneuch. It's the new tutor lad, up at the hoose; a fine, douce, honest chield, an' weel-faured, forby. Lat's see the bit beuky, lassie."

Margaret handed it to her father.

"Col—e—ridge's Poems," read David, with some difficulty.

"Tak' it hame direckly," said Janet.

"Na, na," said David; "a' the apples o' the tree o' knowledge are no stappit wi sut an stew; an' gin this ane be, she'll sune ken by the taste o't what's comin'. It's no muckle o' an ill beuk 'at ye'll read, Maggy, my doo."

"Guid preserve's, man! I'm no sayin' it's an ill beuk. But it's no richt to mak appintments wi' stranger lads i' the wud sae ear' i' the mornin'. Is't noo, yersel, Meg?"

"Mither! mither!" said Margaret, and her eyes flashed through the watery veil that tried to hide them, "hoo can ye? Ye ken yersel I had nae appintment wi' him or ony man."

"Weel, weel!" said Janet; and, apparently either satisfied with or overcome by the emotion she had excited, she turned and went in to pursue her usual house—avocations; while David, handing the book to his daughter, went away down the path that led from the cottage door, in the direction of a road to be seen at a little distance through the trees, which surrounded the cottage on all sides. Margaret followed her mother into the cottage, and was soon as busy as she with her share of the duties of the household; but it was a good many minutes before the cloud caused by her mother's hasty words entirely disappeared from a forehead which might with especial justice be called the sky of her face.

Meantime David emerged upon the more open road, and bent his course, still through fir—trees, towards a house for whose sake alone the road seemed to have been constructed.

CHAPTER II. DAVID ELGINBROD AND THE NEW TUTOR.

```
      Concord between our wit and will
Where highest notes to godliness are raised,
And lowest sink not down to jot of ill.

What Languetus taught Sir Philip Sidney.

THE ARCADIA—Third Eclogue.
```

David Elginbrod

The House of Turriepuffit stood about a furlong from David's cottage. It was the abode of the Laird, or landed proprietor, in whose employment David filled several offices ordinarily distinct. The estate was a small one, and almost entirely farmed by the owner himself; who, with David's help, managed to turn it to good account. Upon week-days, he appeared on horseback in a costume more fitted for following the plough; but he did not work with his own hands; and on Sundays was at once recognizable as a country gentleman.

David was his bailiff or grieve, to overlook the labourers on the estate; his steward to pay them, and keep the farm accounts; his head gardener—for little labour was expended in that direction, there being only one lady, the mistress of the house, and she no patroness of useless flowers: David was in fact the laird's general adviser and executor.

The laird's family, besides the lady already mentioned, consisted only of two boys, of the ages of eleven and fourteen, whom he wished to enjoy the same privileges he had himself possessed, and to whom, therefore, he was giving a classical and mathematical education, in view of the University, by means of private tutors; the last of whom—for the changes were not few, seeing the salary was of the smallest—was Hugh Sutherland, the young man concerning whom David Elginbrod has already given his opinion. But notwithstanding the freedom he always granted his daughter, and his good opinion of Hugh as well, David could not help feeling a little anxious, in his walk along the road towards the house, as to what the apparent acquaintance between her and the new tutor might evolve; but he got rid of all the difficulty, as far as he was concerned, by saying at last:

"What richt hae I to interfere? even supposin' I wanted to interfere. But I can lippen weel to my bonny doo; an' for the rest, she maun tak' her chance like the lave o's. An' wha' kens but it micht jist be stan'in' afore Him, i' the very get that He meant to gang. The Lord forgie me for speakin' o' chance, as gin I believed in ony sic havers. There's no fear o' the lassie. Gude mornin' t'ye, Maister Sutherlan'. That's a braw beuk o' ballants ye gae the len' o' to my Maggy, this mornin', sir."

Sutherland was just entering a side-door of the house when David accosted him. He was not old enough to keep from blushing at David's words; but, having a good conscience, he was ready with a good answer.

David Elginbrod

"It's a good book, Mr. Elginbrod. It will do her no harm, though it be ballads."

"I'm in no dreed o' that, sir. Bairns maun hae ballants. An', to tell the truth, sir, I'm no muckle mair nor a bairn in that respeck mysel'. In fac, this verra mornin', at the beuk, I jist thocht I was readin' a gran' godly ballant, an' it soundet nane the waur for the notion o't."

"You should have been a poet yourself, Mr. Elginbrod."

"Na, na; I ken naething aboot yer poetry. I hae read auld John Milton ower an' ower, though I dinna believe the half o't; but, oh! weel I like some o' the bonny bitties at the en' o't."

"Il Penseroso, for instance?"

"Is that hoo ye ca't? I ken't weel by the sicht, but hardly by the soun'. I aye missed the name o't, an' took to the thing itsel'. Eh, man!—I beg yer pardon, sir—but its wonnerfu' bonny!"

"I'll come in some evening, and we'll have a chat about it," replied Sutherland. "I must go to my work now."

"We'll a' be verra happy to see you, sir. Good mornin', sir."

"Good morning."

David went to the garden, where there was not much to be done in the way of education at this season of the year; and Sutherland to the school–room, where he was busy, all the rest of the morning and part of the afternoon, with Caesar and Virgil, Algebra and Euclid; food upon which intellectual babes are reared to the stature of college youths.

Sutherland was himself only a youth; for he had gone early to college, and had not yet quite completed the curriculum. He was now filling up with teaching, the recess between his third and his fourth winter at one of the Aberdeen Universities. He was the son of an officer, belonging to the younger branch of a family of some historic distinction and considerable wealth. This officer, though not far removed from the estate and title as well, had nothing to live upon but his half—pay; for, to the disgust of his family, he had married a Welsh girl of ancient descent, in whose line the poverty must have been at least coeval with the history, to judge from the perfection of its development in the case of her father; and his relations made this the excuse for quarrelling with him; so relieving themselves from any obligations they might have been supposed to lie under, of rendering him assistance of some sort or other. This, however, rather suited the temperament of Major Robert Sutherland, who was prouder in his poverty than they in their riches. So he disowned them for ever, and accommodated himself, with the best grace in the world, to his yet more straitened circumstances. He resolved, however, cost what it might in pinching and squeezing, to send his son to college before turning him out to shift for himself. In this Mrs. Sutherland was ready to support him to the utmost; and so they had managed to keep their boy at college for three sessions; after the last of which, instead of returning home, as he had done on previous occasions, he had looked about him for a temporary engagement as tutor, and soon found the situation he now occupied in the family of William Glasford, Esq., of Turriepuffit, where he intended to remain no longer than the commencement of the session, which would be his fourth and last. To what he should afterwards devote himself he had by no means made up his mind, except that it must of necessity be hard work of some kind or other. So he had at least the virtue of desiring to be independent. His other goods and bads must come out in the course of the story. His pupils were rather stupid and rather good—natured; so that their temperament operated to confirm their intellectual condition, and to render the labour of teaching them considerably irksome. But he did his work tolerably well, and was not so much interested in the result as to be pained at the moderate degree of his success. At the time of which I write, however, the probability as to his success was scarcely ascertained, for he had been only a fortnight at the task.

It was the middle of the month of April, in a rather backward season. The weather had been stormy, with frequent showers of sleet and snow. Old winter was doing his best to hold young Spring back by the skirts of her garment, and very few of the wild flowers had yet ventured to look out of their warm beds in the mould. Sutherland, therefore, had made but few discoveries in the neighbourhood. Not that the weather would have kept him to the house, had he had any particular desire to go out; but, like many other students, he had no predilection for objectless exertion, and preferred the choice of his own weather indoors, namely, from books and his own imaginings, to an encounter with the keen blasts of the North, charged as they often were with sharp bullets of hail. When the sun did shine out between the showers, his cold glitter upon the pools of rain or melted snow, and on the wet evergreens and gravel walks, always drove him back from the window with a shiver. The house, which was of very moderate size and comfort, stood in the midst of plantations, principally of Scotch firs and larches, some of the former old and of great growth, so that they had arrived at the true condition of the tree, which seems to require old age for the perfection of its idea. There was very little to be seen from the windows except this wood, which, somewhat gloomy at almost any season, was at the present cheerless enough; and Sutherland found it very dreary indeed, as exchanged for the wide view from his own home on the side of an open hill in the Highlands.

In the midst of circumstances so uninteresting, it is not to be wondered at, that the glimpse of a pretty maiden should, one morning, occasion him some welcome excitement. Passing downstairs to breakfast, he observed the drawing–room door ajar, and looked in to see what sort of a room it was; for so seldom was it used that he had never yet entered it. There stood a young girl, peeping, with mingled curiosity and reverence, into a small gilt–leaved volume, which she had lifted from the table by which she stood. He watched her for a moment with some interest; when she, seeming to become mesmerically aware that she was not alone, looked up, blushed deeply, put down the book in confusion, and proceeded to dust some of the furniture. It was his first sight of Margaret. Some of the neighbours were expected to dinner, and her aid was in requisition to get the grand room of the house prepared for the occasion. He supposed her to belong to the household, till, one day, feeling compelled to go out for a stroll, he caught sight of her so occupied at the door of her father's cottage, that he perceived at once that must be her home: she was, in fact, seated upon a stool, paring potatoes. She saw him as well, and, apparently ashamed at the recollection of having been discovered idling in the drawing–room, rose and went in. He had met David once or twice about the house, and, attracted by his appearance, had had some conversation with him; but he did not know where he lived, nor that he was the father of the girl whom he had seen.

CHAPTER III. THE DAISY AND THE PRIMROSE.

```
Dear secret Greenness, nursed below
  Tempests and winds and winter nights!
Vex not that but one sees thee grow;
  That One made all these lesser lights.

HENRY VAUGHAN.
```

David Elginbrod

It was, of course, quite by accident that Sutherland had met Margaret in the fir-wood. The wind had changed during the night, and swept all the clouds from the face of the sky; and when he looked out in the morning, he saw the fir-tops waving in the sunlight, and heard the sound of a south-west wind sweeping through them with the tune of running waters in its course. It is a well-practised ear that can tell whether the sound it hears be that of gently falling waters, or of wind flowing through the branches of firs. Sutherland's heart, reviving like a dormouse in its hole, began to be joyful at the sight of the genial motions of Nature, telling of warmth and blessedness at hand. Some goal of life, vague but sure, seemed to glimmer through the appearances around him, and to stimulate him to action. Be dressed in haste, and went out to meet the Spring. He wandered into the heart of the wood. The sunlight shone like a sunset upon the red trunks and boughs of the old fir-trees, but like the first sunrise of the world upon the new green fringes that edged the young shoots of the larches. High up, hung the memorials of past summers in the rich brown tassels of the clustering cones; while the ground under foot was dappled with sunshine on the fallen fir-needles, and the great fallen cones which had opened to scatter their autumnal seed, and now lay waiting for decay. Overhead, the tops whence they had fallen, waved in the wind, as in welcome of the Spring, with that peculiar swinging motion which made the poets of the sixteenth century call them "sailing pines." The wind blew cool, but not cold; and was filled with a delicious odour from the earth, which Sutherland took as a sign that she was coming alive at last. And the Spring he went out to meet, met him. For, first, at the foot of a tree, he spied a tiny primrose, peeping out of its rough, careful leaves; and he wondered how, by any metamorphosis, such leaves could pass into such a flower. Had he seen the mother of the next spring-messenger he was about to meet, the same thought would have returned in another form. For, next, as he passed on with the primrose in his hand, thinking it was almost cruel to pluck it, the Spring met him, as if in her own shape, in the person of Margaret, whom he spied a little way off, leaning against the stem of a Scotch fir, and looking up to its top swaying overhead in the first billows of the outburst ocean of life. He went up to her with some shyness; for the presence of even a child-maiden was enough to make Sutherland shy—partly from the fear of startling her shyness, as one feels when drawing near a couching fawn. But she, when she heard his footsteps, dropped her eyes slowly from the tree-top, and, as if she were in her own sanctuary, waited his approach. He said nothing at first, but offered her, instead of speech, the primrose he had just plucked, which she received with a smile of the eyes only, and the sweetest "thank you, sir," he had ever heard. But while she held the primrose in her hand, her eyes wandered to the book which, according to his custom, Sutherland had caught up as he left the house. It was the only well-bound book in his possession; and the eyes of Margaret, not yet tutored by experience, naturally expected an entrancing page within such beautiful boards; for the gayest bindings she had seen, were those of a few old annuals up at the house—and were they not full of the most lovely tales and pictures? In this case, however, her expectation was not vain; for the volume was, as I have already disclosed, Coleridge's Poems.

Seeing her eyes fixed upon the book—"Would you like to read it?" said he.

"If you please, sir," answered Margaret, her eyes brightening with the expectation of deliglit.

"Are you fond of poetry?"

Her face fell. The only poetry she knew was the Scotch Psalms and Paraphrases, and such last-century verses as formed the chief part of the selections in her school-books; for this was a very retired parish, and the newer books had not yet reached its school. She had hoped chiefly for tales.

"I dinna ken much about poetry," she answered, trying to speak English. "There's an old book o't on my father's shelf; but the letters o't are auld-fashioned, an' I dinna care aboot it."

"But this is quite easy to read, and very beautiful," said Hugh.

The girl's eyes glistened for a moment, and this was all her reply.

"Would you like to read it?" resumed Hugh, seeing no further answer was on the road.

She held out her hand towards the volume. When he, in his turn, held the volume towards her hand, she almost snatched it from him, and ran towards the house, without a word of thanks or leave-taking—whether from eagerness, or doubt of the propriety of accepting the offer, Hugh could not conjecture. He stood for some moments looking after her, and then retraced his steps towards the house.

It would have been something, in the monotony of one of the most trying of positions, to meet one who snatched at the offered means of spiritual growth, even if that disciple had not been a lovely girl, with the woman waking in her eyes. He commenced the duties of the day with considerably more of energy than he had yet brought to bear on his uninteresting pupils; and this energy did not flag before its effects upon the boys began to react in fresh impulse upon itself.

CHAPTER IV. THE COTTAGE.

```
O little Bethlem! poor in walls,
  But rich in furniture.

JOHN MASON'S Spiritual Songs.
```

There was one great alleviation to the various discomforts of Sutherland's tutor–life. It was, that, except during school–hours, he was expected to take no charge whatever of his pupils. They ran wild all other times; which was far better, in every way, both for them and for him. Consequently, he was entirely his own master beyond the fixed margin of scholastic duties; and he soon found that his absence, even from the table, was a matter of no interest to the family. To be sure, it involved his own fasting till the next meal–time came round—for the lady was quite a household martinet; but that was his own concern.

That very evening, he made his way to David's cottage, about the country supper–time, when he thought he should most likely find him at home. It was a clear, still, moonlit night, with just an air of frost. There was light enough for him to see that the cottage was very neat and tidy, looking, in the midst of its little forest, more like an English than a Scotch habitation. He had had the advantage of a few months' residence in a leafy region on the other side of the Tweed, and so was able to make the comparison. But what a different leafage that was from this! That was soft, floating, billowy; this hard, stiff, and straight–lined, interfering so little with the skeleton form, that it needed not to be put off in the wintry season of death, to make the trees in harmony with the landscape. A light was burning in the cottage, visible through the inner curtain of muslin, and the outer one of frost. As he approached the door, he heard the sound of a voice; and from the even pitch of the tone, he concluded at once that its owner was reading aloud. The measured cadence soon convinced him that it was verse that was being read; and the voice was evidently that of David, and not of Margaret. He knocked at the door. The voice ceased, chairs were pushed back, and a heavy step approached. David opened the door himself.

David Elginbrod

"Eh! Maister Sutherlan'," said he, "I thocht it micht aiblins be yersel. Ye're welcome, sir. Come butt the hoose. Our place is but sma', but ye'll no min' sitttin' doon wi' our ain sels. Janet, ooman, this is Maister Sutherlan'. Maggy, my doo, he's a frien' o' yours, o' a day auld, already. Ye're kindly welcome, Maister Sutherlan'. I'm sure it's verra kin' o' you to come an' see the like o' huz."

As Hugh entered, he saw his own bright volume lying on the table, evidently that from which David had just been reading.

Margaret had already placed for him a cushioned arm–chair, the only comfortable one in the house; and presently, the table being drawn back, they were all seated round the peat–fire on the hearth, the best sort for keeping feet warm at least. On the crook, or hooked iron–chain suspended within the chimney, hung a three–footed pot, in which potatoes were boiling away merrily for supper. By the side of the wide chimney, or more properly lum, hung an iron lamp, of an old classical form common to the country, from the beak of which projected, almost horizontally, the lighted wick—the pith of a rush. The light perched upon it was small but clear, and by it David had been reading. Margaret sat right under it, upon a creepie, or small three–legged wooden stool. Sitting thus, with the light falling on her from above, Hugh could not help thinking she looked very pretty. Almost the only object in the distance from which the feeble light was reflected, was the patch–work counterpane of a little bed filling a recess in the wall, fitted with doors which stood open. It was probably Margaret's refuge for the night.

"Well," said the tutor, after they had been seated a few minutes, and had had some talk about the weather—surely no despicable subject after such a morning—the first of Spring—"well, how do you like the English poet, Mr. Elginbrod?"

"Spier that at me this day week, Maister Sutherlan', an' I'll aiblins answer ye; but no the nicht, no the nicht."

"What for no?" said Hugh, taking up the dialect.

"For ae thing, we're nae clean through wi' the auld sailor's story yet; an' gin I hae learnt ae thing aboon anither, its no to pass jeedgment upo' halves. I hae seen ill weather half the simmer, an' a thrang corn–yard after an' a', an' that o' the best. No that I'm ill pleased wi' the bonny ballant aither."

David Elginbrod

"Weel, will ye jist lat me read the lave o't till ye?"

"Wi' muckle pleesur, sir, an' mony thanks."

He showed Hugh how far they had got in the reading of the "Ancient Mariner"; whereupon he took up the tale, and carried it on to the end. He had some facility in reading with expression, and his few affectations—for it must be confessed he was not free of such faults—were not of a nature to strike uncritical hearers. When he had finished, he looked up, and his eye chancing to light upon Margaret first, he saw that her cheek was quite pale, and her eyes overspread with the film, not of coming tears, but of emotion notwithstanding.

"Well," said Hugh, again, willing to break the silence, and turning towards David, "what do you think of it now you have heard it all?"

Whether Janet interrupted her husband or not, I cannot tell; but she certainly spoke first:

"Tshâvah!"—equivalent to pshaw—"it's a' lees. What for are ye knittin' yer broos ower a leein' ballant—a' havers as weel as lees?"

"I'm no jist prepared to say sae muckle, Janet," replied David; "there's mony a thing 'at's lees, as ye ca't, 'at's no lees a' through. Ye see, Maister Sutherlan', I'm no gleg at the uptak, an' it jist taks me twise as lang as ither fowk to see to the ootside o' a thing. Whiles a sentence 'ill leuk to me clean nonsense a'thegither; an' maybe a haill ook efter, it'll come upo' me a' at ance; an' fegs! it's the best thing in a' the beuk."

Margaret's eyes were fixed on her father with a look which I can only call faithfulness, as if every word he spoke was truth, whether she could understand it or not.

"But perhaps we may look too far for meanings sometimes," suggested Sutherland.

"Maybe, maybe; but when a body has a suspeecion o' a trowth, he sud never lat sit till he's gotten eyther hit, or an assurance that there's nothing there. But there's jist ae thing, in the poem 'at I can pit my finger upo', an' say 'at it's no richt clear to me whether it's a' straucht–foret or no?"

David Elginbrod

"What's that, Mr. Elginbrod?"

"It's jist this—what for a' thae sailor–men fell doon deid, an' the chield 'at shot the bonnie burdie, an' did a' the mischeef, cam' to little hurt i' the 'en comparateevely."

"Well," said Hugh, "I confess I'm not prepared to answer the question. If you get any light on the subject"—

"Ow, I daursay I may. A heap o' things comes to me as I'm takin' a daunder by mysel' i' the gloamin'. I'll no say a thing's wrang till I hae tried it ower an' ower; for maybe I haena a richt grip o' the thing ava."

"What can ye expec, Dawvid, o' a leevin' corp, an' a' that?—ay, twa hunner corps—fower times fifty's twa hunner—an' angels turnin' sailors, an' sangs gaein fleein' aboot like laverocks, and tummelin' doon again, tired like?—Gude preserve's a'!"

"Janet, do ye believe 'at ever a serpent spak?"

"Hoot! Dawvid, the deil was in him, ye ken."

"The deil a word o' that's i' the word itsel, though," rejoined David with a smile.

"Dawvid," said Janet, solemnly, and with some consternation, "ye're no gaein' to tell me, sittin' there, at ye dinna believe ilka word 'at's prentit atween the twa brods o' the Bible? What will Maister Sutherlan' think o' ye?"

"Janet, my bonnie lass—" and here David's eyes beamed upon his wife—"I believe as mony o' them as ye do, an' maybe a wheen mair, my dawtie. Keep yer min' easy aboot that. But ye jist see 'at fowk warna a'thegither saitisfeed aboot a sairpent speikin', an' sae they leukit aboot and aboot till at last they fand the deil in him. Gude kens whether he was there or no. Noo, ye see hoo, gin we was to leuk weel aboot thae corps, an' thae angels, an' a' that queer stuff—but oh! it's bonny stuff tee!—we micht fa' in wi' something we didna awthegither expec, though we was leukin' for't a' the time. Sae I maun jist think aboot it, Mr. Sutherlan'; an' I wad fain read it ower again, afore I lippen on giein' my opingan on the maitter. Ye cud lave the bit beukie, sir? We'se tak' guid care o't."

"Ye're verra welcome to that or ony ither beuk I hae," replied Hugh, who began to feel already as if he were in the hands of a superior.

"Mony thanks; but ye see, sir, we hae eneuch to chow upo' for an aucht days or so."

By this time the potatoes wore considered to be cooked, and were accordingly lifted off the fire. The water was then poured away, the lid put aside, and the pot hung once more upon the crook, hooked a few rings further up in the chimney, in order that the potatoes might be thoroughly dry before they were served. Margaret was now very busy spreading the cloth and laying spoon and plates on the table. Hugh rose to go.

"Will ye no bide," said Janet, in a most hospitable tone, "an' tak' a het pitawta wi' us?"

"I'm afraid of being troublesome," answered he.

"Nae fear o' that, gin ye can jist pit up wi' oor hamely meat."

"Mak nae apologies, Janet, my woman," said David. "A het pitawta's aye guid fare, for gentle or semple. Sit ye doun again, Maister Sutherlan'. Maggy, my doo, whaur's the milk?"

"I thocht Hawkie wad hae a drappy o' het milk by this time," said Margaret, "and sae I jist loot it be to the last; but I'll hae't drawn in twa minutes." And away she went with a jug, commonly called a decanter in that part of the north, in her hand.

"That's hardly fair play to Hawkie," said David to Janet with a smile.

"Hoot! Dawvid, ye see we haena a stranger ilka nicht."

"But really," said Hugh, "I hope this is the last time you will consider me a stranger, for I shall be here a great many times—that is, if you don't get tired of me."

"Gie us the chance at least, Maister Sutherlan'. It's no sma' preevilege to fowk like us to hae a frien' wi' sae muckle buik learnin' as ye hae, sir."

"I am afraid it looks more to you than it really is."

David Elginbrod

"Weel, ye see, we maun a' leuk at the starns frae the hicht o' oor ain een. An' ye seem nigher to them by a lang growth than the lave o's. My man, ye ought to be thankfu'."

With the true humility that comes of worshipping the Truth, David had not the smallest idea that he was immeasurably nearer to the stars than Hugh Sutherland.

Maggie having returned with her jug full of frothy milk, and the potatoes being already heaped up in a wooden bowl or bossie in the middle of the table, sending the smoke of their hospitality to the rafters, Janet placed a smaller wooden bowl, called a caup, filled with deliciously yellow milk of Hawkie's latest gathering, for each individual of the company, with an attendant horn–spoon by its side. They all drew their chairs to the table, and David, asking no blessing, as it was called, but nevertheless giving thanks for the blessing already bestowed, namely, the perfect gift of food, invited Hugh to make a supper. Each, in primitive but not ungraceful fashion, took a potatoe from the dish with the fingers, and ate it, "bite and sup," with the help of the horn–spoon for the milk. Hugh thought he had never supped more pleasantly, and could not help observing how far real good–breeding is independent of the forms and refinements of what has assumed to itself the name of society.

Soon after supper was over, it was time for him to go; so, after kind hand–shakings and good nights, David accompanied him to the road, where he left him to find his way home by the star–light. As he went, he could not help pondering a little over the fact that a labouring man had discovered a difficulty, perhaps a fault, in one of his favourite poems, which had never suggested itself to him. He soon satisfied himself, however, by coming to the conclusion that the poet had not cared about the matter at all, having had no further intention in the poem than Hugh himself had found in it, namely, witchery and loveliness. But it seemed to the young student a wonderful fact, that the intercourse which was denied him in the laird's family, simply from their utter incapacity of yielding it, should be afforded him in the family of a man who had followed the plough himself once, perhaps did so still, having risen only to be the overseer and superior assistant of labourers. He certainly felt, on his way home, much more reconciled to the prospect of his sojourn at Turriepuffit, than he would have thought it possible he ever should.

David lingered a few moments, looking up at the stars, before he re–entered his cottage. When he rejoined his wife and child, he found the Bible already open on the table for their evening devotions. I will close this chapter, as I began the first, with something like his prayer. David's prayers were characteristic of the whole man; but they also partook, in far more than ordinary, of the mood of the moment. His last occupation had been star–gazing:

"O thou, wha keeps the stars alicht, an' our souls burnin' wi' a licht aboon that o' the stars, grant that they may shine afore thee as the stars for ever and ever. An' as thou hauds the stars burnin' a' the nicht, when there's no man to see, so haud thou the licht burnin' in our souls, when we see neither thee nor it, but are buried in the grave o' sleep an' forgetfu'ness. Be thou by us, even as a mother sits by the bedside o' her ailin' wean a' the lang nicht; only be thou nearer to us, even in our verra souls, an' watch ower the warl' o' dreams that they mak' for themsels. Grant that more an' more thochts o' thy thinkin' may come into our herts day by day, till there shall be at last an open road atween thee an' us, an' thy angels may ascend and descend upon us, so that we may be in thy heaven, e'en while we are upo' thy earth: Amen."

CHAPTER V. THE STUDENTS.

In wood and stone, not the softest, but hardest, be always aptest for portraiture, both fairest for pleasure, and most durable for profit. Hard wits be hard to receive, but sure to keep; painful without weariness, heedful without wavering, constant without new–fangleness; bearing heavy things, though not lightly, yet willingly; entering hard things, though not easily, yet deeply; and so come to that perfectness of learning in the end, that quick wits seem in hope but do not in deed, or else very seldom ever attain unto.—ROGER ASCHAM.—The Schoolmaster.

Two or three very simple causes united to prevent Hugh from repeating his visit to David so soon as he would otherwise have done. One was, that, the fine weather continuing, he was seized with the desire of exploring the neighbourhood. The spring, which sets some wild animals to the construction of new dwellings, incites man to the enlarging of his, making, as it were, by discovery, that which lies around him his own. So he spent the greater parts of several evenings in wandering about the neighbourhood; till at length the moonlight failed him. Another cause was, that, in the act of searching for some books for his boys, in an old garret of the house, which was at once lumber room and library, he came upon some stray volumes of the Waverley novels, with which he was as yet only partially acquainted. These absorbed many of his spare hours. But one evening, while reading the Heart of Midlothian, the thought struck him—what a character David would have been for Sir Walter. Whether he was right or not is a question; but the notion brought David so vividly before him, that it roused the desire to see him. He closed the book at once, and went to the cottage.

"We're no lik'ly to ca' ye onything but a stranger yet, Maister Sutherlan'," said David, as he entered.

"I've been busy since I saw you," was all the excuse Hugh offered.

"Weel, ye'r welcome noo; and ye've jist come in time after a', for it's no that mony hours sin' I fand it oot awthegither to my ain settisfaction."

"Found out what?" said Hugh; for he had forgotten all about the perplexity in which he had left David, and which had been occupying his thoughts ever since their last interview.

"Aboot the cross–bow an' the birdie, ye ken," answered David, in a tone of surprise.

"Yes, to be sure. How stupid of me!" said Hugh.

"Weel, ye see, the meanin' o' the haill ballant is no that ill to win at, seein' the poet himsel' tells us that. It's jist no to be proud or ill–natured to oor neebours, the beasts and birds, for God made ane an' a' o's. But there's harder things in't nor that, and yon's the hardest. But ye see it was jist an unlucky thochtless deed o' the puir auld sailor's, an' I'm thinkin' he was sair reprocht in's hert the minit he did it. His mates was fell angry at him, no for killin' the puir innocent craytur, but for fear o' ill luck in consequence. Syne when nane followed, they turned richt roun', an' took awa' the character o' the puir beastie efter 'twas deid. They appruved o' the verra thing 'at he was nae doot sorry for.—But onything to haud aff o' themsels! Nae suner cam the calm, than roun' they gaed again like the weathercock, an' naething wad content them bit hingin' the deid craytur about the auld man's craig, an' abusin' him forby. Sae ye see hoo they war a wheen selfish crayturs, an' a hantle waur nor the man 'at was led astray into an ill deed. But still he maun rue't. Sae Death got them, an' a kin' o' leevin' Death, a she Death as 'twar, an' in some respecks may be waur than the ither, got grips o' him, puir auld body! It's a' fair and richt to the backbane o' the ballant, Maister Sutherlan', an' that I'se uphaud."

David Elginbrod

Hugh could not help feeling considerably astonished to hear this criticism from the lips of one whom he considered an uneducated man. For he did not know that there are many other educations besides a college one, some of them tending far more than that to develope the common-sense, or faculty of judging of things by their nature. Life intelligently met and honestly passed, is the best education of all; except that higher one to which it is intended to lead, and to which it had led David. Both these educations, however, were nearly unknown to the student of books. But he was still more astonished to hear from the lips of Margaret, who was sitting by:

"That's it, father; that's it! I was jist ettlin' efter that same thing mysel, or something like it, but ye put it in the richt words exackly."

The sound of her voice drew Hugh's eyes upon her: he was astonished at the alteration in her countenance. While she spoke it was absolutely beautiful. As soon as she ceased speaking, it settled back into its former shadowless calm. Her father gave her one approving glance and nod, expressive of no surprise at her having approached the same discovery as himself, but testifying pleasure at the coincidence of their opinions. Nothing was left for Hugh but to express his satisfaction with the interpretation of the difficulty, and to add, that the poem would henceforth possess fresh interest for him.

After this, his visits became more frequent; and at length David made a request which led to their greater frequency still. It was to this effect:

"Do ye think, Mr. Sutherlan', I could do onything at my age at the mathematics? I unnerstan' weel eneuch hoo to measur' lan', an' that kin' o' thing. I jist follow the rule. But the rule itsel's a puzzler to me. I dinna understan' it by half. Noo it seems to me that the best o' a rule is, no to mak ye able to do a thing, but to lead ye to what maks the rule richt—to the prenciple o' the thing. It's no 'at I'm misbelievin' the rule, but I want to see the richts o't."

"I've no doubt you could learn fast enough," replied Hugh. "I shall be very happy to help you with it."

"Na, na; I'm no gaein to trouble you. Ye hae eneuch to do in that way. But if ye could jist spare me ane or twa o' yer beuks whiles—ony o' them 'at ye think proper, I sud be muckle obleeged te ye."

David Elginbrod

Hugh promised and fulfilled; but the result was, that, before long, both the father and the daughter were seated at the kitchen–table, every evening, busy with Euclid and Algebra; and that, on most evenings, Hugh was present as their instructor. It was quite a new pleasure to him. Few delights surpass those of imparting knowledge to the eager recipient. What made Hugh's tutor–life irksome, was partly the excess of his desire to communicate, over the desire of his pupils to partake. But here there was no labour. All the questions were asked by the scholars. A single lesson had not passed, however, before David put questions which Hugh was unable to answer, and concerning which he was obliged to confess his ignorance. Instead of being discouraged, as eager questioners are very ready to be when they receive no answer, David merely said, "Weel, weel, we maun bide a wee," and went on with what he was able to master. Meantime Margaret, though forced to lag a good way behind her father, and to apply much more frequently to their tutor for help, yet secured all she got; and that is great praise for any student. She was not by any means remarkably quick, but she knew when she did not understand; and that is a sure and indispensable step towards understanding. It is indeed a rarer gift than the power of understanding itself.

The gratitude of David was too deep to be expressed in any formal thanks. It broke out at times in two or three simple words when the conversation presented an opportunity, or in the midst of their work, as by its own self–birth, ungenerated by association.

During the lesson, which often lasted more than two hours, Janet would be busy about the room, and in and out of it, with a manifest care to suppress all unnecessary bustle. As soon as Hugh made his appearance, she would put off the stout shoes—man's shoes, as we should consider them—which she always wore at other times, and put on a pair of bauchles; that is, an old pair of her Sunday shoes, put down at heel, and so converted into slippers, with which she could move about less noisily. At times her remarks would seem to imply that she considered it rather absurd in her husband to trouble himself with book–learning; but evidently on the ground that he knew everything already that was worthy of the honour of his acquaintance; whereas, with regard to Margaret, her heart was as evidently full of pride at the idea of the education her daughter was getting from the laird's own tutor.

Now and then she would stand still for a moment, and gaze at them, with her bright black eyes, from under the white frills of her mutch, her bare brown arms akimbo, and a look of pride upon her equally brown honest face.

David Elginbrod

Her dress consisted of a wrapper, or short loose jacket, of printed calico, and a blue winsey petticoat, which she had a habit of tucking between her knees, to keep it out of harm's way, as often as she stooped to any wet work, or, more especially, when doing anything by the fire. Margaret's dress was, in ordinary, like her mother's, with the exception of the cap; but, every evening, when their master was expected, she put off her wrapper, and substituted a gown of the same material, a cotton print; and so, with her plentiful dark hair gathered neatly under a net of brown silk, the usual head–dress of girls in her position, both in and out of doors, sat down dressed for the sacrament of wisdom. David made no other preparation than the usual evening washing of his large well–wrought hands, and bathing of his head, covered with thick dark hair, plentifully lined with grey, in a tub of cold water; from which his face, which was "cremsin dyed ingrayne" by the weather, emerged glowing. He sat down at the table in his usual rough blue coat and plain brass buttons; with his breeches of broad–striped corduroy, his blue–ribbed stockings, and leather gaiters, or cuiticans, disposed under the table, and his shoes, with five rows of broad–headed nails in the soles, projecting from beneath it on the other side; for he was a tall man—six feet still, although five–and–fifty, and considerably bent in the shoulders with hard work. Sutherland's style was that of a gentleman who must wear out his dress–coat.

Such was the group which, three or four evenings in the week, might be seen in David Elginbrod's cottage, seated around the white deal table, with their books and slates upon it, and searching, by the light of a tallow candle, substituted as more convenient, for the ordinary lamp, after the mysteries of the universe.

The influences of reviving nature and of genial companionship operated very favourably upon Hugh's spirits, and consequently upon his whole powers. For some time he had, as I have already hinted, succeeded in interesting his boy–pupils in their studies; and now the progress they made began to be appreciable to themselves as well as to their tutor. This of course made them more happy and more diligent. There were no attempts now to work upon their parents for a holiday; no real or pretended head or tooth–aches, whose disability was urged against the greater torture of ill–conceded mental labour. They began in fact to understand; and, in proportion to the beauty and value of the thing understood, to understand is to enjoy. Therefore the laird and his lady could not help seeing that the boys were doing well, far better in fact than they had ever done before; and consequently began not only to prize Hugh's services, but to think more highly of his office than had been their wont. The laird would now and then invite him to join him in a tumbler of toddy after dinner, or in a ride round the farm after school hours. But it must be confessed that these approaches to friendliness were rather irksome to Hugh; for whatever the laird might have been as a collegian, he was certainly now nothing more than a farmer. Where David Elginbrod would have described many a "bonny sicht," the laird only saw the probable results of harvest, in the shape of figures in his banking book. On one occasion, Hugh roused his indignation by venturing to express his admiration of the delightful mingling of colours in a field where a good many scarlet poppies grew among the green blades of the corn, indicating, to the agricultural eye, the poverty of the soil where they were found. This fault in the soil, the laird, like a child, resented upon the poppies themselves.

"Nasty, ugly weyds! We'll hae ye admirin' the smut neist," said he, contemptuously; "'cause the bairns can bleck ane anither's faces wi't."

"But surely," said Hugh, "putting other considerations aside, you must allow that the colour, especially when mingled with that of the corn, is beautiful."

"Deil hae't! It's jist there 'at I canna bide the sicht o't. Beauty ye may ca' 't! I see nane o't. I'd as sune hae a reid—heedit bairn, as see thae reid—coatit rascals i' my corn. I houp ye're no gaen to cram stuff like that into the heeds o' the twa laddies. Faith! we'll hae them sawin' thae ill—faured weyds amang the wheyt neist. Poapies ca' ye them? Weel I wat they're the Popp's ain bairns, an' the scarlet wumman to the mither o' them. Ha! ha! ha!"

Having manifested both wit and Protestantism in the closing sentence of his objurgation, the laird relapsed into good humour and stupidity. Hugh would gladly have spent such hours in David's cottage instead; but he was hardly prepared to refuse his company to Mr. Glasford.

CHAPTER VI. THE LAIRD'S LADY.

```
Ye archewyves, standith at defence,
Sin ye been strong, as is a great camayle;
Ne suffer not that men you don offence.
And slender wives, fell as in battaile,
Beth eager, as is a tiger, yond in Inde;
Aye clappith as a mill, I you counsaile.
```

David Elginbrod

CHAUCER.—The Clerk's Tale.

The length and frequency of Hugh's absences, careless as she was of his presence, had already attracted the attention of Mrs. Glasford; and very little trouble had to be expended on the discovery of his haunt. For the servants knew well enough where he went, and of course had come to their own conclusions as to the object of his visits. So the lady chose to think it her duty to expostulate with Hugh on the subject. Accordingly, one morning after breakfast, the laird having gone to mount his horse, and the boys to have a few minutes' play before lessons, Mrs. Glasford, who had kept her seat at the head of the table, waiting for the opportunity, turned towards Hugh who sat reading the week's news, folded her hands on the tablecloth, drew herself up yet a little more stiffly in her chair, and thus addressed him:

"It's my duty, Mr. Sutherland, seein' ye have no mother to look after ye—"

Hugh expected something matronly about his linen or his socks, and put down his newspaper with a smile; but, to his astonishment, she went on—

—"To remonstrate wi' ye, on the impropriety of going so often to David Elginbrod's. They're not company for a young gentleman like you, Mr. Sutherland."

"They're good enough company for a poor tutor, Mrs. Glasford," replied Hugh, foolishly enough.

"Not at all, not at all," insisted the lady. "With your connexions—"

"Good gracious! who ever said anything about my connexions? I never pretended to have any." Hugh was getting angry already.

Mrs. Glasford nodded her head significantly, as much as to say, "I know more about you than you imagine," and then went on:

"Your mother will never forgive me if you get into a scrape with that smooth–faced hussy; and if her father, honest man hasn't eyes enough in his head, other people have—ay, an' tongues too, Mr. Sutherland."

David Elginbrod

Hugh was on the point of forgetting his manners, and consigning all the above mentioned organs to perdition; but he managed to restrain his wrath, and merely said that Margaret was one of the best girls he had ever known, and that there was no possible danger of any kind of scrape with her. This mode of argument, however, was not calculated to satisfy Mrs. Glasford. She returned to the charge.

"She's a sly puss, with her shy airs and graces. Her father's jist daft wi' conceit o' her, an' it's no to be surprised if she cast a glamour ower you. Mr. Sutherland, ye're but young yet."

Hugh's pride presented any alliance with a lassie who had herded the laird's cows barefoot, and even now tended their own cow, as an all but inconceivable absurdity; and he resented, more than he could have thought possible, the entertainment of such a degrading idea in the mind of Mrs. Glasford. Indignation prevented him from replying; while she went on, getting more vernacular as she proceeded.

"It's no for lack o' company 'at yer driven to seek theirs, I'm sure. There's twa as fine lads an' gude scholars as ye'll fin' in the haill kintra-side, no to mention the laird and mysel'."

But Hugh could bear it no longer; nor would he condescend to excuse or explain his conduct.

"Madam, I beg you will not mention this subject again."

"But I will mention 't, Mr. Sutherlan'; an' if ye'll no listen to rizzon, I'll go to them 'at maun do't."

"I am accountable to you, madam, for my conduct in your house, and for the way in which I discharge my duty to your children—no further."

"Do ye ca' that dischairgin' yer duty to my bairns, to set them the example o' hingin' at a quean's âpron-strings, and fillin' her lug wi' idle havers? Ca' ye that dischairgin' yer duty? My certie! a bonny dischairgin'!"

"I never see the girl but in her father and mother's presence."

"Weel, weel, Mr. Sutherlan'," said Mrs. Glasford, in a final tone, and trying to smother the anger which she felt she had allowed to carry her further than was decorous, "we'll say nae mair aboot it at present; but I maun jist speak to the laird himsel', an' see what he says till 't."

And, with this threat, she walked out of the room in what she considered a dignified manner.

Hugh was exceedingly annoyed at this treatment, and thought, at first, of throwing up his situation at once; but he got calmer by degrees, and saw that it would be to his own loss, and perhaps to the injury of his friends at the cottage. So he took his revenge by recalling the excited face of Mrs. Glasford, whose nose had got as red with passion as the protuberance of a turkey—cock when gobbling out its unutterable feelings of disdain. He dwelt upon this soothing contemplation till a fit of laughter relieved him, and he was able to go and join his pupils as if nothing had happened.

Meanwhile the lady sent for David, who was at work in the garden, into no less an audience—chamber than the drawing—room, the revered abode of all the tutelar deities of the house; chief amongst which were the portraits of the laird and herself: he, plethoric and wrapped in voluminous folds of neckerchief—she long—necked, and lean, and bare—shouldered. The original of the latter work of art seated herself in the most important chair in the room; and when David, after carefully wiping the shoes he had already wiped three times on his way up, entered with a respectful but no wise obsequious bow, she ordered him, with the air of an empress, to shut the door. When he had obeyed, she ordered him, in a similar tone, to be seated; for she sought to mingle condescension and conciliation with severity.

"David," she then began, "I am informed that ye keep open door to our Mr. Sutherland, and that he spends most forenichts in your company."

"Weel, mem, it's verra true," was all David's answer. He sat in an expectant attitude.

"Dawvid, I wonner at ye!" returned Mrs. Glasford, forgetting her dignity, and becoming confidentially remonstrative. "Here's a young gentleman o' talans, wi' ilka prospeck o' waggin' his heid in a poopit some day; an' ye aid an' abet him in idlin' awa' his time at your chimla—lug, duin' waur nor naething ava! I'm surprised at ye, Dawvid. I thocht ye had mair sense."

David looked out of his clear, blue, untroubled eyes, upon the ruffled countenance of his mistress, with an almost paternal smile.

"Weel, mem, I maun say I dinna jist think the young man's in the warst o' company, when he's at our ingle–neuk. An' for idlin' o' his time awa', it's weel waurd for himsel', forby for us, gin holy words binna lees."

"What do ye mean, Dawvid?" said the lady rather sharply, for she loved no riddles.

"I mean this, mem: that the young man is jist actin' the pairt o' Peter an' John at the bonny gate o' the temple, whan they said: 'Such as I have, gie I thee;' an' gin' it be more blessed to gie than to receive, as Sant Paul says 'at the Maister himsel' said, the young man 'ill no be the waur aff in's ain learnin', that he impairts o't to them that hunger for't."

"Ye mean by this, Dawvid, gin ye could express yersel' to the pint, 'at the young man, wha's ower weel paid to instruck my bairns, neglecks them, an' lays himsel' oot upo' ither fowk's weans, wha hae no richt to ettle aboon the station in which their Maker pat them."

This was uttered with quite a religious fervour of expostulation; for the lady's natural indignation at the thought of Meg Elginbrod having lessons from her boys' tutor, was cowed beneath the quiet steady gaze of the noble–minded peasant father.

"He lays himsel' oot mair upo' the ither fowk themsels' than upo' their weans, mem; though, nae doubt, my Maggy comes in for a gude share. But for negleckin' o' his duty to you, mem, I'm sure I kenna hoo that can be; for it was only yestreen 'at the laird himsel' said to me, 'at hoo the bairns had never gotten on naething like it wi' ony ither body."

"The laird's ower ready wi's clavers," quoth the laird's wife, nettled to find herself in the wrong, and forgetful of her own and her lord's dignity at once. "But," she pursued, "all I can say is, that I consider it verra improper o' you, wi' a young lass–bairn, to encourage the nichtly veesits o' a young gentleman, wha's sae far aboon her in station, an' dootless will some day be farther yet."

"Mem!" said David, with dignity, "I'm willin' no to understan' what ye mean. My Maggy's no ane 'at needs luikin' efter; an' a body had need to be carefu' an' no interfere wi' the Lord's herdin', for he ca's himsel' the Shepherd o' the sheep, an' wee! as I loe her I maun lea' him to lead them wha follow him wherever he goeth. She'll be no ill guidit, and I'm no gaeing to kep her at ilka turn."

"Weel, weel! that's yer ain affair, Dawvid, my man," rejoined Mrs. Glasford, with rising voice and complexion. "A' 'at I hae to add is jist this: 'at as lang as my tutor veesits her"—

"He veesits her no more than me, mem," interposed David; but his mistress went on with dignified disregard of the interruption—

"Veesits her, I canna, for the sake o' my own bairns, an' the morals o' my hoosehold, employ her aboot the hoose, as I was in the way o' doin' afore. Good mornin', Dawvid. I'll speak to the laird himsel', sin' ye'll no heed me."

"It's more to my lassie, mem, excuse me, to learn to unnerstan' the works o' her Maker, than it is to be employed in your household. Mony thanks, mem, for what ye hev' done in that way afore; an' good mornin' to ye, mem. I'm sorry we should hae ony misunderstandin', but I canna help it for my pairt."

With these words David withdrew, rather anxious about the consequences to Hugh of this unpleasant interference on the part of Mrs. Glasford. That lady's wrath kept warm without much nursing, till the laird came home; when she turned the whole of her battery upon him, and kept up a steady fire until he yielded, and promised to turn his upon David. But he had more common−sense than his wife in some things, and saw at once how ridiculous it would be to treat the affair as of importance. So, the next time he saw David, he addressed him half jocularly:

"Weel, Dawvid, you an' the mistress hae been haein' a bit o' a dispute thegither, eh?"

"Weel, sir, we warna a'thegither o' ae min'," said David, with a smile.

"Weel, weel, we maun humour her, ye ken, or it may be the waur for us a', ye ken." And the laird nodded with humorous significance.

David Elginbrod

"I'm sure I sud be glaid, sir; but this is no sma' maitter to me an' my Maggie, for we're jist gettin' food for the verra sowl, sir, frae him an' his beuks."

"Cudna ye be content wi the beuks wi'out the man, Dawvid?"

"We sud mak' but sma' progress, sir, that get."

The laird began to be a little nettled himself at David's stiffness about such a small matter, and held his peace. David resumed:

"Besides, sir, that's a maitter for the young man to sattle, an' no for me. It wad ill become me, efter a' he's dune for us, to steek the door in's face. Na, na; as lang's I hae a door to haud open, it's no to be steekit to him."

"Efter a', the door's mine, Dawvid," said the laird.

"As lang's I'm in your hoose an' in your service, sir, the door's mine," retorted David, quietly.

The laird turned and rode away without another word. What passed between him and his wife never transpired. Nothing more was said to Hugh as long as he remained at Turriepuffit. But Margaret was never sent for to the House after this, upon any occasion whatever. The laird gave her a nod as often as he saw her; but the lady, if they chanced to meet, took no notice of her. Margaret, on her part, stood or passed with her eyes on the ground, and no further change of countenance than a slight flush of discomfort.

The lessons went on as usual, and happy hours they were for all those concerned. Often, in after years, and in far different circumstances, the thoughts of Hugh reverted, with a painful yearning, to the dim—lighted cottage, with its clay floor and its deal table; to the earnest pair seated with him at the labours that unfold the motions of the stars; and even to the homely, thickset, but active form of Janet, and that peculiar smile of hers with which, after an apparently snappish speech, spoken with her back to the person addressed, she would turn round her honest face half—apologetically, and shine full upon some one or other of the three, whom she honoured with her whole heart and soul, and who, she feared, might be offended at what she called her "hame—ower fashion of speaking." Indeed it was wonderful what a share the motherhood of this woman, incapable as she was of entering into the intellectual occupations of the others, had in producing that sense of home–blessedness, which inwrapt Hugh also in the folds of its hospitality, and drew him towards its heart. Certain it is that not one of the three would have worked so well without the sense of the presence of Janet, here and there about the room, or in the immediate neighbourhood of it—love watching over labour. Once a week, always on Saturday nights, Hugh stayed to supper with them: and on these occasions, Janet contrived to have something better than ordinary in honour of their guest. Still it was of the homeliest country fare, such as Hugh could partake of without the least fear that his presence occasioned any inconvenience to his entertainers. Nor was Hugh the only giver of spiritual food. Putting aside the rich gifts of human affection and sympathy, which grew more and more pleasant—I can hardly use a stronger word yet—to Hugh every day, many things were spoken by the simple wisdom of David, which would have enlightened Hugh far more than they did, had he been sufficiently advanced to receive them. But their very simplicity was often far beyond the grasp of his thoughts; for the higher we rise, the simpler we become; and David was one of those of whom is the kingdom of Heaven. There is a childhood into which we have to grow, just as there is a childhood which we must leave behind; a childlikeness which is the highest gain of humanity, and a childishness from which but few of those who are counted the wisest among men, have freed themselves in their imagined progress towards the reality of things.

CHAPTER VII. THE SECRET OF THE WOOD.

```
The unthrift sunne shot vitall gold,
  A thousand pieces;
And heaven its azure did unfold,
  Chequered with snowy fleeces.
      The air was all in spice,
        And every bush
      A garland wore: Thus fed my Eyes,
        But all the Eare lay hush.

HENRY VAUGHAN.
```

It was not in mathematics alone that Hugh Sutherland was serviceable to Margaret Elginbrod. That branch of study had been chosen for her father, not for her; but her desire to learn had led her to lay hold upon any mental provision with which the table happened to be spread; and the more eagerly that her father was a guest at the same feast. Before long, Hugh bethought him that it might possibly be of service to her, in the course of her reading, if he taught her English a little more thoroughly than she had probably picked it up at the parish school, to which she had been in the habit of going till within a very short period of her acquaintance with the tutor.—The English reader must not suppose the term parish school to mean what the same term would mean if used in England. Boys and girls of very different ranks go to the Scotch parish schools, and the fees are so small as to place their education within the reach of almost the humblest means.—To his proposal to this effect Margaret responded thankfully; and it gave Hugh an opportunity of directing her attention to many of the more delicate distinctions in literature, for the appreciation of which she manifested at once a remarkable aptitude.

Coleridge's poems had been read long ago; some of them, indeed, almost committed to memory in the process of repeated perusal. No doubt a good many of them must have been as yet too abstruse for her; not in the least, however, from inaptitude in her for such subjects as they treated of, but simply because neither the terms nor the modes of thought could possibly have been as yet presented to her in so many different positions as to enable her to comprehend their scope. Hugh lent her Sir Walter's poems next, but those she read at an eye–glance. She returned the volume in a week, saying merely, they were "verra bonnie stories." He saw at once that, to have done them justice with the girl, he ought to have lent them first. But that could not be helped now; and what should come next? Upon this he took thought. His library was too small to cause much perplexity of choice, but for a few days he continued undecided.

Meantime the interest he felt in his girl–pupil deepened greatly. She became a kind of study to him. The expression of her countenance was far inferior to her intelligence and power of thought. It was still to excess—almost dull in ordinary; not from any fault in the mould of the features, except, perhaps, in the upper lip, which seemed deficient in drawing, if I may be allowed the expression; but from the absence of that light which indicates the presence of active thought and feeling within. In this respect her face was like the earthen pitcher of Gideon: it concealed the light. She seemed to have, to a peculiar degree, the faculty of retiring inside. But now and then, while he was talking to her, and doubtful, from the lack of expression, whether she was even listening with attention to what he was saying, her face would lighten up with a radiant smile of intelligence; not, however, throwing the light upon him, and in a moment reverting to its former condition of still twilight. Her person seemed not to be as yet thoroughly possessed or informed by her spirit. It sat apart within her; and there was no ready transit from her heart to her face. This lack of presence in the face is quite common in pretty school–girls and rustic beauties; but it was manifest to an unusual degree in the case of Margaret. Yet most of the forms and lines in her face were lovely; and when the light did shine through them for a passing moment, her countenance seemed absolutely beautiful. Hence it grew into an almost haunting temptation with Hugh, to try to produce this expression, to unveil the coy light of the beautiful soul. Often he tried; often he failed, and sometimes he succeeded. Had they been alone it might have become dangerous—I mean for Hugh; I cannot tell for Margaret.

When they first met, she had just completed her seventeenth year; but, at an age when a town–bred girl is all but a woman, her manners were those of a child. This childishness, however, soon began to disappear, and the peculiar stillness of her face, of which I have already said so much, made her seem older than she was.

It was now early summer, and all the other trees in the wood—of which there were not many besides the firs of various kinds—had put on their fresh leaves, heaped up in green clouds between the wanderer and the heavens. In the morning the sun shone so clear upon these, that, to the eyes of one standing beneath, the light seemed to dissolve them away to the most ethereal forms of glorified foliage. They were to be claimed for earth only by the shadows that the one cast upon the other, visible from below through the transparent leaf. This effect is very lovely in the young season of the year, when the leaves are more delicate and less crowded; and especially in the early morning, when the light is most clear and penetrating. By the way, I do not think any man is compelled to bid good–bye to his childhood: every man may feel young in the morning, middle–aged in the afternoon, and old at night. A day corresponds to a life, and the portions of the one are "pictures in little" of the seasons of the other. Thus far man may rule even time, and gather up, in a perfect being, youth and age at once.

One morning, about six o'clock, Hugh, who had never been so early in the wood since the day he had met Margaret there, was standing under a beech–tree, looking up through its multitudinous leaves, illuminated, as I have attempted to describe, with the sidelong rays of the brilliant sun. He was feeling young, and observing the forms of nature with a keen discriminating gaze: that was all. Fond of writing verses, he was studying nature, not as a true lover, but as one who would hereafter turn his discoveries to use. For it must be confessed that nature affected him chiefly through the medium of poetry; and that he was

34

far more ambitious of writing beautiful things about nature than of discovering and understanding, for their own sakes, any of her hidden yet patent meanings. Changing his attitude after a few moments, he descried, under another beech–tree, not far from him, Margaret, standing and looking up fixedly as he had been doing a moment before. He approached her, and she, hearing his advance, looked, and saw him, but did not move. He thought he saw the glimmer of tears in her eyes. She was the first to speak, however.

"What were you seeing up there, Mr. Sutherland?"

"I was only looking at the bright leaves, and the shadows upon them."

"Ah! I thocht maybe ye had seen something."

"What do you mean, Margaret?"

"I dinna richtly ken mysel'. But I aye expeck to see something in this fir–wood. I'm here maist mornin's as the day dawns, but I'm later the day."

"We were later than usual at our work last night. But what kind of thing do you expect to see?"

"That's jist what I dinna ken. An' I canna min' whan I began to come here first, luikin' for something. I've tried mony a time, but I canna min', do what I like."

Margaret had never said so much about herself before. I can account for it only on the supposition that Hugh had gradually assumed in her mind a kind of pastoral superiority, which, at a favourable moment, inclined her to impart her thoughts to him. But he did not know what to say to this strange fact in her history. She went on, however, as if, having broken the ice, she must sweep it away as well.

"The only thing 'at helps me to account for't, is a picter in our auld Bible, o' an angel sittin' aneth a tree, and haudin' up his han' as gin he were speakin' to a woman 'at's stan'in' afore him. Ilka time 'at I come across that picter, I feel direckly as gin I war my lane in this fir–wood here; sae I suppose that when I was a wee bairn, I maun hae come oot some mornin' my lane, wi' the expectation o' seein' an angel here waitin' for me, to speak to me like the ane i' the Bible. But never an angel hae I seen. Yet I aye hae an expectation like o' seein' something, I kenna what; for the whole place aye seems fu' o' a presence, an' it's a hantle mair to me nor the kirk an' the sermon forby; an' for the singin', the soun' i' the fir–taps is far mair solemn and sweet at the same time, an' muckle mair like praisin' o' God than a' the psalms thegither. But I aye think 'at gin I could hear Milton playin' on's organ, it would be mair like that soun' o' mony waters, than onything else 'at I can think o'."

Hugh stood and gazed at her in astonishment. To his more refined ear, there was a strange incongruity between the somewhat coarse dialect in which she spoke, and the things she uttered in it. Not that he was capable of entering into her feelings, much less of explaining them to her. He felt that there was something remarkable in them, but attributed both the thoughts themselves and their influence on him, to an uncommon and weird imagination. As of such origin, however, he was just the one to value them highly.

"Those are very strange ideas," he said.

"But what can there be about the wood? The very primroses—ye brocht me the first this spring yersel', Mr. Sutherland—come out at the fit o' the trees, and look at me as if they said, 'We ken—we ken a' aboot it;' but never a word mair they say. There's something by ordinar' in't."

"Do you like no other place besides?" said Hugh, for the sake of saying something.

"Ou ay, mony ane; but nane like this."

"What kind of place do you like best?"

"I like places wi' green grass an' flowers amo't."

"You like flowers then?"

"Like them! whiles they gar me greet an' whiles they gar me lauch; but there's mair i' them than that, an' i' the wood too. I canna richtly say my prayers in ony ither place."

The Scotch dialect, especially to one brought up in the Highlands, was a considerable antidote to the effect of the beauty of what Margaret said.

David Elginbrod

Suddenly it struck Hugh, that if Margaret were such an admirer of nature, possibly she might enjoy Wordsworth. He himself was as yet incapable of doing him anything like justice; and, with the arrogance of youth, did not hesitate to smile at the Excursion, picking out an awkward line here and there as especial food for laughter even. But many of his smaller pieces he enjoyed very heartily, although not thoroughly—the element of Christian Pantheism, which is their soul, being beyond his comprehension, almost perception, as yet. So he made up his mind, after a moment's reflection, that this should be the next author he recommended to his pupil. He hoped likewise so to end an interview, in which he might otherwise be compelled to confess that he could render Margaret no assistance in her search after the something in the wood; and he was unwilling to say he could not understand her; for a power of universal sympathy was one of those mental gifts which Hugh was most anxious to believe he possessed.

"I will bring you another book to-night," said he "which I think you will like, and which may perhaps help you to find out what is in the wood."

He said this smiling, half in playful jest, and without any idea of the degree of likelihood that there was notwithstanding in what he said. For, certainly, Wordsworth, the high-priest of nature, though perhaps hardly the apostle of nature, was more likely than any other writer to contain something of the secret after which Margaret was searching. Whether she can find it there, may seem questionable.

"Thank you, sir," said Margaret, gratefully; but her whole countenance looked troubled, as she turned towards her home. Doubtless, however, the trouble vanished before she reached it, for hers was not a nature to cherish disquietude. Hugh too went home, rather thoughtful.

In the evening, he took a volume of Wordsworth, and repaired, according to his wont, to David's cottage. It was Saturday, and he would stay to supper. After they had given the usual time to their studies, Hugh, setting Margaret some exercises in English to write on her slate, while he helped David with some of the elements of Trigonometry, and again going over those elements with her, while David worked out a calculation—after these were over, and while Janet was putting the supper on the table, Hugh pulled out his volume, and, without any preface, read them the Leech-Gatherer. All listened very intently, Janet included, who delayed several of the operations, that she might lose no word of the verses; David nodding assent every now and then, and ejaculating ay! ay! or eh, man! or producing that strange muffled sound at once common and peculiar to Scotchmen, which cannot be expressed in letters by a nearer approach than hm—hm, uttered, if that can be called uttering, with closed lips and open nasal passage; and Margaret sitting motionless on her creepie, with upturned pale face, and eyes fixed upon the lips of the reader. When he had ceased, all were silent for a moment, when Janet made some little sign of anxiety about her supper, which certainly had suffered by the delay. Then, without a word, David turned towards the table and gave thanks. Turning again to Hugh, who had risen to place his chair, he said,

"That maun be the wark o' a great poet, Mr. Sutherlan'."

"It's Wordsworth's," said Hugh.

"Ay! ay! That's Wordsworth's! Ay! Weel, I hae jist heard him made mention o', but I never read word o' his afore. An' he never repentit o' that same resolution, I'se warrant, 'at he eynds aff wi'. Hoo does it gang, Mr. Sutherlan'?"

Sutherland read:—

```
    "'God,' said I, 'be my help and stay secure!
     I'll think of the leech-gatherer on the lonely moor;'"
```

and added, "It is said Wordsworth never knew what it was to be in want of money all his life."

"Nae doubt, nae doubt: he trusted in Him."

It was for the sake of the minute notices of nature, and not for the religious lesson, which he now seemed to see for the first time, that Hugh had read the poem. He could not help being greatly impressed by the confidence with which David received the statement he had just made on the authority of De Quincey in his unpleasant article about Wordsworth. David resumed:

"He maun hae had a gleg 'ee o' his ain, that Maister Wordsworth, to notice a'thing that get. Weel he maun hae likit leevin' things, puir maukin an' a'—jist like our Robbie Burns for that. An' see hoo they a' ken ane anither, thae poets. What says he aboot Burns?—ye needna tell me, Mr. Sutherlan'; I min't weel aneuch. He says:—

```
'Him wha walked in glory an' in joy,
  Followin' his ploo upo' the muntain-side,'
```

Puir Robbie! puir Robbie! But, man, he was a gran' chield efter a'; an' I trust in God he's won hame by this!"

Both Janet and Hugh, who had had a very orthodox education, started, mentally, at this strange utterance; but they saw the eye of David solemnly fixed, as if in deep contemplation, and lighted in its blue depths with an ethereal brightness; and neither of them ventured to speak. Margaret seemed absorbed for the moment in gazing on her father's face; but not in the least as if it perplexed her like the fir-wood. To the seeing eye, the same kind of expression would have been evident in both countenances, as if Margaret's reflected the meaning of her father's; whether through the medium of intellectual sympathy, or that of the heart only, it would have been hard to say. Meantime supper had been rather neglected; but its operations were now resumed more earnestly, and the conversation became lighter; till at last it ended in hearty laughter, and Hugh rose and took his leave.

CHAPTER VIII. A SUNDAY MORNING.

It is the property of good and sound knowledge, to putrifie and dissolve into a number of subtle, idle, unwholesome, and (as I may tearme them) vermiculate questions; which have indeed a kinde of quicknesse, and life of spirite, but no soundnesse of matter, or goodnesse of quality.—LORD BACON.—Advancement of Learning.

The following morning, the laird's family went to church as usual, and Hugh went with them. Their walk was first across fields, by pleasant footpaths; and then up the valley of a little noisy stream, that obstinately refused to keep Scotch Sabbath, praising the Lord after its own fashion. They emerged into rather a bleak country before reaching the church, which was quite new, and perched on a barren eminence, that it might be as conspicuous by its position, as it was remarkable for its ugliness. One grand aim of the reformers of the Scottish ecclesiastical modes, appears to have been to keep the worship pure and the worshippers sincere, by embodying the whole in the ugliest forms that could be associated with the name of Christianity. It might be wished, however, that some of their followers, and amongst them the clergyman of the church in question, had been content to stop there; and had left the object of worship, as represented by them, in the possession of some lovable attribute; so as not to require a man to love that which is unlovable, or worship that which is not honourable—in a word, to bow down before that which is not divine. The cause of this degeneracy they share in common with the followers of all other great men as well as of Calvin. They take up what their leader, urged by the necessity of the time, spoke loudest, never heeding what he loved most; and then work the former out to a logical perdition of everything belonging to the latter.

Hugh, however, thought it was all right: for he had the same good reasons, and no other, for receiving it all, that a Mohammedan or a Buddhist has for holding his opinions; namely, that he had heard those doctrines, and those alone, from his earliest childhood. He was therefore a good deal startled when, having, on his way home, strayed from the laird's party towards David's, he heard the latter say to Margaret as he came up:

"Dinna ye believe, my bonny doo, 'at there's ony mak' ups or mak' shifts wi' Him. He's aye bringin' things to the licht, no covenin' them up and lattin them rot, an' the moth tak' them. He sees us jist as we are, and ca's us jist what we are. It wad be an ill day for a' o's, Maggy, my doo, gin he war to close his een to oor sins, an' ca' us just in his sicht, whan we cudna possibly be just in oor ain or in ony ither body's, no to say his."

"The Lord preserve's, Dawvid Elginbrod! Dinna ye believe i' the doctrine o' Justification by Faith, an' you a'maist made an elder o'?"

Janet was the respondent, of course, Margaret listening in silence.

"Ou ay, I believe in't, nae doot; but, troth! the minister, honest man, near–han' gart me disbelieve in't a'thegither wi' his gran' sermon this mornin', about imputit richteousness, an' a clean robe hidin' a foul skin or a crookit back. Na, na. May Him 'at woosh the feet o' his friens, wash us a'thegither, and straucht oor crookit banes, till we're clean and weel–faured like his ain bonny sel'."

"Weel, Dawvid—but that's sanctificaition, ye ken."

"Ca't ony name 'at you or the minister likes, Janet, my woman. I daursay there's neither o' ye far wrang after a'; only this is jist my opingan aboot it in sma'—that that man, and that

40

man only, is justifeed, wha pits himsel' into the Lord's han's to sanctifee him. Noo! An' that'll no be dune by pittin' a robe o' richteousness upo' him, afore he's gotten a clean skin aneath't. As gin a father cudna bide to see the puir scabbit skin o' his ain wee bit bairnie, ay, or o' his prodigal son either, but bude to hap it a' up afore he cud lat it come near him! Ahva!"

Here Hugh ventured to interpose a remark.

"But you don't think, Mr. Elginbrod, that the minister intended to say that justification left a man at liberty to sin, or that the robe of Christ's righteousness would hide him from the work of the Spirit?"

"Na; but there is a notion in't o' hidin' frae God himsel'. I'll tell ye what it is Mr. Sutherlan': the minister's a' richt in himsel', an' sae's my Janet here, an' mony mair; an' aiblins there's a kin' o' trowth in a' 'at they say; but this is my quarrel wi' a' thae words an' words an' airguments, an' seemilies as they ca' them, an' doctrines, an' a' that—they jist haud a puir body at airm's lenth oot ower frae God himsel'. An' they raise a mist an' a stour a' aboot him, 'at the puir bairn canna see the Father himsel', stan'in' wi' his airms streekit oot as wide's the heavens, to tak' the worn crater,—and the mair sinner, the mair welcome,—hame to his verra hert. Gin a body wad lea' a' that, and jist get fowk persuâdit to speyk a word or twa to God him lane, the loss, in my opingan, wad be unco sma', and the gain verra great."

Even Janet dared not reply to the solemnity of this speech; for the seer–like look was upon David's face, and the tears had gathered in his eyes and dimmed their blue. A kind of tremulous pathetic smile flickered about his beautifully curved mouth, like the glimmer of water in a valley, betwixt the lofty aquiline nose and the powerful but finely modelled chin. It seemed as if he dared not let the smile break out, lest it should be followed instantly by a burst of tears.

Margaret went close up to her father and took his hand as if she had been still a child, while Janet walked reverentially by him on the other side. It must not be supposed that Janet felt any uneasiness about her husband's opinions, although she never hesitated to utter what she considered her common–sense notions, in attempted modification of some of the more extreme of them. The fact was that, if he was wrong, Janet did not care to be right; and if he was right, Janet was sure to be; "for," said she—and in spirit, if not in the

41

letter, it was quite true—"I never mint at contradickin' him. My man sall hae his ain get, that sall he." But she had one especial grudge at his opinions; which was, that it must have been in consequence of them that he had declined, with a queer smile, the honourable position of Elder of the Kirk; for which Janet considered him, notwithstanding his opinions, immeasurably more fitted than any other man "in the haill country–side—ye may add Scotlan' forby." The fact of his having been requested to fill the vacant place of Elder, is proof enough that David was not in the habit of giving open expression to his opinions. He was looked upon as a douce man, long–headed enough, and somewhat precise in the exaction of the laird's rights, but open–hearted and open–handed with what was his own. Every one respected him, and felt kindly towards him; some were a little afraid of him; but few suspected him of being religious beyond the degree which is commonly supposed to be the general inheritance of Scotchmen, possibly in virtue of their being brought up upon oatmeal porridge and the Shorter Catechism.

Hugh walked behind the party for a short way, contemplating them in their Sunday clothes: David wore a suit of fine black cloth. He then turned to rejoin the laird's company. Mrs. Glasford was questioning her boys, in an intermittent and desultory fashion, about the sermon.

"An' what was the fourth heid, can ye tell me, Willie?"

Willie, the eldest, who had carefully impressed the fourth head upon his memory, and had been anxiously waiting for an opportunity of bringing it out, replied at once:

"Fourthly: The various appellations by which those who have indued the robe of righteousness are designated in Holy Writ."

"Weel done, Willie!" cried the laird.

"That's richt, Willie," said his mother. Then turning to the younger, whose attention was attracted by a strange bird in the hedge in front. "An' what called he them, Johnnie, that put on the robe?" she asked.

"Whited sepulchres," answered Johnnie, indebted for his wit to his wool–gathering.

42

This put an end to the catechising. Mrs. Glasford glanced round at Hugh, whose defection she had seen with indignation, and who, waiting for them by the roadside, had heard the last question and reply, with an expression that seemed to attribute any defect in the answer, entirely to the carelessness of the tutor, and the withdrawal of his energies from her boys to that "saucy quean, Meg Elginbrod."

CHAPTER IX. NATURE.

When the Soul is kindled or enlightened by the Holy Ghost, then it beholds what God its Father does, as a Son beholds what his Father does at Home in his own House.—JACOB BEHMEN'S Aurora—Law's Translation.

Margaret began to read Wordsworth, slowly at first, but soon with greater facility. Ere long she perceived that she had found a friend; for not only did he sympathize with her in her love for nature, putting many vague feelings into thoughts, and many thoughts into words for her, but he introduced her to nature in many altogether new aspects, and taught her to regard it in ways which had hitherto been unknown to her. Not only was the pine wood now dearer to her than before, but its mystery seemed more sacred, and, at the same time, more likely to be one day solved. She felt far more assuredly the presence of a spirit in nature,

> "Whose dwelling is the light of setting suns,
> And the round ocean, and the living air;"

for he taught her to take wider views of nature, and to perceive and feel the expressions of more extended aspects of the world around her. The purple hill—side was almost as dear to her as the fir—wood now; and the star that crowned its summit at eve, sparkled an especial message to her, before it went on its way up the blue. She extended her rambles in all directions, and began to get with the neighbours the character of an idle girl. Little they knew how early she rose, and how diligently she did her share of the work, urged by desire to read the word of God in his own handwriting; or rather, to pore upon that expression of the face of God, which, however little a man may think of it, yet sinks so deeply into his nature, and moulds it towards its own likeness.

Nature was doing for Margaret what she had done before for Wordsworth's Lucy: she was making of her "a lady of her own." She grew taller and more graceful. The lasting quiet of her face began to look as if it were ever upon the point of blossoming into an expression of lovely feeling. The principal change was in her mouth, which became delicate and tender in its curves, the lips seeming to kiss each other for very sweetness. But I am anticipating these changes, for it took a far longer time to perfect them than has yet been occupied by my story.

But even her mother was not altogether proof against the appearance of listlessness and idleness which Margaret's behaviour sometimes wore to her eyes; nor could she quite understand or excuse her long lonely walks; so that now and then she could not help addressing her after this fashion:

"Meg! Meg! ye do try my patience, lass, idlin' awa' yer time that get. It's an awfu' wastery o' time, what wi' beuks, an' what wi' stravaguin', an' what wi' naething ava. Jist pit yer han' to this kirn noo, like a gude bairn."

Margaret would obey her mother instantly, but with a look of silent expostulation which her mother could not resist; sometimes, perhaps, if the words were sharper than usual, with symptoms of gathering tears; upon which Janet would say, with her honest smile of sweet relenting,

"Hootoots, bairn! never heed me. My bark's aye waur nor my bite; ye ken that."

Then Margaret's face would brighten at once, and she would work hard at whatever her mother set her to do, till it was finished; upon which her mother would be more glad than she, and in no haste to impose any further labour out of the usual routine.

In the course of reading Wordsworth, Margaret had frequent occasion to apply to Hugh for help. These occasions, however, generally involved no more than small external difficulties, which prevented her from taking in the scope of a passage. Hugh was always able to meet these, and Margaret supposed that the whole of the light which flashed upon her mind when they were removed, was poured upon the page by the wisdom of her tutor; never dreaming—such was her humility with regard to herself, and her reverence towards him—that it came from the depths of her own lucent nature, ready to perceive what the poet came prepared to show. Now and then, it is true, she applied to him with difficulties in which he was incapable of aiding her; but she put down her failure in discovering the meaning, after all which it must be confessed he sometimes tried to say, to her own stupidity or peculiarity—never to his incapacity. She had been helped to so much by his superior acquirements, and his real gift for communicating what he thoroughly understood; he had been so entirely her guide to knowledge, that she would at once have felt self-condemned of impiety—in the old meaning of the word if she had doubted for a moment his ability to understand or explain any difficulty which she could place clearly before him.

By-and-by he began to lend her harder, that is, more purely intellectual books. He was himself preparing for the class of Moral Philosophy and Metaphysics; and he chose for her some of the simpler of his books on these subjects—of course all of the Scotch school—beginning with Abercrombie's Intellectual Powers. She took this eagerly, and evidently read it with great attention.

One evening in the end of summer, Hugh climbed a waste heathery hill that lay behind the house of Turriepuffit, and overlooked a great part of the neighbouring country, the peaks of some of the greatest of the Scotch mountains being visible from its top. Here he intended to wait for the sunset. He threw himself on the heather, that most delightful and luxurious of all couches, supporting the body with a kindly upholding of every part; and there he lay in the great slumberous sunlight of the late afternoon, with the blue heavens, into which he was gazing full up, closing down upon him, as the light descended the side of the sky. He fell fast asleep. If ever there be an excuse for falling asleep out of bed, surely it is when stretched at full length upon heather in bloom. When he awoke, the last of the sunset was dying away; and between him and the sunset sat Margaret, book in hand, waiting apparently for his waking. He lay still for a few minutes, to come to himself before she should see he was awake. But she rose at the moment, and drawing near very quietly, looked down upon him with her sweet sunset face, to see whether or not he was beginning to rouse, for she feared to let him lie much longer after sundown. Finding him awake, she drew back again without a word, and sat down as before with her book. At length he rose, and, approaching her, said—

"Well, Margaret, what book are you at now?"

"Dr. Abercrombie, sir," replied Margaret.

"How do you like it?"

"Verra weel for some things. It makes a body think; but not a'thegither as I like to think either."

It will be observed that Margaret's speech had begun to improve, that is, to be more like English.

"What is the matter with it?"

"Weel, ye see, sir, it taks a body a' to bits like, and never pits them together again. An' it seems to me that a body's min' or soul, or whatever it may be called—but it's jist a body's ain sel'—can no more be ta'en to pieces like, than you could tak' that red licht there oot o' the blue, or the haill sunset oot o' the heavens an' earth. It may be a' verra weel, Mr. Sutherland, but oh! it's no like this!"

And Margaret looked around her from the hill–top, and then up into the heavens, where the stars were beginning to crack the blue with their thin, steely sparkle.

"It seems to me to tak' a' the poetry oot o' us, Mr. Sutherland."

"Well, well," said Hugh, with a smile, "you must just go to Wordsworth to put it in again; or to set you again up after Dr. Abercrombie has demolished you."

"Na, na, sir, he sanna demolish me: nor I winna trouble Mr. Wordsworth to put the poetry into me again. A' the power on earth shanna tak' that oot o' me, gin it be God's will; for it's his ain gift, Mr. Sutherland, ye ken."

"Of course, of course," replied Hugh, who very likely thought this too serious a way of speaking of poetry, and therefore, perhaps, rather an irreverent way of speaking of God; for he saw neither the divine in poetry, nor the human in God. Could he be said to believe that God made man, when he did not believe that God created poetry—and yet loved it as he did? It was to him only a grand invention of humanity in its loftiest development. In this development, then, he must have considered humanity as farthest from its origin; and God as the creator of savages, caring nothing for poets or their work.

They turned, as by common consent, to go down the hill together.

David Elginbrod

"Shall I take charge of the offending volume? You will not care to finish it, I fear," said Hugh.

"No, sir, if you please. I never like to leave onything unfinished. I'll read ilka word in't. I fancy the thing 'at sets me against it, is mostly this; that, readin' it alang wi' Euclid, I canna help aye thinkin' o' my ain min' as gin it were in some geometrical shape or ither, whiles ane an' whiles anither; and syne I try to draw lines an' separate this power frae that power, the memory frae the jeedgement, an' the imagination frae the rizzon; an' syne I try to pit them a' thegither again in their relations to ane anither. And this aye takes the shape o' some proposition or ither, generally i' the second beuk. It near–han' dazes me whiles. I fancy gin' I understood the pairts o' the sphere, it would be mair to the purpose; but I wat I wish I were clear o't a'thegither."

Hugh had had some experiences of a similar kind himself, though not at all to the same extent. He could therefore understand her.

"You must just try to keep the things altogether apart," said he, "and not think of the two sciences at once."

"But I canna help it," she replied. "I suppose you can, sir, because ye're a man. My father can understan' things ten times better nor me an' my mother. But nae sooner do I begin to read and think about it, than up comes ane o' thae parallelograms, an' nothing will driv't oot o' my head again, but a verse or twa o' Coleridge or Wordsworth."

Hugh immediately began to repeat the first poem of the latter that occurred to him:

    "I wandered lonely as a cloud."

She listened, walking along with her eyes fixed on the ground; and when he had finished, gave a sigh of delight and relief—all the comment she uttered. She seemed never to find it necessary to say what she felt; least of all when the feeling was a pleasant one; for then it was enough for itself. This was only the second time since their acquaintance, that she had spoken of her feelings at all; and in this case they were of a purely intellectual origin. It is to be observed, however, that in both cases she had taken pains to explain thoroughly what she meant, as far as she was able.

David Elginbrod

It was dark before they reached home, at least as dark as it ever is at this season of the year in the north. They found David looking out with some slight anxiety for his daughter's return, for she was seldom out so late as this. In nothing could the true relation between them have been more evident than in the entire absence from her manner of any embarrassment when she met her father. She went up to him and told him all about finding Mr. Sutherland asleep on the hill, and waiting beside him till he woke, that she might walk home with him. Her father seemed perfectly content with an explanation which he had not sought, and, turning to Hugh, said, smiling:

"Weel, no to be troublesome, Mr. Sutherlan', ye maun gie the auld man a turn as weel as the young lass. We didna expec ye the nicht, but I'm sair puzzled wi' a sma' eneuch matter on my sklet in there. Will you no come in and gie me a lift?"

"With all my heart," said Sutherland. So there were five lessons in that week.

When Hugh entered the cottage he had a fine sprig of heather in his hand, which he laid on the table.

He had the weakness of being proud of small discoveries—the tinier the better; and was always sharpening his senses, as well as his intellect, to a fine point, in order to make them. I fear that by these means he shut out some great ones, which could not enter during such a concentration of the faculties. He would stand listening to the sound of goose–feet upon the road, and watch how those webs laid hold of the earth like a hand. He would struggle to enter into their feelings in folding their wings properly on their backs. He would calculate, on chemical and arithmetical grounds, whether one might not hear the nocturnal growth of plants in the tropics. He was quite elated by the discovery, as he considered it, that Shakspeare named his two officers of the watch, Dogberry and Verjuice; the poisonous Dogberry, and the acid liquor of green fruits, affording suitable names for the stupidly innocuous constables, in a play the very essence of which is Much Ado About Nothing. Another of his discoveries he had, during their last lesson, unfolded to David, who had certainly contemplated it with interest. It was, that the original forms of the Arabic numerals were these:

```
1.2.3.4.5.6.7.8.9. {original text has a picture}
```

the number for which each figure stands being indicated by the number of straight lines employed in forming that numeral. I fear the comparative anatomy of figures gives no countenance to the discovery which Hugh flattered himself he had made.

After he had helped David out of his difficulty, he took up the heather, and stripping off the bells, shook them in his hand at Margaret's ear. A half smile, like the moonlight of laughter, dawned on her face; and she listened with something of the same expression with which a child listens to the message from the sea, inclosed in a twisted shell. He did the same at David's ear next.

"Eh, man! that's a bonny wee soun'! It's jist like sma' sheep–bells—fairy–sheep, I reckon, Maggy, my doo."

"Lat me hearken as weel," said Janet.

Hugh obeyed. She laughed.

"It's naething but a reestlin'. I wad raither hear the sheep baain', or the kye routin'."

"Eh, Mr. Sutherlan'! but, ye hae a gleg ee an' a sharp lug. Weel, the warld's fu' o' bonny sichts and souns, doon to the verra sma'est. The Lord lats naething gang. I wadna wonner noo but there micht be thousands sic like, ower sma' a'thegither for human ears, jist as we ken there are creatures as perfect in beowty as ony we see, but far ower sma' for our een wintin' the glass. But for my pairt, I aye like to see a heap o' things at ance, an' tak' them a' in thegither, an' see them playin' into ane anither's han' like. I was jist thinkin', as I came hame the nicht in the sinset, hoo it wad hae been naewise sae complete, wi' a' its red an' gowd an' green, gin it hadna been for the cauld blue east ahint it, wi' the twa–three shiverin' starnies leukin' through't. An' doubtless the warld to come 'ill be a' the warmer to them 'at hadna ower muckle happin here. But I'm jist haverin', clean haverin', Mr. Sutherlan'," concluded David, with a smile of apologetic humour.

"I suppose you could easily believe with Plato, David, that the planets make a grand choral music as they roll about the heavens, only that as some sounds are too small, so that is too loud for us to hear."

"I cud weel believe that," was David's unhesitating answer. Margaret looked as if she not only could believe it, but would be delighted to know that it was true. Neither Janet nor Hugh gave any indication of feeling on the matter.

CHAPTER X. HARVEST.

```
So a small seed that in the earth lies hid
And dies, reviving bursts her cloddy side,
Adorned with yellow locks, of new is born,
And doth become a mother great with corn,
Of grains brings hundreds with it, which when old
Enrich the furrows with a sea of gold.

SIR WILLIAM DRUMMOND.—Hymn of the Resurrection.
```

Hugh had watched the green corn grow, and ear, and turn dim; then brighten to yellow, and ripen at last under the declining autumn sun, and the low skirting moon of the harvest, which seems too full and heavy with mellow and bountiful light to rise high above the fields which it comes to bless with perfection. The long threads, on each of which hung an oat-grain—the harvest here was mostly of oats—had got dry and brittle; and the grains began to spread out their chaff-wings, as if ready to fly, and rustled with sweet sounds against each other, as the wind, which used to billow the fields like the waves of the sea, now swept gently and tenderly over it, helping the sun and moon in the drying and ripening of the joy to be laid up for the dreary winter. Most graceful of all hung those delicate oats; next bowed the bearded barley; and stately and wealthy and strong stood the few fields of wheat, of a rich, ruddy, golden hue. Above the yellow harvest rose the purple hills, and above the hills the pale-blue autumnal sky, full of light and heat, but fading somewhat from the colour with which it deepened above the vanished days of summer. For the harvest here is much later than in England.

At length the day arrived when the sickle must be put into the barley, soon to be followed by the scythe in the oats. And now came the joy of labour. Everything else was abandoned for the harvest field. Books were thrown utterly aside; for, even when there was no fear of a change of weather to urge to labour prolonged beyond the natural hours, there was weariness enough in the work of the day to prevent even David from reading, in the hours of bodily rest, anything that necessitated mental labour.

David Elginbrod

Janet and Margaret betook themselves to the reaping–hook; and the somewhat pale face of the latter needed but a single day to change it to the real harvest hue—the brown livery of Ceres. But when the oats were attacked, then came the tug of war. The laird was in the fields from morning to night, and the boys would not stay behind; but, with their father's permission, much to the tutor's contentment, devoted what powers they had to the gathering of the fruits of the earth. Hugh himself, whose strength had grown amazingly during his stay at Turriepuffit, and who, though he was quite helpless at the sickle, thought he could wield the scythe, would not be behind. Throwing off coat and waistcoat, and tying his handkerchief tight round his loins, he laid hold on the emblematic weapon of Time and Death, determined likewise to earn the name of Reaper. He took the last scythe. It was desperate work for a while, and he was far behind the first bout; but David, who was the best scyther in the whole country side, and of course had the leading scythe, seeing the tutor dropping behind, put more power to his own arm, finished his own bout, and brought up Hugh's before the others had done sharpening their scythes for the next.

"Tak' care an' nae rax yersel' ower sair, Mr. Sutherlan'. Ye'll be up wi' the best o' them in a day or twa; but gin ye tyauve at it aboon yer strenth, ye'll be clean forfochten. Tak' a guid sweep wi' the scythe, 'at ye may hae the weicht o't to ca' through the strae, an' tak' nae shame at bein' hindmost. Here, Maggy, my doo, come an' gather to Mr. Sutherlan'. Ane o' the young gentlemen can tak' your place at the binin'."

The work of Janet and Margaret had been to form bands for the sheaves, by folding together cunningly the heads of two small handfuls of the corn, so as to make them long enough together to go round the sheaf; then to lay this down for the gatherer to place enough of the mown corn upon it; and last, to bind the band tightly around by another skilful twist and an insertion of the ends, and so form a sheaf. From this work David called his daughter, desirous of giving Hugh a gatherer who would not be disrespectful to his awkwardness. This arrangement, however, was far from pleasing to some of the young men in the field, and brought down upon Hugh, who was too hard–wrought to hear them at first, many sly hits of country wit and human contempt. There had been for some time great jealousy of his visits at David's cottage; for Margaret, though she had very little acquaintance with the young men of the neighbourhood, was greatly admired amongst them, and not regarded as so far above the station of many of them as to render aspiration useless. Their remarks to each other got louder and louder, till Hugh at last heard some of them, and could not help being annoyed, not by their wit or personality, but by the tone of contempt in which they were uttered.

51

David Elginbrod

"Tak' care o' yer legs, sir. It'll be ill cuttin' upo' stumps."

"Fegs! he's taen the wings aff o' a pairtrick."

"Gin he gang on that get, he'll cut twa bouts at ance."

"Ye'll hae the scythe ower the dyke, man. Tak' tent."

"Losh! sir; ye've taen aff my leg at the hip!"

"Ye're shavin' ower close: ye'll draw the bluid, sir."

"Hoot, man! lat alane. The gentleman's only mista'en his trade, an' imaigins he's howkin' a grave."

And so on. Hugh gave no further sign of hearing their remarks than lay in increased exertion. Looking round, however, he saw that Margaret was vexed, evidently not for her own sake. He smiled to her, to console her for his annoyance; and then, ambitious to remove the cause of it, made a fresh exertion, recovered all his distance, and was in his own place with the best of them at the end of the bout. But the smile that had passed between them did not escape unobserved; and he had aroused yet more the wrath of the youths, by threatening soon to rival them in the excellencies to which they had an especial claim. They had regarded him as an interloper, who had no right to captivate one of their rank by arts beyond their reach; but it was still less pardonable to dare them to a trial of skill with their own weapons. To the fire of this jealousy, the admiration of the laird added fuel; for he was delighted with the spirit with which Hugh laid himself to the scythe. But all the time, nothing was further from Hugh's thoughts than the idea of rivalry with them. Whatever he might have thought of Margaret in relation to himself, he never thought of her, though labouring in the same field with them, as in the least degree belonging to their class, or standing in any possible relation to them, except that of a common work.

In ordinary, the labourers would have had sufficient respect for Sutherland's superior position, to prevent them from giving such decided and articulate utterance to their feelings. But they were incited by the presence and example of a man of doubtful character from the neighbouring village, a travelled and clever ne'er–do–weel, whose reputation for wit was equalled by his reputation for courage and skill, as well as profligacy. Roused by the effervescence of his genius, they went on from one thing to another, till Hugh saw it must be put a stop to somehow, else he must abandon the field. They dared not have gone so far if David had been present; but he had been called away to superintend some operations in another part of the estate; and they paid no heed to the expostulations of some of the other older men. At the close of the day's work, therefore, Hugh walked up to this fellow, and said:

"I hope you will be satisfied with insulting me all to-day, and leave it alone to-morrow."

The man replied, with an oath and a gesture of rude contempt,

"I dinna care the black afore my nails for ony skelp-doup o' the lot o' ye."

Hugh's highland blood flew to his brain, and before the rascal finished his speech, he had measured his length on the stubble. He sprang to his feet in a fury, threw off the coat which he had just put on, and darted at Hugh, who had by this time recovered his coolness, and was besides, notwithstanding his unusual exertions, the more agile of the two. The other was heavier and more powerful. Hugh sprang aside, as he would have done from the rush of a bull, and again with a quick blow felled his antagonist. Beginning rather to enjoy punishing him, he now went in for it; and, before the other would yield, he had rendered his next day's labour somewhat doubtful. He withdrew, with no more injury to himself than a little water would remove. Janet and Margaret had left the field before he addressed the man.

He went borne and to bed—more weary than he had ever been in his life. Before he went to sleep, however, he made up his mind to say nothing of his encounter to David, but to leave him to hear of it from other sources. He could not help feeling a little anxious as to his judgment upon it. That the laird would approve, he hardly doubted; but for his opinion he cared very little.

"Dawvid, I wonner at ye," said Janet to her husband, the moment he came home, "to lat the young lad warstle himsel' deid that get wi' a scythe. His banes is but saft yet, There wasna a dry steek on him or he wan half the lenth o' the first bout. He's sair disjaskit, I'se warran'."

"Nae fear o' him, Janet; it'll do him guid. Mr. Sutherland's no feckless winlestrae o' a creater. Did he haud his ain at a' wi' the lave?"

"Haud his ain! Gin he be fit for onything the day, he maun be pitten neist yersel', or he'll cut the legs aff o' ony ither man i' the corn."

A glow of pleasure mantled in Margaret's face at her mother's praise of Hugh. Janet went on:

"But I was jist clean affronted wi' the way 'at the young chields behaved themselves till him."

"I thocht I heard a toot—moot o' that kin' afore I left, but I thocht it better to tak' nae notice o't. I'll be wi' ye a' day the morn though, an' I'm thinkin' I'll clap a rouch han' on their mou's 'at I hear ony mair o't frae."

But there was no occasion for interference on David's part. Hugh made his appearance—not, it is true, with the earliest in the hairst—rig, but after breakfast with the laird, who was delighted with the way in which he had handled his scythe the day before, and felt twice the respect for him in consequence. It must be confessed he felt very stiff, but the best treatment for stiffness being the homeoopathic one of more work, he had soon restored the elasticity of his muscles, and lubricated his aching joints. His antagonist of the foregoing evening was nowhere to be seen; and the rest of the young men were shame—faced and respectful enough.

David, having learned from some of the spectators the facts of the combat, suddenly, as they were walking home together, held out his hand to Hugh, shook his hard, and said:

"Mr. Sutherlan', I'm sair obleeged to ye for giein' that vratch, Jamie Ogg, a guid doonsettin'. He's a coorse crater; but the warst maun hae meat, an' sae I didna like to refeese him when he cam for wark. But its a greater kin'ness to clout him nor to cleed him. They say ye made an awfu' munsie o' him. But it's to be houpit he'll live to thank ye. There's some fowk 'at can respeck no airgument but frae steekit neives; an' it's fell cruel to haud it frae them, gin ye hae't to gie them. I hae had eneuch ado to haud my ain han's aff o' the ted, but it comes a hantle better frae you, Mr. Sutherlan'."

Hugh wielded the scythe the whole of the harvest, and Margaret gathered to him. By the time it was over, leading–home and all, he measured an inch less about the waist, and two inches more about the shoulders; and was as brown as a berry, and as strong as an ox, or "owse," as David called it, when thus describing Mr. Sutherland's progress in corporal development; for he took a fatherly pride in the youth, to whom, at the same time, he looked up with submission, as his master in learning.

CHAPTER XI. A CHANGE AND NO CHANGE.

```
Affliction, when I know it, is but this—
A deep alloy, whereby man tougher is
To bear the hammer; and the deeper still,
We still arise more image of his will.
Sickness—an humorous cloud 'twist us and light;
And death, at longest, but another night.
Man is his own star; and that soul that can
Be honest, is the only perfect Man.

JOHN FLETCHER.—Upon an Honest Man's Fortune.
```

Had Sutherland been in love with Margaret, those would have been happy days; and that a yet more happy night, when, under the mystery of a low moonlight and a gathering storm, the crop was cast in haste into the carts, and hurried home to be built up in safety; when a strange low wind crept sighing across the stubble, as if it came wandering out of the past and the land of dreams, lying far off and withered in the green west; and when Margaret and he came and went in the moonlight like creatures in a dream—for the vapours of sleep were floating in Hugh's brain, although he was awake and working.

"Margaret," he said, as they stood waiting a moment for the cart that was coming up to be filled with sheaves, "what does that wind put you in mind of?"

"Ossian's Poems," replied Margaret, without a moment's hesitation.

Hugh was struck by her answer. He had meant something quite different. But it harmonized with his feeling about Ossian; for the genuineness of whose poetry, Highlander as he was, he had no better argument to give than the fact, that they produced in himself an altogether peculiar mental condition; that the spiritual sensations he had in

55

reading them were quite different from those produced by anything else, prose or verse; in fact, that they created moods of their own in his mind. He was unwilling to believe, apart from national prejudices (which have not prevented the opinions on this question from being as strong on the one side as on the other), that this individuality of influence could belong to mere affectations of a style which had never sprung from the sources of real feeling. "Could they," he thought, "possess the power to move us like remembered dreams of our childhood, if all that they possessed of reality was a pretended imitation of what never existed, and all that they inherited from the past was the halo of its strangeness?"

But Hugh was not in love with Margaret, though he could not help feeling the pleasure of her presence. Any youth must have been the better for having her near him; but there was nothing about her quiet, self-contained being, free from manifestation of any sort, to rouse the feelings commonly called love, in the mind of an inexperienced youth like Hugh Sutherland.—I say commonly called, because I believe that within the whole sphere of intelligence there are no two loves the same.—Not that he was less easily influenced than other youths. A designing girl might have caught him at once, if she had had no other beauty than sparkling eyes; but the womanhood of the beautiful Margaret kept so still in its pearly cave, that it rarely met the glance of neighbouring eyes. How Margaret regarded him I do not know; but I think it was with a love almost entirely one with reverence and gratitude. Cause for gratitude she certainly had, though less than she supposed; and very little cause indeed for reverence. But how could she fail to revere one to whom even her father looked up? Of course David's feeling of respect for Hugh must have sprung chiefly from intellectual grounds; and he could hardly help seeing, if he thought at all on the subject, which is doubtful, that Hugh was as far behind Margaret in the higher gifts and graces, as he was before her in intellectual acquirement. But whether David perceived this or not, certainly Margaret did not even think in that direction. She was pure of self-judgment—conscious of no comparing of herself with others, least of all with those next her.

At length the harvest was finished; or, as the phrase of the district was, clyack was gotten—a phrase with the derivation, or even the exact meaning of which, I am unacquainted; knowing only that it implies something in close association with the feast of harvest-home, called the kirn in other parts of Scotland. Thereafter, the fields lay bare to the frosts of morning and evening, and to the wind that grew cooler and cooler with the breath of Winter, who lay behind the northern hills, and waited for his hour. But many lovely days remained, of quiet and slow decay, of yellow and red leaves, of warm noons and lovely sunsets, followed by skies—green from the west horizon to the zenith, and walked by a moon that seemed to draw up to her all the white mists from pond and river and pool, to settle again in hoar-frost, during the colder hours that precede the dawn. At length every leafless tree sparkled in the morning sun, incrusted with fading gems; and the ground was hard under foot; and the hedges were filled with frosted spider-webs; and winter had laid the tips of his fingers on the land, soon to cover it deep with the flickering snow-flakes, shaken from the folds of his outspread mantle. But long ere this, David and Margaret had returned with renewed diligence, and powers strengthened by repose, or at least by intermission, to their mental labours, and Hugh was as constant a visitor at the cottage as before. The time, however, drew nigh when he must return to his studies at Aberdeen; and David and Margaret were looking forward with sorrow to the loss of their friend. Janet, too, "cudna bide to think o't."

"He'll tak' the daylicht wi' him, I doot, my lass," she said, as she made the porridge for breakfast one morning, and looked down anxiously at her daughter, seated on the creepie by the ingle-neuk.

"Na, na, mither," replied Margaret, looking up from her book; "he'll lea' sic gifts ahin' him as'll mak' daylicht i' the dark;" and then she bent her head and went on with her reading, as if she had not spoken.

The mother looked away with a sigh and a slight, sad shake of the head.

But matters were to turn out quite different from all anticipations. Before the day arrived on which Hugh must leave for the university, a letter from home informed him that his father was dangerously ill. He hastened to him, but only to comfort his last hours by all that a son could do, and to support his mother by his presence during the first hours of her loneliness. But anxious thoughts for the future, which so often force themselves on the attention of those who would gladly prolong their brooding over the past, compelled them to adopt an alteration of their plans for the present.

The half-pay of Major Sutherland was gone, of course; and all that remained for Mrs. Sutherland was a small annuity, secured by her husband's payments to a certain fund for the use of officers' widows. From this she could spare but a mere trifle for the completion of Hugh's university-education; while the salary he had received at Turriepuffit, almost the whole of which he had saved, was so small as to be quite inadequate for the very moderate outlay necessary. He therefore came to the resolution to write to the laird, and offer, if they were not yet provided with another tutor, to resume his relation to the young gentlemen for the winter. It was next to impossible to spend money there; and he judged that before the following winter, he should be quite able to meet the expenses of his residence at Aberdeen, during the last session of his course. He would have preferred trying to find another situation, had it not been that David and Janet and Margaret had made there a home for him.

Whether Mrs. Glasford was altogether pleased at the proposal, I cannot tell; but the laird wrote a very gentlemanlike epistle, condoling with him and his mother upon their loss, and urging the usual common−places of consolation. The letter ended with a hearty acceptance of Hugh's offer, and, strange to tell, the unsolicited promise of an increase of salary to the amount of five pounds. This is another to be added to the many proofs that verisimilitude is not in the least an essential element of verity.

He left his mother as soon as circumstances would permit, and returned to Turriepuffit; an abode for the winter very different indeed from that in which he had expected to spend it.

He reached the place early in the afternoon; received from Mrs. Glasford a cold "I hope you're well, Mr. Sutherland;" found his pupils actually reading, and had from them a welcome rather boisterously evidenced; told them to get their books; and sat down with them at once to commence their winter labours. He spent two hours thus; had a hearty shake of the hand from the laird, when he came home; and, after a substantial tea, walked down to David's cottage, where a welcome awaited him worth returning for.

"Come yer wa's butt," said Janet, who met him as he opened the door without any prefatory knock, and caught him with both hands; "I'm blithe to see yer bonny face ance mair. We're a' jist at ane mair wi' expeckin' o' ye."

David stood in the middle of the floor, waiting for him.

"Come awa', my bonny lad," was all his greeting, as he held out a great fatherly hand to the youth, and, grasping his in the one, clapped him on the shoulder with the other, the water standing in his blue eyes the while. Hugh thought of his own father, and could not restrain his tears. Margaret gave him a still look full in the face, and, seeing his emotion, did not even approach to offer him any welcome. She hastened, instead, to place a chair for him as she had done when first he entered the cottage, and when he had taken it sat down at his feet on her creepie. With true delicacy, no one took any notice of him for some time. David said at last,

"An' hoo's yer puir mother, Mr. Sutherlan'?"

"She's pretty well," was all Hugh could answer.

"It's a sair stroke to bide," said David; "but it's a gran' thing whan a man's won weel throw't. When my father deit, I min' weel, I was sae prood to see him lyin' there, in the cauld grandeur o' deith, an' no man 'at daured say he ever did or spak the thing 'at didna become him, 'at I jist gloried i' the mids o' my greetin'. He was but a puir auld shepherd, Mr. Sutherlan', wi' hair as white as the sheep 'at followed him; an' I wat as they followed him, he followed the great Shepherd; an' followed an' followed, till he jist followed Him hame, whaur we're a' boun', an' some o' us far on the road, thanks to Him!"

And with that David rose, and got down the Bible, and, opening it reverently, read with a solemn, slightly tremulous voice, the fourteenth chapter of St. John's Gospel. When he had finished, they all rose, as by one accord, and knelt down, and David prayed:

"O Thou in whase sicht oor deeth is precious, an' no licht maitter; wha through darkness leads to licht, an' through deith to the greater life!—we canna believe that thou wouldst gie us ony guid thing, to tak' the same again; for that would be but bairns' play. We believe that thou taks, that thou may gie again the same thing better nor afore—mair o't and better nor we could ha' received it itherwise; jist as the Lord took himsel' frae the sicht o' them 'at lo'ed him weel, that instead o' bein' veesible afore their een, he micht hide himsel' in their verra herts. Come thou, an' abide in us, an' tak' us to bide in thee; an' syne gin we be a' in thee, we canna be that far frae ane anither, though some sud be in haven, an' some upo' earth. Lord help us to do oor wark like thy men an' maidens doon the stair, remin'in' oursel's, 'at them 'at we miss hae only gane up the stair, as gin 'twar to haud things to thy han' i' thy ain presence–chamber, whaur we houp to be called or lang, an' to see thee an' thy Son, wham we lo'e aboon a'; an' in his name we say, Amen!"

Hugh rose from his knees with a sense of solemnity and reality that he had never felt before. Little was said that evening; supper was eaten, if not in silence, yet with nothing that could be called conversation. And, almost in silence, David walked home with Hugh. The spirit of his father seemed to walk beside him. He felt as if he had been buried with him; and had found that the sepulchre was clothed with green things and roofed with stars—was in truth the heavens and the earth in which his soul walked abroad.

If Hugh looked a little more into his Bible, and tried a little more to understand it, after his father's death, it is not to be wondered at. It is but another instance of the fact that, whether from education or from the leading of some higher instinct, we are ready, in every more profound trouble, to feel as if a solution or a refuge lay somewhere—lay in sounds of wisdom, perhaps, to be sought and found in the best of books, the deepest of all the mysterious treasuries of words. But David never sought to influence Hugh to this end. He read the Bible in his family, but he never urged the reading of it on others. Sometimes he seemed rather to avoid the subject of religion altogether; and yet it was upon those very occasions that, if he once began to speak, he would pour out, before he ceased, some of his most impassioned utterances.

CHAPTER XII.

CHARITY.

Knowledge bloweth up, but charity buildeth up.

LORD BACON'S rendering of 1 Cor. viii. I.

Things went on as usual for a few days, when Hugh began to encounter a source of suffering of a very material and unromantic kind, but which, nevertheless, had been able before now, namely, at the commencement of his tutorship, to cause him a very sufficient degree of distress. It was this; that he had no room in which he could pursue his studies in private, without having to endure a most undesirable degree of cold. In summer this was a matter of little moment, for the universe might then be his secret chamber; but in a Scotch spring or autumn, not to say winter, a bedroom without a fire-place, which, strange to say, was the condition of his, was not a study in which thought could operate to much satisfactory result. Indeed, pain is a far less hurtful enemy to thinking than cold. And to have to fight such suffering and its benumbing influences, as well as to follow out a train of reasoning, difficult at any time, and requiring close attention—is too much for any machine whose thinking wheels are driven by nervous gear. Sometimes—for he must make the attempt—he came down to his meals quite blue with cold, as his pupils remarked to their mother, but their observation never seemed to suggest to her mind the necessity of making some better provision for the poor tutor. And Hugh, after the way in which she had behaved to him, was far too proud to ask her a favour, even if he had had hopes of receiving his request. He knew, too, that, in the house, the laird, to interfere in the smallest degree, must imperil far more than he dared. The prospect, therefore, of the coming winter, in a country where there was scarcely any afternoon, and where the snow might lie feet deep for weeks, was not at all agreeable. He had, as I have said, begun to suffer already, for the mornings and evenings were cold enough now, although it was a bright, dry October. One evening Janet remarked that he had caught cold, for he was 'hostin' sair;' and this led Hugh to state the discomfort he was condemned to experience up at the ha' house.

"Weel," said David, after some silent deliberation, "that sattles't; we maun set aboot it immedantly."

Of course Hugh was quite at a loss to understand what he meant, and begged him to explain.

"Ye see," replied David, "we hae verra little hoose–room i' this bit cot; for, excep this kitchen, we hae but the ben whaur Janet and me sleeps; and sae last year I spak' to the laird to lat me hae muckle timmer as I wad need to big a kin' o' a lean–to to the house ahin', so 'at we micht hae a kin' o' a bit parlour like, or rather a roomie 'at ony o' us micht retire till for a bit, gin we wanted to be oor lanes. He had nae objections, honest man. But somehoo or ither I never sat han' till't; but noo the wa's maun be up afore the wat weather sets in. Sae I'se be at it the morn, an' maybe ye'll len' me a han', Mr. Sutherlan', and tak' oot yer wages in house–room an' firin' efter it's dune."

"Thank you heartily!" said Hugh; that would be delightful. It seems too good to be possible. But will not wooden walls be rather a poor protection against such winters as I suppose you have in these parts?"

"Hootoot, Mr. Sutherlan', ye micht gie me credit for raither mair rumgumption nor that comes till. Timmer was the only thing I not (needed) to spier for; the lave lies to ony

David Elginbrod

body's han'—a few cart-fu's o' sods frae the hill ahint the hoose, an' a han'fu' or twa o' stanes for the chimla oot o' the quarry—there's eneuch there for oor turn ohn blastit mair; an' we'll saw the wood oorsels; an' gin we had ance the wa's up, we can carry on the inside at oor leisur'. That's the way 'at the Maker does wi' oorsels; he gie's us the wa's an' the material, an' a whole lifetime, maybe mair, to furnish the house."

"Capital!" exclaimed Hugh. "I'll work like a horse, and we'll be at it the morn."

"I'se be at it afore daylicht, an' ane or twa o' the lads'll len' me a han' efter wark-hours; and there's yersel', Mr. Sutherlan', worth ane an' a half o' ordinary workers; an' we'll hae truff aneuch for the wa's in a jiffey. I'll mark a feow saplin's i' the wud here at denner-time, an' we'll hae them for bauks, an' couples, an' things; an' there's plenty dry eneuch for beurds i' the shed, an' bein' but a lean-to, there'll be but half wark, ye ken."

They went out directly, in the moonlight, to choose the spot; and soon came to the resolution to build it so, that a certain back door, which added more to the cold in winter than to the convenience in summer, should be the entrance to the new chamber. The chimney was the chief difficulty; but all the materials being in the immediate neighbourhood, and David capable of turning his hands to anything, no obstruction was feared. Indeed, he set about that part first, as was necessary; and had soon built a small chimney, chiefly of stones and lime; while, under his directions, the walls were making progress at the same time, by the labour of Hugh and two or three of the young men from the farm, who were most ready to oblige David with their help, although they were still rather unfriendly to the colliginer, as they called him. But Hugh's frankness soon won them over, and they all formed within a day or two a very comfortable party of labourers. They worked very hard; for if the rain should set in before the roof was on, their labour would be almost lost from the soaking of the walls. They built them of turf, very thick, with a slight slope on the outside towards the roof; before commencing which, they partially cut the windows out of the walls, putting wood across to support the top. I should have explained that the turf used in building was the upper and coarser part of the peat, which was plentiful in the neighbourhood. The thatch-eaves of the cottage itself projected over the joining of the new roof, so as to protect it from the drip; and David soon put a thick thatch of new straw upon the little building. Second-hand windows were procured at the village, and the holes in the walls cut to their size. They next proceeded to the saw-pit on the estate—for almost everything necessary for keeping up the offices was done on the farm itself—where they sawed thin planks of deal, to floor and line the room, and make it more cosie. These David planed upon one side; and when they were nailed against slight posts all round the walls, and the joints filled in with putty, the room began to look most enticingly habitable. The roof had not been thatched two days before the rain set in; but now they could work quite comfortably inside, and as the space was small, and the forenights were long, they had it quite finished before the end of November. David bought an old table in the village, and one or two chairs; mended them up; made a kind of rustic sofa or settle; put a few bookshelves against the wall; had a peat fire lighted on the hearth every day; and at length, one Saturday evening, they had supper in the room, and the place was consecrated henceforth to friendship and learning. From this time, every evening, as soon as lessons, and the meal which immediately followed them, were over, Hugh betook himself to the cottage, on the shelves of which all his books by degrees collected themselves; and there spent the whole long evening, generally till ten o'clock; the first part alone reading or writing; the last in company with his pupils, who, diligent as ever, now of course made more rapid progress than before, inasmuch as the lessons were both longer and more frequent. The only drawback to their comfort was, that they seemed to have shut Janet out; but she soon remedied this, by contriving to get through with her house work earlier than she had ever done before; and, taking her place on the settle behind them, knitted away diligently at her stocking, which, to inexperienced eyes, seemed always the same, and always in the same state of progress, notwithstanding that she provided the hose of the whole family, blue and grey, ribbed and plain. Her occasional withdrawings, to observe the progress of the supper, were only a cheerful break in the continuity of labour. Little would the passer–by imagine that beneath that roof, which seemed worthy only of the name of a shed, there sat, in a snug little homely room, such a youth as Hugh, such a girl as Margaret, such a grand peasant king as David, and such a true–hearted mother to them all as Janet. There were no pictures and no music; for Margaret kept her songs for solitary places; but the sound of verse was often the living wind which set a–waving the tops of the trees of knowledge, fast growing in the sunlight of Truth. The thatch of that shed–roof was like the grizzled hair of David, beneath which lay the temple not only of holy but of wise and poetic thought. It was like the sylvan abode of the gods, where the architecture and music are all of their own making, in their kind the more beautiful, the more simple and rude; and if more doubtful in their intent, and less precise in their finish, yet therein the fuller of life and its grace, and the more suggestive of deeper harmonies.

CHAPTER XIII.

HERALDRY.

And like his father of face and of stature, And false of love—it came him of nature; As doth the fox Renard, the fox's son; Of kinde, he coud his old father's wone, Without lore, as can a drake swim, When it is caught, and carried to the brim.

CHAUCER.—Legend of Phillis.

Of course, the yet more lengthened absences of Hugh from the house were subjects of remark as at the first; but Hugh had made up his mind not to trouble himself the least about that. For some time Mrs. Glasford took no notice of them to himself; but one evening, just as tea was finished, and Hugh was rising to go, her restraint gave way, and she uttered one spiteful speech, thinking it, no doubt, so witty that it ought to see the light.

"Ye're a day–labourer it seems, Mr. Sutherlan', and gang hame at night."

"Exactly so, madam," rejoined Hugh. "There is no other relation between you and me, than that of work and wages. You have done your best to convince me of that, by making it impossible for me to feel that this house is in any sense my home."

With this grand speech he left the room, and from that time till the day of his final departure from Turriepuffit, there was not a single allusion made to the subject.

He soon reached the cottage. When he entered the new room, which was always called Mr. Sutherland's study, the mute welcome afforded him by the signs of expectation, in the glow of the waiting fire, and the outspread arms of the elbow–chair, which was now called his, as well as the room, made ample amends to him for the unfriendliness of Mrs. Glasford. Going to the shelves to find the books he wanted, he saw that they had been carefully arranged on one shelf, and that the others were occupied with books belonging to the house. He looked at a few of them. They were almost all old books, and such as may be found in many Scotch cottages; for instance, Boston's Fourfold State, in which the ways of God and man may be seen through a fourfold fog; Erskine's Divine Sonnets, which will repay the reader in laughter for the pain it costs his reverence, producing much the same effect that a Gothic cathedral might, reproduced by the pencil and from the remembrance of a Chinese artist, who had seen it once; Drelincourt on Death, with the

64

famous ghost–hoax of De Foe, to help the bookseller to the sale of the unsaleable; the Scots Worthies, opening of itself at the memoir of Mr. Alexander Peden; the Pilgrim's Progress, that wonderful inspiration, failing never save when the theologian would sometimes snatch the pen from the hand of the poet; Theron and Aspasio; Village Dialogues; and others of a like class. To these must be added a rare edition of Blind Harry. It was clear to Hugh, unable as he was fully to appreciate the wisdom of David, that it was not from such books as these that he had gathered it; yet such books as these formed all his store. He turned from them, found his own, and sat down to read. By and by David came in.

"I'm ower sune, I doubt, Mr. Sutherlan'. I'm disturbin' ye."

"Not at all," answered Hugh. "Besides, I am not much in a reading mood this evening: Mrs. Glasford has been annoying me again."

"Poor body! What's she been sayin' noo?"

Thinking to amuse David, Hugh recounted the short passage between them recorded above. David, however, listened with a very different expression of countenance from what Hugh had anticipated; and, when he had finished, took up the conversation in a kind of apologetic tone.

"Weel, but ye see," said he, folding his palms together, "she hasna' jist had a'thegither fair play. She does na come o' a guid breed. Man, it's a fine thing to come o' a guid breed. They hae a hantle to answer for 'at come o' decent forbears."

"I thought she brought the laird a good property," said Hugh, not quite understanding David.

"Ow, ay, she brocht him gowpenfu's o' siller; but hoo was't gotten? An' ye ken it's no riches 'at 'ill mak' a guid breed—'cep' it be o' maggots. The richer cheese the mair maggots, ye ken. Ye maunna speyk o' this; but the mistress's father was weel kent to hae made his siller by fardins and bawbees, in creepin', crafty ways. He was a bit merchan' in Aberdeen, an' aye keepit his thoom weel ahint the peint o' the ellwan', sae 'at he made an inch or twa upo' ilka yard he sauld. Sae he took frae his soul, and pat intill his siller–bag, an' had little to gie his dochter but a guid tocher. Mr. Sutherlan', it's a fine thing to come o' dacent fowk. Noo, to luik at yersel': I ken naething aboot yer family; but ye seem at eesicht to come o' a guid breed for the bodily part o' ye. That's a sma' matter; but frae what I ha'e seen—an' I trust in God I'm no' mista'en—ye come o' the richt breed for the min' as weel. I'm no flatterin' ye, Mr. Sutherlan'; but jist layin' it upo' ye, 'at gin ye had an honest father and gran'father, an' especially a guid mither, ye hae a heap to answer for; an' ye ought never to be hard upo' them 'at's sma' creepin' creatures, for they canna help it sae weel as the like o' you and me can."

David was not given to boasting. Hugh had never heard anything suggesting it from his lips before. He turned full round and looked at him. On his face lay a solemn quiet, either from a feeling of his own responsibility, or a sense of the excuse that must be made for others. What he had said about the signs of breed in Hugh's exterior, certainly applied to himself as well. His carriage was full of dignity, and a certain rustic refinement; his voice was wonderfully gentle, but deep; and slowest when most impassioned. He seemed to have come of some gigantic antediluvian breed: there was something of the Titan slumbering about him. He would have been a stern man, but for an unusual amount of reverence that seemed to overflood the sternness, and change it into strong love. No one had ever seen him thoroughly angry; his simple displeasure with any of the labourers, the quality of whose work was deficient, would go further than the laird's oaths.

Hugh sat looking at David, who supported the look with that perfect calmness that comes of unconscious simplicity. At length Hugh's eye sank before David's, as he said:

"I wish I had known your father, then, David."

"My father was sic a ane as I tauld ye the ither day, Mr. Sutherlan'. I'm a' richt there. A puir, semple, God—fearin' shepherd, 'at never gae his dog an ill—deserved word, nor took the skin o' ony puir lammie, wha's woo' he was clippin', atween the shears. He was weel worthy o' the grave 'at he wan till at last. An' my mither was jist sic like, wi' aiblins raither mair heid nor my father. They're her beuks maistly upo' the skelf there abune yer ain, Mr. Sutherlan'. I honour them for her sake, though I seldom trouble them mysel'. She gae me a kin' o' a scunner at them, honest woman, wi' garrin' me read at them o' Sundays, till they near scomfisht a' the guid 'at was in me by nater. There's doctrine for ye, Mr. Sutherlan'!" added David, with a queer laugh.

"I thought they could hardly be your books," said Hugh.

David Elginbrod

"But I hae ae odd beuk, an' that brings me upo' my pedigree, Mr. Sutherlan'; for the puirest man has as lang a pedigree as the greatest, only he kens less aboot it, that's a'. An' I wat, for yer lords and ladies, it's no a' to their credit 'at's tauld o' their hither—come; an' that's a' against the breed, ye ken. A wilfu' sin in the father may be a sinfu' weakness i' the son; an' that's what I ca' no fair play."

So saying, David went to his bedroom, whence he returned with a very old—looking book, which he laid on the table before Hugh. He opened it, and saw that it was a volume of Jacob Beohmen, in the original language. He found out afterwards, upon further inquiry, that it was in fact a copy of the first edition of his first work, The Aurora, printed in 1612. On the title—page was written a name, either in German or old English character, he was not sure which; but he was able to read it—Martin Elginbrodde. David, having given him time to see all this, went on:

"That buik has been in oor family far langer nor I ken. I needna say I canna read a word o't, nor I never heard o' ane 'at could. But I canna help tellin' ye a curious thing, Mr. Sutherlan', in connexion wi' the name on that buik: there's a gravestane, a verra auld ane—hoo auld I canna weel mak' out, though I gaed ends—errand to Aberdeen to see't—an' the name upo' that gravestane is Martin Elginbrod, but made mention o' in a strange fashion; an' I'm no sure a'thegither aboot hoo ye'll tak' it, for it soun's rather fearsome at first hearin' o't. But ye'se hae't as I read it:

```
 "'Here lie I, Martin Elginbrodde:
  Hae mercy o' my soul, Lord God;
  As I wad do, were I Lord God,
  And ye were Martin Elginbrodde.'"
```

Certainly Hugh could not help a slight shudder at what seemed to him the irreverence of the epitaph, if indeed it was not deserving of a worse epithet. But he made no remark; and, after a moment's pause, David resumed:

"I was unco ill—pleased wi't at the first, as ye may suppose, Mr. Sutherlan'; but, after a while, I begude (began) an' gaed through twa or three bits o' reasonin's aboot it, in this way: By the natur' o't, this maun be the man's ain makin', this epitaph; for no ither body cud ha' dune't; and he had left it in's will to be pitten upo' the deid—stane, nae doot: I' the contemplation o' deith, a man wad no be lik'ly to desire the perpetuation o' a blasphemy upo' a table o' stone, to stan' against him for centuries i' the face o' God an' man: therefore it cudna ha' borne the luik to him o' the presumptuous word o' a proud man evenin' himsel' wi' the Almichty. Sae what was't, then, 'at made him mak' it? It seems to me—though I confess, Mr. Sutherlan', I may be led astray by the nateral desire 'at a man has to think weel o' his ain forbears—for 'at he was a forbear o' my ain, I canna weel doot, the name bein' by no means a common ane, in Scotland ony way—I'm sayin', it seems to me, that it's jist a darin' way, maybe a childlike way, o' judgin', as Job micht ha' dune, 'the Lord by himsel';' an' sayin', 'at gin he, Martin Elginbrod, wad hae mercy, surely the Lord was not less mercifu' than he was. The offspring o' the Most High was, as it were, aware o' the same spirit i' the father o' him, as muved in himsel'. He felt 'at the mercy in himsel' was ane o' the best things; an' he cudna think 'at there wad be less o't i' the father o' lichts, frae whom cometh ilka guid an' perfeck gift. An' may be he remembered 'at the Saviour himsel' said: 'Be ye perfect as your father in Heaven is perfect;' and that the perfection o' God, as He had jist pinted oot afore, consisted in causin' his bonny sun to shine on the evil an' the good, an' his caller rain to fa' upo' the just an' the unjust."

It may well be doubted whether David's interpretation of the epitaph was the correct one. It will appear to most of my readers to breathe rather of doubt lighted up by hope, than of that strong faith which David read in it. But whether from family partiality, and consequent unwillingness to believe that his ancestor had been a man who, having led a wild, erring, and evil life, turned at last towards the mercy of God as his only hope, which the words might imply; or simply that he saw this meaning to be the best; this was the interpretation which David had adopted.

"But," interposed Hugh, "supposing he thought all that, why should he therefore have it carved on his tombstone?"

"I hae thocht aboot that too," answered David. "For ae thing, a body has but feow ways o' sayin' his say to his brithermen. Robbie Burns cud do't in sang efter sang; but maybe this epitaph was a' that auld Martin was able to mak'. He michtna hae had the gift o' utterance. But there may be mair in't nor that. Gin the clergy o' thae times warna a gey hantle mair enlichtened nor a fowth o' the clergy hereabouts, he wad hae heard a heap aboot the glory o' God, as the thing 'at God himsel' was maist anxious aboot uphaudin', jist like a prood creater o' a king; an' that he wad mak' men, an' feed them, an' cleed them, an' gie them braw wives an' toddlin' bairnies, an' syne damn them, a' for's ain glory. Maybe ye wadna get mony o' them 'at wad speyk sae fair–oot noo–a–days, for they gang wi' the tide jist like the lave; but i' my auld minny's buiks, I hae read jilt as muckle as that, an' waur too. Mony ane 'at spak like that, had nae doot a guid meanin' in't; but, hech man! it's an awesome deevilich way o' sayin' a holy thing. Noo, what better could puir auld Martin do, seein' he had no ae word to say i' the kirk a' his lifelang, nor jist say his ae word, as pithily as might be, i' the kirkyard, efter he was deid; an' ower an' ower again, wi' a tongue o' stane, let them tak' it or lat it alane 'at likit? That's a' my defence o' my auld luckie–daddy—Heaven rest his brave auld soul!"

"But are we not in danger," said Hugh, "of thinking too lightly and familiarly of the Maker, when we proceed to judge him so by ourselves?"

"Mr. Sutherlan'," replied David, very solemnly, "I dinna thenk I can be in muckle danger o' lichtlyin' him, whan I ken in my ain sel', as weel as she 'at was healed o' her plague, 'at I wad be a horse i' that pleuch, or a pig in that stye, not merely if it was his will—for wha can stan' against that—but if it was for his glory; ay, an' comfort mysel', a' the time the change was passin' upo' me, wi' the thocht that, efter an' a', his blessed han's made the pigs too."

"But, a moment ago, David, you seemed to me to be making rather little of his glory."

"O' his glory, as they consider glory—ay; efter a warldly fashion that's no better nor pride, an' in him would only be a greater pride. But his glory! consistin' in his trowth an' lovin'kindness—(man! that's a bonny word)—an' grand self–forgettin' devotion to his creaters—lord! man, it's unspeakable. I care little for his glory either, gin by that ye mean the praise o' men. A heap o' the anxiety for the spread o' his glory, seems to me to be but a desire for the sempathy o' ither fowk. There's no fear but men 'll praise him, a' in guid time—that is, whan they can. But, Mr. Sutherlan', for the glory o' God, raither than, if it were possible, one jot or one tittle should fail of his entire perfection of holy beauty, I call God to witness, I would gladly go to hell itsel'; for no evil worth the full name can befall the earth or ony creater in't, as long as God is what he is. For the glory o' God, Mr. Sutherlan', I wad die the deith . For the will o' God, I'm ready for onything he likes. I canna surely be in muckle danger o' lichtlyin' him. I glory in my God."

The almost passionate earnestness with which David spoke, would alone have made it impossible for Hugh to reply at once. After a few moments, however, he ventured to ask the question:

"Would you do nothing that other people should know God, then, David?"

"Onything 'at he likes. But I would tak' tent o' interferin'. He's at it himsel' frae mornin' to nicht, frae year's en' to year's en'."

"But you seem to me to make out that God is nothing but love!"

"Ay, naething but love. What for no?"

"Because we are told he is just."

"Would he be lang just if he didna lo'e us?"

"But does he not punish sin?"

"Would it be ony kin'ness no to punish sin? No to us a' means to pit awa' the ae ill thing frae us? Whatever may be meant by the place o' meesery, depen' upo't, Mr. Sutherlan', it's only anither form o' love, love shinin' through the fogs o' ill, an' sae gart leuk something verra different thereby. Man, raither nor see my Maggy—an' ye'll no doot 'at I lo'e her—raither nor see my Maggy do an ill thing, I'd see her lyin' deid at my feet. But supposin' the ill thing ance dune, it's no at my feet I wad lay her, but upo' my heart, wi' my auld arms aboot her, to hand the further ill aff o' her. An' shall mortal man be more just than God? Shall a man be more pure than his Maker? O my God! my God!"

The entrance of Margaret would have prevented the prosecution of this conversation, even if it had not already drawn to a natural close. Not that David would not have talked thus before his daughter, but simply that minds, like instruments, need to be brought up to the same pitch, before they can "atone together," and that one feels this instinctively on the entrance of another who has not gone through the same immediate process of gradual elevation of tone.

Their books and slates were got out, and they sat down to their work; but Hugh could not help observing that David, in the midst of his lines and angles and algebraic computations, would, every now and then, glance up at Margaret, with a look of tenderness in his face yet deeper and more delicate in its expression than ordinary. Margaret was, however, quite unconscious of it, pursuing her work with her ordinary even diligence. But Janet observed it.

"What ails the bairn, Dawvid, 'at ye leuk at her that get? said she.

"Naething ails her, woman. Do ye never leuk at a body but when something ails them?"

"Ow, ay—but no that get."

"Weel, maybe I was thinkin' hoo I wad leuk at her gin onything did ail her."

"Hoot! hoot! dinna further the ill hither by makin' a bien doonsittin' an' a bed for't."

All David's answer to this was one of his own smiles.

At supper, for it happened to be Saturday, Hugh said:

"I've been busy, between whiles, inventing, or perhaps discovering, an etymological pedigree for you, David!"

"Weel, lat's hear't," said David.

"First—do you know that that volume with your ancestor's name on it, was written by an old German shoemaker, perhaps only a cobbler, for anything I know?"

"I know nothing aboot it, more or less," answered David.

"He was a wonderful man. Some people think he was almost inspired."

"Maybe, maybe," was all David's doubtful response.

"At all events, though I know nothing about it myself, he must have written wonderfully for a cobbler."

David Elginbrod

"For my pairt," replied David, "if I see no wonder in the man, I can see but little in the cobbler. What for shouldna a cobbler write wonnerfully, as weel as anither? It's a trade 'at furthers meditation. My grandfather was a cobbler, as ye ca't; an' they say he was no fule in his ain way either."

"Then it does go in the family!" cried Hugh, triumphantly. "I was in doubt at first whether your name referred to the breadth of your shoulders, David, as transmitted from some ancient sire, whose back was an Ellwand—broad; for the g might come from a w or v, for anything I know to the contrary. But it would have been braid in that case. And, now, I am quite convinced that that Martin or his father was a German, a friend of old Jacob Beohmen, who gave him the book himself, and was besides of the same craft; and he coming to this country with a name hard to be pronounced, they found a resemblance in the sound of it to his occupation; and so gradually corrupted his name, to them uncouth, into Elsynbrod, Elshinbrod, thence Elginbrod, with a soft g, and lastly Elginbrod, as you pronounce it now, with a hard g. This name, turned from Scotch into English, would then be simply Martin Awlbore. The cobbler is in the family, David, descended from Jacob Beohmen himself, by the mother's side."

This heraldic blazon amused them all very much, and David expressed his entire concurrence with it, declaring it to be incontrovertible. Margaret laughed heartily.

Besides its own beauty, two things made Margaret's laugh of some consequence; one was, that it was very rare; and the other, that it revealed her two regular rows of dainty white teeth, suiting well to the whole build of the maiden. She was graceful and rather tall, with a head which, but for its smallness, might have seemed too heavy for the neck that supported it, so ready it always was to droop like a snowdrop. The only parts about her which Hugh disliked, were her hands and feet. The former certainly had been reddened and roughened by household work: but they were well formed notwithstanding. The latter he had never seen, notwithstanding the bare—foot habits of Scotch maidens; for he saw Margaret rarely except in the evenings, and then she was dressed to receive him. Certainly, however, they were very far from following the shape of the clumsy country shoes, by which he misjudged their proportions. Had he seen them, as he might have seen them some part of any day during the summer, their form at least would have satisfied him.

CHAPTER XIV. WINTER.

```
Out of whose womb came the ice? and the hoary frost of heaven, who
hath gendered it?  The waters are hid as with a stone, and the face
of the deep is frozen.
```

```
He giveth snow like wool; he scattereth the hoar frost like ashes.
```

```
JOB xxxviii. 29, 30; PSALM cxlvii. 16.
```

Winter was fairly come at last. A black frost had bound the earth for many days; and at length a peculiar sensation, almost a smell of snow in the air, indicated an approaching storm. The snow fell at first in a few large unwilling flakes, that fluttered slowly and heavily to the earth, where they lay like the foundation of the superstructure that was about to follow. Faster and faster they fell—wonderful multitudes of delicate crystals, adhering in shapes of beauty which outvied all that jeweller could invent or execute of ethereal, starry forms, structures of evanescent yet prodigal loveliness—till the whole air was obscured by them, and night came on, hastened by an hour, from the gathering of their white darkness. In the morning, all the landscape was transfigured. The snow had ceased to fall; but the whole earth, houses, fields, and fences, ponds and streams, were changed to whiteness. But most wonderful looked the trees—every bough and every twig thickened, and bent earthward with its own individual load of the fairy ghost–birds. Each retained the semblance of its own form, wonderfully, magically altered by its thick garment of radiant whiteness, shining gloriously in the sunlight. It was the shroud of dead nature; but a shroud that seemed to prefigure a lovely resurrection; for the very death–robe was unspeakably, witchingly beautiful. Again at night the snow fell; and again and again, with intervening days of bright sunshine. Every morning, the first fresh footprints were a new wonder to the living creatures, the young–hearted amongst them at least, who lived and moved in this death–world, this sepulchral planet, buried in the shining air before the eyes of its sister–stars in the blue, deathless heavens. Paths had to be cleared in every direction towards the out–houses, and again cleared every morning; till at last the walls of solid rain stood higher than the head of little Johnnie, as he was still called, though he was twelve years old. It was a great delight to him to wander through the snow–avenues in every direction; and great fun it was, both to him and his brother, when they were tired of snowballing each other and every living thing about the place except their parents and tutor, to hollow out mysterious caves and vaulted passages. Sometimes they would carry these passages on from one path to within an inch or two of

73

another, and there lie in wait till some passer–by, unweeting of harm, was just opposite their lurking cave; when they would dash through the solid wall of snow with a hideous yell, almost endangering the wits of the maids, and causing a recoil and startled ejaculation even of the strong man on whom they chanced to try their powers of alarm. Hugh himself was once glad to cover the confusion of his own fright with the hearty fit of laughter into which the perturbation of the boys, upon discovering whom they had startled, threw him. It was rare fun to them; but not to the women about the house, who moved from place to place in a state of chronic alarm, scared by the fear of being scared; till one of them going into hysterics, real or pretended, it was found necessary to put a stop to the practice; not, however, before Margaret had had her share of the jest. Hugh happened to be looking out of his window at the moment—watching her, indeed, as she passed towards the kitchen with some message from her mother; when an indescribable monster, a chaotic mass of legs and snow, burst, as if out of the earth, upon her. She turned pale as the snow around her (and Hugh had never observed before how dark her eyes were), as she sprang back with the grace of a startled deer. She uttered no cry, however, perceiving in a moment who it was, gave a troubled little smile, and passed on her way as if nothing had happened. Hugh was not sorry when maternal orders were issued against the practical joke. The boys did not respect their mother very much, but they dared not disobey her, when she spoke in a certain tone.

There was no pathway cut to David's cottage; and no track trodden, except what David, coming to the house sometimes, and Hugh going every afternoon to the cottage, made between them. Hugh often went to the knees in snow, but was well dried and warmed by Janet's care when he arrived. She had always a pair of stockings and slippers ready for him at the fire, to be put on the moment of his arrival; and exchanged again for his own, dry and warm, before he footed once more the ghostly waste. When neither moon was up nor stars were out, there was a strange eerie glimmer from the snow that lighted the way home; and he thought there must be more light from it than could be accounted for merely by the reflection of every particle of light that might fall upon it from other sources.

Margaret was not kept to the house by the snow, even when it was falling. She went out as usual—not of course wandering far, for walking was difficult now. But she was in little danger of losing her way, for she knew the country as well as any one; and although its face was greatly altered by the filling up of its features, and the uniformity of the colour, yet those features were discernible to her experienced eye through the sheet that covered them. It was only necessary to walk on the tops of dykes, and other elevated ridges, to keep clear of the deep snow.

There were many paths between the cottages and the farms in the neighbourhood, in which she could walk with comparative ease and comfort. But she preferred wandering away through the fields and toward the hills. Sometimes she would come home like a creature of the snow, born of it, and living in it; so covered was she from head to foot with its flakes. David used to smile at her with peculiar complacency on such occasions. It was evident that it pleased him she should be the playmate of Nature. Janet was not altogether indulgent to these freaks, as she considered them, of Marget—she had quite given up calling her Meg, "sin' she took to the beuk so eident." But whatever her mother might think of it, Margaret was in this way laying up a store not only of bodily and mental health, but of resources for thought and feeling, of secret understandings and communions with Nature, and everything simple, and strong, and pure through Nature, than which she could have accumulated nothing more precious.

This kind of weather continued for some time, till the people declared they had never known a storm last so long "ohn ever devallt," that is, without intermission. But the frost grew harder; and then the snow, instead of falling in large adhesive flakes, fell in small dry flakes, of which the boys could make no snaw–ba's. All the time, however, there was no wind; and this not being a sheep country, there was little uneasiness or suffering occasioned by the severity of the weather, beyond what must befall the poorer classes in every northern country during the winter.

One day, David heard that a poor old man of his acquaintance was dying, and immediately set out to visit him, at a distance of two or three miles. He returned in the evening, only in time for his studies; for there was of course little or nothing to be done at present in the way of labour. As he sat down to the table, he said:

"I hae seen a wonnerfu' sicht sin' I saw you, Mr. Sutherlan'. I gaed to see an auld Christian, whase body an' brain are nigh worn oot. He was never onything remarkable for intellec, and jist took what the minister tellt him for true, an' keepit the guid o't; for his hert was aye richt, an' his faith a hantle stronger than maybe it had ony richt to be, accordin' to his ain opingans; but, hech! there's something far better nor his opingans i' the hert o' ilka God–fearin' body. Whan I gaed butt the hoose, he was sittin' in's auld arm–chair by the side o' the fire, an' his face luikit dazed like. There was no licht in't but

75

what cam' noo an' than frae a low i' the fire. The snaw was driftin' a wee aboot the bit winnock, an' his auld een was fixed upo't; an' a' 'at he said, takin' no notice o' me, was jist, 'The birdies is flutterin'; the birdies is flutterin'.' I spak' till him, an' tried to roose him, wi' ae thing after anither, bit I micht as weel hae spoken to the door–cheek, for a' the notice that he took. Never a word he spak', but aye 'The birdies is flutterin'.' At last, it cam' to my min' 'at the body was aye fu' o' ane o' the psalms in particler; an' sae I jist said till him at last: 'John, hae ye forgotten the twenty–third psalm?' 'Forgotten the twenty–third psalm!' quo' he; an' his face lighted up in a moment frae the inside: 'The Lord's my shepherd,—an' I hae followed Him through a' the smorin' drift o' the warl', an' he'll bring me to the green pastures an' the still waters o' His summer–kingdom at the lang last. I shall not want. An' I hae wanted for naething, naething.' He had been a shepherd himsel' in's young days. And so on he gaed, wi' a kin' o' a personal commentary on the haill psalm frae beginnin' to en', and syne he jist fell back into the auld croonin' sang, 'The birdies is flutterin'; the birdies is flutterin'.' The licht deed oot o' his face, an' a' that I could say could na' bring back the licht to his face, nor the sense to his tongue. He'll sune be in a better warl'. Sae I was jist forced to leave him. But I promised his dochter, puir body, that I would ca' again an' see him the morn's afternoon. It's unco dowie wark for her; for they hae scarce a neebor within reach o' them, in case o' a change; an' there had hardly been a creatur' inside o' their door for a week."

The following afternoon, David set out according to his promise. Before his return, the wind, which had been threatening to wake all day, had risen rapidly, and now blew a snowstorm of its own. When Hugh opened the door to take his usual walk to the cottage, just as darkness was beginning to fall, the sight he saw made his young strong heart dance with delight. The snow that fell made but a small part of the wild, confused turmoil and uproar of the ten–fold storm. For the wind, raving over the surface of the snow, which, as I have already explained, lay nearly as loose as dry sand, swept it in thick fierce clouds along with it, tearing it up and casting it down again no one could tell where—for the whole air was filled with drift, as they call the snow when thus driven. A few hours of this would alter the face of the whole country, leaving some parts bare, and others buried beneath heaps on heaps of snow, called here snaw–wreaths. For the word snow–wreaths does not mean the lovely garlands hung upon every tree and bush in its feathery fall; but awful mounds of drifted snow, that may be the smooth, soft, white sepulchres of dead men, smothered in the lapping folds of the almost solid wind. Path or way was none before him. He could see nothing but the surface of a sea of froth and foam, as it appeared to him, with the spray torn from it, whirled in all shapes and contortions, and driven in every direction; but chiefly, in the main direction of the wind, in long sloping spires of misty whiteness, swift as arrows, and as keen upon the face of him who dared to oppose them.

Hugh plunged into it with a wild sense of life and joy. In the course of his short walk, however, if walk it could be called, which was one chain of plungings and emergings, struggles with the snow, and wrestles with the wind, he felt that it needed not a stout heart only, but sound lungs and strong limbs as well, to battle with the storm, even for such a distance. When he reached the cottage, he found Janet in considerable anxiety, not only about David, who had not yet returned, but about Margaret as well, whom she had not seen for some time, and who must be out somewhere in the storm—"the wull hizzie." Hugh suggested that she might have gone to meet her father.

"The Lord forbid!" ejaculated Janet. "The road lies ower the tap o' the Halshach, as eerie and bare a place as ever was hill—moss, wi' never a scoug or bield in't, frae the tae side to the tither. The win' there jist gangs clean wud a'thegither. An' there's mony a well—ee forbye, that gin ye fell intill't, ye wud never come at the boddom o't. The Lord preserve's! I wis' Dawvid was hame."

"How could you let him go, Janet?"

"Lat him gang, laddie! It's a strang tow 'at wad haud or bin' Dawvid, whan he considers he bud to gang, an' 'twere intill a deil's byke. But I'm no that feared aboot him. I maist believe he's under special protection, if ever man was or oucht to be; an' he's no more feared at the storm, nor gin the snaw was angels' feathers flauchterin' oot o' their wings a' aboot him. But I'm no easy i' my min' aboot Maggy—the wull hizzie! Gin she be meetin' her father, an' chance to miss him, the Lord kens what may come o' her."

Hugh tried to comfort her, but all that could be done was to wait David's return. The storm seemed to increase rather than abate its force. The footprints Hugh had made, had all but vanished already at the very door of the house, which stood quite in the shelter of the fir—wood. As they looked out, a dark figure appeared within a yard or two of the house.

"The Lord grant it be my bairn!" prayed poor Janet. But it was David, and alone. Janet gave a shriek.

David Elginbrod

"Dawvid, whaur's Maggie?"

"I haena seen the bairn," replied David, in repressed perturbation. "She's no theroot, is she, the nicht?"

"She's no at hame, Dawvid, that's a' 'at I ken."

"Whaur gaed she?"

"The Lord kens. She's smoored i' the snaw by this time."

"She's i' the Lord's han's, Janet, be she aneath a snaw—vraith. Dinna forget that, wuman. Hoo lang is't sin' ye missed her?"

"An hour an' mair—I dinna ken hoo lang. I'm clean doitit wi' dreid."

"I'll awa' an' leuk for her. Just haud the hert in her till I come back, Mr. Sutherlan'."

"I won't be left behind, David. I'm going with you."

"Ye dinna ken what ye're sayin', Mr. Sutherlan'. I wad sune hae twa o' ye to seek in place o' ane."

"Never heed me; I'm going on my own account, come what may."

"Weel, weel; I downa bide to differ. I'm gaein up the burn—side; baud ye ower to the farm, and spier gin onybody's seen her; an' the lads 'll be out to leuk for her in a jiffey. My puir lassie!"

The sigh that must have accompanied the last words, was lost in the wind, as they vanished in the darkness. Janet fell on her knees in the kitchen, with the door wide open, and the wind drifting in the powdery snow, and scattering it with the ashes from the hearth over the floor. A picture of more thorough desolation can hardly be imagined. She soon came to herself, however; and reflecting that, if the lost child was found, there must be a warm bed to receive her, else she might be a second time lost, she rose and shut the door, and mended the fire. It was as if the dumb attitude of her prayer was answered; for

78

though she had never spoken or even thought a word, strength was restored to her distracted brain. When she had made every preparation she could think of, she went to the door again, opened it, and looked out. It was a region of howling darkness, tossed about by pale snow-drifts; out of which it seemed scarce more hopeful that welcome faces would emerge, than that they should return to our eyes from the vast unknown in which they vanish at last. She closed the door once more, and knowing nothing else to be done, sat down on a chair, with her hands on her knees, and her eyes fixed on the door. The clock went on with its slow swing, tic—tac, tic—tac, an utterly inhuman time-measurer; but she heard the sound of every second, through the midst of the uproar in the fir-trees, which bent their tall heads hissing to the blast, and swinging about in the agony of their strife. The minutes went by, till an hour was gone, and there was neither sound nor hearing, but of the storm and the clock. Still she sat and stared, her eyes fixed on the door-latch. Suddenly, without warning it was lifted, and the door opened. Her heart bounded and fluttered like a startled bird; but alas! the first words she heard were: "Is she no come yet?" It was her husband, followed by several of the farm servants. He had made a circuit to the farm, and finding that Hugh had never been there, hoped, though with trembling, that Margaret had already returned home. The question fell upon Janet's heart like the sound of the earth on the coffin-lid, and her silent stare was the only answer David received.

But at that very moment, like a dead man burst from the tomb, entered from behind the party at the open door, silent and white, with rigid features and fixed eyes, Hugh. He stumbled in, leaning forward with long strides, and dragging something behind him. He pushed and staggered through them as if he saw nothing before him; and as they parted horror-stricken, they saw that it was Margaret, or her dead body, that he dragged after him. He dropped her at her mother's feet, and fell himself on the floor, before they were able to give him any support. David, who was quite calm, got the whisky bottle out, and tried to administer some to Margaret first; but her teeth were firmly set, and to all appearance she was dead. One of the young men succeeded better with Hugh, whom at David's direction they took into the study; while he and Janet got Margaret undressed and put to bed, with hot bottles all about her; for in warmth lay the only hope of restoring her. After she had lain thus for a while, she gave a sigh; and when they had succeeded in getting her to swallow some warm milk, she began to breathe, and soon seemed to be only fast asleep. After half an hour's rest and warming, Hugh was able to move and speak. David would not allow him to say much, however, but got him to bed, sending word to the house that he could not go home that night. He and Janet sat by the fireside all night, listening to the storm that still raved without, and thanking God for both of the lives. Every few minutes a tip–toe excursion was made to the bedside, and now and then to the other room. Both the patients slept quietly. Towards morning Margaret opened her eyes, and faintly called her mother; but soon fell asleep once more, and did not awake again till nearly noon. When sufficiently restored to be able to speak, the account she gave was, that she had set out to meet her father; but the storm increasing, she had thought it more prudent to turn. It grew in violence, however, so rapidly, and beat so directly in her face, that she was soon exhausted with struggling, and benumbed with the cold. The last thing she remembered was, dropping, as she thought, into a hole, and feeling as if she were going to sleep in bed, yet knowing it was death; and thinking how much sweeter it was than sleep. Hugh's account was very strange and defective, but he was never able to add anything to it. He said that, when he rushed out into the dark, the storm seized him like a fury, beating him about the head and face with icy wings, till he was almost stunned. He took the road to the farm, which lay through the fir–wood; but he soon became aware that he had lost his way and might tramp about in the fir–wood till daylight, if he lived as long. Then, thinking of Margaret, he lost his presence of mind, and rushed wildly along. He thought he must have knocked his head against the trunk of a tree, but he could not tell; for he remembered nothing more but that he found himself dragging Margaret, with his arms round her, through the snow, and nearing the light in the cottage–window. Where or how he had found her, or what the light was that he was approaching, he had not the least idea. He had only a vague notion that he was rescuing Margaret from something dreadful. Margaret, for her part, had no recollection of reaching the fir–wood, and as, long before morning, all traces were obliterated, the facts remained a mystery. Janet thought that David had some wonderful persuasion about it; but he was never heard even to speculate on the subject. Certain it was, that Hugh had saved Margaret's life. He seemed quite well next day, for he was of a very powerful and enduring frame for his years. She recovered more slowly, and perhaps never altogether overcame the effects of Death's embrace that night. From the moment when Margaret was brought home, the storm gradually died away, and by the morning all was still; but many starry and moonlit nights glimmered and passed, before that snow was melted away from the earth; and many a night Janet awoke from her sleep with a cry, thinking she heard her daughter moaning, deep in the smooth ocean of snow, and could not find where she lay.

The occurrences of this dreadful night could not lessen the interest his cottage friends felt in Hugh; and a long winter passed with daily and lengthening communion both in study and in general conversation. I fear some of my younger readers will think my story slow; and say: "What! are they not going to fall in love with each other yet? We have been expecting it ever so long." I have two answers to make to this. The first is: "I do not pretend to know so much about love as you excuse me think you do; and must confess, I do not know whether they were in love with each other or not." The second is: "That I dare not pretend to understand thoroughly such a sacred mystery as the heart of Margaret; and I should feel it rather worse than presumptuous to talk as if I did. Even Hugh's is known to me only by gleams of light thrown, now and then, and here and there, upon it." Perhaps the two answers are only the same answer in different shapes.

Mrs. Glasford, however, would easily answer the question, if an answer is all that is wanted; for she, notwithstanding the facts of the story, which she could not fail to have heard correctly from the best authority, and notwithstanding the nature of the night, which might have seemed sufficient to overthrow her conclusions, uniformly remarked, as often as their escape was alluded to in her hearing,

"Lat them tak' it They had no business to be oot aboot thegither."

CHAPTER XV. TRANSITION.

```
Tell me, bright boy, tell me, my golden lad,
Whither away so frolic?  Why so glad?
What all thy wealth in council? all thy state?
Are husks so dear? troth, 'tis a mighty rate.

RICHARD CRASHAW.
```

The long Scotch winter passed by without any interruption to the growing friendship. But the spring brought a change; and Hugh was separated from his friends sooner than he had anticipated, by more than six months. For his mother wrote to him in great distress, in consequence of a claim made upon her for some debt which his father had contracted, very probably for Hugh's own sake. Hugh could not bear that any such should remain undischarged, or that his father's name should not rest in peace as well as his body and soul. He requested, therefore, from the laird, the amount due to him, and despatched almost the whole of it for the liquidation of this debt, so that he was now as unprovided as before for the expenses of the coming winter at Aberdeen. But, about the same time, a fellow–student wrote to him with news of a situation for the summer, worth three times as much as his present one, and to be procured through his friend's interest. Hugh having engaged himself to the laird only for the winter, although he had intended to stay till the commencement of the following session, felt that, although he would much rather remain where he was, he must not hesitate a moment to accept his friend's offer; and therefore wrote at once.

I will not attempt to describe the parting. It was very quiet, but very solemn and sad. Janet showed far more distress than Margaret, for she wept outright. The tears stood in David's eyes, as he grasped the youth's hand in silence. Margaret was very pale; that was all. As soon as Hugh disappeared with her father, who was going to walk with him to the village through which the coach passed, she hurried away, and went to the fir-wood for comfort.

Hugh found his new situation in Perthshire very different from the last. The heads of the family being themselves a lady and a gentleman, he found himself a gentleman too. He had more to do, but his work left him plenty of leisure notwithstanding. A good portion of his spare time he devoted to verse-making, to which he felt a growing impulse; and whatever may have been the merit of his compositions, they did him intellectual good at least, if it were only through the process of their construction. He wrote to David after his arrival, telling him all about his new situation; and received in return a letter from Margaret, written at her father's dictation. The mechanical part of letter-writing was rather laborious to David; but Margaret wrote well, in consequence of the number of papers, of one sort and another, which she had written for Hugh. Three or four letters more passed between them at lengthening intervals. Then they ceased—on Hugh's side first; until, when on the point of leaving for Aberdeen, feeling somewhat conscience-stricken at not having written for so long, he scribbled a note to inform them of his approaching departure, promising to let them know his address as soon as he found himself settled. Will it be believed that the session went by without the redemption of this pledge? Surely he could not have felt, to any approximate degree, the amount of obligation he was under to his humble friends. Perhaps, indeed, he may have thought that the obligation was principally on their side; as it would have been, if intellectual assistance could outweigh heart-kindness, and spiritual impulse and enlightenment; for, unconsciously in a great measure to himself, he had learned from David to regard in a new and more real aspect, many of those truths which he had hitherto received as true, and which yet had till then produced in him no other than a feeling of the common-place and uninteresting at the best.

David Elginbrod

Besides this, and many cognate advantages, a thousand seeds of truth must have surely remained in his mind, dropped there from the same tongue of wisdom, and only waiting the friendly aid of a hard winter, breaking up the cold, selfish clods of clay, to share in the loveliness of a new spring, and be perfected in the beauty of a new summer.

However this may have been, it is certain that he forgot his old friends far more than he himself could have thought it possible he should; for, to make the best of it, youth is easily attracted and filled with the present show, and easily forgets that which, from distance in time or space, has no show to show. Spending his evenings in the midst of merry faces, and ready tongues fluent with the tones of jollity, if not always of wit, which glided sometimes into no too earnest discussion of the difficult subjects occupying their student hours; surrounded by the vapours of whisky–toddy, and the smoke of cutty pipes, till far into the short hours; then hurrying home, and lapsing into unrefreshing slumbers over intended study; or sitting up all night to prepare the tasks which had been neglected for a ball or an evening with Wilson, the great interpreter of Scottish song—it is hardly to be wondered at that he should lose the finer consciousness of higher powers and deeper feelings, not from any behaviour in itself wrong, but from the hurry, noise, and tumult in the streets of life, that, penetrating too deep into the house of life, dazed and stupefied the silent and lonely watcher in the chamber of conscience, far apart. He had no time to think or feel.

The session drew to a close. He eschewed all idleness; shut himself up, after class hours, with his books; ate little, studied hard, slept irregularly, working always best between midnight and two in the morning; carried the first honours in most of his classes; and at length breathed freely, but with a dizzy brain, and a face that revealed, in pale cheeks, and red, weary eyes, the results of an excess of mental labour—an excess which is as injurious as any other kind of intemperance, the moral degradation alone kept out of view. Proud of his success, he sat down and wrote a short note, with a simple statement of it, to David; hoping, in his secret mind, that he would attribute his previous silence to an absorption in study which had not existed before the end of the session was quite at hand. Now that he had more time for reflection, he could not bear the idea that that noble rustic face should look disapprovingly or, still worse, coldly upon him; and he could not help feeling as if the old ploughman had taken the place of his father, as the only man of whom he must stand in awe, and who had a right to reprove him. He did reprove him now, though unintentionally. For David was delighted at having such good news from him; and the uneasiness which he had felt, but never quite expressed, was almost swept away in the conclusion, that it was unreasonable to expect the young man to give his time to them both absent and present, especially when he had been occupied to such good purpose as this letter signified. So he was nearly at peace about him—though not quite. Hugh received from him the following letter in reply to his; dictated, as usual, to his secretary, Margaret:—

"MY DEAR SIR,

"Ye'll be a great man some day, gin ye haud at it. But things maunna be gotten at the outlay o' mair than they're worth. Ye'll ken what I mean. An' there's better things nor bein' a great man, efter a'. Forgie the liberty I tak' in remin'in' ye o' sic like. I'm only remin'in' ye o' what ye ken weel aneuch. But ye're a brave lad, an' ye hae been an unco frien' to me an' mine; an' I pray the Lord to thank ye for me, for ye hae dune muckle guid to his bairns—meanin' me an' mine. It's verra kin' o' ye to vrite till's in the verra moment o' victory; but weel ye kent that amid a' yer frien's—an' ye canna fail to hae mony a ane, wi' a head an' a face like yours—there was na ane—na, no ane, that wad rejoice mair ower your success than Janet, or my doo, Maggie, or yer ain auld obleeged frien' an' servant,

"DAVID ELGINBROD.

"P.S.—We're a' weel, an' unco blythe at your letter.

Maggy—

"P.S. 2.—Dear Mr. Sutherland,—I wrote all the above at my father's dictation, and just as he said it, for I thought you would like his Scotch better than my English. My mother and I myself are rejoiced at the good news. My mother fairly grat outright. I gaed out to the tree where I met you first. I wonder sair sometimes if you was the angel I was to meet in the fir–wood. I am,

"Your obedient servant,

"MARGARET ELGINBROD."

This letter certainly touched Hugh. But he could not help feeling rather offended that David should write to him in such a warning tone. He had never addressed him in this fashion when he saw him every day. Indeed, David could not very easily have spoken to him thus. But writing is a different thing; and men who are not much accustomed to use a pen, often assume a more solemn tone in doing so, as if it were a ceremony that required state. As for David, having been a little uneasy about Hugh, and not much afraid of offending him—for he did not know his weaknesses very thoroughly, and did not take into account the effect of the very falling away which he dreaded, in increasing in him pride, and that impatience of the gentlest reproof natural to every man—he felt considerably relieved after he had discharged his duty in this memento vivere. But one of the results, and a very unexpected one, was, that a yet longer period elapsed before Hugh wrote again to David. He meant to do so, and meant to do so; but, as often as the thought occurred to him, was checked both by consciousness and by pride. So much contributes, not the evil alone that is in us, but the good also sometimes, to hold us back from doing the thing we ought to do.

It now remained for Hugh to look about for some occupation. The state of his funds rendered immediate employment absolutely necessary; and as there was only one way in which he could earn money without yet further preparation, he must betake himself to that way, as he had done before, in the hope that it would lead to something better. At all events, it would give him time to look about him, and make up his mind for the future. Many a one, to whom the occupation of a tutor is far more irksome than it was to Hugh, is compelled to turn his acquirements to this immediate account; and, once going in this groove, can never get out of it again. But Hugh was hopeful enough to think, that his reputation at the university would stand him in some stead; and, however much he would have disliked the thought of being a tutor all his days, occupying a kind of neutral territory between the position of a gentleman and that of a menial, he had enough of strong Saxon good sense to prevent him, despite his Highland pride, from seeing any great hardship in labouring still for a little while, as he had laboured hitherto. But he hoped to find a situation more desirable than either of those he had occupied before; and, with this expectation, looked towards the South, as most Scotchmen do, indulging the national impulse to spoil the Egyptians. Nor did he look long, sending his tentacles afloat in every direction, before he heard, through means of a college friend, of just such a situation as he wanted, in the family of a gentleman of fortune in the county of Surrey, not much more than twenty miles from London. This he was fortunate enough to obtain without difficulty.

David Elginbrod

Margaret was likewise on the eve of a change. She stood like a young fledged bird on the edge of the nest, ready to take its first long flight. It was necessary that she should do something for herself, not so much from the compulsion of immediate circumstances, as in prospect of the future. Her father was not an old man, but at best he could leave only a trifle at his death; and if Janet outlived him, she would probably require all that, and what labour she would then be capable of as well, to support herself. Margaret was anxious, too, though not to be independent, yet, not to be burdensome. Both David and Janet saw that, by her peculiar tastes and habits, she had separated herself so far from the circle around her, that she could never hope to be quite comfortable in that neighbourhood. It was not that by any means she despised or refused the labours common to the young women of the country; but, all things considered, they thought that something more suitable for her might be procured.

The laird's lady continued to behave to her in the most supercilious fashion. The very day of Hugh's departure, she had chanced to meet Margaret walking alone with a book, this time unopened, in her hand. Mrs. Glasford stopped. Margaret stopped too, expecting to be addressed. The lady looked at her, all over, from head to foot, as if critically examining the appearance of an animal she thought of purchasing; then, without a word, but with a contemptuous toss of the head, passed on, leaving poor Margaret both angry and ashamed.

But David was much respected by the gentry of the neighbourhood, with whom his position, as the laird's steward, brought him not unfrequently into contact; and to several of them he mentioned his desire of finding some situation for Margaret. Janet could not bear the idea of her lady–bairn leaving them, to encounter the world alone; but David, though he could not help sometimes feeling a similar pang, was able to take to himself hearty comfort from the thought, that if there was any safety for her in her father's house, there could not be less in her heavenly Father's, in any nook of which she was as full in His eye, and as near His heart, as in their own cottage. He felt that anxiety in this case, as in every other, would just be a lack of confidence in God, to suppose which justifiable would be equivalent to saying that He had not fixed the foundations of the earth that it should not be moved; that He was not the Lord of Life, nor the Father of His children; in short, that a sparrow could fall to the ground without Him, and that the hairs of our head are not numbered. Janet admitted all this, but sighed nevertheless. So did David too, at times; for he knew that the sparrow must fall; that many a divine truth is hard to learn, all–blessed as it is when learned; and that sorrow and suffering must come to Margaret, ere she could be fashioned into the perfection of a child of the kingdom. Still, she was as safe abroad as at home.

An elderly lady of fortune was on a visit to one of the families in the neighbourhood. She was in want of a lady's–maid, and it occurred to the housekeeper that Margaret might suit her. This was not quite what her parents would have chosen, but they allowed her to go and see the lady. Margaret was delighted with the benevolent–looking gentlewoman; and she, on her part, was quite charmed with Margaret. It was true she knew nothing of the duties of the office; but the present maid, who was leaving on the best of terms, would soon initiate her into its mysteries. And David and Janet were so much pleased with Margaret's account of the interview, that David himself went to see the lady. The sight of him only increased her desire to have Margaret, whom she said she would treat like a daughter, if only she were half as good as she looked. Before David left her, the matter was arranged; and within a month, Margaret was borne in her mistress's carriage, away from father and mother and cottage–home.

END OF THE FIRST BOOK.

BOOK II. ARNSTEAD.

The earth hath bubbles as the water has.

MACBETH.—I.3

CHAPTER I. A NEW HOME.

A wise man's home is whereso'er he's wise.

JOHN MARSTON.—Antonio's Revenge.

Hugh left the North dead in the arms of grey winter, and found his new abode already alive in the breath of the west wind. As he walked up the avenue to the house, he felt that the buds were breaking all about, though, the night being dark and cloudy, the green shadows of the coming spring were invisible.

David Elginbrod

He was received at the hall-door, and shown to his room, by an old, apparently confidential, and certainly important butler; whose importance, however, was inoffensive, as founded, to all appearance, on a sense of family and not of personal dignity. Refreshment was then brought him, with the message that, as it was late, Mr. Arnold would defer the pleasure of meeting him till the morning at breakfast.

Left to himself, Hugh began to look around him. Everything suggested a contrast between his present position and that which he had first occupied about the same time of the year at Turriepuffit. He was in an old handsome room of dark wainscot, furnished like a library, with book-cases about the walls. One of them, with glass doors, had an ancient escritoire underneath, which was open, and evidently left empty for his use. A fire was burning cheerfully in an old high grate; but its light, though assisted by that of two wax candles on the table, failed to show the outlines of the room, it was so large and dark. The ceiling was rather low in proportion, and a huge beam crossed it. At one end, an open door revealed a room beyond, likewise lighted with fire and candles. Entering, he found this to be an equally old-fashioned bedroom, to which his luggage had been already conveyed.

"As far as creature comforts go," thought Hugh, "I have fallen on my feet." He rang the bell, had the tray removed, and then proceeded to examine the book-cases. He found them to contain much of the literature with which he was most desirous of making an acquaintance. A few books of the day were interspersed. The sense of having good companions in the authors around him, added greatly to his feeling of comfort; and he retired for the night filled with pleasant anticipations of his sojourn at Arnstead. All the night, however, his dreams were of wind and snow, and Margaret out in them alone. Janet was waiting in the cottage for him to bring her home. He had found her, but could not move her; for the spirit of the storm had frozen her to ice, and she was heavy as a marble statue.

When he awoke, the shadows of boughs and budding twigs were waving in changeful network-tracery, across the bright sunshine on his window-curtains. Before he was called he was ready to go down; and to amuse himself till breakfast-time, he proceeded to make another survey of the books. He concluded that these must be a colony from the mother-library; and also that the room must, notwithstanding, be intended for his especial occupation, seeing his bedroom opened out of it. Next, he looked from all the windows, to discover into what kind of a furrow on the face of the old earth he had fallen.

David Elginbrod

All he could see was trees and trees. But oh! how different from the sombre, dark, changeless fir–wood at Turriepuffit! whose trees looked small and shrunken in his memory, beside this glory of boughs, breaking out into their prophecy of an infinite greenery at hand. His rooms seemed to occupy the end of a small wing at the back of the house, as well as he could judge. His sitting–room windows looked across a small space to another wing; and the windows of his bedroom, which were at right–angles to those of the former, looked full into what seemed an ordered ancient forest of gracious trees of all kinds, coming almost close to the very windows. They were the trees which had been throwing their shadows on these windows for two or three hours of the silent spring sunlight, at once so liquid and so dazzling. Then he resolved to test his faculty for discovery, by seeing whether he could find his way to the breakfast–room without a guide. In this he would have succeeded without much difficulty, for it opened from the main–entrance hall, to which the huge square–turned oak staircase, by which he had ascended, led; had it not been for the somewhat intricate nature of the passages leading from the wing in which his rooms were (evidently an older and more retired portion of the house) to the main staircase itself. After opening many doors and finding no thoroughfare, he became convinced that, in place of finding a way on, he had lost the way back. At length he came to a small stair, which led him down to a single door. This he opened, and straightway found himself in the library, a long, low, silent–looking room, every foot of the walls of which was occupied with books in varied and rich bindings. The lozenge–paned windows, with thick stone mullions, were much overgrown with ivy, throwing a cool green shadowiness into the room. One of them, however, had been altered to a more modern taste, and opened with folding–doors upon a few steps, descending into an old–fashioned, terraced garden. To approach this window he had to pass a table, lying on which he saw a paper with verses on it, evidently in a woman's hand, and apparently just written, for the ink of the corrective scores still glittered. Just as he reached the window, which stood open, a lady had almost gained it from the other side, coming up the steps from the garden. She gave a slight start when she saw him, looked away, and as instantly glanced towards him again. Then approaching him through the window, for he had retreated to allow her to enter, she bowed with a kind of studied ease, and a slight shade of something French in her manner. Her voice was very pleasing, almost bewitching; yet had, at the same time, something assumed, if not affected, in the tone. All this was discoverable, or rather spiritually palpable, in the two words she said—merely, "Mr. Sutherland?" interrogatively. Hugh bowed, and said:

David Elginbrod

"I am very glad you have found me, for I had quite lost myself. I doubt whether I should ever have reached the breakfast–room."

"Come this way," she rejoined.

As they passed the table on which the verses lay, she stopped and slipped them into a writing–case. Leading him through a succession of handsome, evidently modern passages, she brought him across the main hall to the breakfast–room, which looked in the opposite direction to the library, namely, to the front of the house. She rang the bell; the urn was brought in; and she proceeded at once to make the tea; which she did well, rising in Hugh's estimation thereby. Before he had time, however, to make his private remarks on her exterior, or his conjectures on her position in the family, Mr. Arnold entered the room, with a slow, somewhat dignified step, and a dull outlook of grey eyes from a grey head well–balanced on a tall, rather slender frame. The lady rose, and, addressing him as uncle, bade him good morning; a greeting which he returned cordially, with a kiss on her forehead. Then accosting Hugh, with a manner which seemed the more polite and cold after the tone in which he had spoken to his niece, he bade him welcome to Arnstead.

"I trust you were properly attended to last night, Mr. Sutherland? Your pupil wanted very much to sit up till you arrived, but he is altogether too delicate, I am sorry to say, for late hours, though he has an unfortunate preference for them himself. Jacob," (to the man in waiting), "is not Master Harry up yet?"

Master Harry's entrance at that moment rendered reply unnecessary.

"Good morning, Euphra," he said to the lady, and kissed her on the cheek.

"Good morning, dear," was the reply, accompanied by a pretence of returning the kiss. But she smiled with a kind of confectionary sweetness on him; and, dropping an additional lump of sugar into his tea at the same moment, placed it for him beside herself; while he went and shook hands with his father, and then glancing shyly up at Hugh from a pair of large dark eyes, put his hand in his, and smiled, revealing teeth of a pearly whiteness. The lips, however, did not contrast them sufficiently, being pale and thin, with indication of suffering in their tremulous lines. Taking his place at table, he trifled with his breakfast; and after making pretence of eating for a while, asked Euphra if he might

90

go. She giving him leave, he hastened away.

Mr. Arnold took advantage of his retreat to explain to Hugh what he expected of him with regard to the boy.

"How old would you take Harry to be, Mr. Sutherland?"

"I should say about twelve from his size," replied Hugh; "but from his evident bad health, and intelligent expression—"

"Ah! you perceive the state he is in," interrupted Mr. Arnold, with some sadness in his voice. "You are right; he is nearly fifteen. He has not grown half–an–inch in the last twelve months."

"Perhaps that is better than growing too fast," said Hugh.

"Perhaps—perhaps; we will hope so. But I cannot help being uneasy about him. He reads too much, and I have not yet been able to help it; for he seems miserable, and without any object in life, if I compel him to leave his books."

"Perhaps we can manage to get over that in a little while."

"Besides," Mr. Arnold went on, paying no attention to what Hugh said, "I can get him to take no exercise. He does not even care for riding. I bought him a second pony a month ago, and he has not been twice on its back yet."

Hugh could not help thinking that to increase the supply was not always the best mode of increasing the demand; and that one who would not ride the first pony, would hardly be likely to ride the second. Mr. Arnold concluded with the words:

"I don't want to stop the boy's reading, but I can't have him a milksop."

"Will you let me manage him as I please, Mr. Arnold?" Hugh ventured to say.

Mr. Arnold looked full at him, with a very slight but quite manifest expression of surprise; and Hugh was aware that the eyes of the lady, called by the boy Euphra, were likewise fixed upon him penetratingly. As if he were then for the first time struck by the manly development of Hugh's frame, Mr. Arnold answered:

"I don't want you to overdo it, either. You cannot make a muscular Christian of him." (The speaker smiled at his own imagined wit.) "The boy has talents, and I want him to use them."

"I will do my best for him both ways," answered Hugh, "if you will trust me. For my part, I think the only way is to make the operation of the intellectual tendency on the one side, reveal to the boy himself his deficiency on the other. This once done, all will be well."

As he said this, Hugh caught sight of a cloudy, inscrutable dissatisfaction slightly contracting the eyebrows of the lady. Mr. Arnold, however, seemed not to be altogether displeased.

"Well," he answered, "I have my plans; but let us see first what you can do with yours. If they fail, perhaps you will oblige me by trying mine."

This was said with the decisive politeness of one who is accustomed to have his own way, and fully intends to have it—every word as articulate and deliberate as organs of speech could make it. But he seemed at the same time somewhat impressed by Hugh, and not unwilling to yield.

Throughout the conversation, the lady had said nothing, but had sat watching, or rather scrutinizing, Hugh's countenance, with a far keener and more frequent glance than, I presume, he was at all aware of. Whether or not she was satisfied with her conclusions, she allowed no sign to disclose; but, breakfast being over, rose and withdrew, turning, however, at the door, and saying:

"When you please, Mr. Sutherland, I shall be glad to show you what Harry has been doing with me; for till now I have been his only tutor."

"Thank you," replied Hugh; "but for some time we shall be quite independent of school-books. Perhaps we may require none at all. He can read, I presume, fairly well?"

"Reading is not only his forte but his fault," replied Mr. Arnold; while Euphra, fixing one more piercing look upon him, withdrew.

"Yes," responded Hugh; "but a boy may shuffle through a book very quickly, and have no such accurate perceptions of even the mere words, as to be able to read aloud intelligibly."

How little this applied to Harry, Hugh was soon to learn.

"Well, you know best about these things, I daresay. I leave it to you. With such testimonials as you have, Mr. Sutherland, I can hardly be wrong in letting you try your own plans with him. Now, I must bid you good morning. You will, in all probability, find Harry in the library."

CHAPTER II. HARRY'S NEW HORSE.

Spielender Unterricht heisst nicht, dem Kinde Anstrengungen ersparen und abnehmen, sondern eine Leidenschaft in ihm erwecken, welche ihm die stärksten aufnöthigt und erleichtert.

JEAN PAUL.—Die Unsichtbare Loge.

It is not the intention of sportive instruction that the child should be spared effort, or delivered from it; but that thereby a passion should be wakened in him, which shall both necessitate and facilitate the strongest exertion.

Hugh made no haste to find his pupil in the library; thinking it better, with such a boy, not to pounce upon him as if he were going to educate him directly. He went to his own rooms instead; got his books out and arranged them,—supplying thus, in a very small degree, the scarcity of modern ones in the book–cases; then arranged his small wardrobe, looked about him a little, and finally went to seek his pupil.

He found him in the library, as he had been given to expect, coiled up on the floor in a corner, with his back against the book–shelves, and an old folio on his knees, which he was reading in silence.

David Elginbrod

"Well, Harry," said Hugh, in a half–indifferent tone, as he threw himself on a couch, "what are you reading?"

Harry had not heard him come in. He started, and almost shuddered; then looked up, hesitated, rose, and, as if ashamed to utter the name of the book, brought it to Hugh, opening it at the title–page as he held it out to him. It was the old romance of Polexander. Hugh knew nothing about it; but, glancing over some of the pages, could not help wondering that the boy should find it interesting.

"Do you like this very much?" said he.

"Well—no. Yes, rather."

"I think I could find you something more interesting in the book–shelves."

"Oh! please, sir, mayn't I read this?" pleaded Harry, with signs of distress in his pale face.

"Oh, yes, certainly, if you wish. But tell me why you want to read it so very much."

"Because I have set myself to read it through."

Hugh saw that the child was in a diseased state of mind, as well as of body.

"You should not set yourself to read anything, before you know whether it is worth reading."

"I could not help it. I was forced to say I would."

"To whom?"

"To myself. Mayn't I read it?"

"Certainly," was all Hugh's answer; for he saw that he must not pursue the subject at present: the boy was quite hypochondriacal. His face was keen, with that clear definition of feature which suggests superior intellect. He was, though very small for his age, well proportioned, except that his head and face were too large. His forehead indicated thought; and Hugh could not doubt that, however uninteresting the books which he read might be, they must have afforded him subjects of mental activity. But he could not help seeing as well, that this activity, if not altered in its direction and modified in its degree, would soon destroy itself, either by ruining his feeble constitution altogether, or, which was more to be feared, by irremediably injuring the action of the brain. He resolved, however, to let him satisfy his conscience by reading the book; hoping, by the introduction of other objects of thought and feeling, to render it so distasteful, that he would be in little danger of yielding a similar pledge again, even should the temptation return, which Hugh hoped to prevent.

"But you have read enough for the present, have you not?" said he, rising, and approaching the book–shelves.

"Yes; I have been reading since breakfast."

"Ah! there's a capital book. Have you ever read it—Gulliver's Travels?"

"No. The outside looked always so uninteresting."

"So does Polexander's outside."

"Yes. But I couldn't help that one."

"Well, come along. I will read to you."

"Oh! thank you. That will be delightful. But must we not go to our lessons?"

"I'm going to make a lesson of this. I have been talking to your papa; and we're going to begin with a holiday, instead of ending with one. I must get better acquainted with you first, Harry, before I can teach you right. We must be friends, you know."

The boy crept close up to him, laid one thin hand on his knee, looked in his face for a moment, and then, without a word, sat down on the couch close beside him. Before an hour had passed, Harry was laughing heartily at Gulliver's adventures amongst the Lilliputians. Having arrived at this point of success, Hugh ceased reading, and began to talk to him.

David Elginbrod

"Is that lady your cousin?"

"Yes. Isn't she beautiful?"

"I hardly know yet. I have not got used to her enough yet. What is her name?"

"Oh! such a pretty name—Euphrasia."

"Is she the only lady in the house?"

"Yes; my mamma is dead, you know. She was ill for a long time, they say; and she died when I was born."

The tears came in the poor boy's eyes. Hugh thought of his own father, and put his hand on Harry's shoulder. Harry laid his head on Hugh's shoulder.

"But," he went on, "Euphra is so kind to me! And she is so clever too! She knows everything."

"Have you no brothers or sisters?"

"No, none. I wish I had."

"Well, I'll be your big brother. Only you must mind what I say to you; else I shall stop being him. Is it a bargain?"

"Yes, to be sure!" cried Harry in delight; and, springing from the couch, he began hopping feebly about the room on one foot, to express his pleasure.

"Well, then, that's settled. Now, you must come and show me the horses—your ponies, you know—and the pigs—"

"I don't like the pigs—I don't know where they are."

"Well, we must find out. Perhaps I shall make some discoveries for you. Have you any rabbits?"

David Elginbrod

"No."

"A dog though, surely?"

"No. I had a canary, but the cat killed it, and I have never had a pet since."

"Well, get your cap, and come out with me. I will wait for you here."

Harry walked away—he seldom ran. He soon returned with his cap, and they sallied out together.

Happening to look back at the house, when a few paces from it, Hugh thought he saw Euphra standing at the window of a back staircase. They made the round of the stables, and the cow–house, and the poultry–yard; and even the pigs, as proposed, came in for a share of their attention. As they approached the stye, Harry turned away his head with a look of disgust. They were eating out of the trough.

"They make such a nasty noise!" he said.

"Yes, but just look: don't they enjoy it?" said Hugh.

Harry looked at them. The notion of their enjoyment seemed to dawn upon him as something quite new. He went nearer and nearer to the stye. At last a smile broke out over his countenance.

"How tight that one curls his tail!" said he, and burst out laughing.

"How dreadfully this boy must have been mismanaged!" thought Hugh to himself. "But there is no fear of him now, I hope."

By this time they had been wandering about for more than an hour; and Hugh saw, by Harry's increased paleness, that he was getting tired.

"Here, Harry, get on my back, my boy, and have a ride. You're tired."

And Hugh knelt down.

David Elginbrod

Harry shrunk back.

"I shall spoil your coat with my shoes."

"Nonsense! Rub them well on the grass there. And then get on my back directly."

Harry did as he was bid, and found his tutor's broad back and strong arms a very comfortable saddle. So away they went, wandering about for a long time, in their new relation of horse and his rider. At length they got into the middle of a long narrow avenue, quite neglected, overgrown with weeds, and obstructed with rubbish. But the trees were fine beeches, of great growth and considerable age. One end led far into a wood, and the other towards the house, a small portion of which could be seen at the end, the avenue appearing to reach close up to it.

"Don't go down this," said Harry.

"Well, it's not a very good road for a horse certainly, but I think I can go it. What a beautiful avenue! Why is it so neglected?"

"Don't go down there, please, dear horse."

Harry was getting wonderfully at home with Hugh already.

"Why?" asked Hugh.

"They call it the Ghost's Walk, and I don't much like it. It has a strange distracted look!"

"That's a long word, and a descriptive one too," thought Hugh; but, considering that there would come many a better opportunity of combating the boy's fears than now, he simply said: "Very well, Harry,"—and proceeded to leave the avenue by the other side. But Harry was not yet satisfied.

"Please, Mr. Sutherland, don't go on that side, just now. Ride me back, please. It is not safe, they say, to cross her path. She always follows any one who crosses her path."

David Elginbrod

Hugh laughed; but again said, "Very well, my boy;" and, returning, left the avenue by the side by which he had entered it.

"Shall we go home to luncheon now?" said Harry.

"Yes," replied Hugh. "Could we not go by the front of the house? I should like very much to see it."

"Oh, certainly," said Harry, and proceeded to direct Hugh how to go; but evidently did not know quite to his own satisfaction. There being, however, but little foliage yet, Hugh could discover his way pretty well. He promised himself many a delightful wander in the woody regions in the evenings.

They managed to get round to the front of the house, not without some difficulty; and then Hugh saw to his surprise that, although not imposing in appearance, it was in extent more like a baronial residence than that of a simple gentleman. The front was very long, apparently of all ages, and of all possible styles of architecture, the result being somewhat mysterious and eminently picturesque. All kinds of windows; all kinds of projections and recesses; a house here, joined to a hall there; here a pointed gable, the very bell on the top overgrown and apparently choked with ivy; there a wide front with large bay windows; and next a turret of old stone, with not a shred of ivy upon it, but crowded over with grey-green lichens, which looked as if the stone itself had taken to growing; multitudes of roofs, of all shapes and materials, so that one might very easily be lost amongst the chimneys and gutters and dormer windows and pinnacles—made up the appearance of the house on the outside to Hugh's first inquiring glance, as he paused at a little distance with Harry on his back, and scanned the wonderful pile before him. But as he looked at the house of Arnstead, Euphra was looking at him with the boy on his back, from one of the smaller windows. Was she making up her mind?

"You are as kind to me as Euphra," said Harry, as Hugh set him down in the hall. "I've enjoyed my ride very much, thank you, Mr. Sutherland. I am sure Euphra will like you very much—she likes everybody."

CHAPTER III. EUPHRASIA.

```
     then purged with Euphrasy and Rue
The visual nerve, for he had much to see.

Paradise Lost, b. xi.
```

Soft music came to mine ear. It was like the rising breeze, that whirls, at first, the thistle's beard; then flies, dark–shadowy, over the grass. It was the maid of Fuärfed wild: she raised the nightly song; for she knew that my soul was a stream, that flowed at pleasant sounds.

Ossian.—Oina–Morul.

Harry led Hugh by the hand to the dining–room, a large oak hall with Gothic windows, and an open roof supported by richly carved woodwork, in the squares amidst which were painted many escutcheons parted by fanciful devices. Over the high stone carving above the chimney hung an old piece of tapestry, occupying the whole space between that and the roof. It represented a hunting–party of ladies and gentlemen, just setting out. The table looked very small in the centre of the room, though it would have seated twelve or fourteen. It was already covered for luncheon; and in a minute Euphra entered and took her place without a word. Hugh sat on one side and Harry on the other. Euphra, having helped both to soup, turned to Harry and said, "Well, Harry, I hope you have enjoyed your first lesson."

"Very much," answered Harry with a smile. "I have learned pigs and horseback."

"The boy is positively clever," thought Hugh.

"Mr. Sutherland"—he continued, "has begun to teach me to like creatures."

"But I thought you were very fond of your wild–beast book, Harry."

"Oh! yes; but that was only in the book, you know. I like the stories about them, of course. But to like pigs, you know, is quite different. They are so ugly and ill–bred. I like them though."

David Elginbrod

"You seem to have quite gained Harry already," said Euphra, glancing at Hugh, and looking away as quickly.

"We are very good friends, and shall be, I think," replied he.

Harry looked at him affectionately, and said to him, not to Euphra, "Oh! yes, that we shall, I am sure." Then turning to the lady—"Do you know, Euphra, he is my big brother?"

"You must mind how you make new relations, though, Harry; for you know that would make him my cousin."

"Well, you will be a kind cousin to him, won't you?"

"I will try," replied Euphra, looking up at Hugh with a naïve expression of shyness, and the slightest possible blush.

Hugh began to think her pretty, almost handsome. His next thought was to wonder how old she was. But about this he could not at once make up his mind. She might be four–and–twenty; she might be two–and–thirty. She had black, lustreless hair, and eyes to match, as far as colour was concerned—but they could sparkle, and probably flash upon occasion; a low forehead, but very finely developed in the faculties that dwell above the eyes; slender but very dark eyebrows—just black arched lines in her rather sallow complexion; nose straight, and nothing remarkable—"an excellent thing in woman," a mouth indifferent when at rest, but capable of a beautiful laugh. She was rather tall, and of a pretty enough figure; hands good; feet invisible. Hugh came to these conclusions rapidly enough, now that his attention was directed to her; for, though naturally unobservant, his perception was very acute as soon as his attention was roused.

"Thank you," he replied to her pretty speech. "I shall do my best to deserve it."

"I hope you will, Mr. Sutherland," rejoined she, with another arch look. "Take some wine, Harry."

She poured out a glass of sherry, and gave it to the boy, who drank it with some eagerness. Hugh could not approve of this, but thought it too early to interfere. Turning to

Harry, he said:

"Now, Harry, you have had rather a tiring morning. I should like you to go and lie down a while."

"Very well, Mr. Sutherland," replied Harry, who seemed rather deficient in combativeness, as well as other boyish virtues. "Shall I lie down in the library?"

"No—have a change."

"In my bed–room?"

"No, I think not. Go to my room, and lie on the couch till I come to you."

Harry went; and Hugh, partly for the sake of saying something, and partly to justify his treatment of Harry, told Euphra, whose surname he did not yet know, what they had been about all the morning, ending with some remark on the view of the house in front. She heard the account of their proceedings with apparent indifference, replying only to the remark with which he closed it:

"It is rather a large house, is it not, for three—I beg your pardon, for four persons to live in, Mr. Sutherland?"

"It is, indeed; it quite bewilders me."

"To tell the truth, I don't quite know above the half of it myself."

Hugh thought this rather a strange assertion, large as the house was; but she went on:

"I lost myself between the housekeeper's room and my own, no later than last week."

I suppose there was a particle of truth in this; and that she had taken a wrong turning in an abstracted fit. Perhaps she did not mean it to be taken as absolutely true.

"You have not lived here long, then?"

"Not long for such a great place. A few years. I am only a poor relation."

She accompanied this statement with another swift uplifting of the eyelids. But this time her eyes rested for a moment on Hugh's, with something of a pleading expression; and when they fell, a slight sigh followed. Hugh felt that he could not quite understand her. A vague suspicion crossed his mind that she was bewitching him, but vanished instantly. He replied to her communication by a smile, and the remark:

"You have the more freedom, then.—Did you know Harry's mother?" he added, after a pause.

"No. She died when Harry was born. She was very beautiful, and, they say, very clever, but always in extremely delicate health. Between ourselves, I doubt if there was much sympathy—that is, if my uncle and she quite understood each other. But that is an old story."

A pause followed. Euphra resumed:

"As to the freedom you speak of, Mr. Sutherland, I do not quite know what to do with it. I live here as if the place were my own, and give what orders I please. But Mr. Arnold shows me little attention—he is so occupied with one thing and another, I hardly know what; and if he did, perhaps I should get tired of him. So, except when we have visitors, which is not very often, the time hangs rather heavy on my hands."

"But you are fond of reading—and writing, too, I suspect;" Hugh ventured to say.

She gave him another of her glances, in which the apparent shyness was mingled with something for which Hugh could not find a name. Nor did he suspect, till long after, that it was in reality slyness, so tempered with archness, that, if discovered, it might easily pass for an expression playfully assumed.

"Oh! yes," she said; "one must read a book now and then; and if a verse"—again a glance and a slight blush—"should come up from nobody knows where, one may as well write it down. But, please, do not take me for a literary lady. Indeed, I make not the slightest pretensions. I don't know what I should do without Harry; and indeed, indeed, you must not steal him from me, Mr. Sutherland."

"I should be very sorry," replied Hugh. "Let me beg you, as far as I have a right to do so, to join us as often and as long as you please. I will go and see how he is. I am sure the boy only wants thorough rousing, alternated with perfect repose."

He went to his own room, where he found Harry, to his satisfaction, fast asleep on the sofa. He took care not to wake him, but sat down beside him to read till his sleep should be over. But, a moment after, the boy opened his eyes with a start and a shiver, and gave a slight cry. When he saw Hugh he jumped up, and with a smile which was pitiful to see upon a scared face, said:

"Oh! I am so glad you are there."

"What is the matter, dear Harry?"

"I had a dreadful dream."

"What was it?"

"I don't know. It always comes. It is always the same. I know that. And yet I can never remember what it is."

Hugh soothed him as well as he could; and he needed it, for the cold drops were standing on his forehead. When he had grown calmer, he went and fetched Gulliver, and, to the boy's great delight, read to him till dinner–time. Before the first bell rang, he had quite recovered, and indeed seemed rather interested in the approach of dinner.

Dinner was an affair of some state at Arnstead. Almost immediately after the second bell had rung, Mr. Arnold made his appearance in the drawing–room, where the others were already waiting for him. This room had nothing of the distinctive character of the parts of the house which Hugh had already seen. It was merely a handsome modern room, of no great size. Mr. Arnold led Euphra to dinner, and Hugh followed with Harry.

Mr. Arnold's manner to Hugh was the same as in the morning—studiously polite, without the smallest approach to cordiality. He addressed him as an equal, it is true; but an equal who could never be in the smallest danger of thinking he meant it. Hugh, who, without having seen a great deal of the world, yet felt much the same wherever he was, took care to give him all that he seemed to look for, as far at least as was consistent with his own self-respect. He soon discovered that he was one of those men, who, if you will only grant their position, and acknowledge their authority, will allow you to have much your own way in everything. His servants had found this out long ago, and almost everything about the house was managed as they pleased; but as the oldest of them were respectable family servants, nothing went very far wrong. They all, however, waited on Euphra with an assiduity that showed she was, or could be, quite mistress when and where she pleased. Perhaps they had found out that she had great influence with Mr. Arnold; and certainly he seemed very fond of her indeed, after a stately fashion. She spoke to the servants with peculiar gentleness; never said, if you please; but always, thank you. Harry never asked for anything, but always looked to Euphra, who gave the necessary order. Hugh saw that the boy was quite dependent upon her, seeming of himself scarcely capable of originating the simplest action. Mr. Arnold, however, dull as he was, could not help seeing that Harry's manner was livelier than usual, and seemed pleased at the slight change already visible for the better. Turning to Hugh he said:

"Do you find Harry very much behind with his studies, Mr. Sutherland?"

"I have not yet attempted to find out," replied Hugh.

"Not?" said Mr. Arnold, with surprise.

"No. If he be behind, I feel confident it will not be for long."

"But," began Mr. Arnold, pompously; and then he paused.

"You were kind enough to say, Mr. Arnold, that I might try my own plans with him first. I have been doing so."

"Yes—certainly. But—"

Here Harry broke in with some animation:

"Mr. Sutherland has been my horse, carrying me about on his back all the morning—no, not all the morning—but an hour, or an hour and a half—or was it two hours, Mr. Sutherland?"

David Elginbrod

"I really don't know, Harry," answered Hugh; "I don't think it matters much."

Harry seemed relieved, and went on:

"He has been reading Gulliver's Travels to me—oh, such fall! And we have been to see the cows and the pigs; and Mr. Sutherland has been teaching me to jump. Do you know, papa, he jumped right over the pony's back without touching it."

Mr. Arnold stared at the boy with lustreless eyes and hanging checks. These grew red, as if he were going to choke. Such behaviour was quite inconsistent with the dignity of Arnstead and its tutor, who had been recommended to him as a thorough gentleman. But for the present he said nothing; probably because he could think of nothing to say.

"Certainly Harry seems better already," interposed Euphra.

"I cannot help thinking Mr. Sutherland has made a good beginning."

Mr. Arnold did not reply, but the cloud wore away from his face by degrees; and at length he asked Hugh to take a glass of wine with him.

When Euphra rose from the table, and Harry followed her example, Hugh thought it better to rise as well. Mr. Arnold seemed to hesitate whether or not to ask him to resume his seat and have a glass of claret. Had he been a little wizened pedagogue, no doubt he would have insisted on his company, sure of acquiescence from him in every sentiment he might happen to utter. But Hugh really looked so very much like a gentleman, and stated his own views, or adopted his own plans, with so much independence, that Mr. Arnold judged it safer to keep him at arm's length for a season at least, till he should thoroughly understand his position—not that of a guest, but that of his son's tutor, belonging to the household of Arnstead only on approval.

On leaving the dining–room, Hugh hesitated, in his turn, whether to betake himself to his own room, or to accompany Euphra to the drawing–room, the door of which stood open on the opposite side of the hall, revealing a brightness and warmth, which the chill of the evening, and the lowness of the fire in the dining–room, rendered quite enticing. But Euphra, who was half–across the hall, seeming to divine his thoughts, turned, and said, "Are you not going to favour us with your company, Mr. Sutherland?"

David Elginbrod

"With pleasure," replied Hugh; but, to cover his hesitation, added, "I will be with you presently;" and ran up stairs to his own room. "The old gentleman sits on his dignity—can hardly be said to stand on it," thought he, as he went. "The poor relation, as she calls herself, treats me like a guest. She is mistress here, however; that is clear enough."

As he descended the stairs to the drawing−room, a voice rose through the house, like the voice of an angel. At least so thought Hugh, hearing it for the first time. It seemed to take his breath away, as he stood for a moment on the stairs, listening. It was only Euphra singing The Flowers of the Forest. The drawing−room door was still open, and her voice rang through the wide lofty hall. He entered almost on tip−toe, that he might lose no thread of the fine tones.—Had she chosen the song of Scotland out of compliment to him?—She saw him enter, but went on without hesitating even. In the high notes, her voice had that peculiar vibratory richness which belongs to the nightingale's; but he could not help thinking that the low tones were deficient both in quality and volume. The expression and execution, however, would have made up for a thousand defects. Her very soul seemed brooding over the dead upon Flodden field, as she sang this most wailful of melodies—this embodiment of a nation's grief. The song died away as if the last breath had gone with it; failing as it failed, and ceasing with its inspiration, as if the voice that sang lived only for and in the song. A moment of intense silence followed. Then, before Hugh had half recovered from the former, with an almost grand dramatic recoil, as if the second sprang out of the first, like an eagle of might out of an ocean of weeping, she burst into Scots wha hae. She might have been a new Deborah, heralding her nation to battle. Hugh was transfixed, turned icy cold, with the excitement of his favourite song so sung.—Was that a glance of satisfied triumph with which Euphra looked at him for a single moment?—She sang the rest of the song as if the battle were already gained; but looked no more at Hugh.

The excellence of her tones, and the lambent fluidity of her transitions, if I may be allowed the phrase, were made by her art quite subservient to the expression, and owed their chief value to the share they bore in producing it. Possibly there was a little too much of the dramatic in her singing, but it was all in good taste; and, in a word, Hugh had never heard such singing before. As soon as she had finished, she rose, and shut the piano.

"Do not, do not," faltered Hugh, seeking to arrest her hand, as she closed the instrument.

"I can sing nothing after that," she said with emotion, or perhaps excitement; for the trembling of her voice might be attributed to either cause. "Do not ask me."

Hugh respectfully desisted; but after a few minutes' pause ventured to remark:

"I cannot understand how you should be able to sing Scotch songs so well. I never heard any but Scotch women sing them, even endurably, before: your singing of them is perfect."

"It seems to me," said Euphra, speaking as if she would rather have remained silent, "that a true musical penetration is independent of styles and nationalities. It can perceive, or rather feel, and reproduce, at the same moment. If the music speaks Scotch, the musical nature hears Scotch. It can take any shape, indeed cannot help taking any shape, presented to it."

Hugh was yet further astonished by this criticism from one whom he had been criticising with so much carelessness that very day.

"You think, then," said he, modestly, not as if he would bring her to book, but as really seeking to learn from her, "that a true musical nature can pour itself into the mould of any song, in entire independence of association and education?"

"Yes; in independence of any but what it may provide for itself."

Euphrasia, however, had left one important element unrepresented in the construction of her theory—namely, the degree of capability which a mind may possess of sympathy with any given class of feelings. The blossom of the mind, whether it flower in poetry, music, or any other art, must be the exponent of the nature and condition of that whose blossom it is. No mind, therefore, incapable of sympathising with the feelings whence it springs, can interpret the music of another. And Euphra herself was rather a remarkable instance of this forgotten fact.

Further conversation on the subject was interrupted by the entrance of Mr. Arnold, who looked rather annoyed at finding Hugh in the drawing–room, and ordered Harry off to bed, with some little asperity of tone. The boy rose at once, rang the bell, bade them all good night, and went. A servant met him at the door with a candle, and accompanied him.

Thought Hugh: "Here are several things to be righted at once. The boy must not have wine; and he must have only one dinner a-day—especially if he is ordered to bed so early. I must make a man of him if I can."

He made inquiries, and, with some difficulty, found out where the boy slept. During the night he was several times in Harry's room, and once in happy time to wake him from a nightmare dream. The boy was so overcome with terror, that Hugh got into bed beside him and comforted him to sleep in his arms. Nor did he leave him till it was time to get up, when he stole back to his own quarters, which, happily, were at no very great distance.

I may mention here, that it was not long before Hugh succeeded in stopping the wine, and reducing the dinner to a mouthful of supper. Harry, as far as he was concerned, yielded at once; and his father only held out long enough to satisfy his own sense of dignity.

CHAPTER IV. THE CAVE IN THE STRAW.

All knowledge and wonder (which is the seed of knowledge) is an impression of pleasure in itself.

LORD BACON.—Advancement of Learning.

The following morning dawned in a cloud; which, swathed about the trees, wetted them down to the roots, without having time to become rain. They drank it in like sorrow, the only material out of which true joy can be fashioned. This cloud of mist would yet glimmer in a new heaven, namely, in the cloud of blooms which would clothe the limes and the chestnuts and the beeches along the ghost's walk. But there was gloomy weather within doors as well; for poor Harry was especially sensitive to variations of the barometer, without being in the least aware of the fact himself. Again Hugh found him in the library, seated in his usual corner, with Polexander on his knees. He half dropped the book when Hugh entered, and murmured with a sigh:

"It's no use; I can't read it."

"What's the matter, Harry?" said his tutor.

"I should like to tell you, but you will laugh at me."

"I shall never laugh at you, Harry."

"Never?"

"No, never."

"Then tell me how I can be sure that I have read this book."

"I do not quite understand you."

"All! I was sure nobody could be so stupid as I am. Do you know, Mr. Sutherland, I seem to have read a page from top to bottom sometimes, and when I come to the bottom I know nothing about it, and doubt whether I have read it at all; and then I stare at it all over again, till I grow so queer, and sometimes nearly scream. You see I must be able to say I have read the book."

"Why? Nobody will ever ask you."

"Perhaps not; but you know that is nothing. I want to know that I have read the book—really and truly read it."

Hugh thought for a moment, and seemed to see that the boy, not being strong enough to be a law to himself, just needed a benign law from without, to lift him from the chaos of feeble and conflicting notions and impulses within, which generated a false law of slavery. So he said:

"Harry, am I your big brother?"

"Yes, Mr. Sutherland."

"Then, ought you to do what I wish, or what you wish yourself?"

"What you wish, sir."

David Elginbrod

"Then I want you to put away that book for a month at least."

"Oh, Mr. Sutherland! I promised."

"To whom?"

"To myself." "But I am above you; and I want you to do as I tell you. Will you, Harry?"

"Yes."

"Put away the book, then."

Harry sprang to his feet, put the book on its shelf, and, going up to Hugh, said,

"You have done it, not me."

"Certainly, Harry."

The notions of a hypochondriacal child will hardly be interesting to the greater part of my readers; but Hugh learned from this a little lesson about divine law which he never forgot.

"Now, Harry," added he, "you must not open a book till I allow you."

"No poetry, either?" said poor Harry; and his face fell.

"I don't mind poetry so much; but of prose I will read as much to you as will be good for you. Come, let us have a bit of Gulliver again."

"Oh, how delightful!" cried Harry. "I am so glad you made me put away that tiresome book. I wonder why it insisted so on being read."

Hugh read for an hour, and then made Harry put on his cloak, notwithstanding the rain, which fell in a slow thoughtful spring shower. Taking the boy again on his back, he carried him into the woods. There he told him how the drops of wet sank into the ground, and then went running about through it in every direction, looking for seeds: which were all thirsty little things, that wanted to grow, and could not, till a drop came and gave them drink. And he told him how the rain–drops were made up in the skies, and then came down, like millions of angels, to do what they were told in the dark earth. The good drops went into all the cellars and dungeons of the earth, to let out the imprisoned flowers. And he told him how the seeds, when they had drunk the rain–drops, wanted another kind of drink next, which was much thinner and much stronger, but could not do them any good till they had drunk the rain first.

"What is that?" said Harry. "I feel as if you were reading out of the Bible, Mr. Sutherland."

"It is the sunlight," answered his tutor. "When a seed has drunk of the water, and is not thirsty any more, it wants to breathe next; and then the sun sends a long, small finger of fire down into the grave where the seed is lying; and it touches the seed, and something inside the seed begins to move instantly and to grow bigger and bigger, till it sends two green blades out of it into the earth, and through the earth into the air; and then it can breathe. And then it sends roots down into the earth; and the roots keep drinking water, and the leaves keep breathing the air, and the sun keeps them alive and busy; and so a great tree grows up, and God looks at it, and says it is good."

"Then they really are living things?" said Harry.

"Certainly."

"Thank you, Mr. Sutherland. I don't think I shall dislike rain so much any more."

Hugh took him next into the barn, where they found a great heap of straw. Recalling his own boyish amusements, he made him put off his cloak, and help to make a tunnel into this heap. Harry was delighted—the straw was so nice, and bright, and dry, and clean. They drew it out by handfuls, and thus excavated a round tunnel to the distance of six feet or so; when Hugh proceeded to more extended operations. Before it was time to go to lunch, they had cleared half of a hollow sphere, six feet in diameter, out of the heart of the heap.

After lunch, for which Harry had been very unwilling to relinquish the straw hut, Hugh sent him to lie down for a while; when he fell fast asleep as before. After he had left the room, Euphra said:

David Elginbrod

"How do you get on with Harry, Mr. Sutherland?"

"Perfectly to my satisfaction," answered Hugh.

"Do you not find him very slow?"

"Quite the contrary."

"You surprise me. But you have not given him any lessons yet."

"I have given him a great many, and he is learning them very fast."

"I fear he will have forgotten all my poor labours before you take up the work where we left it. When will you give him any book-lessons?"

"Not for a while yet."

Euphra did not reply. Her silence seemed intended to express dissatisfaction; at least so Hugh interpreted it.

"I hope you do not think it is to indulge myself that I manage Master Harry in this peculiar fashion," he said. "The fact is, he is a very peculiar child, and may turn out a genius or a weakling, just as he is managed. At least so it appears to me at present. May I ask where you left the work you were doing with him?"

"He was going through the Eton grammar for the third time," answered Euphra, with a defiant glance, almost of dislike, at Hugh. "But I need not enumerate his studies, for I daresay you will not take them up at all after my fashion. I only assure you I have been a very exact disciplinarian. What he knows, I think you will find he knows thoroughly."

So saying, Euphra rose, and with a flush on her cheek, walked out of the room in a more stately manner than usual.

Hugh felt that he had, somehow or other, offended her. But, to tell the truth, he did not much care, for her manner had rather irritated him. He retired to his own room, wrote to his mother, and, when Harry awoke, carried him again to the barn for an hour's work in the straw. Before it grew dusk, they had finished a little, silent, dark chamber, as round as they could make it, in the heart of the straw. All the excavated material they had thrown on the top, reserving only a little to close up the entrance when they pleased.

The next morning was still rainy; and when Hugh found Harry in the library as usual, he saw that the clouds had again gathered over the boy's spirit. He was pacing about the room in a very odd manner. The carpet was divided diamond–wise in a regular pattern. Harry's steps were, for the most part, planted upon every third diamond, as he slowly crossed the floor in a variety of directions; for, as on previous occasions, he had not perceived the entrance of his tutor. But, every now and then, the boy would make the most sudden and irregular change in his mode of progression, setting his foot on the most unexpected diamond, at one time the nearest to him, at another the farthest within his reach. When he looked up, and saw his tutor watching him, he neither started nor blushed: but, still retaining on his countenance the perplexed, anxious expression which Hugh had remarked, said to him:

"How can God know on which of those diamonds I am going to set my foot next?"

"If you could understand how God knows, Harry, then you would know yourself; but before you have made up your mind, you don't know which you will choose; and even then you only know on which you intend to set your foot; for you have often changed your mind after making it up."

Harry looked as puzzled as before.

"Why, Harry, to understand how God understands, you would need to be as wise as he is; so it is no use trying. You see you can't quite understand me, though I have a real meaning in what I say."

"Ah! I see it is no use; but I can't bear to be puzzled."

"But you need not be puzzled; you have no business to be puzzled. You are trying to get into your little brain what is far too grand and beautiful to get into it. Would you not think it very stupid to puzzle yourself how to put a hundred horses into a stable with twelve stalls?"

Harry laughed, and looked relieved.

"It is more unreasonable a thousand times to try to understand such things. For my part, it would make me miserable to think that there was nothing but what I could understand. I should feel as if I had no room anywhere. Shall we go to our cave again?"

"Oh! yes, please," cried Harry; and in a moment he was on Hugh's back once more, cantering joyously to the barn.

After various improvements, including some enlargement of the interior, Hugh and Harry sat down together in the low yellow twilight of their cave, to enjoy the result of their labours. They could just see, by the light from the tunnel, the glimmer of the golden hollow all about them. The rain was falling heavily out-of-doors; and they could hear the sound of the multitudinous drops of the broken cataract of the heavens like the murmur of the insects in a summer wood. They knew that everything outside was rained upon, and was again raining on everything beneath it, while they were dry and warm.

"This is nice!" exclaimed Harry, after a few moments of silent enjoyment.

"This is your first lesson in architecture," said Hugh.

"Am I to learn architecture?" asked Harry, in a rueful tone.

"It is well to know how things came to be done, if you should know nothing more about them, Harry. Men lived in the cellars first of all, and next on the ground floor; but they could get no further till they joined the two, and then they could build higher."

"I don't quite understand you, sir."

"I did not mean you should, Harry."

"Then I don't mind, sir. But I thought architecture was building."

"So it is; and this is one way of building. It is only making an outside by pulling out an inside, instead of making an inside by setting up an outside."

David Elginbrod

Harry thought for a while, and then said joyfully:

"I see it, sir! I see it. The inside is the chief thing—not the outside."

"Yes, Harry; and not in architecture only. Never forget that."

They lay for some time in silence, listening to the rain. At length Harry spoke:

"I have been thinking of what you told me yesterday, Mr. Sutherland, about the rain going to look for the seeds that were thirsty for it. And now I feel just as if I were a seed, lying in its little hole in the earth, and hearing the rain–drops pattering down all about it, waiting—oh, so thirsty!—for some kind drop to find me out, and give me itself to drink. I wonder what kind of flower I should grow up," added he, laughing.

"There is more truth than you think, in your pretty fancy, Harry," rejoined Hugh, and was silent—self–rebuked; for the memory of David came back upon him, recalled by the words of the boy; of David, whom he loved and honoured with the best powers of his nature, and whom yet he had neglected and seemed to forget; nay, whom he had partially forgotten—he could not deny. The old man, whose thoughts were just those of a wise child, had said to him once:

"We ken no more, Maister Sutherlan', what we're growin' till, than that neep–seed there kens what a neep is, though a neep it will be. The only odds is, that we ken that we dinna ken, and the neep–seed kens nothing at all aboot it. But ae thing, Maister Sutherlan', we may be sure o': that, whatever it be, it will be worth God's makin' an' our growin'."

A solemn stillness fell upon Hugh's spirit, as he recalled these words; out of which stillness, I presume, grew the little parable which follows; though Hugh, after he had learned far more about the things therein hinted at, could never understand how it was, that he could have put so much more into it, than he seemed to have understood at that period of his history.

For Harry said:

"Wouldn't this be a nice place for a story, Mr. Sutherland? Do you ever tell stories, sir?"

"I was just thinking of one, Harry; but it is as much yours as mine, for you sowed the seed of the story in my mind."

"Do you mean a story that never was in a book—a story out of your own head? Oh! that will be grand!"

"Wait till we see what it will be, Harry; for I can't tell you how it will turn out."

After a little further pause, Hugh began:

"Long, long ago, two seeds lay beside each other in the earth, waiting. It was cold, and rather wearisome; and, to beguile the time, the one found means to speak to the other.

"'What are you going to be?' said the one.

"'I don't know,' answered the other.

"'For me,' rejoined the first, 'I mean to be a rose. There is nothing like a splendid rose. Everybody will love me then!'

"'It's all right,' whispered the second; and that was all he could say; for somehow when he had said that, he felt as if all the words in the world were used up. So they were silent again for a day or two.

"'Oh, dear!' cried the first, 'I have had some water. I never knew till it was inside me. I'm growing! I'm growing! Good–bye!'

"'Good–bye!' repeated the other, and lay still; and waited more than ever.

"The first grew and grew, pushing itself straight up, till at last it felt that it was in the open air, for it could breathe. And what a delicious breath that was! It was rather cold, but so refreshing. The flower could see nothing, for it was not quite a flower yet, only a plant; and they never see till their eyes come, that is, till they open their blossoms—then they are flowers quite. So it grew and grew, and kept its head up very steadily, meaning to see the sky the first thing, and leave the earth quite behind as well as beneath it. But somehow or other, though why it could not tell, it felt very much inclined to cry. At length it opened its eye. It was morning, and the sky was over its head; but, alas! itself was no rose—only a tiny white flower. It felt yet more inclined to hang down its head and to cry; but it still resisted, and tried hard to open its eye wide, and to hold its head upright, and to look full at the sky.

"'I will be a star of Bethlehem at least!' said the flower to itself.

"But its head felt very heavy; and a cold wind rushed over it, and bowed it down towards the earth. And the flower saw that the time of the singing of birds was not come, that the snow covered the whole land, and that there was not a single flower in sight but itself. And it half−closed its leaves in terror and the dismay of loneliness. But that instant it remembered what the other flower used to say; and it said to itself: 'It's all right; I will be what I can.' And thereon it yielded to the wind, drooped its head to the earth, and looked no more on the sky, but on the snow. And straightway the wind stopped, and the cold died away, and the snow sparkled like pearls and diamonds; and the flower knew that it was the holding of its head up that had hurt it so; for that its body came of the snow, and that its name was Snow−drop. And so it said once more, 'It's all right!' and waited in perfect peace. All the rest it needed was to hang its head after its nature."

"And what became of the other?" asked Harry.

"I haven't done with this one yet," answered Hugh. "I only told you it was waiting. One day a pale, sad−looking girl, with thin face, large eyes, and long white hands, came, hanging her head like the snowdrop, along the snow where the flower grew. She spied it, smiled joyously, and saying, 'Ah! my little sister, are you come?' stooped and plucked the snowdrop. It trembled and died in her hand; which was a heavenly death for a snowdrop; for had it not cast a gleam of summer, pale as it had been itself, upon the heart of a sick girl?"

"And the other?" repeated Harry.

"The other had a long time to wait; but it did grow one of the loveliest roses ever seen. And at last it had the highest honour ever granted to a flower: two lovers smelled it together, and were content with it."

David Elginbrod

Harry was silent, and so was Hugh; for he could not understand himself quite. He felt, all the time he was speaking, is if he were listening to David, instead of talking himself. The fact was, he was only expanding, in an imaginative soil, the living seed which David had cast into it. There seemed to himself to be more in his parable than he had any right to invent. But is it not so with all stories that are rightly rooted in the human?

"What a delightful story, Mr. Sutherland!" said Harry, at last. "Euphra tells me stories sometimes; but I don't think I ever heard one I liked so much. I wish we were meant to grow into something, like the flower–seeds."

"So we are, Harry."

"Are we indeed? How delightful it would be to think that I am only a seed, Mr. Sutherland! Do you think I might think so?"

"Yes, I do."

"Then, please, let me begin to learn something directly. I haven't had anything disagreeable to do since you came; and I don't feel as if that was right."

Poor Harry, like so many thousands of good people, had not yet learned that God is not a hard task–master.

"I don't intend that you should have anything disagreeable to do, if I can help it. We must do such things when they come to us; but we must not make them for ourselves, or for each other."

"Then I'm not to learn any more Latin, am I?" said Harry, in a doubtful kind of tone, as if there were after all a little pleasure in doing what he did not like.

"Is Latin so disagreeable, Harry?"

"Yes; it is rule after rule, that has nothing in it I care for. How can anybody care for Latin? But I am quite ready to begin, if I am only a seed—really, you know."

"Not yet, Harry. Indeed, we shall not begin again—I won't let you—till you ask me with your whole heart, to let you learn Latin."

"I am afraid that will be a long time, and Euphra will not like it."

"I will talk to her about it. But perhaps it will not be so long as you think. Now, don't mention Latin to me again, till you are ready to ask me, heartily, to teach you. And don't give yourself any trouble about it either. You never can make yourself like anything."

Harry was silent. They returned to the house, through the pouring rain; Harry, as usual, mounted on his big brother.

As they crossed the hall, Mr. Arnold came in. He looked surprised and annoyed. Hugh set Harry down, who ran upstairs to get dressed for dinner; while he himself half–stopped, and turned towards Mr. Arnold. But Mr. Arnold did not speak, and so Hugh followed Harry.

Hugh spent all that evening, after Harry had gone to bed, in correcting his impressions of some of the chief stories of early Roman history; of which stories he intended commencing a little course to Harry the next day.

Meantime there was very little intercourse between Hugh and Euphra, whose surname, somehow or other, Hugh had never inquired after. He disliked asking questions about people to an uncommon degree, and so preferred waiting for a natural revelation. Her later behaviour had repelled him, impressing him with the notion that she was proud, and that she had made up her mind, notwithstanding her apparent frankness at first, to keep him at a distance. That she was fitful, too, and incapable of showing much tenderness even to poor Harry, he had already concluded in his private judgment–hall. Nor could he doubt that, whether from wrong theories, incapacity, or culpable indifference, she must have taken very bad measures indeed with her young pupil.

The next day resembled the two former; with this difference, that the rain fell in torrents. Seated in their strawy bower, they cared for no rain. They were safe from the whole world, and all the tempers of nature.

Then Hugh told Harry about the slow beginnings and the mighty birth of the great Roman people. He told him tales of their battles and conquests; their strifes at home, and their wars abroad. He told him stories of their grand men, great with the individuality of their nation and their own. He told him their characters, their peculiar opinions and grounds of action, and the results of their various schemes for their various ends. He told him about their love to their country, about their poetry and their religion; their courage, and their hardihood; their architecture, their clothes, and their armour; their customs and their laws; but all in such language, or mostly in such language, as one boy might use in telling another of the same age; for Hugh possessed the gift of a general simplicity of thought, one of the most valuable a man can have. It cost him a good deal of labour (well–repaid in itself, not to speak of the evident delight of Harry), to make himself perfectly competent for this; but he had a good foundation of knowledge to work upon.

This went on for a long time after the period to which I am now more immediately confined. Every time they stopped to rest from their rambles or games—as often, in fact, as they sat down alone, Harry's constant request was:

"Now, Mr. Sutherland, mightn't we have something more about the Romans?"

And Mr. Sutherland gave him something more. But all this time he never uttered the word—Latin.

CHAPTER V. LARCH AND OTHER HUNTING.

```
For there is neither buske nor hay
In May, that it n'ill shrouded bene,
And it with newé leavés wrene;
These woodés eke recoveren grene,
That drie in winter ben to sene,
And the erth waxeth proud withall,
For swoté dewes that on it fall,
And the poore estate forget,
In which that winter had it set:
And than becomes the ground so proude,
That it wol have a newé shroude,
And maketh so queint his robe and faire,
That it hath hewes an hundred paire,
Of grasse and floures, of Ind and Pers,
```

David Elginbrod

```
And many hewés full divers:
That is the robe I mean, ywis,
Through which the ground to praisen is.
```

CHAUCER'S translation of the Romaunt of the Rose.

So passed the three days of rain. After breakfast the following morning, Hugh went to find Harry, according to custom, in the library. He was reading.

"What are you reading, Harry?" asked he.

"A poem," said Harry; and, rising as before, he brought the book to Hugh. It was Mrs. Hemans's Poems.

"You are fond of poetry, Harry."

"Yes, very."

"Whose poems do you like best?"

"Mrs. Hemans's, of course. Don't you think she is the best, sir?"

"She writes very beautiful verses, Harry. Which poem are you reading now?"

"Oh! one of my favourites—The Voice of Spring."

"Who taught you to like Mrs. Hemans?"

"Euphra, of course."

"Will you read the poem to me?"

Harry began, and read the poem through, with much taste and evident enjoyment; an enjoyment which seemed, however, to spring more from the music of the thought and its embodiment in sound, than from sympathy with the forms of nature called up thereby. This was shown by his mode of reading, in which the music was everything, and the sense little or nothing. When he came to the line,

"And the larch has hung all his tassels forth,"

he smiled so delightedly, that Hugh said:

"Are you fond of the larch, Harry?"

"Yes, very."

"Are there any about here?"

"I don't know. What is it like?"

"You said you were fond of it."

"Oh, yes; it is a tree with beautiful tassels, you know. I think I should like to see one. Isn't it a beautiful line?"

"When you have finished the poem, we will go and see if we can find one anywhere in the woods. We must know where we are in the world, Harry—what is all round about us, you know."

"Oh, yes," said Harry; "let us go and hunt the larch."

"Perhaps we shall meet Spring, if we look for her—perhaps hear her voice, too."

"That would be delightful," answered Harry, smiling. And away they went.

I may just mention here that Mrs. Hemans was allowed to retire gradually, till at last she was to be found only in the more inaccessible recesses of the library—shelves; while by that time Harry might be heard, not all over the house, certainly, but as far off as outside the closed door of the library, reading aloud to himself one or other of Macaulay's ballads, with an evident enjoyment of the go in it. A story with drum and trumpet accompaniment was quite enough, for the present, to satisfy Harry; and Macaulay could give him that, if little more.

David Elginbrod

As they went across the lawn towards the shrubbery, on their way to look for larches and Spring, Euphra joined them in walking dress. It was a lovely morning.

"I have taken you at your word, you see, Mr. Sutherland," said she. "I don't want to lose my Harry quite."

"You dear kind Euphra!" said Harry, going round to her side and taking her hand. He did not stay long with her, however, nor did Euphra seem particularly to want him.

"There was one thing I ought to have mentioned to you the other night, Mr. Sutherland; and I daresay I should have mentioned it, had not Mr. Arnold interrupted our tête-à-tête. I feel now as if I had been guilty of claiming far more than I have a right to, on the score of musical insight. I have Scotch blood in me, and was indeed born in Scotland, though I left it before I was a year old. My mother, Mr. Arnold's sister, married a gentleman who was half Sootch; and I was born while they were on a visit to his relatives, the Camerons of Lochnie. His mother, my grandmother, was a Bohemian lady, a countess with sixteen quarterings—not a gipsy, I beg to say."

Hugh thought she might have been, to judge from present appearances.

But how was he to account for this torrent of genealogical information, into which the ice of her late constraint had suddenly thawed? It was odd that she should all at once volunteer so much about herself. Perhaps she had made up one of those minds which need making up, every now and then, like a monthly magazine; and now was prepared to publish it. Hugh responded with a question:

"Do I know your name, then, at last? You are Miss Cameron?"

"Euphrasia Cameron; at your service, sir." And she dropped a gay little courtesy to Hugh, looking up at him with a flash of her black diamonds.

"Then you must sing to me to-night."

"With all the pleasure in gipsy-land," replied she, with a second courtesy, lower than the first; taking for granted, no doubt, his silent judgment on her person and complexion.

David Elginbrod

By this time they had reached the woods in a different quarter from that which Hugh had gone through the other day with Harry. And here, in very deed, the Spring met them, with a profusion of richness to which Hugh was quite a stranger. The ground was carpeted with primroses, and anemones, and other spring flowers, which are the loveliest of all flowers. They were drinking the sunlight, which fell upon them through the budded boughs. By the time the light should be hidden from them by the leaves, which are the clouds of the lower firmament of the woods, their need of it would be gone: exquisites in living, they cared only for the delicate morning of the year.

"Do look at this darling, Mr. Sutherland!" exclaimed Euphrasia suddenly, as she bent at the root of a great beech, where grew a large bush of rough leaves, with one tiny but perfectly-formed primrose peeping out between. "Is it not a little pet?—all eyes—all one eye staring out of its curtained bed to see what ever is going on in the world.—You had better lie down again: it is not a nice place."

She spoke to it as if it had been a kitten or a baby. And as she spoke, she pulled the leaves yet closer over the little starer so as to hide it quite.

As they went on, she almost obtrusively avoided stepping on the flowers, saying she almost felt cruel, or at least rude, when she did so. Yet she trailed her dress over them in quite a careless way, not lifting it at all. This was a peculiarity of hers, which Hugh never understood till he understood herself.

All about in shady places, the ferns were busy untucking themselves from their grave-clothes, unrolling their mysterious coils of life, adding continually to the hidden growth as they unfolded the visible. In this, they were like the other revelations of God the Infinite. All the wild lovely things were coming up for their month's life of joy. Orchis-harlequins, cuckoo-plants, wild arums, more properly lords-and-ladies, were coming, and coming—slowly; for had they not a long way to come, from the valley of the shadow of death into the land of life? At last the wanderers came upon a whole company of bluebells—not what Hugh would have called bluebells, for the bluebells of Scotland are the single-poised harebells—but wild hyacinths, growing in a damp and shady spot, in wonderful luxuriance. They were quite three feet in height, with long, graceful, drooping heads; hanging down from them, all along one side, the largest and loveliest of bells—one lying close above the other, on the lower part; while they parted thinner and thinner as they rose towards the lonely one at the top. Miss Cameron went into ecstasies over these; not saying much, but breaking up what she did say with many prettily passionate pauses.

She had a very happy turn for seeing external resemblances, either humorous or pathetic; for she had much of one element that goes to the making of a poet—namely, surface impressibility.

"Look, Harry; they are all sad at having to go down there again so soon. They are looking at their graves so ruefully."

Harry looked sad and rather sentimental immediately. When Hugh glanced at Miss Cameron, he saw tears in her eyes.

"You have nothing like this in your country, have you, Mr. Sutherland?" said she, with an apparent effort.

"No, indeed," answered Hugh.

And he said no more. For a vision rose before him of the rugged pine—wood and the single primrose; and of the thoughtful maiden, with unpolished speech and rough hands, and—but this he did not see—a soul slowly refining itself to a crystalline clearness. And he thought of the grand old grey-haired David, and of Janet with her quaint motherhood, and of all the blessed bareness of the ancient time—in sunlight and in snow; and he felt again that he had forgotten and forsaken his friends.

"How the fairies will be ringing the bells in these airy steeples in the moonlight!" said Miss Cameron to Harry, who was surprised and delighted with it all. He could not help wondering, however, after he went to bed that night, that Euphra had never before taken him to see these beautiful things, and had never before said anything half so pretty to him, as the least pretty thing she had said about the flowers that morning when they were out with Mr. Sutherland. Had Mr. Sutherland anything to do with it? Was he giving Euphra a lesson in flowers such as he had given him in pigs?

Miss Cameron presently drew Hugh into conversation again, and the old times were once more forgotten for a season. They were worthy of distinguishing note—that trio in those spring woods: the boy waking up to feel that flowers and buds were lovelier in the woods than in verses; Euphra finding everything about her sentimentally useful, and really delighting in the prettinesses they suggested to her; and Hugh regarding the whole chiefly as a material and means for reproducing in verse such impressions of delight as he had received and still received from all (but the highest) poetry about nature. The presence of Harry and his necessities was certainly a saving influence upon Hugh; but, however much he sought to realize Harry's life, he himself, at this period of his history, enjoyed everything artistically far more than humanly.

Margaret would have walked through all this infant summer without speaking at all, but with a deep light far back in her quiet eyes. Perhaps she would not have had many thoughts about the flowers. Rather she would have thought the very flowers themselves; would have been at home with them, in a delighted oneness with their life and expression. Certainly she would have walked through them with reverence, and would not have petted or patronised nature by saying pretty things about her children. Their life would have entered into her, and she would have hardly known it from her own. I daresay Miss Cameron would have called a mountain a darling or a beauty. But there are other ways of showing affection than by patting and petting—though Margaret, for her part, would have needed no art-expression, because she had the things themselves. It is not always those who utter best who feel most; and the dumb poets are sometimes dumb because it would need the "large utterance of the early gods" to carry their thoughts through the gates of speech.

But the fancy and skin–sympathy of Miss Cameron began already to tell upon Hugh. He knew very little of women, and had never heard a woman talk as she talked. He did not know how cheap this accomplishment is, and took it for sensibility, imaginativeness, and even originality. He thought she was far more en rapport with nature than he was. It was much easier to make this mistake after hearing the really delightful way in which she sang. Certainly she could not have sung so, perhaps not even have talked so, except she had been capable of more; but to be capable of more, and to be able for more, are two very distinct conditions.

Many walks followed this, extending themselves farther and farther from home, as Harry's strength gradually improved. It was quite remarkable how his interest in everything external increased, in exact proportion as he learned to see into the inside or life of it. With most children, the interest in the external comes first, and with many ceases there. But it is in reality only a shallower form of the deeper sympathy; and in

David Elginbrod

those cases where it does lead to a desire after the hidden nature of things, it is perhaps the better beginning of the two. In such exceptional cases as Harry's, it is of unspeakable importance that both the difference and the identity should be recognized; and in doing so, Hugh became to Harry his big brother indeed, for he led him where he could not go alone.

As often as Mr. Arnold was from home, which happened not unfrequently, Miss Cameron accompanied them in their rambles. She gave as her reason for doing so only on such occasions, that she never liked to be out of the way when her uncle might want her. Traces of an inclination to quarrel with Hugh, or even to stand upon her dignity, had all but vanished; and as her vivacity never failed her, as her intellect was always active, and as by the exercise of her will she could enter sympathetically, or appear to enter, into everything, her presence was not in the least a restraint upon them.

On one occasion, when Harry had actually run a little way after a butterfly, Hugh said to her:

"What did you mean, Miss Cameron, by saying you were only a poor relation? You are certainly mistress of the house."

"On sufferance, yes. But I am only a poor relation. I have no fortune of my own."

"But Mr. Arnold does not treat you as such."

"Oh! no. He likes me. He is very kind to me.—He gave me this ring on my last birthday. Is it not a beauty?"

She pulled off her glove and showed a very fine diamond on a finger worthy of the ornament.

"It is more like a gentleman's, is it not?" she added, drawing it off. "Let me see how it would look on your hand."

She gave the ring to Hugh; who, laughing, got it with some difficulty just over the first joint of his little finger, and held it up for Euphra to see.

"Ah! I see I cannot ask you to wear it for me," said she. "I don't like it myself. I am afraid, however," she added, with an arch look, "my uncle would not like it either—on your finger. Put it on mine again."

Holding her hand towards Hugh, she continued:

"It must not be promoted just yet. Besides, I see you have a still better one of your own."

As Hugh did according to her request, the words sprang to his lips, "There are other ways of wearing a ring than on the finger." But they did not cross the threshold of speech. Was it the repression of them that caused that strange flutter and slight pain at the heart, which he could not quite understand?

CHAPTER VI. FATIMA.

```
Those lips that Love's own hand did make
Breathed forth the sound that said, "I hate,"
To me that languished for her sake:
But when she saw my woeful state,
Straight in her heart did mercy come,
Chiding that tongue that, ever sweet,
Was used in giving gentle doom,
And taught it thus anew to greet:
"I hate" she altered with an end,
That followed it as gentle day
Doth follow night, who, like a fiend,
From heaven to hell is flown away.
"I hate" from hate away she threw,
And saved my life, saying—"Not you."
```

SHAKSPERE.

Mr. Arnold was busy at home for a few days after this, and Hugh and Harry had to go out alone. One day, when the wind was rather cold, they took refuge in the barn; for it was part of Hugh's especial care that Harry should be rendered hardy, by never being exposed to more than he could bear without a sense of suffering. As soon as the boy began to feel fatigue, or cold, or any other discomfort, his tutor took measures accordingly.

Harry would have crept into the straw–house; but Hugh said, pulling a book out of his pocket,

"I have a poem here for you, Harry. I want to read it to you now; and we can't see in there."

They threw themselves down on the straw, and Hugh, opening a volume of Robert Browning's Poems, read the famous ride from Ghent to Aix. He knew the poem well, and read it well. Harry was in raptures.

"I wish I could read that as you do," said he.

"Try," said Hugh.

Harry tried the first verse, and threw the book down in disgust with himself.

"Why cannot I read it?" said he.

"Because you can't ride."

"I could ride, if I had such a horse as that to ride upon."

"But you could never have such a horse as that except you could ride, and ride well, first. After that, there is no saying but you might get one. You might, in fact, train one for yourself—till from being a little foal it became your own wonderful horse."

"Oh! that would be delightful! Will you teach me horses as well, Mr. Sutherland?"

"Perhaps I will."

That evening, at dinner, Hugh said to Mr. Arnold:

"Could you let me have a horse to–morrow morning, Mr. Arnold?"

Mr. Arnold stared a little, as he always did at anything new. But Hugh went on:

"Harry and I want to have a ride to–morrow; and I expect we shall like it so much, that we shall want to ride very often."

"Yes, that we shall!" cried Harry.

"Could not Mr. Sutherland have your white mare, Euphra?" said Mr. Arnold, reconciled at once to the proposal.

"I would rather not, if you don't mind, uncle. My Fatty is not used to such a burden as I fear Mr. Sutherland would prove. She drops a little now, on the hard road."

The fact was, Euphra would want Fatima.

"Well, Harry," said Mr. Arnold, graciously pleased to be facetious, "don't you think your Welsh dray–horse could carry Mr. Sutherland?"

"Ha! ha! ha! Papa, do you know, Mr. Sutherland set him up on his hind legs yesterday, and made him walk on them like a dancing–dog. He was going to lift him, but he kicked about so when he felt himself leaving the ground, that he tumbled Mr. Sutherland into the horse–trough."

Even the solemn face of the butler relaxed into a smile, but Mr. Arnold's clouded instead. His boy's tutor ought to be a gentleman.

"Wasn't it fun, Mr. Sutherland?"

"It was to you, you little rogue!" said Sutherland, laughing.

"And how you did run home, dripping like a water–cart!—and all the dogs after you!"

Mr. Arnold's monotonous solemnity soon checked Harry's prattle.

"I will see, Mr. Sutherland, what I can do to mount you."

"I don't care what it is," said Hugh; who though by no means a thorough horseman, had been from boyhood in the habit of mounting everything in the shape of a horse that he

131

could lay hands upon, from a cart–horse upwards and downwards.

"There's an old bay that would carry me very well."

"That is my own horse, Mr. Sutherland."

This stopped the conversation in that direction. But next morning after breakfast, an excellent chestnut horse was waiting at the door, along with Harry's new pony. Mr. Arnold would see them go off. This did not exactly suit Miss Cameron, but if she frowned, it was when nobody saw her. Hugh put Harry up himself, told him to stick fast with his knees, and then mounted his chestnut. As they trotted slowly down the avenue, Euphrasia heard Mr. Arnold say to himself, "The fellow sits well, at all events." She took care to make herself agreeable to Hugh by reporting this, with the omission of the initiatory epithet, however.

Harry returned from his ride rather tired, but in high spirits.

"Oh, Euphra!" he cried, "Mr. Sutherland is such a rider! He jumps hedges and ditches and everything. And he has promised to teach me and my pony to jump too. And if I am not too tired, we are to begin to–morrow, out on the common. Oh! jolly!"

The little fellow's heart was full of the sense of growing life and strength, and Hugh was delighted with his own success. He caught sight of a serpentine motion in Euphra's eyebrows, as she bent her face again over the work from which she had lifted it on their entrance. He addressed her.

"You will be glad to hear that Harry has ridden like a man."

"I am glad to hear it, Harry."

Why did she reply to the subject of the remark, and not to the speaker? Hugh perplexed himself in vain to answer this question; but a very small amount of experience would have made him able to understand at once as much of her behaviour as was genuine. At luncheon she spoke only in reply; and then so briefly, as not to afford the smallest peg on which to hang a response.

"What can be the matter?" thought Hugh. "What a peculiar creature she is! But after what has passed between us, I can't stand this."

When dinner was over that evening, she rose as usual and left the room, followed by Hugh and Harry; but as soon as they were in the drawing–room, she left it; and, returning to the dining–room, resumed her seat at the table.

"Take a glass of claret, Euphra, dear?" said Mr. Arnold.

"I will, if you please, uncle. I should like it. I have seldom a minute with you alone now."

Evidently flattered, Mr. Arnold poured out a glass of claret, rose and carried it to his niece himself, and then took a chair beside her.

"Thank you, dear uncle," she said, with one of her bewitching flashes of smile.

"Harry has been getting on bravely with his riding, has he not?" she continued.

"So it would appear."

Harry had been full of the story of the day at the dinner–table, where he still continued to present himself; for his father would not be satisfied without hint. It was certainly good moral training for the boy, to sit there almost without eating; and none the worse that he found it rather hard sometimes. He talked much more freely now, and asked the servants for anything he wanted without referring to Euphra. Now and then he would glance at her, as if afraid of offending her; but the cords which bound him to her were evidently relaxing; and she saw it plainly enough, though she made no reference to the unpleasing fact.

"I am only a little fearful, uncle, lest Mr. Sutherland should urge the boy to do more than his strength will admit of. He is exceedingly kind to him, but he has evidently never known what weakness is himself."

"True, there is danger of that. But you see he has taken him so entirely into his own hands. I don't seem to be allowed a word in the matter of his education any more." Mr. Arnold spoke with the peevishness of weak importance. "I wish you would take care that he does not carry things too far, Euphra."

This was just what Euphra wanted.

"I think, if you do not disapprove, uncle, I will have Fatima saddled to—morrow morning, and go with them myself."

"Thank you, my love; I shall be much obliged to you." The glass of claret was soon finished after this. A little more conversation about nothing followed, and Euphra rose the second time, and returned to the drawing—room. She found it unoccupied. She sat down to the piano, and sang song after song—Scotch, Italian, and Bohemian. But Hugh did not make his appearance. The fact was, he was busy writing to his mother, whom he had rather neglected since he came. Writing to her made him think of David, and he began a letter to him too; but it was never finished, and never sent. He did not return to the drawing—room that evening. Indeed, except for a short time, while Mr. Arnold was drinking his claret, he seldom showed himself there. Had Euphra repelled him too much—hurt him? She would make up for it to—morrow.

Breakfast was scarcely over, when the chestnut and the pony passed the window, accompanied by a lovely little Arab mare, broad—chested and light—limbed, with a wonderfully small head. She was white as snow, with keen, dark eyes. Her curb—rein was red instead of white. Hearing their approach, and begging her uncle to excuse her, Euphra rose from the table, and left the room; but re—appeared in a wonderfully little while, in a well—fitted riding—habit of black velvet, with a belt of dark red leather clasping a waist of the roundest and smallest. Her little hat, likewise black, had a single long, white feather, laid horizontally within the upturned brim, and drooping over it at the back. Her white mare would be just the right pedestal for the dusky figure—black eyes, tawny skin, and all. As she stood ready to mount, and Hugh was approaching to put her up, she called the groom, seemed just to touch his hand, and was in the saddle in a moment, foot in stirrup, and skirt falling over it. Hugh thought she was carrying out the behaviour of yesterday, and was determined to ask her what it meant. The little Arab began to rear and plunge with pride, as soon as she felt her mistress on her back; but she seemed as much at home as if she had been on the music—stool, and patted her arching neck, talking to her in the same tone almost in which she had addressed the flowers.

"Be quiet, Fatty dear; you're frightening Mr. Sutherland."

David Elginbrod

But Hugh, seeing the next moment that she was in no danger, sprang into his saddle. Away they went, Fatima infusing life and frolic into the equine as Euphra into the human portion of the cavalcade. Having reached the common, out of sight of the house, Miss Cameron, instead of looking after Harry, lest he should have too much exercise, scampered about like a wild girl, jumping everything that came in her way, and so exciting Harry's pony, that it was almost more than he could do to manage it, till at last Hugh had to beg her to go more quietly, for Harry's sake. She drew up alongside of them at once, and made her mare stand as still as she could, while Harry made his first essay upon a little ditch. After crossing it two or three times, he gathered courage; and setting his pony at a larger one beyond, bounded across it beautifully.

"Bravo! Harry!" cried both Euphra and Hugh. Harry galloped back, and over it again; then came up to them with a glow of proud confidence on his pale face.

"You'll be a horseman yet, Harry," said Hugh.

"I hope so," said Harry, in an aspiring tone, which greatly satisfied his tutor. The boy's spirit was evidently reviving. Euphra must have managed him ill. Yet she was not in the least effeminate herself. It puzzled Hugh a good deal. But he did not think about it long; for Harry cantering away in front, he had an opportunity of saying to Euphra:

"Are you offended with me, Miss Cameron?"

"Offended with you! What do you mean? A girl like me offended with a man like you?"

She looked two and twenty as she spoke; but even at that she was older than Hugh. He, however, certainly looked considerably older than he really was.

"What makes you think so?" she added, turning her face towards him.

"You would not speak to me when we came home yesterday."

"Not speak to you?—I had a little headache—and perhaps I was a little sullen, from having been in such bad company all the morning."

"What company had you?" asked Hugh, gazing at her in some surprise.

135

David Elginbrod

"My own," answered she, with a lovely laugh, thrown full in his face. Then after a pause: "Let me advise you, if you want to live in peace, not to embark on that ocean of discovery."

"What ocean? what discovery?" asked Hugh, bewildered, and still gazing.

"The troubled ocean of ladies' looks," she replied. "You will never be able to live in the same house with one of our kind, if it be necessary to your peace to find out what every expression that puzzles you may mean."

"I did not intend to be inquisitive—it really troubled me."

"There it is. You must never mind us. We show so much sooner than men—but, take warning, there is no making out what it is we do show. Your faces are legible; ours are so scratched and interlined, that you had best give up at once the idea of deciphering them."

Hugh could not help looking once more at the smooth, simple, naïve countenance shining upon him.

"There you are at it again," she said, blushing a little, and turning her head away. "Well, to comfort you, I will confess I was rather cross yesterday—because—because you seemed to have been quite happy with only one of your pupils."

As she spoke the words, she gave Fatima the rein, and bounded off, overtaking Harry's pony in a moment. Nor did she leave her cousin during all the rest of their ride.

Most women in whom the soul has anything like a chance of reaching the windows, are more or less beautiful in their best moments. Euphra's best was when she was trying to fascinate. Then she was—fascinating. During the first morning that Hugh spent at Arnstead, she had probably been making up her mind whether, between her and Hugh, it was to be war to the knife, or fascination. The latter had carried the day, and was now carrying him. But had she calculated that fascination may re-act as well?

Hugh's heart bounded, like her Arab steed, as she uttered the words last recorded. He gave his chestnut the rein in his turn, to overtake her; but Fatima's canter quickened into a gallop, and, inspirited by her companionship, and the fact that their heads were turned stablewards, Harry's pony, one of the quickest of its race, laid itself to the ground, and kept up, taking three strides for Fatty's two, so that Hugh never got within three lengths of them till they drew rein at the hall–door, where the grooms were waiting them. Euphra was off her mare in a moment, and had almost reached her own room before Hugh and Harry had crossed the hall. She came down to luncheon in a white muslin dress, with the smallest possible red spot in it; and, taking her place at the table, seemed to Hugh to have put off not only her riding habit, but the self that was in it as well; for she chatted away in the most unconcerned and easy manner possible, as if she had not been out of her room all the morning. She had ridden so hard, that she had left her last speech in the middle of the common, and its mood with it; and there seemed now no likelihood of either finding its way home.

CHAPTER VII. THE PICTURE GALLERY.

```
      the house is crencled to and fro,
And hath so queint waies for to go,
For it is shapen as the mase is wrought.
```

CHAUCER—Legend of Ariadne.

Luncheon over, and Harry dismissed as usual to lie down, Miss Cameron said to Hugh:

"You have never been over the old house yet, I believe, Mr. Sutherland. Would you not like to see it?"

"I should indeed," said Hugh. "It is what I have long hoped for, and have often been on the point of begging."

"Come, then; I will be your guide—if you will trust yourself with a madcap like me, in the solitudes of the old hive."

"Lead on to the family vaults, if you will," said Hugh.

"That might be possible, too, from below. We are not so very far from them. Even within the house there is an old chapel, and some monuments worth looking at. Shall we take it last?"

137

David Elginbrod

"As you think best," answered Hugh.

She rose and rang the bell. When it was answered,

"Jacob," she said, "get me the keys of the house from Mrs. Horton."

Jacob vanished, and reappeared with a huge bunch of keys. She took them.

"Thank you. They should not be allowed to get quite rusty, Jacob."

"Please, Miss, Mrs. Horton desired me to say, she would have seen to them, if she had known you wanted them."

"Oh! never mind. Just tell my maid to bring me an old pair of gloves."

Jacob went; and the maid came with the required armour.

"Now, Mr. Sutherland. Jane, you will come with us. No, you need not take the keys. I will find those I want as we go."

She unlocked a door in the corner of the hall, which Hugh had never seen open. Passing through a long low passage, they came to a spiral staircase of stone, up which they went, arriving at another wide hall, very dusty, but in perfect repair. Hugh asked if there was not some communication between this hall and the great oak staircase.

"Yes," answered Euphra; "but this is the more direct way."

As she said this, he felt somehow as if she cast on him one of her keenest glances; but the place was very dusky, and he stood in a spot where the light fell upon him from an opening in a shutter, while she stood in deep shadow.

"Jane, open that shutter."

The girl obeyed; and the entering light revealed the walls covered with paintings, many of them apparently of no value, yet adding much to the effect of the place. Seeing that Hugh was at once attracted by the pictures, Euphra said:

David Elginbrod

"Perhaps you would like to see the picture gallery first?"

Hugh assented. Euphra chose key after key, and opened door after door, till they came into a long gallery, well lighted from each end. The windows were soon opened.

"Mr. Arnold is very proud of his pictures, especially of his family portraits; but he is content with knowing he has them, and never visits them except to show them; or perhaps once or twice a year, when something or other keeps him at home for a day, without anything particular to do."

In glancing over the portraits, some of them by famous masters, Hugh's eyes were arrested by a blonde beauty in the dress of the time of Charles II. There was such a reality of self—willed boldness as well as something worse in her face, that, though arrested by the picture, Hugh felt ashamed of looking at it in the presence of Euphra and her maid. The pictured woman almost put him out of countenance, and yet at the same time fascinated him. Dragging his eyes from it, he saw that Jane had turned her back upon it, while Euphra regarded it steadily.

"Open that opposite window, Jane," said she; "there is not light enough on this portrait."

Jane obeyed. While she did so, Hugh caught a glimpse of her face, and saw that the formerly rosy girl was deadly pale. He said to Euphra:

"Your maid seems ill, Miss Cameron."

"Jane, what is the matter with you?"

She did not reply, but, leaning against the wall, seemed ready to faint.

"The place is close," said her mistress. "Go into the next room there,"—she pointed to a door—"and open the window. You will soon be well."

"If you please, Miss, I would rather stay with you. This place makes me feel that strange."

She had come but lately, and had never been over the house before.

David Elginbrod

"Nonsense!" said Miss Cameron, looking at her sharply. "What do you mean?"

"Please, don't be angry, Miss; but the first night e'er I slept here, I saw that very lady—"

"Saw that lady!"

"Well, Miss, I mean, I dreamed that I saw her; and I remembered her the minute I see her up there; and she give me a turn like. I'm all right now, Miss."

Euphra fixed her eyes on her, and kept them fixed, till she was very nearly all wrong again. She turned as pale as before, and began to draw her breath hard.

"You silly goose!" said Euphra, and withdrew her eyes; upon which the girl began to breathe more freely.

Hugh was making some wise remarks in his own mind on the unsteady condition of a nature in which the imagination predominates over the powers of reflection, when Euphra turned to him, and began to tell him that that was the picture of her three or four times great–grandmother, painted by Sir Peter Lely, just after she was married.

"Isn't she fair?" said she.—"She turned nun at last, they say."

"She is more fair than honest," thought Hugh. "It would take a great deal of nun to make her into a saint." But he only said, "She is more beautiful than lovely. What was her name?"

"If you mean her maiden name, it was Halkar—Lady Euphrasia Halkar—named after me, you see. She had foreign blood in her, of course; and, to tell the truth, there were strange stories told of her, of more sorts than one. I know nothing of her family. It was never heard of in England, I believe, till after the Restoration."

All the time Euphra was speaking, Hugh was being perplexed with that most annoying of perplexities—the flitting phantom of a resemblance, which he could not catch. He was forced to dismiss it for the present, utterly baffled.

"Were you really named after her, Miss Cameron?"

"No, no. It is a family name with us. But, indeed, I may be said to be named after her, for she was the first of us who bore it. You don't seem to like the portrait."

"I do not; but I cannot help looking at it, for all that."

"I am so used to the lady's face," said Euphra, "that it makes no impression on me of any sort. But it is said," she added, glancing at the maid, who stood at some distance, looking uneasily about her—and as she spoke she lowered her voice to a whisper—"it is said, she cannot lie still."

"Cannot lie still! What do you mean?"

"I mean down there in the chapel," she answered, pointing.

The Celtic nerves of Hugh shuddered. Euphra laughed; and her voice echoed in silvery billows, that broke on the faces of the men and women of old time, that had owned the whole; whose lives had flowed and ebbed in varied tides through the ancient house; who had married and been given in marriage; and gone down to the chapel below—below the prayers and below the psalms—and made a Sunday of all the week.

Ashamed of his feeling of passing dismay, Hugh said, just to say something:

"What a strange ornament that is! Is it a brooch or a pin? No, I declare it is a ring—large enough for three cardinals, and worn on her thumb. It seems almost to sparkle. Is it ruby, or carbuncle, or what?"

"I don't know: some clumsy old thing," answered Euphra, carelessly.

"Oh! I see," said Hugh; "it is not a red stone. The glow is only a reflection from part of her dress. It is as clear as a diamond. But that is impossible—such a size. There seems to me something curious about it; and the longer I look at it, the more strange it appears."

Euphra stole another of her piercing glances at him, but said nothing.

"Surely," Hugh went on, "a ring like that would hardly be likely to be lost out of the family? Your uncle must have it somewhere."

Euphra laughed; but this laugh was very different from the last. It rattled rather than rang.

"You are wonderfully taken with a bauble—for a man of letters, that is, Mr. Sutherland. The stone may have been carried down any one of the hundred streams into which a family river is always dividing."

"It is a very remarkable ornament for a lady's finger, notwithstanding," said Hugh, smiling in his turn.

"But we shall never get through the pictures at this rate," remarked Euphra; and going on, she directed Hugh's attention now to this, now to that portrait, saying who each was, and mentioning anything remarkable in the history of their originals. She manifested a thorough acquaintance with the family story, and made, in fact, an excellent show-woman. Having gone nearly to the other end of the gallery,

"This door," said she, stopping at one, and turning over the keys, "leads to one of the oldest portions of the house, the principal room in which is said to have belonged especially to the lady over there."

As she said this, she fixed her eyes once more on the maid.

"Oh! don't ye now, Miss," interrupted Jane. "Hannah du say as how a whitey-blue light shines in the window of a dark night, sometimes—that lady's window, you know, Miss. Don't ye open the door—pray, Miss."

Jane seemed on the point of falling into the same terror as before.

"Really, Jane," said her mistress, "I am ashamed of you; and of myself, for having such silly servants about me."

"I beg your pardon, Miss, but—"

"So Mr. Sutherland and I must give up our plan of going over the house, because my maid's nerves are too delicate to permit her to accompany us. For shame!"

"Oh, du ye now go without me!" cried the girl, clasping her hands.

David Elginbrod

"And you will wait here till we come back?"

"Oh! don't ye leave me here. Just show me the way out."

And once more she turned pale as death.

"Mr. Sutherland, I am very sorry, but we must put off the rest of our ramble till another time. I am, like Hamlet, very vilely attended, as you see. Come, then, you foolish girl," she added, more mildly.

The poor maid, what with terror of Lady Euphrasia, and respect for her mistress, was in a pitiable condition of moral helplessness. She seemed almost too frightened to walk behind them. But if she had been in front it would have been no better; for, like other ghost–fearers, she seemed to feel very painfully that she had no eyes in her back.

They returned as they came; and Jane receiving the keys to take to the housekeeper, darted away. When she reached Mrs. Horton's room, she sank on a chair in hysterics.

"I must get rid of that girl, I fear," said Miss Cameron, leading the way to the library; "she will infect the whole household with her foolish terrors. We shall not hear the last of this for some time to come. We had a fit of it the same year I came; and I suppose the time has come round for another attack of the same epidemic."

"What is there about the room to terrify the poor thing?"

"Oh! they say it is haunted; that is all. Was there ever an old house anywhere over Europe, especially an old family house, but was said to be haunted? Here the story centres in that room—or at least in that room and the avenue in front of its windows."

"Is that the avenue called the Ghost's Walk?"

"Yes. Who told you?"

"Harry would not let me cross it."

"Poor boy! This is really too bad. He cannot stand anything of that kind, I am sure. Those servants!"

"Oh! I hope we shall soon get him too well to be frightened at anything. Are these places said to be haunted by any particular ghost?"

"Yes. By Lady Euphrasia—Rubbish!"

Had Hugh possessed a yet keener perception of resemblance, he would have seen that the phantom–likeness which haunted him in the portrait of Euphrasia Halkar, was that of Euphrasia Cameron—by his side all the time. But the mere difference of complexion was sufficient to throw him out—insignificant difference as that is, beside the correspondence of features and their relations. Euphra herself was perfectly aware of the likeness, but had no wish that Hugh should discover it.

As if the likeness, however, had been dimly identified by the unconscious part of his being, he sat in one corner of the library sofa, with his eyes fixed on the face of Euphra, as she sat in the other. Presently he was made aware of his unintentional rudeness, by seeing her turn pale as death, and sink back in the sofa. In a moment she started up, and began pacing about the room, rubbing her eyes and temples. He was bewildered and alarmed.

"Miss Cameron, are you ill?" he exclaimed.

She gave a kind of half–hysterical laugh, and said:

"No—nothing worth speaking of. I felt a little faint, that was all. I am better now."

She turned full towards him, and seemed to try to look all right; but there was a kind of film over the clearness of her black eyes.

"I fear you have headache."

"A little, but it is nothing. I will go and lie down."

"Do, pray; else you will not be well enough to appear at dinner."

She retired, and Hugh joined Hairy.

Euphra had another glass of claret with her uncle that evening, in order to give her report of the morning's ride.

"Really, there is not much to be afraid of, uncle. He takes very good care of Harry. To be sure, I had occasion several times to check him a little; but he has this good quality in addition to a considerable aptitude for teaching, that he perceives a hint, and takes it at once."

Knowing her uncle's formality, and preference for precise and judicial modes of expression, Euphra modelled her phrase to his mind.

"I am glad he has your good opinion so far, Euphra; for I confess there is something about the youth that pleases me. I was afraid at first that I might be annoyed by his overstepping the true boundaries of his position in my family: he seems to have been in good society, too. But your assurance that he can take a hint, lessens my apprehension considerably. To—morrow, I will ask him to resume his seat after dessert."

This was not exactly the object of Euphra's qualified commendation of Hugh. But she could not help it now.

"I think, however, if you approve, uncle, that it will be more prudent to keep a little watch over the riding for a while. I confess, too, I should be glad of a little more of that exercise than I have had for some time: I found my seat not very secure to—day."

"Very desirable on both considerations, my love."

And so the conference ended.

CHAPTER VIII. NEST–BUILDING.

```
If you will have a tree bear more fruit than it hath used to do, it
is not anything you can do to the boughs, but it is the stirring of
the earth, and putting new mould about the roots, that must work it.
```

David Elginbrod

LORD BACON'S Advancement of Learning, b. ii.

In a short time Harry's health was so much improved, and consequently the strength and activity of his mind so much increased, that Hugh began to give him more exact mental operations to perform. But as if he had been a reader of Lord Bacon, which as yet he was not, and had learned from him that "wonder is the seed of knowledge," he came, by a kind of sympathetic instinct, to the same conclusion practically, in the case of Harry. He tried to wake a question in him, by showing him something that would rouse his interest. The reply to this question might be the whole rudiments of a science.

Things themselves should lead to the science of them. If things are not interesting in themselves, how can any amount of knowledge about them be? To be sure, there is such a thing as a purely or abstractly intellectual interest—the pleasure of the mere operation of the intellect upon the signs of things; but this must spring from a highly exercised intellectual condition, and is not to be expected before the pleasures of intellectual motion have been experienced through the employment of its means for other ends. Whether this is a higher condition or not, is open to much disquisition.

One day Hugh was purposely engaged in taking the altitude of the highest turret of the house, with an old quadrant he had found in the library, when Harry came up.

"What are you doing, big brother?" said he; for now that he was quite at home with Hugh, there was a wonderful mixture of familiarity and respect in him, that was quite bewitching.

"Finding out how high your house is, little brother," answered Hugh.

"How can you do it with that thing? Will it measure the height of other things besides the house?"

"Yes, the height of a mountain, or anything you like."

"Do show me how."

Hugh showed him as much of it as he could.

David Elginbrod

"But I don't understand it."

"Oh! that is quite another thing. To do that, you must learn a great many things—Euclid to begin with."

That very afternoon Harry began Euclid, and soon found quite enough of interest on the road to the quadrant, to prevent him from feeling any tediousness in its length.

Of an afternoon Hugh had taken to reading Shakspere to Harry. Euphra was always a listener. On one occasion Harry said:

"I am so sorry, Mr. Sutherland, but I don't understand the half of it. Sometimes when Euphra and you are laughing,—and sometimes when Euphra is crying," added he, looking at her slyly, "I can't understand what it is all about. Am I so very stupid, Mr. Sutherland?" And he almost cried himself.

"Not a bit of it, Harry, my boy; only you must learn a great many other things first."

"How can I learn them? I am willing to learn anything. I don't find it tire me now as it used."

"There are many things necessary to understand Shakspere that I cannot teach you, and that some people never learn. Most of them will come of themselves. But of one thing you may be sure, Harry, that if you learn anything, whatever it be, you are so far nearer to understanding Shakspere."

The same afternoon, when Harry had waked from his siesta, upon which Hugh still insisted, they went out for a walk in the fields. The sun was half way down the sky, but very hot and sultry.

"I wish we had our cave of straw to creep into now," said Harry. "I felt exactly like the little field–mouse you read to me about in Burns's poems, when we went in that morning, and found it all torn up, and half of it carried away. We have no place to go to now for a peculiar own place; and the consequence is, you have not told me any stories about the Romans for a whole week."

David Elginbrod

"Well, Harry, is there any way of making another?"

"There's no more straw lying about that I know of," answered Harry; "and it won't do to pull the inside out of a rick, I am afraid."

"But don't you think it would be pleasant to have a change now; and as we have lived underground, or say in the snow like the North people, try living in the air, like some of the South people?"

"Delightful!" cried Harry.—"A balloon?"

"No, not quite that. Don't you think a nest would do?"

"Up in a tree?"

"Yes."

Harry darted off for a run, as the only means of expressing his delight. When he came back, he said:

"When shall we begin, Mr. Sutherland?"

"We will go and look for a place at once; but I am not quite sure when we shall begin yet. I shall find out to–night, though."

They left the fields, and went into the woods in the neighbourhood of the house, at the back. Here the trees had grown to a great size, some of them being very old indeed. They soon fixed upon a grotesque old oak as a proper tree in which to build their nest; and Harry, who, as well as Hugh, had a good deal of constructiveness in his nature, was so delighted, that the heat seemed to have no more influence upon him; and Hugh, fearful of the reaction, was compelled to restrain his gambols.

Pursuing their way through the dark warp of the wood, with its golden weft of crossing sunbeams, Hugh began to tell Harry the story of the killing of Cæsar by Brutus and the rest, filling up the account with portions from Shakspere. Fortunately, he was able to give the orations of Brutus and Antony in full. Harry was in ecstasy over the eloquence of the two men.

"Well, what language do you think they spoke, Harry?" said Hugh.

"Why," said Harry, hesitating, "I suppose—" then, as if a sudden light broke upon him—"Latin of course. How strange!"

"Why strange?"

"That such men should talk such a dry, unpleasant language."

"I allow it is a difficult language, Harry; and very ponderous and mechanical; but not necessarily dry or unpleasant. The Romans, you know, were particularly fond of law in everything; and so they made a great many laws for their language; or rather, it grew so, because they were of that sort. It was like their swords and armour generally, not very graceful, but very strong;—like their architecture too, Harry. Nobody can ever understand what a people is, without knowing its language. It is not only that we find all these stories about them in their language, but the language itself is more like them than anything else can be. Besides, Harry, I don't believe you know anything about Latin yet."

"I know all the declensions and conjugations."

"But don't you think it must have been a very different thing to hear it spoken?"

"Yes, to be sure—and by such men. But how ever could they speak it?"

"They spoke it just as you do English. It was as natural to them. But you cannot say you know anything about it, till you read what they wrote in it; till your ears delight in the sound of their poetry;—"

"Poetry?"

"Yes; and beautiful letters; and wise lessons; and histories and plays."

"Oh! I should like you to teach me. Will it be as hard to learn always as it is now?"

David Elginbrod

"Certainly not. I am sure you will like it."

"When will you begin me?"

"To-morrow. And if you get on pretty well, we will begin our nest, too, in the afternoon."

"Oh, how kind you are! I will try very hard."

"I am sure you will, Harry."

Next morning, accordingly, Hugh did begin him, after a fashion of his own; namely, by giving him a short simple story to read, finding out all the words with him in the dictionary, and telling him what the terminations of the words signified; for he found that he had already forgotten a very great deal of what, according to Euphra, he had been thoroughly taught. No one can remember what is entirely uninteresting to him.

Hugh was as precise about the grammar of a language as any Scotch Professor of Humanity, old Prosody not excepted; but he thought it time enough to begin to that, when some interest in the words themselves should have been awakened in the mind of his pupil. He hated slovenliness as much as any one; but the question was, how best to arrive at thoroughness in the end, without losing the higher objects of study; and not how, at all risks, to commence teaching the lesson of thoroughness at once, and so waste on the shape of a pin-head the intellect which, properly directed, might arrive at the far more minute accuracies of a steam-engine. The fault of Euphra in teaching Harry, had been that, with a certain kind of tyrannical accuracy, she had determined to have the thing done—not merely decently and in order, but prudishly and pedantically; so that she deprived progress of the pleasure which ought naturally to attend it. She spoiled the walk to the distant outlook, by stopping at every step, not merely to pick flowers, but to botanise on the weeds, and to calculate the distance advanced. It is quite true that we ought to learn to do things irrespective of the reward; but plenty of opportunities will be given in the progress of life, and in much higher kinds of action, to exercise our sense of duty in severe loneliness. We have no right to turn intellectual exercises into pure operations of conscience: these ought to involve essential duty; although no doubt there is plenty of room for mingling duty with those; while, on the other hand, the highest act of suffering self-denial is not without its accompanying reward. Neither is there any exercise of the higher intellectual powers in learning the mere grammar of a language, necessary as it is for a means. And language having been made before grammar, a language must be in some measure understood, before its grammar can become intelligible.

Harry's weak (though true and keen) life could not force its way into any channel. His was a nature essentially dependent on sympathy. It could flow into truth through another loving mind: left to itself, it could not find the way, and sank in the dry sand of ennui and self–imposed obligations. Euphra was utterly incapable of understanding him; and the boy had been dying for lack of sympathy, though neither he nor any one about him had suspected the fact.

There was a strange disproportion between his knowledge and his capacity. He was able, when his attention was directed, his gaze fixed, and his whole nature supported by Hugh, to see deep into many things, and his remarks were often strikingly original; but he was one of the most ignorant boys, for his years, that Hugh had ever come across. A long and severe illness, when he was just passing into boyhood, had thrown him back far into his childhood; and he was only now beginning to show that he had anything of the boy–life in him. Hence arose that unequal development which has been sufficiently evident in the story.

In the afternoon, they went to the wood, and found the tree they had chosen for their nest. To Harry's intense admiration, Hugh, as he said, went up the tree like a squirrel, only he was too big for a bear even. Just one layer of foliage above the lowest branches, he came to a place where he thought there was a suitable foundation for the nest. From the ground Harry could scarcely see him, as, with an axe which he had borrowed for the purpose (for there was a carpenter's work–shop on the premises), he cut away several small branches from three of the principal ones; and so had these three as rafters, ready dressed and placed, for the foundation of the nest. Having made some measurements, he descended; and repairing with Harry to the work–shop, procured some boarding and some tools, which Harry assisted in carrying to the tree. Ascending again, and drawing up his materials, by the help of Harry, with a piece of string, Hugh in a very little while had a level floor, four feet square, in the heart of the oak tree, quite invisible from below—buried in a cloud of green leaves. For greater safety, he fastened ropes as handrails all around it from one branch to another. And now nothing remained but to construct a bench to sit on, and such a stair as Harry could easily climb. The boy was quite restless with anxiety to get up and see the nest; and kept calling out constantly to know if he might not come up yet. At length Hugh allowed him to try; but the poor boy was not half strong enough to climb the tree without help. So Hugh descended, and with his aid Harry was soon standing on the new–built platform.

"I feel just like an eagle," he cried; but here his voice faltered, and he was silent.

"What is the matter, Harry?" said his tutor.

"Oh, nothing," replied he; "only I didn't exactly know whereabouts we were till I got up here."

"Whereabouts are we, then?"

"Close to the end of the Ghost's Walk."

"But you don't mind that now, surely, Harry?"

"No, sir; that is, not so much as I used."

"Shall I take all this down again, and build our nest somewhere else?"

"Oh, no, if you don't think it matters. It would be a great pity, after you have taken so much trouble with it. Besides, I shall never be here without you; and I do not think I should be afraid of the ghost herself, if you were with me."

Yet Harry shuddered involuntarily at the thought of his own daring speech.

"Very well, Harry, my boy; we will finish it here. Now, if you stand there, I will fasten a plank across here between these two stumps—no, that won't do exactly. I must put a piece on to this one, to raise it to a level with the other—then we shall have a seat in a few minutes."

Hammer and nails were busy again; and in a few minutes they sat down to enjoy the "soft pipling cold" which swung all the leaves about like little trap–doors that opened into the Infinite. Harry was highly contented. He drew a deep breath of satisfaction as, looking above and beneath and all about him, he saw that they were folded in an almost impenetrable net of foliage, through which nothing could steal into their sanctuary, save "the chartered libertine, the air," and a few stray beams of the setting sun, filtering through the multitudinous leaves, from which they caught a green tint as they passed.

"Fancy yourself a fish," said Hugh, "in the depth of a cavern of sea weed, which floats about in the slow swinging motion of the heavy waters."

"What a funny notion!"

"Not so absurd as you may think, Harry; for just as some fishes crawl about on the bottom of the sea, so do we men at the bottom of an ocean of air; which, if it be a thinner one, is certainly a deeper one."

"Then the birds are the swimming fishes, are they not?"

"Yes, to be sure."

"And you and I are two mermen—doing what? Waiting for mother mermaid to give us our dinner. I am getting hungry. But it will be a long time before a mermaid gets up here, I am afraid."

"That reminds me," said Hugh, "that I must build a stair for you, Master Harry; for you are not merman enough to get up with a stroke of your scaly tail. So here goes. You can sit there till I fetch you."

Nailing a little rude bracket here and there on the stem of the tree, just where Harry could avail himself of hand–hold as well, Hugh had soon finished a strangely irregular staircase, which it took Harry two or three times trying, to learn quite off.

CHAPTER IX. GEOGRAPHY POINT.

```
I will fetch you a tooth-picker now from the farthest inch of Asia;
bring you the length of Prester John's foot; fetch you a hair off
the great Cham's beard; do you any embassage to the Pigmies.
```

David Elginbrod

Much Ado about Nothing.

The next day, after dinner, Mr. Arnold said to the tutor:

"Well, Mr. Sutherland, how does Harry get on with his geography?"

Mr. Arnold, be it understood, had a weakness for geography.

"We have not done anything at that yet, Mr. Arnold."

"Not done anything at geography! And the boy getting quite robust now! I am astonished, Mr. Sutherland. Why, when he was a mere child, he could repeat all the counties of England."

"Perhaps that may be the reason for the decided distaste he shows for it now, Mr. Arnold. But I will begin to teach him at once, if you desire it."

"I do desire it, Mr. Sutherland. A thorough geographical knowledge is essential to the education of a gentleman. Ask me any question you please, Mr. Sutherland, on the map of the world, or any of its divisions."

Hugh asked a few questions, which Mr. Arnold answered at once.

"Pooh! pooh!" said he, "this is mere child's play. Let me ask you some, Mr. Sutherland."

His very first question posed Hugh, whose knowledge in this science was not by any means minute.

"I fear I am no gentleman," said he, laughing; "but I can at least learn as well as teach. We shall begin to—morrow."

"What books have you?"

"Oh! no books, if you please, just yet. If you are satisfied with Harry's progress so far, let me have my own way in this too."

David Elginbrod

"But geography does not seem your strong point."

"No; but I may be able to teach it all the better from feeling the difficulties of a learner myself."

"Well, you shall have a fair trial."

Next morning Hugh and Harry went out for a walk to the top of a hill in the neighbourhood. When they reached it, Hugh took a small compass from his pocket, and set it on the ground, contemplating it and the horizon alternately.

"What are you doing, Mr. Sutherland?"

"I am trying to find the exact line that would go through my home," said he.

"Is that funny little thing able to tell you?"

"Yes; this along with other things. Isn't it curious, Harry, to have in my pocket a little thing with a kind of spirit in it, that understands the spirit that is in the big world, and always points to its North Pole?"

"Explain it to me."

"It is nearly as much a mystery to me as to you."

"Where is the North Pole?"

"Look, the little thing points to it."

"But I will turn it away. Oh! it won't go. It goes back and back, do what I will."

"Yes, it will, if you turn it away all day long. Look, Harry, if you were to go straight on in this direction, you would come to a Laplander, harnessing his broad-horned reindeer to his sledge. He's at it now, I daresay. If you were to go in this line exactly, you would go through the smoke and fire of a burning mountain in a land of ice. If you were to go this way, straight on, you would find yourself in the middle of a forest with a lion glaring at your feet, for it is dark night there now, and so hot! And over there, straight on, there is such a lovely sunset. The top of a snowy mountain is all pink with light, though the sun is down—oh! such colours all about, like fairyland! And there, there is a desert of sand, and a camel dying, and all his companions just disappearing on the horizon. And there, there is an awful sea, without a boat to be seen on it, dark and dismal, with huge rocks all about it, and waste borders of sand—so dreadful!"

"How do you know all this, Mr. Sutherland? You have never walked along those lines, I know, for you couldn't."

"Geography has taught me."

"No, Mr. Sutherland!" said Harry, incredulously. "Well, shall we travel along this line, just across that crown of trees on the hill?"

"Yes, do let us."

"Then," said Hugh, drawing a telescope from his pocket, "this hill is henceforth Geography Point, and all the world lies round about it. Do you know we are in the very middle of the earth?"

"Are we, indeed?"

"Yes. Don't you know any point you like to choose on a ball is the middle of it?"

"Oh! yes—of course."

"Very well. What lies at the bottom of the hill down there?"

"Arnstead, to be sure."

"And what beyond there?"

"I don't know."

"Look through here."

"Oh! that must be the village we rode to yesterday—I forget the name of it."

Hugh told him the name; and then made him look with the telescope all along the receding line to the trees on the opposite hill. Just as he caught them, a voice beside them said:

"What are you about, Harry?"

Hugh felt a glow of pleasure as the voice fell on his ear.

It was Euphra's.

"Oh!" replied Harry, "Mr. Sutherland is teaching me geography with a telescope. It's such fun!"

"He's a wonderful tutor, that of yours, Harry!"

"Yes, isn't he just? But," Harry went on, turning to Hugh, "what are we to do now? We can't get farther for that hill."

"Ah! we must apply to your papa now, to lend us some of his beautiful maps. They will teach us what lies beyond that hill. And then we can read in some of his books about the places; and so go on and on, till we reach the beautiful, wide, restless sea; over which we must sail in spite of wind and tide—straight on and on, till we come to land again. But we must make a great many such journeys before we really know what sort of a place we are living in; and we shall have ever so many things to learn that will surprise us."

"Oh! it will be nice!" cried Harry.

After a little more geographical talk, they put up their instruments, and began to descend the hill. Harry was in no need of Hugh's back now, but Euphra was in need of his hand. In fact, she spelled for its support.

"How awkward of me! I am stumbling over the heather shamefully!"

David Elginbrod

She was, in fact, stumbling over her own dress, which she would not hold up. Hugh offered his hand; and her small one seemed quite content to be swallowed up in his large one.

"Why do you never let me put you on your horse?" said Hugh. "You always manage to prevent me somehow or other. The last time, I just turned my head, and, behold! when I looked, you were gathering your reins."

"It is only a trick of independence, Hugh—Mr. Sutherland—I beg your pardon."

I can make no excuse for Euphra, for she had positively never heard him called Hugh: there was no one to do so. But, the slip had not, therefore, the less effect; for it sounded as if she had been saying his name over and over again to herself.

"I beg your pardon," repeated Euphra, hastily; for, as Hugh did not reply, she feared her arrow had swerved from its mark.

"For a sweet fault, Euphra—I beg your pardon—Miss Cameron."

"You punish me with forgiveness," returned she, with one of her sweetest looks.

Hugh could not help pressing the little hand.

Was the pressure returned? So slight, so airy was the touch, that it might have been only the throb of his own pulses, all consciously vital about the wonderful woman–hand that rested in his. If he had claimed it, she might easily have denied it, so ethereal and uncertain was it. Yet he believed in it. He never dreamed that she was exercising her skill upon him. What could be her object in bewitching a poor tutor? Ah! what indeed?

Meantime this much is certain, that she was drawing Hugh closer and closer to her side; that a soothing dream of delight had begun to steal over his spirit, soon to make it toss in feverous unrest—as the first effects of some poisons are like a dawn of tenfold strength. The mountain wind blew from her to him, sometimes sweeping her garments about him, and bathing him in their faint sweet odours—odours which somehow seemed to belong to her whom they had only last visited; sometimes, so kindly strong did it blow, compelling her, or at least giving her excuse enough, to leave his hand and cling closely to his arm. A fresh spring began to burst from the very bosom of what had seemed before a perfect summer. A spring to summer! What would the following summer be? Ah! and what the autumn? And what the winter? For if the summer be tenfold summer, then must the winter be tenfold winter.

But though knowledge is good for man, foreknowledge is not so good.

And, though Love be good, a tempest of it in the brain will not ripen the fruits like a soft steady wind, or waft the ships home to their desired haven.

Perhaps, what enslaved Hugh most, was the feeling that the damsel stooped to him, without knowing that she stooped. She seemed to him in every way above him. She knew so many things of which he was ignorant; could say such lovely things; could, he did not doubt, write lovely verses; could sing like an angel; (though Scotch songs are not of essentially angelic strain, nor Italian songs either, in general; and they were all that she could do); was mistress of a great rich wonderful house, with a history; and, more than all, was, or appeared to him to be—a beautiful woman. It was true that his family was as good as hers; but he had disowned his family—so his pride declared; and the same pride made him despise his present position, and look upon a tutor's employment as—as—well, as other people look upon it; as a rather contemptible one in fact, especially for a young, powerful, six–foot fellow.

The influence of Euphrasia was not of the best upon him from the first; for it had greatly increased this feeling about his occupation. It could not affect his feelings towards Harry; so the boy did not suffer as yet. But it set him upon a very unprofitable kind of castle–building: he would be a soldier like his father; he would leave Arnstead, to revisit it with a sword by his side, and a Sir before his name. Sir Hugh Sutherland would be somebody even in the eyes of the master of Arnstead. Yes, a six–foot fellow, though he may be sensible in the main, is not, therefore, free from small vanities, especially if he be in love. But how leave Euphra?

Again I outrun my story.

CHAPTER X. ITALIAN.

Per me si va nella città dolente.

DANTE

Through me thou goest into the city of grief.

Of necessity, with so many shafts opened into the mountain of knowledge, a far greater amount of time must be devoted by Harry and his tutor to the working of the mine, than they had given hitherto. This made a considerable alteration in the intercourse of the youth and the lady; for, although Euphra was often present during school–hours, it must be said for Hugh that, during those hours, he paid almost all his attention to Harry; so much of it, indeed, that perhaps there was not enough left to please the lady. But she did not say so. She sat beside them in silence, occupied with her work, and saving up her glances for use. Now and then she would read; taking an opportunity sometimes, but not often, when a fitting pause occurred, to ask him to explain some passage about which she was in doubt. It must be conceded that such passages were well chosen for the purpose; for she was too wise to do her own intellect discredit by feigning a difficulty where she saw none; intellect being the only gift in others for which she was conscious of any reverence.

By–and–by she began to discontinue these visits to the schoolroom. Perhaps she found them dull. Perhaps—but we shall see.

One morning, in the course of their study—Euphra not present—Hugh had occasion to go from his own room, where, for the most part, they carried on the severer portion of their labours, down to the library for a book, to enlighten them upon some point on which they were in doubt. As he was passing an open door, Euphra's voice called him. He entered, and found himself in her private sitting–room. He had not known before where it was.

"I beg your pardon, Mr. Sutherland, for calling you, but I am at this moment in a difficulty. I cannot manage this line in the Inferno. Do help me."

She moved the book towards him, as he now stood by her side, she remaining seated at her table. To his mortification, he was compelled to confess his utter ignorance of the language.

"Oh! I am disappointed," said Euphra.

"Not so much as I am," replied Hugh. "But could you spare me one or two of your Italian books?"

"With pleasure," she answered, rising and going to her bookshelves.

"I want only a grammar, a dictionary, and a New Testament."

"There they are," she said, taking them down one after the other, and bringing them to him. "I daresay you will soon get up with poor stupid me."

"I shall do my best to get within hearing of your voice, at least, in which Italian must be lovely."

No reply, but a sudden droop of the head.

"But," continued Hugh, "upon second thoughts, lest I should be compelled to remain dumb, or else annoy your delicate ear with discordant sounds, just give me one lesson in the pronunciation. Let me hear you read a little first."

"With all my heart."

Euphra began, and read delightfully; for she was an excellent Italian scholar. It was necessary that Hugh should look over the book. This was difficult while he remained standing, as she did not offer to lift it from the table. Gradually, therefore, and hardly knowing how, he settled into a chair by her side. Half–an–hour went by like a minute, as he listened to the silvery tones of her voice, breaking into a bell–like sound upon the double consonants of that sweet lady–tongue. Then it was his turn to read and be corrected, and read again and be again corrected. Another half–hour glided away, and yet another. But it must be confessed he made good use of the time—if only it had been his own to use; for at the end of it he could pronounce Italian very tolerably—well enough, at least, to keep him from fixing errors in his pronunciation, while studying the language alone. Suddenly he came to himself, and looked up as from a dream. Had she been bewitching him? He was in Euphra's room—alone with her. And the door was shut—how or when? And—he looked at his watch—poor little Harry had been waiting his return from the library, for the last hour and a half. He was conscience–stricken. He gathered up the books hastily, thanked Euphra in the same hurried manner, and left the room with considerable disquietude, closing the door very gently, almost guiltily, behind him.

I am afraid Euphra had been perfectly aware that he knew nothing about Italian. Did she see her own eyes shine in the mirror before her, as he closed the door? Was she in love with him, then?

When Hugh returned with the Italian books, instead of the encyclopædia he had gone to seek, he found Harry sitting where he had left him, with his arms and head on the table, fast asleep.

"Poor boy!" said Hugh to himself; but he could not help feeling glad he was asleep. He stole out of the room again, passed the fatal door with a longing pain, found the volume of his quest in the library, and, returning with it, sat down beside Harry. There he sat till he awoke.

When he did awake at last, it was almost time for luncheon. The shame–faced boy was exceedingly penitent for what was no fault, while Hugh could not relieve him by confessing his. He could only say:

"It was my fault, Harry dear. I stayed away too long. You were so nicely asleep, I would not wake you. You will not need a siesta, that is all."

He was ashamed of himself, as he uttered the false words to the true–hearted child. But this, alas! was not the end of it all.

Desirous of learning the language, but far more desirous of commending himself to Euphra, Hugh began in downright earnest. That very evening, he felt that he had a little hold of the language. Harry was left to his own resources. Nor was there any harm in this in itself: Hugh had a right to part of every day for his own uses. But then, he had been with Harry almost every evening, or a great part of it, and the boy missed him much; for he was not yet self–dependent. He would have gone to Euphrasia, but somehow she happened to be engaged that evening. So he took refuge in the library, where, in the desolation of his spirit, Polexander began, almost immediately, to exercise its old dreary fascination upon him. Although he had not opened the book since Hugh had requested him to put it away, yet he had not given up the intention of finishing it some day; and now he took it down, and opened it listlessly, with the intention of doing something towards the gradual redeeming of the pledge he had given to himself. But he found it more irksome than ever. Still he read on; till at length he could discover no meaning at all in the sentences. Then he began to doubt whether he had read the words. He fixed his attention by main force on every individual word; but even then he began to doubt whether he could say he had read the words, for he might have missed seeing some of the letters composing each word. He grew so nervous and miserable over it, almost counting every letter, that at last he burst into tears, and threw the book down.

His intellect, which in itself was excellent, was quite of the parasitic order, requiring to wind itself about a stronger intellect, to keep itself in the region of fresh air and possible growth. Left to itself, its weak stem could not raise it above the ground: it would grow and mass upon the earth, till it decayed and corrupted, for lack of room, light, and air. But, of course, there was no danger in the meantime. This was but the passing sadness of an occasional loneliness.

He crept to Hugh's room, and received an invitation to enter, in answer to his gentle knock; but Hugh was so absorbed in his new study, that he hardly took any notice of him, and Harry found it almost as dreary here as in the study. He would have gone out, but a drizzling rain was falling; and he shrank into himself at the thought of the Ghost's Walk. The dinner–bell was a welcome summons.

Hugh, inspirited by the reaction from close attention, by the presence of Euphra, and by the desire to make himself generally agreeable, which sprung from the consciousness of having done wrong, talked almost brilliantly, delighting Euphra, overcoming Harry with reverent astonishment, and even interesting slow Mr. Arnold. With the latter Hugh had been gradually becoming a favourite; partly because he had discovered in him what he considered high–minded sentiments; for, however stupid and conventional Mr. Arnold might be, he had a foundation of sterling worthiness of character. Euphra, instead of showing any jealousy of this growing friendliness, favoured it in every way in her power, and now and then alluded to it in her conversations with Hugh, as affording her great satisfaction.

David Elginbrod

"I am so glad he likes you!" she would say.

"Why should she be glad?" thought Hugh.

This gentle claim of a kind of property in him, added considerably to the strength of the attraction that drew him towards her, as towards the centre of his spiritual gravitation; if indeed that could be called spiritual which had so little of the element of moral or spiritual admiration, or even approval, mingled with it. He never felt that Euphra was good. He only felt that she drew him with a vague force of feminine sovereignty—a charm which he could no more resist or explain, than the iron could the attraction of the loadstone. Neither could he have said, had he really considered the matter, that she was beautiful—only that she often, very often, looked beautiful. I suspect if she had been rather ugly, it would have been all the same for Hugh.

He pursued his Italian studies with a singleness of aim and effort that carried him on rapidly. He asked no assistance from Euphra, and said nothing to her about his progress. But he was so absorbed in it, that it drew him still further from his pupil. Of course he went out with him, walking or riding every day that the weather would permit; and he had regular school hours with him within doors. But during the latter, while Harry was doing something on his slate, or writing, or learning some lesson (which kind of work happened oftener now than he could have approved of), he would take up his Italian; and, notwithstanding Harry's quiet hints that he had finished what had been set him, remain buried in it for a long time. When he woke at last to the necessity of taking some notice of the boy, he would only appoint him something else to occupy him again, so as to leave himself free to follow his new bent. Now and then he would become aware of his blameable neglect, and make a feeble struggle to rectify what seemed to be growing into a habit—and one of the worst for a tutor; but he gradually sank back into the mire, for mire it was, comforting himself with the resolution that as soon as he was able to read Italian without absolutely spelling his way, he would let Euphra see what progress he had made, and then return with renewed energy to Harry's education, keeping up his own new accomplishment by more moderate exercise therein. It must not be supposed, however, that a long course of time passed in this way. At the end of a fortnight, he thought he might venture to request Euphra to show him the passage which had perplexed her. This time he knew where she was—in her own room; for his mind had begun to haunt her whereabouts. He knocked at her door, heard the silvery, thrilling, happy sound, "Come in;" and entered trembling.

David Elginbrod

"Would you show me the passage in Dante that perplexed you the other day?"

Euphra looked a little surprised; but got the book and pointed it out at once.

Hugh glanced at it. His superior acquaintance with the general forms of language enabled him, after finding two words in Euphra's larger dictionary, to explain it, to her immediate satisfaction.

"You astonish me," said Euphra.

"Latin gives me an advantage, you see," said Hugh modestly.

"It seems to be very wonderful, nevertheless."

These were sweet sounds to Hugh's ear. He had gained his end. And she hers.

"Well," she said, "I have just come upon another passage that perplexes me not a little. Will you try your powers upon that for me?"

So saying, she proceeded to find it.

"It is school–time," said Hugh "I fear I must not wait now."

"Pooh! pooh! Don't make a pedagogue of yourself. You know you are here more as a guardian—big brother, you know—to the dear child. By the way, I am rather afraid you are working him a little more than his constitution will stand."

"Do you think so?" returned Hugh quite willing to be convinced. "I should be very sorry."

"This is the passage," said Euphra.

Hugh sat down once more at the table beside her. He found this morsel considerably tougher than the last. But at length he succeeded in pulling it to pieces and reconstructing it in a simpler form for the lady. She was full of thanks and admiration. Naturally enough, they went on to the next line, and the next stanza, and the next and the next; till—shall I be believed?—they had read a whole canto of the poem. Euphra knew more words by a

165

great many than Hugh; so that, what with her knowledge of the words, and his insight into the construction, they made rare progress.

"What a beautiful passage it is!" said Euphra.

"It is indeed," responded Hugh; "I never read anything more beautiful."

"I wonder if it would be possible to turn that into English. I should like to try."

"You mean verse, of course?"

"To be sure."

"Let us try, then. I will bring you mine when I have finished it. I fear it will take some time, though, to do it well. Shall it be in blank verse, or what?"

"Oh! don't you think we had better keep the Terza Rima of the original?"

"As you please. It will add much to the difficulty."

"Recreant knight! will you shrink from following where your lady leads?"

"Never! so help me, my good pen!" answered Hugh, and took his departure, with burning cheeks and a trembling at the heart. Alas! the morning was gone. Harry was not in his study: he sought and found him in the library, apparently buried in Polexander.

"I am so glad you are come," said Harry; "I am so tired."

"Why do you read that stupid book, then?"

"Oh! you know, I told you."

"Tut! tut! nonsense! Put it away," said Hugh, his dissatisfaction with himself making him cross with Harry, who felt, in consequence, ten times more desolate than before. He could not understand the change.

David Elginbrod

If it went ill before with the hours devoted to common labour, it went worse now. Hugh seized every gap of time, and widened its margins shamefully, in order to work at his translation. He found it very difficult to render the Italian in classical and poetic English. The three rhyming words, and the mode in which the stanzas are looped together, added greatly to the difficulty. Blank verse he would have found quite easy compared to this. But he would not blench. The thought of her praise, and of the yet better favour he might gain, spurred him on; and Harry was the sacrifice. But he would make it all up to him, when this was once over. Indeed, he would.

Thus he baked cakes of clay to choke the barking of Cerberian conscience. But it would growl notwithstanding.

The boy's spirit was sinking; but Hugh did not or would not see it. His step grew less elastic. He became more listless, more like his former self—sauntering about with his hands in his pockets. And Hugh, of course, found himself caring less about him; for the thought of him, rousing as it did the sense of his own neglect, had become troublesome. Sometimes he even passed poor Harry without speaking to him.

Gradually, however, he grew still further into the favour of Mr. Arnold, until he seemed to have even acquired some influence with him. Mr. Arnold would go out riding with them himself sometimes, and express great satisfaction, not only with the way Harry sat his pony, for which he accorded Hugh the credit due to him, but with the way in which Hugh managed his own horse as well. Mr. Arnold was a good horseman, and his praise was especially grateful to Hugh, because Euphra was always near, and always heard it. I fear, however, that his progress in the good graces of Mr. Arnold, was, in a considerable degree, the result of the greater anxiety to please, which sprung from the consciousness of not deserving approbation. Pleasing was an easy substitute for well-doing. Not acceptable to himself, he had the greater desire to be acceptable to others; and so reflect the side-beams of a false approbation on himself—who needed true light and would be ill-provided for with any substitute. For a man who is received as a millionaire can hardly help feeling like one at times, even if he knows he has overdrawn his banker's account. The necessity to Hugh's nature of feeling right, drove him to this false mode of producing the false impression. If one only wants to feel virtuous, there are several royal roads to that end. But, fortunately, the end itself would be unsatisfactory if gained; while not one of these roads does more than pretend to lead even to that land of delusion.

The reaction in Hugh's mind was sometimes torturing enough. But he had not strength to resist Euphra, and so reform.

Well or ill done, at length his translation was finished. So was Euphra's. They exchanged papers for a private reading first; and arranged to meet afterwards, in order to compare criticisms.

CHAPTER XI. THE FIRST MIDNIGHT.

```
    Well, if anything be damned,
It will be twelve o'clock at night; that twelve
Will never scape.

CYRIL TOURNEUR.—The Revenger's Tragedy.
```

Letters arrived at Arnstead generally while the family was seated at breakfast. One morning, the post—bag having been brought in, Mr. Arnold opened it himself, according to his unvarying custom; and found, amongst other letters, one in an old—fashioned female hand, which, after reading it, he passed to Euphra.

"You remember Mrs. Elton, Euphra?"

"Quite well, uncle—a dear old lady!"

But the expression which passed across her face, rather belied her words, and seemed to Hugh to mean: "I hope she is not going to bore us again."

She took care, however, to show no sign with regard to the contents of the letter; but, laying it beside her on the table, waited to hear her uncle's mind first.

"Poor, dear girl!" said he at last. "You must try to make her as comfortable as you can. There is consumption in the family, you see," he added, with a meditative sigh.

"Of course I will, uncle. Poor girl! I hope there is not much amiss though, after all."

But, as she spoke, an irrepressible flash of dislike, or displeasure of some sort, broke from her eyes, and vanished. No one but himself seemed to Hugh to have observed it; but he was learned in the lady's eyes, and their weather–signs. Mr. Arnold rose from the table and left the room, apparently to write an answer to the letter. As soon as he was gone, Euphra gave the letter to Hugh. He read as follows.—

"MY DEAR MR. ARNOLD,

"Will you extend the hospitality of your beautiful house to me and my young friend, who has the honour of being your relative, Lady Emily Lake? For some time her health has seemed to be failing, and she is ordered to spend the winter abroad, at Pau, or somewhere in the south of France. It is considered highly desirable that in the meantime she should have as much change as possible; and it occurred to me, remembering the charming month I passed at your seat, and recalling the fact that Lady Emily is cousin only once removed to your late most lovely wife, that there would be no impropriety in writing to ask you whether you could, without inconvenience, receive us as your guests for a short time. I say us; for the dear girl has taken such a fancy to unworthy old me, that she almost refuses to set out without me. Not to be cumbersome either to our friends or ourselves, we shall bring only our two maids, and a steady old man–servant, who has been in my family for many years.—I trust you will not hesitate to refuse my request, should I happen to have made it at an unsuitable season; assured, as you must be, that we cannot attribute the refusal to any lack of hospitality or friendliness on your part. At all events, I trust you will excuse what seems—now I have committed it to paper—a great liberty, I hope not presumption, on mine. I am, my dear Mr. Arnold,

"Yours most sincerely,

"HANNAH ELTON."

Hugh refolded the letter, and laid it down without remark. Harry had left the room.

"Isn't it a bore?" said Euphra.

Hugh answered only by a look. A pause followed.

"Who is Mrs. Elton?" he said at last.

"Oh, a good–hearted creature enough. Frightfully prosy."

"But that is a well–written letter?"

"Oh, yes. She is famed for her letter–writing; and, I believe, practises every morning on a slate. It is the only thing that redeems her from absolute stupidity."

Euphra, with her taper fore–finger, tapped the table–cloth impatiently, and shifted back in her chair, as if struggling with an inward annoyance.

"And what sort of person is Lady Emily?" asked Hugh.

"I have never seen her. Some blue–eyed milk–maid with a title, I suppose. And in a consumption, too! I presume the dear girl is as religious as the old one.—Good heavens! what shall we do?" she burst out at length; and, rising from her chair, she paced about the room hurriedly, but all the time with a gliding kind of footfall, that would have shaken none but the craziest floor.

"Dear Euphra!" Hugh ventured to say, "never mind. Let us try to make the best of it."

She stopped in her walk, turned towards him, smiled as if ashamed and delighted at the same moment, and slid out of the room. Had Euphra been the same all through, she could hardly have smiled so without being in love with Hugh.

That morning he sought her again in her room. They talked over their versions of Dante. Hugh's was certainly the best, for he was more practised in such things than Euphra. He showed her many faults, which she at once perceived to be faults, and so rose in his estimation. But at the same time there were individual lines and passages of hers, which he considered not merely better than the corresponding lines and passages, but better than any part of his version. This he was delighted to say; and she seemed as delighted that he should think so. A great part of the morning was spent thus.

"I cannot stay longer," said Hugh.

"Let us read for an hour, then, after we come up stairs to–night."

David Elginbrod

"With more pleasure than I dare to say."

"But you mean what you do say?"

"You can doubt it no more than myself."

Yet he did not like Euphra's making the proposal. No more did he like the flippant, almost cruel way in which she referred to Lady Emily's illness. But he put it down to annoyance and haste—got over it somehow—anyhow; and began to feel that if she were a devil he could not help loving her, and would not help it if he could. The hope of meeting her alone that night, gave him spirit and energy with Harry; and the poor boy was more cheery and active than he had been for some time. He thought his big brother was going to love him again as at the first. Hugh's treatment of his pupil might still have seemed kind from another, but Harry felt it a great change in him.

In the course of the day, Euphra took an opportunity of whispering to him:

"Not in my room—in the library." I presume she thought it would be more prudent, in the case of any interruption.

After dinner that evening, Hugh did not go to the drawingroom with Mr. Arnold, but out into the woods about the house. It was early in the twilight; for now the sun set late. The month was June; and the even a rich, dreamful, rosy even—the sleep of a gorgeous day. "It is like the soul of a gracious woman," thought Hugh, charmed into a lucid interval of passion by the loveliness of the nature around him. Strange to tell, at that moment, instead of the hushed gloom of the library, towards which he was hoping and leaning in his soul, there arose before him the bare, stern, leafless pine–wood—for who can call its foliage leaves?—with the chilly wind of a northern spring morning blowing through it with a wailing noise of waters; and beneath a weird fir–tree, lofty, gaunt, and huge, with bare goblin arms, contorted sweepily, in a strange mingling of the sublime and the grotesque—beneath this fir–tree, Margaret sitting on one of its twisted roots, the very image of peace, with a face that seemed stilled by the expected approach of a sacred and unknown gladness; a face that would blossom the more gloriously because its joy delayed its coming. And above it, the tree shone a "still," almost "awful red," in the level light of the morning.

David Elginbrod

The vision came and passed, for he did not invite its stay: it rebuked him to the deepest soul. He strayed in troubled pleasure, restless and dissatisfied. Woods of the richest growth were around him; heaps on heaps of leaves floating above him like clouds, a trackless wilderness of airy green, wherein one might wish to dwell for ever, looking down into the vaults and aisles of the long-ranging boles beneath. But no peace could rest on his face; only, at best, a false mask, put on to hide the trouble of the unresting heart. Had he been doing his duty to Harry, his love for Euphra, however unworthy she might be, would not have troubled him thus.

He came upon an avenue. At the further end the boughs of the old trees, bare of leaves beneath, met in a perfect pointed arch, across which were barred the lingering colours of the sunset, transforming the whole into a rich window full of stained glass and complex tracery, closing up a Gothic aisle in a temple of everlasting worship. A kind of holy calm fell upon him as he regarded the dim, dying colours; and the spirit of the night, a something that is neither silence nor sound, and yet is like both, sank into his soul, and made a moment of summer twilight there. He walked along the avenue for some distance; and then, leaving it, passed on through the woods.—Suddenly it flashed upon him that he had crossed the Ghost's Walk. A slight but cold shudder passed through the region of his heart. Then he laughed at himself, and, as it were in despite of his own tremor, turned, and crossed yet again the path of the ghost.

A spiritual epicure in his pleasures, he would not spoil the effect of the coming meeting, by seeing Euphra in the drawingroom first: he went to his own study, where he remained till the hour had nearly arrived. He tried to write some verses. But he found that, although the lovely form of its own Naiad lay on the brink of the Well of Song, its waters would not flow: during the sirocco of passion, its springs withdraw into the cool caves of the Life beneath. At length he rose, too much preoccupied to mind his want of success; and, going down the back stair, reached the library. There he seated himself, and tried to read by the light of his chamber-candle. But it was scarcely even an attempt, for every moment he was looking up to the door by which he expected her to enter.

Suddenly an increase of light warned him that she was in the room. How she had entered he could not tell. One hand carried her candle, the light of which fell on her pale face, with its halo of blackness—her hair, which looked like a well of darkness, that threatened to break from its bonds and overflood the room with a second night, dark enough to blot out that which was now looking in, treeful and deep, at the uncurtained windows. The other hand was busy trying to incarcerate a stray tress which had escaped from its net, and made her olive shoulders look white beside it.

"Let it alone," said Hugh, "let it be beautiful."

But she gently repelled the hand he raised to hers, and, though she was forced to put down her candle first, persisted in confining the refractory tress; then seated herself at the table, and taking from her pocket the manuscript which Hugh had been criticising in the morning, unfolded it, and showed him all the passages he had objected to, neatly corrected or altered. It was wonderfully done for the time she had had. He went over it all with her again, seated close to her, their faces almost meeting as they followed the lines. They had just finished it, and were about to commence reading from the original, when Hugh, who missed a sheet of Euphra's translation, stooped under the table to look for it. A few moments were spent in the search, before he discovered that Euphra's foot was upon it. He begged her to move a little, but received no reply either by word or act. Looking up in some alarm, he saw that she was either asleep or in a faint. By an impulse inexplicable to himself at the time, he went at once to the windows, and drew down the green blinds. When he turned towards her again, she was reviving or awaking, he could not tell which.

"How stupid of me to go to sleep!" she said. "Let us go on with our reading."

They had read for about half an hour, when three taps upon one of the windows, slight, but peculiar, and as if given with the point of a finger, suddenly startled them. Hugh turned at once towards the windows; but, of course, he could see nothing, having just lowered the blinds. He turned again towards Euphra. She had a strange wild look; her lips were slightly parted, and her nostrils wide; her face was rigid, and glimmering pale as death from the cloud of her black hair.

"What was it?" said Hugh, affected by her fear with the horror of the unknown. But she made no answer, and continued staring towards one of the windows. He rose and was about to advance to it, when she caught him by the hand with a grasp of which hers would have been incapable except under the influence of terror. At that moment a clock in the room began to strike. It was a slow clock, and went on deliberately, striking one...two...three...till it had struck twelve. Every stroke was a blow from the hammer of fear, and his heart was the bell. He could not breathe for dread so long as the awful clock was striking. When it had ended, they looked at each other again, and Hugh breathed once.

"Euphra!" he sighed.

But she made no answer; she turned her eyes again to one of the windows. They were both standing. He sought to draw her to him, but she yielded no more than a marble statue.

"I crossed the Ghost's Walk to–night," said he, in a hard whisper, scarcely knowing that he uttered it, till he heard his own words. They seemed to fall upon his ear as if spoken by some one outside the room. She looked at him once more, and kept looking with a fixed stare. Gradually her face became less rigid, and her eyes less wild. She could move at last.

"Come, come," she said, in a hurried whisper. "Let us go—no, no, not that way;"—as Hugh would have led her towards the private stair—"let us go the front way, by the oak staircase."

They went up together. When they reached the door of her room, she said, "Good night," without even looking at him, and passed in. Hugh went on, in a state of utter bewilderment, to his own apartment; shut the door and locked it—a thing he had never done before; lighted both the candles on his table; and then walked up and down the room, trying, like one aware that he is dreaming, to come to his real self.

"Pshaw!" he said at last. "It was only a little bird, or a large moth. How odd it is that darkness can make a fool of one! I am ashamed of myself. I wish I had gone out at the window, if only to show Euphra I was not afraid, though of course there was nothing to be seen."

As he said this in his mind,—he could not have spoken it aloud, for fear of hearing his own voice in the solitude,—he went to one of the windows of his sitting–room, which was nearly over the library, and looked into the wood.—Could it be?—Yes.—He did see something white, gliding through the wood, away in the direction of the Ghost's Walk. It vanished; and he saw it no more.

David Elginbrod

The morning was far advanced before he could go to bed. When the first light of the aurora broke the sky, he looked out again;—and the first glimmerings of the morning in the wood were more dreadful than the deepest darkness of the past night. Possessed by a new horror, he thought how awful it would be to see a belated ghost, hurrying away in helpless haste. The spectre would be yet more terrible in the grey light of the coming day, and the azure breezes of the morning, which to it would be like a new and more fearful death, than amidst its own homely sepulchral darkness; while the silence all around—silence in light—could befit only that dread season of loneliness when men are lost in sleep, and ghosts, if they walk at all, walk in dismay.

But at length fear yielded to sleep, though still he troubled her short reign.

When he awoke, he found it so late, that it was all he could do to get down in time for breakfast. But so anxious was he not to be later than usual, that he was in the room before Mr. Arnold made his appearance. Euphra, however, was there before him. She greeted him in the usual way, quite circumspectly. But she looked troubled. Her face was very pale, and her eyes were red, as if from sleeplessness or weeping. When her uncle entered, she addressed him with more gaiety than usual, and he did not perceive that anything was amiss with her. But the whole of that day she walked as in a reverie, avoiding Hugh two or three times that they chanced to meet without a third person in the neighbourhood. Once in the forenoon—when she was generally to be found in her room—he could not refrain from trying to see her. The change and the mystery were insupportable to him. But when he tapped at her door, no answer came; and he walked back to Harry, feeling, as if, by an unknown door in his own soul, he had been shut out of the half of his being. Or rather—a wall seemed to have been built right before his eyes, which still was there wherever he went.

As to the gliding phantom of the previous night, the day denied it all, telling him it was but the coinage of his own over-wrought brain, weakened by prolonged tension of the intellect, and excited by the presence of Euphra at an hour claimed by phantoms when not yielded to sleep. This was the easiest and most natural way of disposing of the difficulty. The cloud around Euphra hid the ghost in its skirts.

Although fear in some measure returned with the returning shadows, he yet resolved to try to get Euphra to meet him again in the library that night. But she never gave him a chance of even dropping a hint to that purpose. She had not gone out with them in the morning; and when he followed her into the drawing–room, she was already at the piano. He thought he might convey his wish without interrupting the music; but as often as he approached her, she broke, or rather glided, out into song, as if she had been singing in an undertone all the while. He could not help seeing she did not intend to let him speak to her. But, all the time, whatever she sang was something she knew he liked; and as often as she spoke to him in the hearing of her uncle or cousin, it was in a manner peculiarly graceful and simple.

He could not understand her; and was more bewitched, more fascinated than ever, by seeing her through the folds of the incomprehensible, in which element she had wrapped herself from his nearer vision. She had always seemed above him—now she seemed miles away as well; a region of Paradise, into which he was forbidden to enter. Everything about her, to her handkerchief and her gloves, was haunted by a vague mystery of worshipfulness, and drew him towards it with wonder and trembling. When they parted for the night, she shook hands with him with a cool frankness, that put him nearly beside himself with despair; and when he found himself in his own room, it was some time before he could collect his thoughts. Having succeeded, however, he resolved, in spite of growing fears, to go to the library, and see whether it were not possible she might be there. He took up a candle, and went down the back stair. But when he opened the library door, a gust of wind blew his candle out; all was darkness within; a sudden horror seized him; and, afraid of yielding to the inclination to bound up the stair, lest he should go wild with the terror of pursuit, he crept slowly back, feeling his way to his own room with a determined deliberateness.—Could the library window have been left open? Else whence the gust of wind?

Next day, and the next, and the next, he fared no better: her behaviour continued the same; and she allowed him no opportunity of requesting an explanation.

CHAPTER XII. A SUNDAY.

A man may be a heretic in the truth; and if he believe things only because his pastor says so, or the assembly so determines, without knowing other reason, though his belief be true, yet the very truth he holds becomes his heresy.—MILTON.—Areopagitica.

David Elginbrod

At length the expected visitors arrived. Hugh saw nothing of them till they assembled for dinner. Mrs. Elton was a benevolent old lady—not old enough to give in to being old—rather tall, and rather stout, in rich widow–costume, whose depth had been moderated by time. Her kindly grey eyes looked out from a calm face, which seemed to have taken comfort from loving everybody in a mild and moderate fashion. Lady Emily was a slender girl, rather shy, with fair hair, and a pale innocent face. She wore a violet dress, which put out her blue eyes. She showed to no advantage beside the suppressed glow of life which made Euphra look like a tropical twilight—I am aware there is no such thing, but if there were, it would be just like her.

Mrs. Elton seemed to have concentrated the motherhood of her nature, which was her most prominent characteristic, notwithstanding—or perhaps in virtue of—her childlessness, upon Lady Emily. To her Mrs. Elton was solicitously attentive; and she, on her part, received it all sweetly and gratefully, taking no umbrage at being treated as more of an invalid than she was.

Lady Emily ate nothing but chicken, and custard–pudding or rice, all the time she was at Arnstead.

The richer and more seasoned any dish, the more grateful it was to Euphra.

Mr. Arnold was a saddle–of–mutton man.

Hugh preferred roast–beef, but ate anything.

"What sort of a clergyman have you now, Mr. Arnold?" asked Mrs. Elton, at the dinner–table.

"Oh! a very respectable young gentleman, brother to Sir Richard, who has the gift, you know. A very moderate, excellent clergyman he makes, too!"

"All! but you know, Lady Emily and I"—here she looked at Lady Emily, who smiled and blushed faintly, "are very dependent on our Sundays, and"—

"We all go to church regularly, I assure you, Mrs. Elton; and of course my carriage shall be always at your disposal."

David Elginbrod

"I was in no doubt about either of those things, indeed, Mr. Arnold. But what sort of a preacher is he?"

"Ah, well! let me see.—What was the subject of his sermon last Sunday, Euphra, my dear?"

"The devil and all his angels," answered Euphra, with a wicked flash in her eyes.

"Yes, yes; so it was. Oh! I assure you, Mrs. Elton, he is quite a respectable preacher, as well as clergyman. He is an honour to the cloth."

Hugh could not help thinking that the tailor should have his due, and that Mr. Arnold gave it him.

"He is no Puseyite either," added Mr. Arnold, seeing but not understanding Mrs. Elton's baffled expression, "though he does preach once a month in his surplice."

"I am afraid you will not find him very original, though," said Hugh, wishing to help the old lady.

"Original!" interposed Mr. Arnold. "Really, I am bound to say I don't know how the remark applies. How is a man to be original on a subject that is all laid down in plain print—to use a vulgar expression—and has been commented upon for eighteen hundred years and more?"

"Very true, Mr. Arnold," responded Mrs. Elton. "We don't want originality, do we? It is only the gospel we want. Does he preach the gospel?"

"How can he preach anything else? His text is always out of some part of the Bible."

"I am glad to see you hold by the Inspiration of the Scriptures, Mr. Arnold," said Mrs. Elton, chaotically bewildered.

"Good heavens! Madam, what do you mean? Could you for a moment suppose me to be an atheist? Surely you have not become a student of German Neology?" And Mr. Arnold smiled a grim smile.

"Not I, indeed!" protested poor Mrs. Elton, moving uneasily in her seat;—"I quite agree with you, Mr. Arnold."

"Then you may take my word for it, that you will hear nothing but what is highly orthodox, and perfectly worthy of a gentleman and a clergyman, from the pulpit of Mr. Penfold. He dined with us only last week."

This last assertion was made in an injured tone, just sufficient to curl the tail of the sentence. After which, what was to be said?

Several vain attempts followed, before a new subject was started, sufficiently uninteresting to cause, neither from warmth nor stupidity, any danger of dissension, and quite worthy of being here omitted.

Dinner over, and the ceremony of tea—in Lady Emily's case, milk and water—having been observed, the visitors withdrew.

The next day was Sunday. Lady Emily came down stairs in black, which suited her better. She was a pretty, gentle creature, interesting from her illness, and good, because she knew no evil, except what she heard of from the pulpit. They walked to church, which was at no great distance, along a meadow–path paved with flags, some of them worn through by the heavy shoes of country generations. The church was one of those which are, in some measure, typical of the Church itself; for it was very old, and would have been very beautiful, had it not been all plastered over, and whitened to a smooth uniformity of ugliness—the attempt having been more successful in the case of the type. The open roof had had a French heaven added to it—I mean a ceiling; and the pillars, which, even if they were not carved—though it was impossible to come to a conclusion on that point—must yet have been worn into the beauty of age, had been filled up, and stained with yellow ochre. Even the remnants of stained glass in some of the windows, were half concealed by modern appliances for the partial exclusion of the light. The church had fared as Chaucer in the hands of Dryden. So had the truth, that flickered through the sermon, fared in the hands of the clergyman, or of the sermon–wright whose manuscript he had bought for eighteen pence—I am told that sermons are to be procured at that price—on his last visit to London. Having, although a Scotchman, had an episcopalian education, Hugh could not help rejoicing that not merely the Bible, but the Church–service as well, had been fixed beyond the reach of such degenerating influences

179

as those which had operated on the more material embodiments of religion; for otherwise such would certainly have been the first to operate, and would have found the greatest scope in any alteration. We may hope that nothing but a true growth in such religion as needs and seeks new expression for new depth and breadth of feeling, will ever be permitted to lay the hand of change upon it—a hand, otherwise, of desecration and ruin.

The sermon was chiefly occupied with proving that God is no respecter of persons; a mark of indubitable condescension in the clergyman, the rank in society which he could claim for himself duly considered. But, unfortunately, the church was so constructed, that its area contained three platforms of position, actually of differing level; the loftiest, in the chancel, on the right hand of the pulpit, occupied by the gentry; the middle, opposite the pulpit, occupied by the tulip–beds of their servants; and the third, on the left of the pulpit, occupied by the common parishioners. Unfortunately, too, by the perpetuation of some old custom, whose significance was not worn out, all on the left of the pulpit were expected, as often as they stood up to sing—which was three times—to turn their backs to the pulpit, and so face away from the chancel where the gentry stood. But there was not much inconsistency, after all; the sermon founding its argument chiefly on the antithetical facts, that death, lowering the rich to the level of the poor, was a dead leveller; and that, on the other hand, the life to come would raise the poor to the level of the rich. It was a pity that there was no phrase in the language to justify him in carrying out the antithesis, and so balancing his sentence like a rope–walker, by saying that life was a live leveller. The sermon ended with a solemn warning: "Those who neglect the gospel–scheme, and never think of death and judgment—be they rich or poor, be they wise or ignorant—whether they dwell in the palace or the hut—shall be damned. Glory be to the Father, and to the Son, and to the Holy Ghost,"

Lady Emily was forced to confess that she had not been much interested in the sermon. Mrs. Elton thought he spoke plainly, but there was not much of the gospel in it. Mr. Arnold opined that people should not go to church to hear sermons, but to make the responses; whoever read prayers, it made no difference, for the prayers were the Church's, not the parson's; and for the sermon, as long as it showed the uneducated how to be saved, and taught them to do their duty in the station of life to which God had called them, and so long as the parson preached neither Puseyism nor Radicalism—(he frowned solemnly and disgustedly as he repeated the word)—nor Radicalism, it was of comparatively little moment whether he was a man of intellect or not, for he could not go wrong.

Little was said in reply to this, except something not very audible or definite, by Mrs. Elton, about the necessity of faith. The conversation, which took place at luncheon, flagged, and the visitors withdrew to their respective rooms, to comfort themselves with their Daily Portions.

At dinner, Mr. Arnold, evidently believing he had made an impression by his harangue of the morning, resumed the subject. Hugh was a little surprised to find that he had, even of a negative sort, strong opinions on the subject of religion.

"What do you think, then, Mrs. Elton, my dear madam, that a clergyman ought to preach?"

"I think, Mr. Arnold, that he ought to preach salvation by faith in the merits of the Saviour."

"Oh! of course, of course. We shall not differ about that. Everybody believes that."

"I doubt it very much.—He ought, in order that men may believe, to explain the divine plan, by which the demands of divine justice are satisfied, and the punishment due to sin averted from the guilty, and laid upon the innocent; that, by bearing our sins, he might make atonement to the wrath of a justly offended God; and so—"

"Now, my dear madam, permit me to ask what right we, the subjects of a Supreme Authority, have to inquire into the reasons of his doings? It seems to me—I should be sorry to offend any one, but it seems to me quite as presumptuous as the present arrogance of the lower classes in interfering with government, and demanding a right to give their opinion, forsooth, as to the laws by which they shall be governed; as if they were capable of understanding the principles by which kings rule, and governors decree justice.—I believe I quote Scripture."

"Are we, then, to remain in utter ignorance of the divine character?"

"What business have we with the divine character? Or how could we understand it? It seems to me we have enough to do with our own. Do I inquire into the character of my sovereign? All we have to do is, to listen to what we are told by those who are educated for such studies, whom the Church approves, and who are appointed to take care of the

181

souls committed to their charge; to teach them to respect their superiors, and to lead honest, hard—working lives."

Much more of the same sort flowed from the oracular lips of Mr. Arnold. When he ceased, he found that the conversation had ceased also. As soon as the ladies withdrew, he said, without looking at Hugh, as he filled his glass:

"Mr. Sutherland, I hate cant."

And so he canted against it.

But the next day, and during the whole week, he seemed to lay himself out to make amends for the sharpness of his remarks on the Sunday. He was afraid he had made his guests uncomfortable, and so sinned against his own character as a host. Everything that he could devise, was brought to bear for their entertainment; daily rides in the open carriage, in which he always accompanied them, to show his estate, and the improvements he was making upon it; visits sometimes to the more deserving, as he called them, of the poor upon his property—the more deserving being the most submissive and obedient to the wishes of their lord; inspections of the schools, in all of which matters he took a stupid, benevolent interest. For if people would be content to occupy the corner in which he chose to place them, he would throw them morsel after morsel, as long as ever they chose to pick it up. But woe to them if they left this corner a single pace!

Euphra made one of the party always; and it was dreary indeed for Hugh to be left in the desolate house without her, though but for a few hours. And when she was at home, she never yet permitted him to speak to her alone.

There might have been some hope for Harry in Hugh's separation from Euphra; but the result was, that, although he spent school—hours more regularly with him, Hugh was yet more dull, and uninterested in the work, than he had been before. Instead of caring that his pupil should understand this or that particular, he would be speculating on Euphra's behaviour, trying to account for this or that individual look or tone, or seeking, perhaps, a special symbolic meaning in some general remark that she had happened to let fall. Meanwhile, poor Harry would be stupifying himself with work which he could not understand for lack of some explanation or other that ought to have been given him weeks ago. Still, however, he clung to Hugh with a far–off, worshipping love, never suspecting that he could be to blame, but thinking at one time that he must be ill, at another that he himself was really too stupid, and that his big brother could not help getting tired of him. When Hugh would be wandering about the place, seeking to catch a glimpse of the skirt of Euphra's dress, as she went about with her guests, or devising how he could procure an interview with her alone, Harry would be following him at a distance, like a little terrier that had lost its master, and did not know whether this man would be friendly or not; never spying on his actions, but merely longing to be near him—for had not Hugh set him going in the way of life, even if he had now left him to walk in it alone? If Hugh could have once seen into that warm, true, pining little heart, he would not have neglected it as he did. He had no eyes, however, but for Euphra.

Still, it may be that even now Harry was able to gather, though with tears, some advantage from Hugh's neglect. He used to wander about alone; and it may be that the hints which his tutor had already given him, enabled him now to find for himself the interest belonging to many objects never before remarked. Perhaps even now he began to take a few steps alone; the waking independence of which was of more value for the future growth of his nature, than a thousand miles accomplished by the aid of the strong arm of his tutor. One certain advantage was, that the constitutional trouble of the boy's nature had now assumed a definite form, by gathering around a definite object, and blending its own shadowy being with the sorrow he experienced from the loss of his tutor's sympathy. Should that sorrow ever be cleared away, much besides might be cleared away along with it.

Meantime, nature found some channels, worn by his grief, through which her comforts, that, like waters, press on all sides, and enter at every cranny and fissure in the house of life, might gently flow into him with their sympathetic soothing. Often he would creep away to the nest which Hugh had built and then forsaken; and seated there in the solitude of the wide–bourgeoned oak, he would sometimes feel for a moment as if lifted up above the world and its sorrows, to be visited by an all–healing wind from God, that came to him, through the wilderness of leaves around him——gently, like all powerful things.

But I am putting the boy's feelings into forms and words for him. He had none of either for them.

CHAPTER XIII. A STORM.

```
    When the mind's free,
The body's delicate: the tempest in my mind
Doth from my senses take all feeling else
Save what beats there.

King Lear.
```

While Harry took to wandering abroad in the afternoon sun, Hugh, on the contrary, found the bright weather so distasteful to him, that he generally trifled away his afternoons with some old romance in the dark library, or lay on the couch in his study, listless and suffering. He could neither read nor write. What he felt he must do he did; but nothing more.

One day, about noon, the weather began to change. In the afternoon it grew dark; and Hugh, going to the window, perceived with delight—the first he had experienced for many days—that a great thunder–storm was at hand. Harry was rather frightened; but under his fear, there evidently lay a deep delight. The storm came nearer and nearer; till at length a vivid flash broke from the mass of darkness over the woods, lasted for one brilliant moment, and vanished. The thunder followed, like a pursuing wild beast, close on the traces of the vanishing light; as if the darkness were hunting the light from the earth, and bellowing with rage that it could not overtake and annihilate it. Without the usual prelude of a few great drops, the rain poured at once, in continuous streams, from the dense canopy overhead; and in a few moments there were six inches of water all round the house, which the force of the falling streams made to foam, and fume, and flash like a seething torrent. Harry had crept close to Hugh, who stood looking out of the window; and as if the convulsion of the elements had begun to clear the spiritual and moral, as well as the physical atmosphere, Hugh looked down on the boy kindly, and put his arm round his shoulders. Harry nestled closer, and wished it would thunder for ever. But longing to hear his tutor's voice, he ventured to speak, looking up to his face:

"Euphra says it is only electricity, Mr. Sutherland. What is that?"

A common tutor would have seized the opportunity of explaining what he knew of the laws and operations of electricity. But Hugh had been long enough a pupil of David to feel that to talk at such a time of anything in nature but God, would be to do the boy a serious wrong. One capable of so doing would, in the presence of the Saviour himself, speculate on the nature of his own faith; or upon the death of his child, seize the opportunity of lecturing on anatomy. But before Hugh could make any reply, a flash, almost invisible from excess of light, was accompanied rather than followed by a roar that made the house shake; and in a moment more the room was filled with the terrified household, which, by an unreasoning impulse, rushed to the neighbourhood of him who was considered the strongest.—Mr. Arnold was not at home.

"Come from the window instantly, Mr. Sutherland. How can you be so imprudent!" cried Mrs. Elton, her usually calm voice elevated in command, but tremulous with fear.

"Why, Mrs. Elton," answered Hugh on whose temper, as well as conduct, recent events had had their operation, "do you think the devil makes the thunder?"

Lady Emily gave a faint shriek, whether out of reverence for the devil, or fear of God, I hesitate to decide; and flitting out of the room, dived into her bed, and drew the clothes over her head—at least so she was found at a later period of the day. Euphra walked up to the window beside Hugh, as if to show her approval of his rudeness; and stood looking out with eyes that filled their own night with home–born flashes, though her lip was pale, and quivered a little. Mrs. Elton, confounded at Hugh's reply, and perhaps fearing the house might in consequence share the fate of Sodom, notwithstanding the presence of a goodly proportion of the righteous, fled, accompanied by the housekeeper, to the wine–cellar. The rest of the household crept into corners, except the coachman, who, retaining his composure, in virtue of a greater degree of insensibility from his nearer approximation to the inanimate creation, emptied the jug of ale intended for the dinner of the company, and went out to look after his horses.

But there was one in the house who, left alone, threw the window wide open; and, with gently clasped hands and calm countenance, looked up into the heavens; and the clearness of whose eye seemed the prophetic symbol of the clearness that rose all untroubled above the turmoil of the earthly storm. Truly God was in the storm; but there was more of God in the clear heaven beyond; and yet more of Him in the eye that regarded the whole with a still joy, in which was mingled no dismay.

Euphra, Hugh, and Harry were left together, looking out upon the storm. Hugh could not speak in Harry's presence. At length the boy sat down in a dark corner on the floor, concealed from the others by a window—curtain. Hugh thought he had left the room.

"Euphra," he began.

Euphra looked round for Harry, and not seeing him, thought likewise that he had left the room: she glided away without making any answer to Hugh's invocation.

He stood for a few moments in motionless despair; then glancing round the room, and taking in all its desertedness, caught up his hat, and rushed out into the storm. It was the best relief his feelings could have had; for the sullen gloom, alternated with bursts of flame, invasions of horrid uproar, and long wailing blasts of tyrannous wind, gave him his own mood to walk in; met his spirit with its own element; widened, as it were, his microcosm to the expanse of the macrocosm around him. All the walls of separation were thrown down, and he lived, not in his own frame, but in the universal frame of nature. The world was for the time, to the reality of his feeling, what Schleiermacher, in his Monologen, describes it as being to man, an extension of the body in which he dwells. His spirit flashed in the lightning, raved in the thunder, moaned in the wind, and wept in the rain.

But this could not last long, either without or within him.

He came to himself in the woods. How far he had wandered, or whereabout he was, he did not know. The storm had died away, and all that remained was the wind and the rain. The tree—tops swayed wildly in the irregular blasts, and shook new, fitful, distracted, and momentary showers upon him. It was evening, but what hour of the evening he could not tell. He was wet to the skin; but that to a young Scotchman is a matter of little moment.

Although he had no intention of returning home for some time, and meant especially to avoid the dinner—table—for, in the mood he was in, it seemed more than he could endure—he yet felt the weakness to which we are subject as embodied beings, in a common enough form; that, namely, of the necessity of knowing the precise portion of space which at the moment we fill; a conviction of our identity not being sufficient to make us comfortable, without a knowledge of our locality. So, looking all about him, and finding where the wood seemed thinnest, he went in that direction; and soon, by forcing his way through obstacles of all salvage kinds, found himself in the high road, within a quarter of a mile of the country town next to Arnstead, removed from it about three miles.

186

This little town he knew pretty well; and, beginning to feel exhausted, resolved to go to an inn there, dry his clothes, and then walk back in the moonlight; for he felt sure the storm would be quite over in an hour or so. The fatigue he now felt was proof enough in itself, that the inward storm had, for the time, raved itself off; and now—must it be confessed?—he wished very much for something to eat and drink.

He was soon seated by a blazing fire, with a chop and a jug of ale before him.

CHAPTER XIV. AN EVENING LECTURE.

```
    The Nightmare
Shall call thee when it walks.

MIDDLETON.—The Witch.
```

The inn to which Hugh had betaken himself, though not the first in the town, was yet what is called a respectable house, and was possessed of a room of considerable size, in which the farmers of the neighbourhood were accustomed to hold their gatherings. While eating his dinner, Hugh learned from the conversation around him—for he sat in the kitchen for the sake of the fire—that this room was being got ready for a lecture on Bilology, as the landlady called it. Bills in red and blue had been posted all over the town; and before he had finished his dinner, the audience had begun to arrive. Partly from curiosity about a subject of which he knew nothing, and partly because it still rained, and, having got nearly dry, he did not care about a second wetting if he could help it, Hugh resolved to make one of them. So he stood by the fire till he was informed that the lecturer had made his appearance, when he went up-stairs, paid his shilling, and was admitted to one of the front seats. The room was tolerably lighted with gas; and a platform had been constructed for the lecturer and his subjects. When the place was about half-filled, he came from another room alone—a little, thick-set, bull-necked man, with vulgar face and rusty black clothes; and, mounting the platform, commenced his lecture; if lecture it could be called, in which there seemed to be no order, and scarcely any sequence. No attempt even at a theory, showed itself in the mass of what he called facts and scientific truths; and he perpeturated the most awful blunders in his English. It will not be desired that I should give any further account of such a lecture. The lecturer himself seemed to depend chiefly for his success, upon the manifestations of his art which he proceeded to bring forward. He called his familiar by the name of Willi–am,

187

and a stunted, pale–faced, dull–looking youth started up from somewhere, and scrambled upon the platform beside his master. Upon this tutored slave a number of experiments was performed. He was first cast into whatever abnormal condition is necessary for the operations of biology, and then compelled to make a fool of himself by exhibiting actions the most inconsistent with his real circumstances and necessities. But, aware that all this was open to the most palpable objection of collusion, the operator next invited any of the company that pleased, to submit themselves to his influences. After a pause of a few moments, a stout country fellow, florid and healthy, got up and slouched to the platform. Certainly, whatever might be the nature of the influence that was brought to bear, its operative power could not, with the least probability, be attributed to an over–activity of imagination in either of the subjects submitted to its exercise. In the latter, as well as in the former case, the operator was eminently successful; and the clown returned to his seat, looking remarkably foolish and conscious of disgrace—a sufficient voucher to most present, that in this case at least there had been no collusion. Several others volunteered their negative services; but with no one of them did he succeed so well; and in one case the failure was evident. The lecturer pretended to account for this, in making some confused and unintelligible remarks about the state of the weather, the thunder–storm, electricity, of which things he evidently did not understand the best known laws.

"The blundering idiot!" growled, close to Hugh's ear, a voice with a foreign accent.

He looked round sharply.

A tall, powerful, eminently handsome man, with a face as foreign as his tone and accent, sat beside him.

"I beg your pardon," he said to Hugh; "I thought aloud."

"I should like to know, if you wouldn't mind telling me, what you detect of the blunderer in him. I am quite ignorant of these matters."

"I have had many opportunities of observing them; and I see at once that this man, though he has the natural power, is excessively ignorant of the whole subject."

This was all the answer he vouchsafed to Hugh's modest inquiry. Hugh had not yet learned that one will always fare better by concealing than by acknowledging ignorance.

David Elginbrod

The man, whatever his capacity, who honestly confesses even a partial ignorance, will instantly be treated as more or less incapable, by the ordinary man who has already gained a partial knowledge, or is capable of assuming a knowledge which he does not possess. But, for God's sake! let the honest and modest man stick to his honesty and modesty, cost what they may.

Hugh was silent, and fixed his attention once more on what was going on. But presently he became aware that the foreigner was scrutinizing him with the closest attention. He knew this, somehow, without having looked round; and the knowledge was accompanied with a feeling of discomfort that caused him to make a restless movement on his seat. Presently he felt that the annoyance had ceased; but not many minutes had passed, before it again commenced. In order to relieve himself from a feeling which he could only compare to that which might be produced by the presence of the dead, he turned towards his neighbour so suddenly, that it seemed for a moment to embarrass him, his eyes being caught in the very act of devouring the stolen indulgence. But the stranger recovered himself instantly with the question:

"Will you permit me to ask of what country you are?"

Hugh thought he made the request only for the sake of covering his rudeness; and so merely answered:

"Why, an Englishman, of course."

"Ah! yes; it is not necessary to be told that. But it seems to me, from your accent, that you are a Scotchman."

"So I am."

"A Highlander?"

"I was born in the Highlands. But if you are very anxious to know my pedigree, I have no reason for concealing the fact that I am, by birth, half a Scotchman and half a Welchman."

189

David Elginbrod

The foreigner riveted his gaze, though but for the briefest moment sufficient to justify its being called a gaze, once more upon Hugh; and then, with a slight bow, as of acquiescence, turned towards the lecturer.

When the lecture was over, and Hugh was walking away in the midst of the withdrawing audience, the stranger touched him on the shoulder.

"You said that you would like to know more of this science: will you come to my lodging?" said he.

"With pleasure," Hugh answered; though the look with which he accompanied the words, must have been one rather of surprise.

"You are astonished that a stranger should invite you so. Ah! you English always demand an introduction. There is mine."

He handed Hugh a card: Herr von Funkelstein. Hugh happened to be provided with one in exchange.

The two walked out of the inn, along the old High Street, full of gables and all the delightful irregularities of an old country–town, till they came to a court, down which Herr von Funkelstein led the way.

He let himself in with a pass–key at a low door, and then conducted Hugh, by a stair whose narrowness was equalled by its steepness, to a room, which, though not many yards above the level of the court, was yet next to the roof of the low house. Hugh could see nothing till his conductor lighted a candle. Then he found himself in a rather large room with a shaky floor and a low roof. A chintz–curtained bed in one corner had the skin of a tiger thrown over it; and a table in another had a pair of foils lying upon it. The German—for such he seemed to Hugh—offered him a chair in the politest manner; and Hugh sat down.

"I am only in lodgings here," said the host; "so you will forgive the poverty of my establishment."

"There is no occasion for forgiveness, I assure you," answered Hugh.

David Elginbrod

"You wished to know something of the subject with which that lecturer was befooling himself and the audience at the same time."

"I shall be grateful for any enlightenment."

"Ah! it is a subject for the study of a benevolent scholar, not for such a clown as that. He jumps at no conclusions; yet he shares the fate of one who does: he flounders in the mire between. No man will make anything of it who has not the benefit of the human race at heart. Humanity is the only safe guide in matters such as these. This is a dangerous study indeed in unskilful hands."

Here a frightful caterwauling interrupted Herr von Funkelstein. The room had a storm-window, of which the lattice stood open. In front of it, on the roof, seen against a white house opposite, stood a demon of a cat, arched to half its length, with a tail expanded to double its natural thickness. Its antagonist was invisible from where Hugh sat. Von Funkelstein started up without making the slightest noise, trod as softly as a cat to the table, took up one of the foils, removed the button, and, creeping close to the window, made one rapid pass at the enemy, which vanished with a shriek of hatred and fear. He then, replacing the button, laid the foil down, and resumed his seat and his discourse. This, after dealing with generalities and commonplaces for some time, gave no sign of coming either to an end or to the point. All the time he was watching Hugh—at least so Hugh thought—as if speculating on him in general. Then appearing to have come to some conclusion, he gave his mind more to his talk, and encouraged Hugh to speak as well. The conversation lasted for nearly half an hour. At its close, Hugh felt that the stranger had touched upon a variety of interesting subjects, as one possessed of a minute knowledge of them. But he did not feel that he had gained any insight from his conversation. It seemed rather as if he had been giving him a number of psychological, social, literary, and scientific receipts. During the course of the talk, his eye had appeared to rest on Hugh by a kind of compulsion; as if by its own will it would have retired from the scrutiny, but the will of its owner was too strong for it. In seemed, in relation to him, to be only a kind of tool, which he used for a particular purpose.

At length Funkelstein rose, and, marching across the room to a cupboard, brought out a bottle and glasses, saying, in the most by-the-bye way, as he went:

"Have you the second-sight, Mr. Sutherland?"

David Elginbrod

"Certainly not, as far as I am aware."

"Ah! the Welch do have it, do they not?"

"Oh! yes, of course," answered Hugh laughing. "I should like to know, though," he added, "whether they inherit the gift as Celts or as mountaineers."

"Will you take a glass of—?"

"Of nothing, thank you," answered and interrupted Hugh. "It is time for me to be going. Indeed, I fear I have stayed too long already. Good night, Herr von Funkelstein."

"You will allow me the honour of returning your visit?"

Hugh felt he could do no less, although he had not the smallest desire to keep up the acquaintance. He wrote Arnstead on his card.

As he left the house, he stumbled over something in the court. Looking down, he saw it was a cat, apparently dead.

"Can it be the cat Herr Funkelstein made the pass at?" thought he. But presently he forgot all about it, in the visions of Euphra which filled his mind during his moonlight walk home. It just occurred to him, however, before those visions had blotted everything else from his view, that he had learned simply nothing whatever about biology from his late host.

When he reached home, he was admitted by the butler, and retired to bed at once, where he slept soundly, for the first time for many nights.

But, as he drew near his own room, he might have seen, though he saw not, a little white figure gliding away in the far distance of the long passage. It was only Harry, who could not lie still in his bed, till he knew that his big brother was safe at home.

CHAPTER XV. ANOTHER EVENING LECTURE.

```
This Eneas is come to Paradise
Out of the swolows of Hell.
```

CHAUCER.—Legend of Dido.

The next day, Hugh was determined to find or make an opportunity of speaking to Euphra; and fortune seemed to favour him.—Or was it Euphra herself, in one or other of her inexplicable moods? At all events, she had that morning allowed the ladies and her uncle to go without her; and Hugh met her as he went to his study.

"May I speak to you for one moment?" said he, hurriedly, and with trembling lips.

Yes, certainly," she replied with a smile, and a glance in his face as of wonder as to what could trouble him so much. Then turning, and leading the way, she said:

"Come into my room."

He followed her. She turned and shut the door, which he had left open behind him. He almost knelt to her; but something held him back from that.

"Euphra," he said, "what have I done to offend you?"

"Offend me! Nothing."—This was uttered in a perfect tone of surprise.

"How is it that you avoid me as you do, and will not allow me one moment's speech with you? You are driving me to distraction."

"Why, you foolish man!" she answered, half playfully, pressing the palms of her little hands together, and looking up in his face, "how can I? Don't you see how those two dear old ladies swallow me up in their faddles? Oh, dear? Oh, dear! I wish they would go. Then it would be all right again—wouldn't it?"

But Hugh was not to be so easily satisfied.

David Elginbrod

"Before they came, ever since that night—"

"Hush—sh!" she interrupted, putting her finger on his lips, and looking hurriedly round her with an air of fright, of which he could hardly judge whether it was real or assumed—"hush!"

Comforted wondrously by the hushing finger, Hugh would yet understand more.

"I am no baby, dear Euphra," he said, taking hold of the hand to which the finger belonged, and laying it on his mouth; "do not make one of me. There is some mystery in all this—at least something I do not understand."

"I will tell you all about it one day. But, seriously, you must be careful how you behave to me; for if my uncle should, but for one moment, entertain a suspicion—good–bye to you—perhaps good–bye to Arnstead. All my influence with him comes from his thinking that I like him better than anybody else. So you must not make the poor old man jealous. By the bye," she went on—rapidly, as if she would turn the current of the conversation aside—"what a favourite you have grown with him! You should have heard him talk of you to the old ladies. I might well be jealous of you. There never was a tutor like his."

Hugh's heart smote him that the praise of even this common man, proud of his own vanity, should be undeserved by him. He was troubled, too, at the flippancy with which Euphra spoke; yet not the less did he feel that he loved her passionately.

"I daresay," he replied, "he praised me as he would anything else that happened to be his. Isn't that old bay horse of his the best hack in the county?"

"You naughty man! Are you going to be satirical?"

"You claim that as your privilege, do you?"

"Worse and worse! I will not talk to you. But, seriously, for I must go—bring your Italian to—to—" She hesitated.

"To the library—why not?" suggested Hugh.

"No—o," she answered, shaking her head, and looking quite solemn.

"Well, will you come to my study? Will that please you better?"

"Yes, I will," she answered, with a definitive tone. "Good—bye, now."

She opened the door, and having looked out to see that no one was passing, told him to go. As he went, he felt as if the oaken floor were elastic beneath his tread.

It was sometime after the household had retired, however, before Euphra made her appearance at the door of his study. She seemed rather shy of entering, and hesitated, as if she felt she was doing something she ought not to do. But as soon as she had entered, and the door was shut, she appeared to recover herself quite; and they sat down at the table with their books. They could not get on very well with their reading, however. Hugh often forgot what he was about, in looking at her; and she seemed nowise inclined to avert his gazes, or check the growth of his admiration.

Rather abruptly, but apparently starting from some suggestion in the book, she said to him:

"By the bye, has Mr. Arnold ever said anything to you about the family jewels?"

"No," said Hugh. "Are there many?"

"Yes, a great many. Mr. Arnold is very proud of them, as well as of the portraits; so he treats them in the same way—keeps them locked up. Indeed he seldom allows them to see daylight, except it be as a mark of especial favour to some one."

"I should like much to see them. I have always been curious about stones. They are wonderful, mysterious things to me."

Euphra gave him a very peculiar, searching glance, as he spoke.

"Shall I," he continued, "give him a hint that I should like to see them?"

David Elginbrod

"By no means," answered Euphra, emphatically, "except he should refer to them himself. He is very jealous of his possessions—his family possessions, I mean. Poor old man! he has not much else to plume himself upon; has he?"

"He is kind to you, Euphra."

She looked at him as if she did not understand him.

"Yes. What then?"

"You ought not to be unkind to him."

"You odd creature! I am not unkind to him. I like him. But we are not getting on with our reading. What could have led me to talk about family–jewels? Oh! I see. What a strange thing the association of ideas is! There is not a very obvious connexion here; is there?"

"No. One cannot account for such things. The links in the chain of ideas are sometimes slender enough. Yet the slenderest is sufficient to enable the electric flash of thought to pass along the line."

She seemed pondering for a moment.

"That strikes me as a fine simile," she said. "You ought to be a poet yourself."

Hugh made no reply.

"I daresay you have hundreds of poems in that old desk, now?"

"I think they might be counted by tens."

"Do let me see them."

"You would not care for them."

"Wouldn't I, Hugh?"

David Elginbrod

"I will, on one condition—two conditions, I mean."

"What are they?"

"One is, that you show me yours."

"Mine?"

"Yes."

"Who told you I wrote verses? That silly boy?"

"No—I saw your verses before I saw you. You remember?"

"It was very dishonourable in you to read them."

"I only saw they were verses. I did not read a word."

"I forgive you, then. You must show me yours first, till I see whether I could venture to let you see mine. If yours were very bad indeed, then I might risk showing mine."

And much more of this sort, with which I will not weary my readers. It ended in Hugh's taking from the old escritoire a bundle of papers, and handing them to Euphra. But the reader need not fear that I am going to print any of these verses. I have more respect for my honest prose page than to break it up so. Indeed, the whole of this interview might have been omitted, but for two circumstances. One of them was, that in getting these papers, Hugh had to open a concealed portion of the escritoire, which his mathematical knowledge had enabled him to discover. It had evidently not been opened for many years before he found it. He had made use of it to hold the only treasures he had—poor enough treasures, certainly! Not a loving note, not a lock of hair even had he—nothing but the few cobwebs spun from his own brain. It is true, we are rich or poor according to what we are, not what we have. But what a man has produced, is not what he is. He may even impoverish his true self by production.

When Euphra saw him open this place, she uttered a suppressed cry of astonishment.

David Elginbrod

"Ah!" said Hugh, "you did not know of this hidie–hole, did you?"

"Indeed, I did not. I had used the desk myself, for this was a favourite room of mine before you came, but I never found that. Dear me! Let me look."

She put her hand on his shoulder and leaned over him, as he pointed out the way of opening it.

"Did you find nothing in it?" she said, with a slight tremour in her voice.

"Nothing whatever."

"There may be more places."

"No. I have accounted for the whole bulk, I believe."

"How strange!"

"But now you must give me my guerdon," said Hugh timidly.

The fact was, the poor youth had bargained, in a playful manner, and yet with an earnest, covetous heart, for one, the first kiss, in return for the poems she begged to see.

She turned her face towards him.

The second circumstance which makes the interview worth recording is, that, at this moment, three distinct knocks were heard on the window. They sprang asunder, and saw each other's face pale as death. In Euphra's, the expression of fright was mingled with one of annoyance. Hugh, though his heart trembled like a bird, leaped to the window. Nothing was to be seen but the trees that "stretched their dark arms" within a few feet of the oriel. Turning again towards Euphra, he found, to his mortification, that she had vanished—and had left the packet of poems behind her.

He replaced them in their old quarters in the escritoire; and his vague dismay at the unaccountable noises, was drowned in the bitter waters of miserable humiliation. He slept at last, from the exhaustion of disappointment.

David Elginbrod

When he awoke, however, he tried to persuade himself that he had made far too much of the trifling circumstance of her leaving the verses behind. For was she not terrified?—Why, then, did she leave him and go alone to her own room?—She must have felt that she ought not to be in his, at that hour, and therefore dared not stay.—Why dared not? Did she think the house was haunted by a ghost of propriety? What rational theory could he invent to account for the strange and repeated sounds?—He puzzled himself over it to the verge of absolute intellectual prostration.

He was generally the first in the breakfast-room; that is, after Euphra, who was always the first. She went up to him as he entered, and said, almost in a whisper:

"Have you got the poems for me? Quick!"

Hugh hesitated. She looked at him.

"No," he said at last.—"You never wanted them."

"That is very unkind; when you know I was frightened out of my wits. Do give me them."

"They are not worth giving you. Besides, I have not got them. I don't carry them in my pocket. They are in the escritoire. I couldn't leave them lying about. Never mind them."

"I have a right to them," she said, looking up at him slyly and shyly.

"Well, I gave you them, and you did not think them worth keeping. I kept my part of the bargain."

She looked annoyed.

"Never mind, dear Euphra; you shall have them, or anything else I have;—the brain that made them, if you like."

"Was it only the brain that had to do with the making of them?"

"Perhaps the heart too; but you have that already."

David Elginbrod

Her face flushed like a damask rose.

At that moment Mrs. Elton entered, and looked a little surprised. Euphra instantly said:

"I think it is rather too bad of you, Mr. Sutherland, to keep the poor boy so hard to his work, when you know he is not strong. Mrs. Elton, I have been begging a holiday for poor Harry, to let him go with us to Wotton House; but he has such a hard task–master! He will not hear of it."

The flush, which she could not get rid of all at once, was thus made to do duty as one of displeasure. Mrs. Elton was thoroughly deceived, and united her entreaties to those of Miss Cameron. Hugh was compelled to join in the deception, and pretend to yield a slow consent. Thus a holiday was extemporised for Harry, subject to the approbation of his father. This was readily granted; and Mr. Arnold, turning to Hugh, said:

"You will have nothing to do, Mr. Sutherland: had you not better join us?"

"With pleasure," replied he; "but the carriage will be full."

"You can take your horse."

"Thank you very much. I will."

The day was delightful; one of those grey summer–days, that are far better for an excursion than bright ones. In the best of spirits, mounted on a good horse, riding alongside of the carriage in which was the lady who was all womankind to him, and who, without taking much notice of him, yet contrived to throw him a glance now and then, Hugh would have been overflowingly happy, but for an unquiet, distressed feeling, which all the time made him aware of the presence of a sick conscience somewhere within. Mr. Arnold was exceedingly pleasant, for he was much taken with the sweetness and modesty of Lady Emily, who, having no strong opinions upon anything, received those of Mr. Arnold with attentive submission. He saw, or fancied he saw in her, a great resemblance to his deceased wife, to whom he had been as sincerely attached as his nature would allow. In fact, Lady Emily advanced so rapidly in his good graces, that either Euphra was, or thought fit to appear, rather jealous of her. She paid her every attention, however, and seemed to gratify Mr. Arnold by her care of the invalid. She even joined in the entreaties which, on their way home, he made with evident earnestness, for an extension of their visit to a month. Lady Emily was already so much better for the change, that Mrs. Elton made no objection to the proposal. Euphra gave Hugh one look of misery, and, turning again, insisted with increased warmth on their immediate consent. It was gained without much difficulty before they reached home.

Harry, too, was captivated by the gentle kindness of Lady Emily, and hardly took his eyes off her all the way; while, on the other hand, his delicate little attentions had already gained the heart of good Mrs. Elton, who from the first had remarked and pitied the sad looks of the boy.

CHAPTER XVI. A NEW VISITOR AND AN OLD ACQUAINTANCE.

```
     He's enough
To bring a woman to confusion,
More than a wiser man, or a far greater.

MIDDLETON.—The Witch.
```

When they reached the lodge, Lady Emily expressed a wish to walk up the avenue to the house. To this Mr. Arnold gladly consented. The carriage was sent round the back way; and Hugh, dismounting, gave his horse to the footman in attendance. As they drew near the house, the rest of the party having stopped to look at an old tree which was a favourite with its owner, Hugh and Harry were some yards in advance; when the former spied, approaching them from the house, the distinguished figure of Herr von Funkelstein. Saluting as they met, the visitor informed Hugh that he had just been leaving his card for him, and would call some other morning soon; for, as he was rusticating, he had little to occupy him. Hugh turned with him towards the rest of the party, who were now close at hand; when Funkelstein exclaimed, in a tone of surprise,

"What! Miss Cameron here!" and advanced with a profound obeisance, holding his hat in his hand.

Hugh thought he saw her look annoyed; but she held out her hand to him, and, in a voice indicating—still as it appeared to Hugh—some reluctance, introduced him to her uncle, with the words:

"We met at Sir Edward Laston's, when I was visiting Mrs. Elkingham, two years ago, uncle."

Mr. Arnold lifted his hat and bowed politely to the stranger. Had Euphra informed him that, although a person of considerable influence in Sir Edward's household, Herr von Funkelstein had his standing there only as Sir Edward's private secretary, Mr. Arnold's aversion to foreigners generally would not have been so scrupulously banished into the background of his behaviour. Ordinary civilities passed between them, marked by an air of flattering deference on Funkelstein's part, which might have been disagreeable to a man less uninterruptedly conscious of his own importance than Mr. Arnold; and the new visitor turned once more, as if forgetful of his previous direction, and accompanied them towards the house. Before they reached it he had, even in that short space, ingratiated himself so far with Mr. Arnold, that he asked him to stay and dine with them—an invitation which was accepted with manifest pleasure.

"Mr. Sutherland," said Mr. Arnold, "will you show your friend anything worth note about the place? He has kindly consented to dine with us; and in the meantime I have some letters to write."

"With pleasure," answered Hugh.

But all this time he had been inwardly commenting on the appearance of his friend, as Mr. Arnold called him, with the jealousy of a youth in love; for was not Funkelstein an old acquaintance of Miss Cameron? What might not have passed between them in that old hidden time?—for love is jealous of the past as well as of the future. Love, as well as metaphysics, has a lasting quarrel with time and space: the lower love fears them, while the higher defies them.—And he could not help seeing that Funkelstein was one to win favour in ladies' eyes. Very regular features and a dark complexion were lighted up by eyes as black as Euphra's, and capable of a wonderful play of light; while his form was remarkable for strength and symmetry. Hugh felt that in any company he would attract immediate attention. His long dark beard, of which just the centre was removed to expose a finely-turned chin, blew over each shoulder as often as they met the wind in going round the house. From what I have heard of him from other deponents besides Hugh, I should judge that he did well to conceal the lines of his mouth in a long moustache,

202

which flowed into his bifurcated beard. He had just enough of the foreign in his dress to add to the appearance of fashion which it bore.

As they walked, Hugh could not help observing an odd peculiarity in the carriage of his companion. It was, that, every few steps, he gave a backward and downward glance to the right, with a sweeping bend of his body, as if he were trying to get a view of the calf of his leg, or as if he fancied he felt something trailing at his foot. So probable, from his motion, did the latter supposition seem, that Hugh changed sides to satisfy himself whether or not there was some dragging briar or straw annoying him; but no follower was to be discovered.

"You are a happy man, Mr. Sutherland," said the guest, "to live under the same roof with that beautiful Miss Cameron."

"Am I?" thought Hugh; but he only said, affecting some surprise:

"Do you think her so beautiful?"

Funkelstein's eyes were fixed upon him, as if to see the effect of his remark. Hugh felt them, and could not conform his face to the indifference of his words. But his companion only answered indifferently:

"Well, I should say so; but beauty is not, that is not beauty for us."

Whether or not there was poison in the fork of this remark, Hugh could only conjecture. He made no reply.

As they walked about the precincts of the house, Funkelstein asked many questions of Hugh, which his entire ignorance of domestic architecture made it impossible for him to answer. This seemed only to excite the questioner's desire for information to a higher pitch; and as if the very stones could reply to his demands, he examined the whole range of the various buildings constituting the house of Arnstead "as he would draw it."

"Certainly," said he, "there is at least variety enough in the style of this mass of material. There is enough for one pyramid."

203

David Elginbrod

"That would be rather at the expense of the variety, would it not?" said Hugh, in spiteful response to the inconsequence of the second member of Funkelstein's remark. But the latter was apparently too much absorbed in his continued inspection of the house, from every attainable point of near view, to heed the comment.

"This they call the Ghost's Walk," said Hugh.

"Ah! about these old houses there are always such tales."

"What sort of tales do you mean?"

"I mean of particular spots and their ghosts. You must have heard many such?"

"No, not I."

"I think Germany is more prolific of such stories. I could tell you plenty."

"But you don't mean you believe such things?"

"To me it is equal. I look at them entirely as objects of art."

"That is a new view of a ghost to me. An object of art? I should have thought them considerably more suitable objects previous to their disembodiment."

"Ah! you do not understand. You call art painting, don't you—or sculpture at most? I give up sculpture certainly—and painting too. But don't you think a ghost a very effective object in literature now? Confess: do you not like a ghost–story very much?"

"Yes, if it is a very good one."

"Hamlet now?"

"Ah! we don't speak of Shakspere's plays as stories. His characters are so real to us, that, in thinking of their development, we go back even to their fathers and mothers—and sometimes even speculate about their future."

David Elginbrod

"You islanders are always in earliest somehow. So are we Germans. We are all one."

"I hope you can be in earnest about dinner, then, for I hear the bell."

"We must render ourselves in the drawing–room, then? Yes."

When they entered the drawing–room, they found Miss Cameron alone. Funkelstein advanced, and addressed a few words to her in German, which Hugh's limited acquaintance with the language prevented him from catching. At the same moment, Mr. Arnold entered, and Funkelstein, turning to him immediately, proceeded, as if by way of apology for speaking in an unknown tongue, to interpret for Mr. Arnold's benefit:

"I have just been telling Miss Cameron in the language of my country, how much better she looks than when I saw her at Sir Edward Lastons."

"I know I was quite a scare–crow then," said Euphra, attempting to laugh.

"And now you are quite a decoy–duck, eh, Euphra?" said Mr. Arnold, laughing in reality at his own joke, which put him in great good–humour for the whole time of dinner and dessert.

"Thank you, uncle," said Euphra, with a prettily pretended affectation of humility. Then she added gaily:

"When did you rise on our Sussex horizon, Herr von Funkelstein?"

"Oh! I have been in the neighbourhood for a few days; but I owe my meeting with you to one of those coincidences which, were they not so pleasant—to me in this case, at least—one would think could only result from the blundering of old Dame Nature over her knitting. If I had not had the good fortune to meet Mr. Sutherland the other evening, I should have remained in utter ignorance of your neighbourhood and my own felicity, Miss Cameron. Indeed, I called now to see him, not you."

Hugh saw Mr. Arnold looking rather doubtful of the foreigner's fine speeches.

Dinner was announced. Funkelstein took Miss Cameron, Hugh Mrs. Elton, and Mr. Arnold followed with Lady Emily, who would never precede her older friend. Hugh tried to talk to Mrs. Elton, but with meagre success. He was suddenly a nobody, and felt more than he had felt for a long time what, in his present deteriorated moral state, he considered the degradation of his position. A gulf seemed to have suddenly yawned between himself and Euphra, and the loudest voice of his despairing agony could not reach across that gulf. An awful conviction awoke within him, that the woman he worshipped would scarcely receive his worship at the worth of incense now; and yet in spirit he fell down grovelling before his idol. The words "euphrasy and rue" kept ringing in his brain, coming over and over with an awful mingling of chime and toll. When he thought about it afterwards, he seemed to have been a year in crossing the hall with Mrs. Elton on his arm. But as if divining his thoughts—just as they passed through the dining-room door, Euphra looked round at him, almost over Funkelstein's shoulder, and, without putting into her face the least expression discernible by either of the others following, contrived to banish for the time all Hugh's despair, and to convince him that he had nothing to fear from Funkelstein. How it was done Hugh himself could not tell. He could not even recall the look. He only knew that he had been as miserable as one waking in his coffin, and that now he was out in the sunny air.

During dinner, Funkelstein paid no very particular attention to Euphrasia, but was remarkably polite to Lady Emily. She seemed hardly to know how to receive his attentions, but to regard him as a strange animal, which she did not know how to treat, and of which she was a little afraid. Mrs. Elton, on the contrary, appeared to be delighted with his behaviour and conversation; for, without showing the least originality, he yet had seen so much, and knew so well how to bring out what he had seen, that he was a most interesting companion. Hugh took little share in the conversation beyond listening as well as he could, to prevent himself from gazing too much at Euphra.

"Had Mr. Sutherland and you been old acquaintances then, Herr von Funkelstein?" asked Mr. Arnold, reverting to the conversation which had been interrupted by the announcement of dinner.

"Not at all. We met quite accidentally, and introduced ourselves. I believe a thunderstorm and a lecture on biology were the mediating parties between us. Was it not so, Mr. Sutherland?"

David Elginbrod

"I beg your pardon," stammered Hugh. But Mr. Arnold interposed:

"A lecture on what, did you say?"

"On biology."

Mr. Arnold looked posed. He did not like to say he did not know what the word meant; for, like many more ignorant men, he thought such a confession humiliating. Von Funkelstein hastened to his relief.

"It would be rather surprising if you were acquainted with the subject, Mr. Arnold. I fear to explain it to you, lest both Mr. Sutherland and myself should sink irrecoverably in your estimation. But young men want to know all that is going on."

Herr Funkelstein was not exactly what one would call a young man; but, as he chose to do so himself, there was no one to dispute the classification.

"Oh! of course," replied Mr. Arnold; "quite right. What, then, pray, is biology?"

"A science, falsely so called," said Hugh, who, waking up a little, wanted to join in the conversation.

"What does the word mean?" said Mr. Arnold.

Von Funkelstein answered at once:

"The science of life. But I must say, the name, as now applied, is no indication of the thing signified."

"How, then, is a gentleman to know what it is?" said Mr. Arnold, half pettishly, and forgetting that his knowledge had not extended even to the interpretation of the name.

"It is one of the sciences, true or false, connected with animal magnetism."

"Bah!" exclaimed Mr. Arnold, rather rudely.

David Elginbrod

"You would have said so, if you had heard the lecture," said Funkelstein.

The conversation had not taken this turn till quite late in the dining ceremony. Euphra rose to go; and Hugh remarked that her face was dreadfully pale. But she walked steadily out of the room.

This interrupted the course of the talk, and the subject was not resumed. Immediately after tea, which was served very soon, Funkelstein took his leave of the ladies.

"We shall be glad to see you often while in this neighbourhood," said Mr. Arnold, as he bade him good night.

"I shall, without fail, do myself the honour of calling again soon," replied he, and bowed himself out.

Lady Emily, evidently relieved by his departure, rose, and, approaching Euphra, said, in a sweet coaxing tone, which even she could hardly have resisted:

"Dear Miss Cameron, you promised to sing, for me in particular, some evening. May I claim the fulfilment of your promise?"

Euphra had recovered her complexion, and she too seemed to Hugh to be relieved by the departure of Funkelstein.

"Certainly," she answered, rising at once. "What shall I sing?"

Hugh was all ear now.

"Something sacred, if you please."

Euphra hesitated, but not long.

"Shall I sing Mozart's Agnus Dei, then?"

Lady Emily hesitated in her turn.

David Elginbrod

"I should prefer something else. I don't approve of singing popish music, however beautiful it may be."

"Well, what shall it be?"

"Something of Handel or Mendelssohn, please. Do you sing, 'I know that my Redeemer liveth?'"

"I daresay I can sing it," replied Euphra, with some petulance; and went to the piano.

This was a favourite air with Hugh; and he placed himself so as to see the singer without being seen himself, and to lose no slightest modulation of her voice. But what was his disappointment to find that oratorio—music was just what Euphra was incapable of! No doubt she sang it quite correctly; but there was no religion in it. Not a single tone worshipped or rejoiced. The quality of sound necessary to express the feeling and thought of the composer was lacking: the palace of sound was all right constructed, but of wrong material. Euphra, however, was quite unconscious of failure. She did not care for the music; but she attributed her lack of interest in it to the music itself, never dreaming that, in fact, she had never really heard it, having no inner ear for its deeper harmonies. As soon as she had finished, Lady Emily thanked her, but did not praise her more than by saying:

"I wish I had a voice like yours, Miss Cameron."

"I daresay you have a better of your own," said Euphra, falsely.

Lady Emily laughed.

"It is the poorest little voice you ever heard; yet I confess I am glad, for my own sake, that I have even that. What should I do if I never heard Handel!"

Every simple mind has a little well of beauty somewhere in its precincts, which flows and warbles, even when the owner is unheedful. The religion of Lady Emily had led her into a region far beyond the reach of her intellect, in which there sprang a constant fountain of sacred song. To it she owed her highest moods.

David Elginbrod

"Then Handel is your musician?" said Euphra. "You should not have put me to such a test. It was very unfair of you, Lady Emily."

Lady Emily laughed, as if quite amused at the idea of having done Euphra any wrong. Euphra added:

"You must sing now, Lady Emily. You cannot refuse, after the admission you have just made."

"I confess it is only fair; but I warn you to expect nothing."

She took her place at the piano, and sang—He shall feed his flock. Her health had improved so much during her sojourn at Arnstead, that, when she began to sing, the quantity of her voice surprised herself; but after all, it was a poor voice; and the execution, if clear of any great faults, made no other pretence to merit. Yet she effected the end of the music, the very result which every musician would most desire, wherein Euphra had failed utterly. This was worthy of note, and Hugh was not even yet too blind to perceive it. Lady Emily, with very ordinary intellect, and paltry religious opinions, yet because she was good herself, and religious—could, in the reproduction of the highest kind of music, greatly surpass the spirited, intellectual musician, whose voice was as superior to hers as a nightingale's to a sparrow's, and whose knowledge of music and musical power generally, surpassed hers beyond all comparison.

It must be allowed for Euphra, that she seemed to have gained some perception of the fact. Perhaps she had seen signs of emotion in Hugh's face, which he had shaded with his hand as Lady Emily sang; or perhaps the singing produced in her a feeling which she had not had when singing herself. All I know is, that the same night—while Hugh was walking up and down his room, meditating on this defect of Euphra's, and yet feeling that if she could sing only devil's music, he must love her—a tap came to the door which made him start with the suggestion of the former mysterious noises of a similar kind; that he sprang to the door; and that, instead of looking out on a vacant corridor, as he all but anticipated, he saw Euphra standing there in the dark—who said in a whisper:

"Ah! you do not love me any longer, because Lady Emily can sing psalms better than I can!"

David Elginbrod

There was both pathos and spite in the speech.

"Come in, Euphra."

"No. I am afraid I have been very naughty in coming here at all."

"Do come in. I want you to tell me something about Funkelstein."

"What do you want to know about him? I suppose you are jealous of him. Ah! you men can both be jealous and make jealous at the same moment." A little broken sigh followed. Hugh answered:

"I only want to know what he is."

"Oh! some twentieth cousin of mine."

"Mr. Arnold does not know that?"

"Oh dear! no. It is so far off I can't count it, In fact I doubt it altogether. It must date centuries back."

"His intimacy, then, is not to be accounted for by his relationship?"

"Ah! ah! I thought so. Jealous of the poor count!"

"Count?"

"Oh dear! what does it matter? He doesn't like to be called Count, because all foreigners are counts or barons, or something equally distinguished. I oughtn't to have let it out."

"Never mind. Tell me something about him."

"He is a Bohemian. I met him first, some years ago, on the continent."

"Then that was not your first meeting—at Sir Edward Laston's?"

"No."

"How candid she is!" thought Hugh.

"He calls me his cousin; but if he be mine, he is yet more Mr. Arnold's. But he does not want it mentioned yet. I am sure I don't know why."

"Is he in love with you?"

"How can I tell?" she answered archly. "By his being very jealous? Is that the way to know whether a man is in love with one? But if he is in love with me, it does not follow that I am in love with him—does it? Confess. Am I not very good to answer all your impertinent downright questions? They are as point blank as the church–catechism;—mind, I don't say as rude.—How can I be in love with two at—a—?"

She seemed to cheek herself. But Hugh had heard enough—as she had intended he should. She turned instantly, and sped—surrounded by the "low melodious thunder" of her silken garments—to her own door, where she vanished noiselessly.

"What care I for oratorios?" said Hugh to himself, as he put the light out, towards morning.

Where was all this to end? What goal had Hugh set himself? Could he not go away, and achieve renown in one of many ways, and return fit, in the eyes of the world, to claim the hand of Miss Cameron? But would he marry her if he could? He would not answer the question. He closed the ears of his heart to it, and tried to go to sleep. He slept, and dreamed of Margaret in the storm.

A few days passed without anything occurring sufficiently marked for relation. Euphra and he seemed satisfied without meeting in private. Perhaps both were afraid of carrying it too far; at least, too far to keep clear of the risk of discovery, seeing that danger was at present greater than usual. Mr. Arnold continued to be thoroughly attentive to his guests, and became more and more devoted to Lady Emily. There was no saying where it might end; for he was not an old man yet, and Lady Emily appeared to have no special admirers. Arnstead was such an abode, and surrounded with such an estate, as few even of the nobility could call their own. And a reminiscence of his first wife seemed to haunt all Mr. Arnold's contemplations of Lady Emily, and all his attentions to her. These were delicate in the extreme, evidently bringing out the best life that yet remained in a heart that was almost a fossil. Hugh made some fresh efforts to do his duty by Harry, and so far succeeded, that at least the boy made some progress—evident enough to the moderate expectations of his father. But what helped Harry as much as anything, was the motherly kindness, even tenderness, of good Mrs. Elton, who often had him to sit with her in her own room. To her he generally fled for refuge, when he felt deserted and lonely.

CHAPTER XVII. MATERIALISM alias GHOST–HUNTING.

Wie der Mond sich leuchtend dränget
Durch den dunkeln Wolkenflor,
Also taucht aus dunkeln Zeiten
Mir ein lichtes Bild hervor.

HEINRICH HEINE

As the moon her face advances Through the darkened cloudy veil; So, from darkened times arising, Dawns on me a vision pale.

In consequence of what Euphra had caused him to believe without saying it, Hugh felt more friendly towards his new acquaintance; and happening—on his side at least it did happen—to meet him a few days after, walking in the neighbourhood, he joined him in a stroll. Mr. Arnold met them on horseback, and invited Von Funkelstein to dine with them that evening, to which he willingly consented. It was noticeable that no sooner was the count within the doors of Arnstead House, than he behaved with cordiality to every one of the company except Hugh. With him he made no approach to familiarity of any kind, treating him, on the contrary, with studious politeness.

In the course of the dinner, Mr. Arnold said:

"It is curious, Herr von Funkelstein, how often, if you meet with something new to you, you fall in with it again almost immediately. I found an article on Biology in the newspaper, the very day after our conversation on the subject. But absurd as the whole thing is, it is quite surpassed by a letter in to–day's Times about spirit–rapping and mediums, and what not!"

This observation of the host at once opened the whole question of those physico—psychological phenomena to which the name of spiritualism has been so absurdly applied. Mr. Arnold was profound in his contempt of the whole system, if not very profound in his arguments against it. Every one had something to remark in opposition to the notions which were so rapidly gaining ground in the country, except Funkelstein, who maintained a rigid silence.

This silence could not continue long without attracting the attention of the rest of the party; upon which Mr. Arnold said:

"You have not given us your opinion on the subject, Herr von Funkelstein."

"I have not, Mr. Arnold;—I should not like to encounter the opposition of so many fair adversaries, as well as of my host."

"We are in England, sir; and every man is at liberty to say what he thinks. For my part, I think it all absurd, if not improper."

"I would not willingly differ from you, Mr. Arnold. And I confess that a great deal that finds its way into the public prints, does seem very ridiculous indeed; but I am bound, for truth's sake, to say, that I have seen more than I can account for, in that kind of thing. There are strange stories connected with my own family, which, perhaps, incline me to believe in the supernatural; and, indeed, without making the smallest pretence to the dignity of what they call a medium, I have myself had some curious experiences. I fear I have some natural proclivity towards what you despise. But I beg that my statement of my own feelings on the subject, may not interfere in the least with the prosecution of the present conversation; for I am quite capable of drawing pleasure from listening to what I am unable to agree with."

"But let us hear your arguments, strengthened by your facts, in opposition to ours; for it will be impossible to talk with a silent judge amongst us," Hugh ventured to say.

"I set up for no judge, Mr. Sutherland, I assure you; and perhaps I shall do my opinions more justice by remaining silent, seeing I am conscious of utter inability to answer the a priori arguments which you in particular have brought against them. All I would venture to say is, that an a priori argument may owe its force to a mistaken hypothesis with regard to the matter in question; and that the true Baconian method, which is the glory of your English philosophy, would be to inquire first what the thing is, by recording observations and experiments made in its supposed direction."

"At least Herr von Funkelstein has the best of the argument now, I am compelled to confess," said Hugh.

Funkelstein bowed stiffly, and was silent.

"You rouse our curiosity," said Mr. Arnold; "but I fear, after the free utterance which we have already given to our own judgments, in ignorance, of course, of your greater experience, you will not be inclined to make us wiser by communicating any of the said experience, however much we may desire to hear it."

Had he been speaking to one of less evident social standing than Funkelstein, Mr. Arnold, if dying with curiosity, would not have expressed the least wish to be made acquainted with his experiences. He would have sat in apparent indifference, but in real anxiety that some one else would draw him out, and thus gratify his curiosity without endangering his dignity.

"I do not think," replied Funkelstein, "that it is of any use to bring testimony to bear on such a matter. I have seen—to use the words of some one else, I forget whom, on a similar subject—I have seen with my own eyes what I certainly should never have believed on the testimony of another. Consequently, I have no right to expect that my testimony should be received. Besides, I do not wish it to be received, although I confess I shrink from presenting it with a certainty of its being rejected. I have no wish to make converts to my opinions."

"Really, Herr von Funkelstein, at the risk of your considering me importunate, I would beg—"

"Excuse me, Mr. Arnold. The recital of some of the matters to which you refer, would not only be painful to myself, but would be agitating to the ladies present."

"In that case, I have only to beg your pardon for pressing the matter—I hope no further than to the verge of incivility."

David Elginbrod

"In no degree approaching it, I assure you, Mr. Arnold. In proof that I do not think so, I am ready, if you wish it—although I rather dread the possible effects on the nerves of the ladies, especially as this is an old house—to repeat, with the aid of those present, certain experiments which I have sometimes found perhaps only too successful."

"Oh! I don't," said Euphra, faintly.

An expression of the opposite desire followed, however, from the other ladies. Their curiosity seemed to strive with their fears, and to overcome them.

"I hope we shall have nothing to do with it in any other way than merely as spectators?" said Mrs. Elton.

"Nothing more than you please. It is doubtful if you can even be spectators. That remains to be seen."

"Good gracious!" exclaimed Mrs. Elton.

Lady Emily looked at her with surprise—almost reproof.

"I beg your pardon, my dear; but it sounds so dreadful. What can it be?"

"Let me entreat you, ladies, not to imagine that I am urging you to anything," said Funkelstein.

"Not in the least," replied Mrs. Elton. "I was very foolish." And the old lady looked ashamed, and was silent.

"Then if you will allow me, I will make one small preparation. Have you a tool–chest anywhere, Mr. Arnold?"

"There must be tools enough about the place, I know. I will ring for Atkins."

"I know where the tool chest is," said Hugh; "and, if you will allow me a suggestion, would it not be better the servants should know nothing about this? There are some foolish stories afloat amongst them already."

"A very proper suggestion, Mr. Sutherland," said Mr. Arnold, graciously. "Will you find all that is wanted, then?"

"What tools do you want?" asked Hugh.

"Only a small drill. Could you get me an earthenware plate—not china—too?"

"I will manage that," said Euphra.

Hugh soon returned with the drill, and Euphra with the plate. The Bohemian, with some difficulty, and the remark that the English ware was very hard, drilled a small hole in the rim of the plate—a dinner-plate; then begging an H B drawing-pencil from Miss Cameron, cut off a small piece, and fitted it into the hole, making it just long enough to touch the table with its point when the plate lay in its ordinary position.

"Now I am ready," said he. "But," he added, raising his head, and looking all round the room, as if a sudden thought had struck him—"I do not think this room will be quite satisfactory."

They were now in the drawing-room.

"Choose the room in the house that will suit you," said Mr. Arnold. "The dining-room?"

"Certainly not," answered Funkelstein, as he took from his watch-chain a small compass and laid it on the table. "Not the dining-room, nor the breakfast-room—I think. Let me see—how is it situated?" He went to the hall, as if to refresh his memory, and then looked again at the compass. "No, not the breakfast-room."

Hugh could not help thinking there was more or less of the charlatan about the man.

"The library?" suggested Lady Emily.

They adjourned to the library to see. The library would do. After some further difficulty, they succeeded in procuring a large sheet of paper and fastening it down to the table by drawing-pins. Only two candles were in the great room, and it was scarcely lighted at all by them; yet Funkelstein requested that one of these should be extinguished, and the other removed to a table near the door. He then said, solemnly:

"Let me request silence, absolute silence, and quiescence of thought even."

After stillness had settled down with outspread wings of intensity, he resumed:

"Will any one, or, better, two of you, touch the plate as lightly as possible with your fingers?"

All hung back for a moment. Then Mr. Arnold came forward.

"I will," said he, and laid his fingers on the plate.

"As lightly as possible, if you please. If the plate moves, follow it with your fingers, but be sure not to push it in any direction."

"I understand," said Mr. Arnold; and silence fell again.

The Bohemian, after a pause, spoke once more, but in a foreign tongue. The words sounded first like entreaty, then like command, and at last, almost like imprecation. The ladies shuddered.

"Any movement of the vehicle?" said he to Mr. Arnold.

If by the vehicle you mean the plate, certainly not," said Mr. Arnold solemnly. But the ladies were very glad of the pretext for attempting a laugh, in order to get rid of the oppression which they had felt for some time.

"Hush!" said Funkelstein, solemnly.—"Will no one else touch the plate, as well? It will seldom move with one. It does with me. But I fear I might be suspected of treachery, if I offered to join Mr. Arnold."

"Do not hint at such a thing. You are beyond suspicion."

What ground Mr. Arnold had for making such an assertion, was no better known to himself than to any one else present. Von Funkelstein, without another word, put the fingers of one hand lightly on the plate beside Mr. Arnold's. The plate instantly began to move upon the paper. The motion was a succession of small jerks at first; but soon it tilted up a little, and moved upon a changing point of support. Now it careered rapidly in wavy lines, sweeping back towards the other side, as often as it approached the extremity of the sheet, the men keeping their fingers in contact with it, but not appearing to influence its motion. Gradually the motion ceased. Von Funkelstein withdrew his hand, and requested that the other candle should be lighted. The paper was taken up and examined. Nothing could be discovered upon it, but a labyrinth of wavy and sweepy lines. Funkelstein pored over it for some minutes, and then confessed his inability to make a single letter out of it, still less words and sentences, as he had expected.

"But," said he, "we are at least so far successful: it moves. Let us try again. Who will try next?"

"I will," said Hugh, who had refrained at first, partly from dislike to the whole affair, partly because he shrank from putting himself forward.

A new sheet of paper was fixed. The candle was extinguished. Hugh put his fingers on the plate. In a second or two, it began to move.

"A medium!" murmured Funkelstein. He then spoke aloud some words unintelligible to the rest.

Whether from the peculiarity of his position and the consequent excitement of his imagination, or from some other cause, Hugh grew quite cold, and began to tremble. The plate, which had been careering violently for a few moments, now went more slowly, making regular short motions and returns, at right angles to its chief direction, as if letters were being formed by the pencil. Hugh shuddered, thinking he recognised the letters as they grew. The writing ceased. The candles were brought. Yes; there it was!—not plain, but easily decipherable—David Elginbrod. Hugh felt sick.

Euphra, looking on beside him, whispered:

"What an odd name! Who can it mean?"

He made no reply

Neither of the other ladies saw it; for Mrs. Elton had discovered, the moment the second candle was lighted, that Lady Emily was either asleep or in a faint. She was soon all but satisfied that she was asleep.

Hugh's opinion, gathered from what followed, was, that the Bohemian had not been so intent on the operations with the plate, as he had appeared to be; and that he had been employing part of his energy in mesmerising Lady Emily. Mrs. Elton, remembering that she had had quite a long walk that morning, was not much alarmed. Unwilling to make a disturbance, she rang the bell very quietly, and, going to the door, asked the servant who answered it, to send her maid with some eau–de–cologne. Meantime, the gentlemen had been too much absorbed to take any notice of her proceedings, and, after removing the one and extinguishing the other candle, had reverted to the plate.—Hugh was still the operator.

Von Funkelstein spoke again in an unknown tongue. The plate began to move as before. After only a second or two of preparatory gyration, Hugh felt that it was writing Turriepuffit, and shook from head to foot.

Suddenly, in the middle of the word, the plate ceased its motion, and lay perfectly still. Hugh felt a kind of surprise come upon him, as if he waked from an unpleasant dream, and saw the sun shining. The morbid excitement of his nervous system had suddenly ceased, and a healthful sense of strength and every–day life took its place.

Simultaneously with the stopping of the plate, and this new feeling which I have tried to describe, Hugh involuntarily raised his eyes towards the door of the room. In the all–but–darkness between him and the door, he saw a pale beautiful face—a face only. It was the face of Margaret Elginbrod; not, however, such as he had used to see it—but glorified. That was the only word by which he could describe its new aspect. A mist of darkness fell upon his brain, and the room swam round with him. But he was saved from falling, or attracting attention to a weakness for which he could have made no excuse, by a sudden cry from Lady Emily.

"See! see!" she cried wildly, pointing towards one of the windows.

These looked across to another part of the house, one of the oldest, at some distance.—One of its windows, apparently on the first floor, shone with a faint bluish light.

All the company had hurried to the window at Lady Emily's exclamation.

"Who can be in that part of the house?" said Mr. Arnold, angrily.

"It is Lady Euphrasia's window," said Euphra, in a low voice, the tone of which suggested, somehow, that the speaker was very cold.

"What do you mean by speaking like that?" said Mr. Arnold, forgetting his dignity. "Surely you are above being superstitious. Is it possible the servants could be about any mischief? I will discharge any one at once, that dares go there without permission."

The light disappeared, fading slowly out.

"Indeed, the servants are all too much alarmed, after what took place last year, to go near that wing—much less that room," said Euphra. "Besides, Mrs. Horton has all the keys in her own charge."

"Go yourself and get me them, Euphra. I will see at once what this means. Don't say why you want them."

"Certainly not, uncle."

Hugh had recovered almost instantaneously. Though full of amazement, he had yet his perceptive faculties sufficiently unimpaired to recognise the real source of the light in the window. It seemed to him more like moonlight than anything else; and he thought the others would have seen it to be such, but for the effect of Lady Emily's sudden exclamation. Perhaps she was under the influence of the Bohemian at the moment. Certainly they were all in a tolerable condition for seeing whatever might be required of them. True, there was no moon to be seen; and if it was the moon, why did the light go out? But he found afterwards that he had been right. The house stood upon a rising ground; and, every recurring cycle, the moon would shine, through a certain vista of trees and branches, upon Lady Euphrasia's window; provided there had been no growth of twigs to stop up the channel of the light, which was so narrow that in a few moments the moon had crossed it. A gap in a hedge made by a bull that morning, had removed the last

221

screen.—Lady Euphrasia's window was so neglected and dusty, that it could reflect nothing more than a dim bluish shimmer.

"Will you all accompany me, ladies and gentlemen, that you may see with your own eyes that there is nothing dangerous in the house?" said Mr. Arnold.

Of course Funkelstein was quite ready, and Hugh as well, although he felt at this moment ill–fitted for ghost–hunting. The ladies hesitated; but at last, more afraid of being left behind alone, than of going with the gentlemen, they consented. Euphra brought the keys, and they commenced their march of investigation. Up the grand staircase they went, Mr. Arnold first with the keys, Hugh next with Mrs. Elton and Lady Emily, and the Bohemian, considerably to Hugh's dissatisfaction, bringing up the rear with Euphra.—This misarrangement did more than anything else could have done, to deaden for the time the distraction of feeling produced in Hugh's mind by the events of the last few minutes. Yet even now he seemed to be wandering through the old house in a dream, instead of following Mr. Arnold, whose presence might well have been sufficient to destroy any illusion, except such as a Chinese screen might superinduce; for, possessed of far less imagination than a horse, he was incapable of any terrors, but such as had to do with robbers, or fire, or chartists—which latter fear included both the former. He strode on securely, carrying a candle in one hand, and the keys in the other. Each of the other gentlemen likewise bore a light. They had to go through doors, some locked, some open, following a different route from that taken by Euphra on a former occasion.

But Mr. Arnold found the keys troublesome. He could not easily distinguish those he wanted, and was compelled to apply to Euphra. She left Funkelstein in consequence, and walked in front with her uncle. Her former companion got beside Lady Emily, and as they could not well walk four abreast, she fell behind with him. So Hugh got next to Euphra, behind her, and was comforted.

At length, by tortuous ways, across old rooms, and up and down abrupt little stairs, they reached the door of Lady Euphrasia's room. The key was found, and the door opened with some perturbation—manifest on the part of the ladies, and concealed on the part of the men. The place was quite dark. They entered; and Hugh was greatly struck with its strange antiquity. Lady Euphrasia's ghost had driven the last occupant out of it nearly a hundred years ago; but most of the furniture was much older than that, having probably belonged to Lady Euphrasia herself. The room remained just as the said last occupant had left it. Even the bed–clothes remained, folded down, as if expecting their occupant for the last hundred years. The fine linen had grown yellow; and the rich counterpane lay like a churchyard after the resurrection, full of the open graves of the liberated moths. On the wall hung the portrait of a nun in convent–attire.

"Some have taken that for a second portrait of Lady Euphrasia," said Mr. Arnold, "but it cannot be.—Euphra, we will go back through the picture gallery.—I suspect it of originating the tradition that Lady Euphrasia became a nun at last. I do not believe it myself. The picture is certainly old enough to stand for her, but it does not seem to me in the least like the other."

It was a great room, with large recesses, and therefore irregular in form. Old chairs, with remnants of enamel and gilding, and seats of faded damask, stood all about. But the beauty of the chamber was its tapestry. The walls were entirely covered with it, and the rich colours had not yet receded into the dull grey of the past, though their gorgeousness had become sombre with age. The subject was the story of Samson.

"Come and see this strange piece of furniture," said Euphra to Hugh, who had kept by her side since they entered this room.

She led him into one of the recesses, almost concealed by the bed–hangings. In it stood a cabinet of ebony, reaching nearly to the ceiling, curiously carved in high relief.

"I wish I could show you the inside of it," she went on, "but I cannot now."

This was said almost in a whisper. Hugh replied with only a look of thanks. He gazed at the carving, on whose black surface his candle made little light, and threw no shadows.

"You have looked at this before, Euphra," said he. "Explain it to me."

"I have often tried to find out what it is," she answered; "but I never could quite satisfy myself about it."

She proceeded, however, to tell him what she fancied it might mean, speaking still in the low tone which seemed suitable to the awe of the place. She got interested in showing him the relations of the different figures; and he made several suggestions as to the possible intention of the artist. More than one well–known subject was proposed and rejected.

Suddenly becoming aware of the sensation of silence, they looked up, and saw that theirs was the only light in the room. They were left alone in the haunted chamber.—They looked at each other for one moment; then said, with half–stifled voices:

"Euphra!"

"Hugh!"

Euphra seemed half amused and half perplexed. Hugh looked half perplexed and wholly pleased.

"Come, come," said Euphra, recovering herself, and leading the way to the door.

When they reached it, they found it closed and locked. Euphra raised her hand to beat on it. Hugh caught it.

"You will drive Lady Emily into fits. Did you not see how awfully pale she was?"

Euphra instantly lifted her hand again, as if she would just like to try that result. But Hugh, who was in no haste for any result, held her back.

She struggled for a moment or two, but not very strenuously, and, desisting all at once, let her arms drop by her sides.

"I fear it is too late. This is a double door, and Mr. Arnold will have locked all the doors between this and the picture–gallery. They are there now. What shall we do?"

She said this with an expression of comical despair, which would have made Hugh burst into laughter, had he not been too much pleased to laugh.

"Never mind," he said, "we will go on with our study of the cabinet. They will soon find out that we are left behind, and come back to look for us."

"Yes, but only fancy being found here!"

She laughed; but the laugh did not succeed. It could not hide a real embarrassment. She pondered, and seemed irresolute. Then with the words—"They will say we stayed behind on purpose," she moved her hand to the door, but again withdrew it, and stood irresolute.

"Let us put out the light." said Hugh laughing, "and make no answer."

"Can you starve well?"

"With you."

She murmured something to herself; then said aloud and hastily, as if she had made up her mind by the compulsion of circumstances:

"But this won't do. They are still looking at the portrait, I daresay. Come."

So saying, she went into another recess, and, lifting a curtain of tapestry, opened a door.

"Come quick," she said.

Hugh followed her down a short stair into a narrow passage, nowhere lighted from the outside. The door went to behind them, as if some one had banged it in anger at their intrusion. The passage smelt very musty, and was as quiet as death.

"Not a word of this, Hugh, as you love me. It may be useful yet."

"Not a word."

They came through a sliding panel into an empty room. Euphra closed it behind them.

"Now shade your light."

He did so. She took him by the hand. A few more turns brought them in sight of the lights of the rest of the party. As Euphra had conjectured, they were looking at the picture of Lady Euphrasia, Mr. Arnold prosing away to them, in proof that the nun could not be she.

David Elginbrod

They entered the gallery without being heard; and parting a little way, one pretending to look at one picture, the other at another, crept gradually round till they joined the group. It was a piece of most successful generalship. Euphra was, doubtless, quite prepared with her story in case it should fail.

"Dear Lady Emily," said she, "how tired you look! Do let us go, uncle."

"By all means. Take my arm, Lady Emily. Euphra, will you take the keys again, and lock the doors?"

Mrs. Elton had already taken Hugh's arm, and was leading him away after Mr. Arnold and Lady Emily.

"I will not leave you behind with the spectres, Miss Cameron," said Funkelstein.

"Thank you; they will not detain me long. They don't mind being locked up."

It was some little time, however, before they presented themselves in the drawing–room, to which, and not to the library, the party had gone: they had had enough of horrors for that night.

Lest my readers should think they have had too many wonders at least, I will explain one of them. It was really Margaret Elginbrod whom Hugh had seen. Mrs. Elton was the lady in whose service she had left her home. It was nothing strange that they had not met, for Margaret knew he was in the same house, and had several times seen him, but had avoided meeting him. Neither was it a wonderful coincidence that they should be in such close proximity; for the college friend from whom Hugh had first heard of Mr. Arnold, was the son of the gentleman whom Mrs. Elton was visiting, when she first saw Margaret.

Margaret had obeyed her mistress's summons to the drawing–room, and had entered while Hugh was stooping over the plate. As the room was nearly dark, and she was dressed in black, her pale face alone caught the light and his eye as he looked up, and the giddiness which followed had prevented him from seeing more. She left the room the next moment, while they were all looking out of the window. Nor was it any exercise of his excited imagination that had presented her face as glorified. She was now a woman;

and, there being no divine law against saying so, I say that she had grown a lady as well; as indeed any one might have foreseen who was capable of foreseeing it. Her whole nature had blossomed into a still, stately, lily–like beauty; and the face that Hugh saw was indeed the realised idea of the former face of Margaret.

But how did the plate move? and whence came the writing of old David's name? I must, for the present, leave the whole matter to the speculative power of each of my readers.

But Margaret was in mourning: was David indeed dead?

He was dead.—Yet his name will stand as the name of my story for pages to come; because, if he had not been in it, the story would never have been worth writing; because the influence of that ploughman is the salt of the whole; because a man's life in the earth is not to be measured by the time he is visible upon it; and because, when the story is wound up, it will be in the presence of his spirit.

Do I then believe that David himself did write that name of his?

Heaven forbid that any friend of mine should be able to believe it!

Long before she saw him, Margaret had known, from what she heard among the servants, that Master Harry's tutor could be no other than her own tutor of the old time. By and by she learned a great deal about him from Harry's talk with Mrs. Elton and Lady Emily. But she did not give the least hint that she knew him, or betray the least desire to see him.

Mrs. Elton was amusingly bewildered by the occurrences of the evening. Her theories were something astounding; and followed one another with such alarming rapidity, that had they been in themselves such as to imply the smallest exercise of the thinking faculty, she might well have been considered in danger of an attack of brain–fever. As it was, none such supervened. Lady Emily said nothing, but seemed unhappy. As for Hugh, he simply could not tell what to make of the writing. But he did not for a moment doubt that the vision he had seen was only a vision—a home–made ghost, sent out from his own creative brain. Still he felt that Margaret's face, come whence it might, was a living reproof to him; for he was losing his life in passion, sinking deeper in it day by day. His powers were deserting him. Poetry, usually supposed to be the attendant of love, had deserted him. Only by fits could he see anything beautiful; and then it was but in closest association of thought with the one image which was burning itself deeper and deeper into his mental sensorium. Come what might, he could not tear it away. It had become a part of himself—of his inner life—even while it seemed to be working the death of life. Deeper and deeper it would burn, till it reached the innermost chamber of life. Let it burn.

Yet he felt that he could not trust her. Vague hopes he had, that, by trusting, she might be made trustworthy; but he feared they were vain as well as vague. And yet he would not cast them away, for he could not cast her away.

CHAPTER XVIII. MORE MATERIALISM AND SOME SPIRITUALISM.

```
God wisheth none should wreck on a strange shelf:
  To Him man's dearer than to himself.
```

```
BEN Jonson.—The Forest: To Sir Robert Wroth.
```

At breakfast the following morning, the influences of the past day on the family were evident. There was a good deal of excitement, alternated with listlessness. The moral atmosphere seemed unhealthy; and Harry, although he had, fortunately for him, had nothing to do with the manifestations of the previous evening, was affected by the condition of those around him. Hugh was still careful enough of him to try to divert the conversation entirely from what he knew would have a very injurious effect upon him; and Mr. Arnold, seeing the anxious way in which he glanced now and then at his pupil, and divining the reason, by the instinct of his affection, with far more than his usual acuteness, tried likewise to turn it aside, as often as it inclined that way. Still a few words were let fall by the visitors, which made Harry stare. Hugh took him away as soon as breakfast was over.

In the afternoon, Funkelstein called to inquire after the ladies; and hoped he had no injury to their health to lay on his conscience. Mr. Arnold, who had a full allowance of curiosity, its amount being frequently in an inverse ratio to that of higher intellectual gifts, begged him to spend the rest of the day with them; but not to say a word of what had passed the day before, till after Harry had retired for the night.

Renewed conversation led to renewed experiments in the library. Hugh, however, refused to have anything more to do with the plate–writing; for he dreaded its influence on his physical nature, attributing, as I have said, the vision of Margaret to a cerebral affection. And the plate did not seem to work satisfactorily with any one else, except Funkelstein, who, for his part, had no great wish to operate. Recourse was had to a more vulgar method—that of expectant solicitation of those noises whereby the prisoners in the aërial vaults are supposed capable of communicating with those in this earthly cell. Certainly, raps were heard from some quarter or another; and when the lights were extinguished, and the crescent moon only allowed to shine in the room, some commotion was discernible amongst the furniture. Several light articles flew about. A pen–wiper alighted on Euphra's lap, and a sofa–pillow gently disarranged Mrs. Elton's cap. Most of the artillery, however, was directed against Lady Emily; and she it was who saw, in a faint stream of moonlight, a female arm uplifted towards her, from under a table, with a threatening motion. It was bare to the elbow, and draped above. It showed first a clenched fist, and next an open hand, palm outwards, making a repellent gesture. Then the back of the hand was turned, and it motioned her away, as if she had been an importunate beggar. But at this moment, one of the doors opened, and a dark figure passed through the room towards the opposite door. Everything that could be called ghostly, ceased instantaneously. The arm vanished. The company breathed more freely.

Lady Emily, who had been on the point of going into hysterics, recovered herself, and overcame the still lingering impulse: she felt as if she had awaked from a momentary aberration of the intellect. Mr. Arnold proceeded to light the candles, saying, in a righteous tone:

"I think we have had enough of this nonsense."

When the candles were lighted, there was no one to be seen in the room besides themselves. Several, Hugh amongst them, had observed the figure; but all had taken it for part of the illusive phantasmagoria. Hugh would have concluded it a variety of his vision of the former night; but others had seen it as well as he.

There was no renewal of the experiments that night. But all were in a very unhealthy state of excitement. Vague fear, vague wonder, and a certain indescribable oppression, had dimmed for the time all the clearer vision, and benumbed all the nobler faculties of the soul. Lady Emily was affected the most. Her eyes looked scared; there was a bright spot on one cheek amidst deathly paleness; and she seemed very unhappy. Mrs. Elton became alarmed, and this brought her back to a more rational condition. She persuaded Lady Emily to go to bed.

But the contagion spread; and indistinct terrors were no longer confined to the upper portions of the family. The bruit revived, which had broken out a year before—that the house was haunted. It was whispered that, the very night after these occurrences, the Ghost's Walk had been in use as the name signified: a figure in death-garments had been seen gliding along the deserted avenue, by one of the maid-servants; the truth of whose story was corroborated by the fact that, to support it, she did not hesitate to confess that she had escaped from the house, nearly at midnight, to meet one of the grooms in a part of the wood contiguous to the avenue in question. Mr. Arnold instantly dismissed her—not on the ground of the intrigue, he took care to let her know, although that was bad enough, but because she was a fool, and spread absurd and annoying reports about the house. Mr. Arnold's usual hatred of what he called superstition, was rendered yet more spiteful by the fact, that the occurrences of the week had had such an effect on his own mind, that he was mortally afraid lest he should himself sink into the same limbo of vanity. The girl, however, was, or pretended to be, quite satisfied with her discharge, protesting she would not have staid for the world; and as the groom, whose wages happened to have been paid the day before, took himself off the same evening, it may be hoped her satisfaction was not altogether counterfeit.

"If all tales be true," said Mrs. Elton, "Lady Euphrasia is where she can't get out."

"But if she repented before she died?" said Euphra, with a muffled scorn in her tone.

"My dear Miss Cameron, do you call becoming a nun—repentance? We Protestants know very well what that means. Besides, your uncle does not believe it."

"Haven't you found out yet, dear Mrs. Elton, what my uncle's favourite phrase is?"

"No. What is it?"

"I don't believe it."

"You naughty girl!"

"I'm not naughty," answered Euphra, affecting to imitate the simplicity of a chidden child. "My uncle is so fond of casting doubt upon everything! If salvation goes by quantity, his faith won't save him."

Euphra knew well enough that Mrs. Elton was no tell–tale. The good lady had hopes of her from this moment, because she all but quoted Scripture to condemn her uncle; the verdict corresponding with her own judgment of Mr. Arnold, founded on the clearest assertions of Scripture; strengthened somewhat, it must be confessed, by the fact that the spirits, on the preceding evening but one, had rapped out the sentence: "Without faith it is impossible to please him."

Lady Emily was still in bed, but apparently more sick in mind than in body. She said she had tossed about all the previous night without once falling asleep; and her maid, who had slept in the dressing–room without waking once, corroborated the assertion. In the morning, Mrs. Elton, wishing to relieve the maid, sent Margaret to Lady Emily. Margaret arranged the bedclothes and pillows, which were in a very uncomfortable condition, sat down behind the curtain; and, knowing that it would please Lady Emily, began to sing, in what the French call a, veiled voice, The Land o' the Leal. Now the air of this lovely song is the same as that of Scots wha hae; but it is the pibroch of onset changed into the coronach of repose, singing of the land beyond the battle, of the entering in of those who have fought the good fight, and fallen in the field. It is the silence after the thunder. Before she had finished, Lady Emily was fast asleep. A sweet peaceful half smile lighted her troubled face graciously, like the sunshine that creeps out when it can, amidst the rain of an autumn day, saying, "I am with you still, though we are all troubled." Finding her thus at rest, Margaret left the room for a minute, to fetch some work. When she returned, she found her tossing, and moaning, and apparently on the point of waking. As soon as she sat down by her, her trouble diminished by degrees, till she lay in the same peaceful sleep as before. In this state she continued for two or three hours, and awoke much refreshed. She held out her little hand to Margaret, and said:

"Thank you. Thank you. What a sweet creature you are!"

And Lady Emily lay and gazed in loving admiration at the face of the lady's–maid.

"Shall I send Sarah to you now, my lady?" said Margaret; "or would you like me to stay with you?"

David Elginbrod

"Oh! you, you, please—if Mrs. Elton can spare you."

"She will only think of your comfort, I know, my lady."

"That recalls me to my duty, and makes me think of her."

"But your comfort will be more to her than anything else."

"In that case you must stay, Margaret."

"With pleasure, my lady."

Mrs. Elton entered, and quite confirmed what Margaret had said.

"But," she added, "it is time Lady Emily had something to eat. Go to the cook, Margaret, and see if the beef–tea Miss Cameron ordered is ready."

Margaret went.

"What a comfort it is," said Mrs. Elton, wishing to interest Lady Emily, "that now–a–days, when infidelity is so rampant, such corroborations of Sacred Writ are springing up on all sides! There are the discoveries at Nineveh; and now these Spiritual Manifestations, which bear witness so clearly to another world."

But Lady Emily made no reply. She began to toss about as before, and show signs of inexplicable discomfort. Margaret had hardly been gone two minutes, when the invalid moaned out:

"What a time Margaret is gone!—when will she be back?"

"I am here, my love," said Mrs. Elton.

"Yes, yes; thank you. But I want Margaret."

"She will be here presently. Have patience, my dear."

"Please, don't let Miss Cameron come near me. I am afraid I am very wicked, but I can't bear her to come near me."

"No, no, dear; we will keep you to ourselves."

"Is Mr.—, the foreign gentleman, I mean—below?"

"No. He is gone."

"Are you sure? I can hardly believe it."

"What do you mean, dear? I am sure he is gone."

Lady Emily did not answer. Margaret returned. She took the beef–tea, and grew quiet again.

"You must not leave her ladyship, Margaret," whispered her mistress. "She has taken it into her head to like no one but you, and you must just stay with her."

"Very well, ma'am. I shall be most happy."

Mrs. Elton left the room. Lady Emily said:

"Read something to me, Margaret."

"What shall I read?"

"Anything you like."

Margaret got a Bible, and read to her one of her father's favourite chapters, the fortieth of Isaiah.

"I have no right to trust in God, Margaret."

"Why, my lady?"

"Because I do not feel any faith in him; and you know we cannot be accepted without faith."

"That is to make God as changeable as we are, my lady."

"But the Bible says so."

"I don't think it does; but if an angel from heaven said so, I would not believe it."

"Margaret!"

"My lady, I love God with all my heart, and I cannot bear you should think so of him. You might as well say that a mother would go away from her little child, lying moaning in the dark, because it could not see her, and was afraid to put its hand out into the dark to feel for her."

"Then you think he does care for us, even when we are very wicked. But he cannot bear wicked people."

"Who dares to say that?" cried Margaret. "Has he not been making the world go on and on, with all the wickedness that is in it; yes, making new babies to be born of thieves and murderers and sad women and all, for hundreds of years? God help us, Lady Emily! If he cannot bear wicked people, then this world is hell itself, and the Bible is all a lie, and the Saviour did never die for sinners. It is only the holy Pharisees that can't bear wicked people."

"Oh! how happy I should be, if that were true! I should not be afraid now."

"You are not wicked, dear Lady Emily; but if you were, God would bend over you, trying to get you back, like a father over his sick child. Will people never believe about the lost sheep?"

"Oh! yes; I believe that. But then—"

"You can't trust it quite. Trust in God, then, the very father of you—and never mind the words. You have been taught to turn the very words of God against himself."

David Elginbrod

Lady Emily was weeping.

"Lady Emily," Margaret went on, "if I felt my heart as hard as a stone; if I did not love God, or man, or woman, or little child, I would yet say to God in my heart: 'O God, see how I trust thee, because thou art perfect, and not changeable like me. I do not love thee. I love nobody. I am not even sorry for it. Thou seest how much I need thee to come close to me, to put thy arm round me, to say to me, my child; for the worse my state, the greater my need of my father who loves me. Come to me, and my day will dawn. My beauty and my love will come back; and oh! how I shall love thee, my God! and know that my love is thy love, my blessedness thy being.'"

As Margaret spoke, she seemed to have forgotten Lady Emily's presence, and to be actually praying. Those who cannot receive such words from the lips of a lady's-maid, must be reminded what her father was, and that she had lost him. She had had advantages at least equal to those which David the Shepherd had—and he wrote the Psalms.

She ended with:

"I do not even desire thee to come, yet come thou."

She seemed to pray entirely as Lady Emily, not as Margaret. When she had ceased, Lady Emily said, sobbing:

"You will not leave me, Margaret? I will tell you why another time."

"I will not leave you, my dear lady."

Margaret stooped and kissed her forehead. Lady Emily threw her arms round her neck, and offered her mouth to be kissed by the maid. In another minute she was fast asleep, with Margaret seated by her side, every now and then glancing up at her from her work, with a calm face, over which brooded the mist of tears.

That night, as Hugh paced up and down the floor of his study about midnight, he was awfully startled by the sudden opening of the door and the apparition of Harry in his nightshirt, pale as death, and scarcely able to articulate the words:

David Elginbrod

"The ghost! the ghost!"

He took the poor boy in his arms, held him fast, and comforted him. When he was a little soothed,

"Oh, Harry!" he said, lightly, "you've been dreaming. Where's the ghost?"

"In the Ghost's Walk," cried Harry, almost shrieking anew with terror.

"How do you know it is there?"

"I saw it from my window.—I couldn't sleep. I got up and looked out—I don't know why—and I saw it! I saw it!"

The words were followed by a long cry of terror.

"Come and show it to me," said Hugh, wanting to make light of it.

"No, no, Mr. Sutherland—please not. I couldn't go back into that room."

"Very well, dear Harry; you shan't go back. You shall sleep with me, to—night."

"Oh! thank you, thank you, dear Mr. Sutherland. You will love me again, won't you?"

This touched Hugh's heart. He could hardly refrain from tears. His old love, buried before it was dead, revived. He clasped the boy to his heart, and carried him to his own bed; then, to comfort him, undressed and lay down beside him, without even going to look if he too might not see the ghost. She had brought about one good thing at least that night; though, I fear, she had no merit in it.

Lady Emily's room likewise looked out upon the Ghost's Walk. Margaret heard the cry as she sat by the sleeping Emily; and, not knowing whence it came, went, naturally enough, in her perplexity, to the window. From it she could see distinctly, for it was clear moonlight: a white figure went gliding away along the deserted avenue. She immediately guessed what the cry had meant; but as she had heard a door bang directly after (as Harry shut his behind him with a terrified instinct, to keep the awful window in), she was not very uneasy about him. She felt besides that she must remain where she was, according to her promise to Lady Emily. But she resolved to be prepared for the possible recurrence of the same event, and accordingly revolved it in her mind. She was sure that any report of it coming to Lady Emily's ears, would greatly impede her recovery, for she instinctively felt that her illness had something to do with the questionable occupations in the library. She watched by her bedside all the night, slumbering at times, but roused in a moment by any restlessness of the patient; when she found that, simply by laying her hand on hers, or kissing her forehead, she could restore her at once to quiet sleep.

CHAPTER XIX. THE GHOST'S WALK.

```
Thierry.—'Tis full of fearful shadows.
Ordella.—    So is sleep, sir;
   Or anything that's merely ours, and mortal;
   We were begotten gods else.  But those fears
   Feeling but once the fires of nobler thoughts,
   Fly, like the shapes of clouds we form, to nothing.

BEAUMONT AND FLETCHER.—Thierry and Theodoret.
```

Margaret sat watching the waking of Lady Emily. Knowing how much the first thought colours the feeling of the whole day, she wished that Lady Emily should at once be aware that she was by her side.

She opened her eyes, and a smile broke over her face when she perceived her nurse. But Margaret did not yet speak to her.

Every nurse should remember that waking ought always to be a gradual operation; and, except in the most triumphant health, is never complete on the opening of the eyes.

"Margaret, I am better," said Lady Emily, at last.

"I am very glad, my lady."

"I have been lying awake for some time, and I am sure I am better. I don't see strange-coloured figures floating about the room as I did yesterday. Were you not out of the room a few minutes ago?"

David Elginbrod

"Just for one moment, my lady."

"I knew it. But I did not mind it. Yesterday, when you left me, those figures grew ten times as many, the moment you were gone. But you will stay with me to-day, too, Margaret?" she added, with some anxiety.

"I will, if you find you need me. But I may be forced to leave you a little while this evening—you must try to allow me this, dear Lady Emily."

"Of course I will. I will be quite patient, I promise you, whatever comes to me."

When Harry woke, after a very troubled sleep, from which he had often started with sudden cries of terror, Hugh made him promise not to increase the confusion of the household, by speaking of what he had seen. Harry promised at once, but begged in his turn that Hugh would not leave him all day. It did not need the pale scared face of his pupil to enforce the request; for Hugh was already anxious lest the fright the boy had had, should exercise a permanently deleterious effect on his constitution. Therefore he hardly let him out of his sight.

But although Harry kept his word, the cloud of perturbation gathered thicker in the kitchen and the servants' hall. Nothing came to the ears of their master and mistress; but gloomy looks, sudden starts, and sidelong glances of fear, indicated the prevailing character of the feelings of the household.

And although Lady Emily was not so ill, she had not yet taken a decided turn for the better, but appeared to suffer from some kind of low fever. The medical man who was called in, confessed to Mrs. Elton, that as yet he could say nothing very decided about her condition, but recommended great quiet and careful nursing. Margaret scarcely left her room, and the invalid showed far more than the ordinary degree of dependence upon her nurse. In her relation to her, she was more like a child than an invalid.

About noon she was better. She called Margaret and said to her:

"Margaret, dear, I should like to tell you one thing that annoys me very much."

"What is it, dear Lady Emily?"

"That man haunts me. I cannot bear the thought of him; and yet I cannot get rid of him. I am sure he is a bad man. Are you certain he is not here?"

"Yes, indeed, my lady. He has not been here since the day before yesterday."

"And yet when you leave me for an instant, I always feel as if he were sitting in the very seat where you were the moment before, or just coming to the door and about to open it. That is why I cannot bear you to leave me."

Margaret might have confessed to some slighter sensations of the same kind; but they did not oppress her as they did Lady Emily.

"God is nearer to you than any thought or feeling of yours, Lady Emily. Do not be afraid. If all the evil things in the universe were around us, they could not come inside the ring that he makes about us. He always keeps a place for himself and his child, into which no other being can enter."

"Oh! how you must love God, Margaret!"

"Indeed I do love him, my lady. If ever anything looks beautiful or lovely to me, then I know at once that God is that."

"But, then, what right have we to take the good of that, however true it is, when we are not beautiful ourselves?"

"That only makes God the more beautiful—in that he will pour out the more of his beauty upon us to make us beautiful. If we care for his glory, we shall be glad to believe all this about him. But we are too anxious about feeling good ourselves, to rejoice in his perfect goodness. I think we should find that enough, my lady. For, if he be good, are not we his children, and sure of having it, not merely feeling it, some day?"

Here Margaret repeated a little poem of George Herbert's. She had found his poems amongst Mrs. Elton's books, who, coming upon her absorbed in it one day, had made her a present of the volume. Then indeed Margaret had found a friend.

The poem is called Dialogue:

David Elginbrod

"Sweetest Saviour, if my soul
  Were but worth the having—"

"Oh, what a comfort you are to me, Margaret!" Lady Emily said, after a short silence. Where did you learn such things?"

"From my father, and from Jesus Christ, and from God himself, showing them to me in my heart."

"Ah! that is why, as often as you come into my room, even if I am very troubled, I feel as if the sun shone, and the wind blew, and the birds sang, and the tree–tops went waving in the wind, as they used to do before I was taken ill—I mean before they thought I must go abroad. You seem to make everything clear, and right, and plain. I wish I were you, Margaret."

"If I were you, my lady, I would rather be what God chose to make me, than the most glorious creature that I could think of. For to have been thought about—born in God's thoughts—and then made by God, is the dearest, grandest, most precious thing in all thinking. Is it not, my lady?"

"It is," said Lady Emily, and was silent.

The shadows of evening came on. As soon as it was dark, Margaret took her place at one of the windows hidden from Lady Emily by a bed–curtain. She raised the blind, and pulled aside one curtain, to let her have a view of the trees outside. She had placed the one candle so as not to shine either on the window or on her own eyes. Lady Emily was asleep. One hour and another passed, and still she sat there—motionless, watching.

Margaret did not know, that at another window—the one, indeed, next to her own—stood a second watcher. It was Hugh, in Harry's room: Harry was asleep in Hugh's. He had no light. He stood with his face close against the windowpane, on which the moon shone brightly. All below him the woods were half dissolved away in the moonlight. The Ghost's Walk lay full before him, like a tunnel through the trees. He could see a great way down, by the light that fell into it, at various intervals, from between the boughs overhead. He stood thus for a long time, gazing somewhat listlessly. Suddenly he became all eyes, as he caught the white glimmer of something passing up the avenue. He stole out of the room, down to the library by the back–stair, and so through the library window into the wood. He reached the avenue sideways, at some distance from the house, and peeped from behind a tree, up and down. At first he saw nothing. But, a moment after, while he was looking down the avenue, that is, away from the house, a veiled figure in white passed him noiselessly from the other direction. From the way in which he was looking at the moment, it had passed him before he saw it. It made no sound. Only some early–fallen leaves rustled as they hurried away in uncertain eddies, startled by the sweep of its trailing garments, which yet were held up by hands hidden within them. On it went. Hugh's eyes were fixed on its course. He could not move, and his heart laboured so frightfully that he could hardly breathe. The figure had not advanced far, however, before he heard a repressed cry of agony, and it sank to the earth, and vanished; while from where it disappeared, down the path, came, silently too, turning neither to the right nor the left, a second figure, veiled in black from head to foot.

"It is the nun in Lady Euphrasia's room," said Hugh to himself.

This passed him too, and, walking slowly towards the house, disappeared somewhere, near the end of the avenue. Turning once more, with reviving courage—for his blood had begun to flow more equably—Hugh ventured to approach the spot where the white figure had vanished. He found nothing there but the shadow of a huge tree. He walked through the avenue to the end, and then back to the house, but saw nothing; though he often started at fancied appearances. Sorely bewildered, he returned to his own room. After speculating till thought was weary, he lay down beside Harry, whom he was thankful to find in a still repose, and fell fast asleep.

Margaret lay on a couch in Lady Emily's room, and slept likewise; but she started wide awake at every moan of the invalid, who often moaned in her sleep.

CHAPTER XX. THE BAD MAN.

```
She kent he was nae gentle knight,
  That she had letten in;
For neither when he gaed nor cam',
  Kissed he her cheek or chin.

He neither kissed her when he cam'
  Nor clappit her when he gaed;
```

David Elginbrod

And in and out at her bower window,
  The moon shone like the gleed.

Glenkindie.—Old Scotch Ballad.

When Euphra recovered from the swoon into which she had fallen—for I need hardly explain to my readers, that it was she who walked the Ghost's Walk in white—on seeing Margaret, whom, under the irresistible influences of the moonlight and a bad conscience, she took for the very being whom Euphra herself was personating—when she recovered, I say, she found herself lying in the wood, with Funkelstein, whom she had gone to meet, standing beside her. Her first words were of anger, as she tried to rise, and found she could not.

"How long, Count Halkar, am I to be your slave?"

"Till you have learned to submit."

"Have I not done all I can?"

"You have not found it. You are free from the moment you place that ring, belonging to me, in right of my family, into my hands."

I do not believe that the man really was Count Halkar, although he had evidently persuaded Euphra that such was his name and title. I think it much more probable that, in the course of picking up a mass of trifling information about various families of distinction, for which his position of secretary in several of their houses had afforded him special facilities, he had learned something about the Halkar family, and this particular ring, of which, for some reason or other, he wanted to possess himself.

"What more can I do?" moaned Euphra, succeeding at length in raising herself to a sitting posture, and leaning thus against a tree. "I shall be found out some day. I have been already seen wandering through the house at midnight, with the heart of a thief. I hate you, Count Halkar!"

A low laugh was the count's only reply.

David Elginbrod

"And now Lady Euphrasia herself dogs my steps, to keep me from the ring." She gave a low cry of agony at the remembrance.

"Miss Cameron—Euphra   are you going to give way to such folly?"

"Folly! Is it not worse folly to torture a poor girl as you do me—all for a worthless ring? What can you want with the ring? I do not know that he has it even."

"You lie. You know he has. You need not think to take me in."

"You base man! You dare not give the lie to any but a woman."

"Why?"

"Because you are a coward. You are afraid of Lady Euphrasia yourself. See there!"

Von Funkelstein glanced round him uneasily. It was only the moonlight on the bark of a silver birch. Conscious of having betrayed weakness, he grew spiteful.

"If you do not behave to me better, I will compel you. Rise up!"

After a moment's hesitation, she rose.

"Put your arms round me."

She seemed to grow to the earth, and to drag herself from it, one foot after another. But she came close up to the Bohemian, and put one arm half round him, looking to the earth all the time.

"Kiss me."

"Count Halkar!" her voice sounded hollow and harsh, as if from a dead throat—"I will do what you please. Only release me."

"Go then; but mind you resist me no more. I do not care for your kisses. You were ready enough once. But that idiot of a tutor has taken my place, I see."

243

David Elginbrod

"Would to God I had never seen you!—never yielded to your influence over me! Swear that I shall be free if I find you the ring."

"You find the ring first. Why should I swear? I can compel you. You know you laid yourself out to entrap me first with your arts, and I only turned upon you with mine. And you are in my power. But you shall be free, notwithstanding; and I will torture you till you free yourself. Find the ring."

"Cruel! cruel! You are doing all you can to ruin me."

"On the contrary, I am doing all I can to save myself. If you had loved me as you allowed me to think once, I should never have made you my tool."

"You would all the same."

"Take care. I am irritable to–night."

For a few moments Euphra made no reply.

"To what will you drive me?" she said at last.

"I will not go too far. I should lose my power over you if I did. I prefer to keep it."

"Inexorable man!"

"Yes."

Another despairing pause.

"What am I to do?"

"Nothing. But keep yourself ready to carry out any plan that I may propose. Something will turn up, now that I have got into the house myself. Leave me to find out the means. I can expect no invention from your brains. You can go home."

Euphra turned without another word, and went; murmuring, as if in excuse to herself:

"It is for my freedom. It is for my freedom."

Of course this account must have come originally from Euphra herself, for there was no one else to tell it. She, at least, believed herself compelled to do what the man pleased. Some of my readers will put her down as insane. She may have been; but, for my part, I believe there is such a power of one being over another, though perhaps only in a rare contact of psychologically peculiar natures. I have testimony enough for that. She had yielded to his will once. Had she not done so, he could not have compelled her; but, having once yielded, she had not strength sufficient to free herself again. Whether even he could free her, further than by merely abstaining from the exercise of the power he had gained, I doubt much.

It is evident that he had come to the neighbourhood of Arnstead for the sake of finding her, and exercising his power over her for his own ends; that he had made her come to him once, if not oftener, before he met Hugh, and by means of his acquaintance, obtained admission into Arnstead. Once admitted, he had easily succeeded, by his efforts to please, in so far ingratiating himself with Mr. Arnold, that now the house–door stood open to him, and he had even his recognised seat at the dinner–table.

CHAPTER XXI. SPIRIT VERSUS MATERIALISM.

```
Next this marble venomed seat,
Smeared with gums of glutinous heat,
I touch with chaste palms moist and cold—
Now the spell hath lost his hold.

MILTON.—Comas.
```

Next morning Lady Emily felt better, and wanted to get up: but her eyes were still too bright, and her hands too hot; and Margaret would not hear of it.

Fond as Lady Emily was in general of Mrs. Elton's society, she did not care to have her with her now, and got tired of her when Margaret was absent.

They had taken care not to allow Miss Cameron to enter the room; but to–day there was not much likelihood of her making the attempt, for she did not appear at breakfast, sending a message to her uncle that she had a bad headache, but hoped to take her place at the dinner–table.

During the day, Lady Emily was better, but restless by fits.

"Were you not out of the room for a little while last night, Margaret?" she said, rather suddenly.

"Yes, my lady. I told you I should have to go, perhaps."

"I remember I thought you had gone, but I was not in the least afraid, and that dreadful man never came near me. I do not know when you returned. Perhaps I had fallen asleep; but when I thought about you next, there you were by my bedside."

"I shall not have to leave you to–night," was all Margaret's answer.

As for Hugh, when first he woke, the extraordinary experiences of the previous night appeared to him to belong only to the night, and to have no real relation to the daylight world. But a little reflection soon convinced him of the contrary; and then he went through the duties of the day like one who had nothing to do with them. The phantoms he had seen even occupied some of the thinking space formerly appropriated by the image of Euphra, though he knew to his concern that she was ill, and confined to her room. He had heard the message sent to Mr. Arnold, however, and so kept hoping for the dinner–hour.

With it came Euphra, very pale. Her eyes had an unsettled look, and there were dark hollows under them. She would start and look sideways without any visible cause; and was thus very different from her usual self—ordinarily remarkable for self–possession, almost to coolness, of manner and speech. Hugh saw it, and became both distressed and speculative in consequence. It did not diminish his discomfort that, about the middle of dinner, Funkelstein was announced. Was it, then, that Euphra had been tremulously expectant of him?

"This is an unforeseen pleasure, Herr von Funkelstein," said Mr. Arnold.

"It is very good of you to call it a pleasure, Mr. Arnold," said he. "Miss Cameron—but, good heavens! how ill you look!"

"Don't be alarmed. I have only caught the plague."

"Only?" was all Funkelstein said in reply; yet Hugh thought he had no right to be so solicitous about Euphra's health.

As the gentlemen sat at their wine, Mr. Arnold said:

"I am anxious to have one more trial of those strange things you have brought to our knowledge. I have been thinking about them ever since."

"Of course I am at your service, Mr. Arnold; but don't you think, for the ladies' sakes, we have had enough of it?"

"You are very considerate, Herr von Funkelstein; but they need not be present if they do not like it."

"Very well, Mr. Arnold."

They adjourned once more to the library instead of the drawing–room. Hugh went and told Euphra, who was alone in the drawing–room, what they were about. She declined going, but insisted on his leaving her, and joining the other gentlemen.

Hugh left her with much reluctance.

"Margaret," said Lady Emily, "I am certain that man is in the house."

"He is, my lady," answered Margaret.

"They are about some more of those horrid experiments, as they call them."

"I do not know."

Mrs. Elton entering the room at the moment, Margaret said:

"Do you know, ma'am, whether the gentlemen are—in the library again?"

"I don't know, Margaret. I hope not. We have had enough of that. I will go and find out, though."

"Will you take my place for a few minutes first, please, ma'am?"

Margaret had felt a growing oppression for some time. She had scarcely left the sick–room that day.

"Don't leave me, dear Margaret," said Lady Emily, imploringly.

"Only for a little while, my lady. I shall be back in less than a quarter of an hour."

"Very well, Margaret," she answered dolefully.

Margaret went out into the moonlight, and walked for ten minutes. She sought the more open parts, where the winds were. She then returned to the sick–chamber, refreshed and strong.

"Now I will go and see what the gentlemen are about," said Mrs. Elton.

The good lady did not like these proceedings, but she was irresistibly attracted by them notwithstanding. Having gone to see for Lady Emily, she remained to see for herself.

After she had left, Lady Emily grew more uneasy. Not even Margaret's presence could make her comfortable. Mrs. Elton did not return. Many minutes elapsed. Lady Emily said at last:

"Margaret, I am terrified at the idea of being left alone, I confess; but not so terrified as at the idea of what is going on in that library. Mrs. Elton will not come back. Would you mind just running down to ask her to come to me?"

"I would go with pleasure," said Margaret; "but I don't want to be seen."

Margaret did not want to be seen by Hugh. Lady Emily, with her dislike to Funkelstein, thought Margaret did not want to be seen by him.

David Elginbrod

"You will find a black veil of mine," she said, "in that wardrobe—just throw it over your head, and hold a handkerchief to your face. They will be so busy that they will never see you."

Margaret yielded to the request of Lady Emily, who herself arranged her head–dress for her.

Now I must go back a little.—When Mrs. Elton reached the room, she found it darkened, and the gentlemen seated at the table. A running fire of knocks was going on all around.

She sat down in a corner. In a minute or two, she fancied she saw strange figures moving about, generally near the floor, and very imperfectly developed. Sometimes only a hand, sometimes only a foot, shadowed itself out of the dim obscurity. She tried to persuade herself that it was all done, somehow or other, by Funkelstein, yet she could not help watching with a curious dread. She was not a very excitable woman, and her nerves were safe enough.

In a minute or two more, the table at which they were seated, began to move up and down with a kind of vertical oscillation, and several things in the room began to slide about, by short, apparently purposeless jerks. Everything threatened to assume motion, and turn the library into a domestic chaos. Mrs. Elton declared afterwards that several books were thrown about the room.—But suddenly everything was as still as the moonlight. Every chair and table was at rest, looking perfectly incapable of motion. Mrs. Elton felt that she dared not say they had moved at all, so utterly ordinary was their appearance. Not a sound was to be heard from corner or ceiling. After a moment's silence, Mrs. Elton was quite restored to her sound mind, as she said, and left the room.

"Some adverse influence is at work," said Funkelstein, with some vexation. "What is in that closet?"

So saying he approached the door of the private staircase, and opened it. They saw him start aside, and a veiled dark figure pass him, cross the library, and go out by another door.

"I have my suspicions," said Funkelstein, with a rather tremulous voice.

David Elginbrod

"And your fears too, I think. Grant it now," said Mr. Arnold.

"Granted, Mr. Arnold. Let us go to the drawing–room."

Just as Margaret had reached the library door at the bottom of the private stair, either a puff of wind from an open loophole window, or some other cause, destroyed the arrangement of the veil, and made it fall quite over her face, She stopped for a moment to readjust it. She had not quite succeeded, when Funkelstein opened the door. Without an instant's hesitation, she let the veil fall, and walked forward.

Mrs. Elton had gone to her own room, on her way to Lady Emily's. When she reached the latter, she found Margaret seated as she had left her, by the bedside. Lady Emily said:

"I did not miss you, Margaret, half so much as I expected. But, indeed, you were not many moments gone. I do not care for that man now. He can't hurt me, can he?"

"Certainty not. I hope he will give you no more trouble either, dear Lady Emily. But if I might presume to advise you, I would say—Get well as soon as you can, and leave this place."

"Why should I? You frighten me. Mr. Arnold is very kind to me."

"The place quite suits Lady Emily, I am sure, Margaret."

"But Lady Emily is not so well as when she came."

"No, but that is not the fault of the place," said Lady Emily. "I am sure it is all that horrid man's doing."

"How else will you get rid of him, then? What if he wants to get rid of you?"

"What harm can I be doing him—a poor girl like me?"

"I don't know. But I fear there is something not right going on."

"We will tell Mr. Arnold at once," said Mrs. Elton.

"But what could you tell him, ma'am? Mr. Arnold is hardly one to listen to your maid's suspicions. Dear Lady Emily, you must get well and go."

"I will try," said Lady Emily, submissive as a child.

"I think you will be able to get up for a little while tomorrow."

A tap came to the door. It was Euphrasia, inquiring after Lady Emily.

"Ask Miss Cameron to come in," said the invalid.

She entered. Her manner was much changed—was subdued and suffering.

"Dear Miss Cameron, you and I ought to change places. I am sorry to see you looking so ill," said Lady Emily.

"I have had a headache all day. I shall be quite well to–morrow, thank you."

"I intend to be so too," said Lady Emily, cheerfully.

After some little talk, Euphra went, holding her hand to her forehead. Margaret did not look up, all the time she was in the room, but went on busily with her needle.

That night was a peaceful one.

CHAPTER XXII. THE RING.

```
      shining crystal, which
Out of her womb a thousand rayons threw.
```

BELLAY: translated by Spenser.

The next day, Lady Emily was very nearly as well as she had proposed being. She did not, however, make her appearance below. Mr. Arnold, hearing at luncheon that she was out of bed, immediately sent up his compliments, with the request that he might be permitted to see her on his return from the neighbouring village, where he had some business. To this Lady Emily gladly consented.

He sat with her a long time, talking about various things; for the presence of the girl, reminding him of his young wife, brought out the best of the man, lying yet alive under the incrustation of self–importance, and its inevitable stupidity. At length, subject of further conversation failing,

"I wonder what we can do to amuse you, Lady Emily," said he.

"Thank you, Mr. Arnold; I am not at all dull. With my kind friend, Mrs. Elton, and—"

She would have said Margaret, but became instinctively aware that the mention of her would make Mr. Arnold open his eyes, for he did not even know her name; and that he would stare yet wider when he learned that the valued companion referred to was Mrs. Elton's maid.

Mr. Arnold left the room, and presently returned with his arms filled with all the drawing–room books he could find, with grand bindings outside, and equally grand plates inside. These he heaped on the table beside Lady Emily, who tried to look interested, but scarcely succeeded to Mr. Arnold's satisfaction, for he presently said:

"You don't seem to care much about these, dear Lady Emily. I daresay you have looked at them all already, in this dull house of ours."

This was a wonderful admission from Mr. Arnold. He pondered—then exclaimed, as if he had just made a grand discovery:

"I have it! I know something that will interest you."

"Do not trouble yourself, pray, Mr. Arnold," said Lady Emily. But he was already half way to the door.

He went to his own room, and his own strong closet therein.

Returning towards the invalid's quarters with an ebony box of considerable size, he found it rather heavy, and meeting Euphra by the way, requested her to take one of the silver handles, and help him to carry it to Lady Emily's room. She started when she saw it, but merely said:

"With pleasure, uncle."

"Now, Lady Emily," said he, as, setting down the box, he took out a curious antique enamelled key, "we shall be able to amuse you for a little while."

He opened the box, and displayed such a glitter and show as would have delighted the eyes of any lady. All kinds of strange ornaments; ancient watches—one of them a death's head in gold; cameo necklaces; pearls abundant; diamonds, rubies, and all the colours of precious stones—every one of them having some history, whether known to the owner or not; gems that had flashed on many a fair finger and many a shining neck—lay before Lady Emily's delighted eyes. But Euphrasia's eyes shone, as she gazed on them, with a very different expression from that which sparkled in Lady Emily's. They seemed to search them with fingers of lightning. Mr. Arnold chose two or three, and gave Lady Emily her choice of them.

"I could not think of depriving you."

"They are of no use to me," said Mr. Arnold, making light of the handsome offer.

"You are too kind.—I should like this ring."

"Take it then, dear Lady Emily."

Euphrasia's eyes were not on the speakers, nor was any envy to be seen in her face. She still gazed at the jewels in the box.

The chosen gem was put aside; and then, one after another, the various articles were taken out and examined. At length, a large gold chain, set with emeralds, was lifted from where it lay coiled up in a corner. A low cry, like a muffled moan, escaped from Euphrasia's lips, and she turned her head away from the box.

"What is the matter, Euphra?" said Mr. Arnold.

"A sudden shoot of pain—I beg your pardon, dear uncle. I fear I am not quite so well yet as I thought I was. How stupid of me!"

"Do sit down. I fear the weight of the box was too much for you."

"Not in the least. I want to see the pretty things."

"But you have seen them before."

"No, uncle. You promised to show them to me, but you never did."

"You see what I get by being ill," said Lady Emily.

The chain was examined, admired, and laid aside.

Where it had lain, they now observed, in the corner, a huge stone like a diamond.

"What is this?" said Lady Emily, taking it up. "Oh! I see. It is a ring. But such a ring for size, I never saw. Do look, Miss Cameron."

For Miss Cameron was not looking. She was leaning her head on her hand, and her face was ashy pale. Lady Emily tried the ring on. Any two of her fingers would go into the broad gold circlet, beyond which the stone projected far in every direction. Indeed, the ring was attached to the stone, rather than the stone set in the ring.

"That is a curious thing, is it not?" said Mr. Arnold. "It is of no value in itself, I believe; it is nothing but a crystal. But it seems to have been always thought something of in the family;—I presume from its being evidently the very ring painted by Sir Peter Lely in that portrait of Lady Euphrasia which I showed you the other day. It is a clumsy affair, is it not?"

It might have occurred to Mr. Arnold, that such a thing must have been thought something of, before its owner would have chosen to wear it when sitting for her portrait.

Lady Emily was just going to lay it down, when she spied something that made her look at it more closely.

David Elginbrod

"What curious engraving is this upon the gold?" she asked.

"I do not know, indeed," answered Mr. Arnold. "I have never observed it."

"Look at it, then—all over the gold. What at first looks only like chasing, is, I do believe, words. The character looks to me like German. I wish I could read it. I am but a poor German scholar. Do look at it, please, dear Miss Cameron."

Euphra glanced slightly at it without touching it, and said:

"I am sure I could make nothing of it.—But," she added, as if struck by a sudden thought, "as Lady Emily seems interested in it—suppose we send for Mr. Sutherland. I have no doubt he will be able to decipher it."

She rose as if she would go for him herself; but, apparently on second thoughts, went to the bell and rang it.

"Oh! do not trouble yourself," interposed Lady Emily, in a tone that showed she would like it notwithstanding.

"No trouble at all," answered Euphra and her uncle in a breath.

"Jacob," said Mr. Arnold, "take my compliments to Mr. Sutherland, and ask him to step this way."

The man went, and Hugh came.

"There's a puzzle for you, Mr. Sutherland," said Mr. Arnold, as he entered. "Decipher that inscription, and gain the favour of Lady Emily for ever."

As he spoke he put the ring in Hugh's hand. Hugh recognized it at once.

"Ah! this is Lady Euphrasia's wonderful ring," said he.

Euphra cast on him one of her sudden glances.

David Elginbrod

"What do you know about it?" said Mr. Arnold, hastily.

Euphra flashed at him once more, covertly.

"I only know that this is the ring in her portrait. Any one may see that it is a very wonderful ring indeed, by only looking at it," answered Hugh, smiling.

"I hope it is not too wonderful for you to get at the mystery of it, though, Mr. Sutherland?" said Lady Emily.

"Lady Emily is dying to understand the inscription," said Euphrasia.

By this time Hugh was turning it round and round, trying to get a beginning to the legend. But in this he met with a difficulty. The fact was, that the initial letter of the inscription could only be found by looking into the crystal held close to the eye. The words seemed not altogether unknown to him, though the characters were a little strange, and the words themselves were undivided. The dinner bell rang.

"Dear me! how the time goes in your room, Lady Emily!" said Mr. Arnold, who was never known to keep dinner waiting a moment. "Will you venture to go down with us to–day?"

"I fear I must not to–day. To–morrow, I hope. But do put up these beauties before you go. I dare not touch them without you, and it is so much more pleasure seeing them, when I have you to tell me about them."

"Well, throw them in," said Mr. Arnold, pretending an indifference he did not feel. "The reality of dinner must not be postponed to the fancy of jewels."

All this time Hugh had stood poring over the ring at the window, whither he had taken it for better light, as the shadows were falling. Euphra busied herself replacing everything in the box. When all were in, she hastily shut the lid.

"Well, Mr. Sutherland?" said Mr. Arnold.

"I seem on the point of making it out, Mr. Arnold, but I certainly have not succeeded yet."

"Confess yourself vanquished, then, and come to dinner."

"I am very unwilling to give in, for I feel convinced that if I had leisure to copy the inscription as far as I can read it, I should, with the help of my dictionary, soon supply the rest. I am very unwilling, as well, to lose a chance of the favour of Lady Emily."

"Yes, do read it, if you can. I too am dying to hear it," said Euphra.

"Will you trust me with it, Mr. Arnold? I will take the greatest care of it."

"Oh, certainly!" replied Mr. Arnold—with a little hesitation in his tone, however, of which Hugh was too eager to take any notice.

He carried it to his room immediately, and laid it beside his manuscript verses, in the hiding–place of the old escritoire. He was in the drawing–room a moment after.

There he found Euphra and the Bohemian alone.—Von Funkelstein had, in an incredibly short space of time, established himself as Hausfreund, and came and went as he pleased.—They looked as if they had been interrupted in a hurried and earnest conversation—their faces were so impassive. Yet Euphra's wore a considerably heightened colour—a more articulate indication. She could school her features, but not her complexion.

CHAPTER XXIII. THE WAGER.

```
    He...stakes this ring;
And would so, had it been a carbuncle
Of Pheobus' wheel; and might so safely, had it
Been all the worth of his car.

Cymbeline.
```

Hugh, of course, had an immediate attack of jealousy. Wishing to show it in one quarter, and hide it in every other, he carefully abstained from looking once in the direction of

Euphra; while, throughout the dinner, he spoke to every one else as often as there was the smallest pretext for doing so. To enable himself to keep this up, he drank wine freely. As he was in general very moderate, by the time the ladies rose, it had begun to affect his brain. It was not half so potent, however, in its influences, as the parting glance which Euphra succeeded at last, as she left the room, in sending through his eyes to his heart.

Hugh sat down to the table again, with a quieter tongue, but a busier brain. He drank still, without thinking of the consequences. A strong will kept him from showing any signs of intoxication, but he was certainly nearer to that state than he had ever been in his life before.

The Bohemian started the new subject which generally follows the ladies' departure.

"How long is it since Arnstead was first said to be haunted, Mr. Arnold?"

"Haunted! Herr von Funkelstein? I am at a loss to understand you," replied Mr. Arnold, who resented any such allusion, being subversive of the honour of his house, almost as much as if it had been depreciative of his own.

"I beg your pardon, Mr. Arnold. I thought it was an open subject of remark."

"So it is," said Hugh; "every one knows that."

Mr. Arnold was struck dumb with indignation. Before he had recovered himself sufficiently to know what to say, the conversation between the other two had assumed a form to which his late experiences inclined him to listen with some degree of interest. But, his pride sternly forbidding him to join in it, he sat sipping his wine in careless sublimity.

"You have seen it yourself, then?" said the Bohemian.

"I did not say that," answered Hugh. "But I heard one of the maids say once—when—"

He paused.

David Elginbrod

This hesitation of his witnessed against him afterwards, in Mr. Arnold's judgment. But he took no notice now.—Hugh ended tamely enough:

"Why, it is commonly reported amongst the servants."

"With a blue light?—Such as we saw that night from the library window, I suppose."

"I did not say that," answered Hugh. "Besides, it was nothing of the sort you saw from the library. It was only the moon. But—"

He paused again. Von Funkelstein saw the condition he was in, and pressed him.

"You know something more, Mr. Sutherland."

Hugh hesitated again, but only for a moment.

"Well, then," he said, "I have seen the spectre myself, walking in her white grave–clothes, in the Ghost's Avenue—ha! ha!"

Funkelstein looked anxious.

"Were you frightened?" said he.

"Frightened!" repeated Hugh, in a tone of the greatest contempt. "I am of Don Juan's opinion with regard to such gentry."

"What is that?"

> "'That soul and body, on the whole,
>   Are odds against a disembodied soul.'"

"Bravo!" cried the count. "You despise all these tales about Lady Euphrasia, wandering about the house with a death–candle in her hand, looking everywhere about as if she had lost something, and couldn't find it?"

"Pooh! pooh! I wish I could meet her!"

259

David Elginbrod

"Then you don't believe a word of it?"

"I don't say that. There would be less of courage than boasting in talking so, if I did not believe a word of it."

"Then you do believe it?"

But Hugh was too much of a Scotchman to give a hasty opinion, or rather a direct answer—even when half-tipsy; especially when such was evidently desired. He only shook and nodded his head at the same moment.

"Do you really mean you would meet her if you could?"

"I do."

"Then, if all tales are true, you may, without much difficulty. For the coachman told me only to-day, that you may see her light in the window of that room almost any night, towards midnight. He told me, too (for I made quite a friend of him to-day, on purpose to hear his tales), that one of the maids, who left the other day, told the groom—and he told the coachman—that she had once heard talking; and, peeping through the key-hole of a door that led into that part of the old house, saw a figure, dressed exactly like the picture of Lady Euphrasia, wandering up and down, wringing her hands and beating her breast, as if she were in terrible trouble. She had a light in her hand which burned awfully blue, and her face was the face of a corpse, with pale-green spots."

"You think to frighten me, Funkelstein, and make me tremble at what I said a minute ago. Instead of repeating that. I say now: I will sleep in Lady Euphrasia's room this night, if you like."

"I lay you a hundred guineas you won't!" cried the Bohemian.

"Done!" said Hugh, offering him his hand. Funkelstein took it; and so the bet was committed to the decision of courage.

"Well, gentlemen," interposed Mr. Arnold at last, "you might have left a corner for me somewhere. Without my permission you will hardly settle your wager."

David Elginbrod

"I beg your pardon, Mr. Arnold," said Funkelstein. "We got rather excited over it, and forgot our manners. But I am quite willing to give it up, if Mr. Sutherland will."

"Not I," said Hugh;—"that is, of course, if Mr. Arnold has no objection."

"Of course not. My house, ghost and all, is at your service, gentlemen," responded Mr. Arnold, rising.

They went to the drawing-room. Mr. Arnold, strange to say, was in a good humour. He walked up to Mrs. Elton, and said:

"These wicked men have been betting, Mrs. Elton."

"I am surprised they should be so silly," said she, with a smile, taking it as a joke.

"What have they been betting about?" said Euphra, coming up to her uncle.

"Herr von Funkelstein has laid a hundred guineas that Mr. Sutherland will not sleep in Lady Euphrasia's room to-night."

Euphra turned pale.

"By sleep I suppose you mean spend the night?" said Hugh to Funkelstein. "I cannot be certain of sleeping, you know."

"Of course, I mean that," answered the other; and, turning to Euphrasia, continued:

"I must say I consider it rather courageous of him to dare the spectre as he does, for he cannot say he disbelieves in her. But come and sing me one of the old songs," he added, in an under tone.

Euphra allowed him to lead her to the piano; but instead of singing a song to him, she played some noisy music, through which he and she contrived to talk for some time, without being overheard; after which he left the room. Euphra then looked round to Hugh, and begged him with her eyes to come to her. He could not resist, burning with jealousy as he was.

261

"Are you sure you have nerve enough for this, Hugh?" she said, still playing.

"I have had nerve enough to sit still and look at you for the last half hour," answered Hugh, rudely.

She turned pale, and glanced up at him with a troubled look. Then, without responding to his answer, said:

"I daresay the count is not over−anxious to hold you to your bet."

"Pray intercede for me with the count, madam," answered Hugh, sarcastically. "He would not wish the young fool to be frightened, I daresay. But perhaps he wishes to have an interview with the ghost himself, and grudges me the privilege."

She turned deadly pale this time, and gave him one terrified glance, but made no other reply to his words. Still she played on.

"You will arm yourself?"

"Against a ghost? Yes, with a stout heart."

"But don't forget the secret door through which we came that night, Hugh. I distrust the count."

The last words were spoken in a whisper, emphasized into almost a hiss.

"Tell him I shall be armed. I tell you I shall meet him bare−handed. Betray me if you like."

Hugh had taken his revenge, and now came the reaction. He gazed at Euphra; but instead of the injured look, which was the best he could hope to see, an expression of "pity and ruth" grew slowly in her face, making it more lovely than ever in his eyes. At last she seemed on the point of bursting into tears; and, suddenly changing the music, she began playing a dead−march. She kept her eyes on the keys. Once more, only, she glanced round, to see whether Hugh was still by her side; and he saw that her face was pale as death, and wet with silent tears. He had never seen her weep before. He would have fallen at her feet, had he been alone with her. To hide his feelings, he left the room, and then the house.

He wandered into the Ghost's Walk; and, finding himself there, walked up and down in it. This was certainly throwing the lady a bold challenge, seeing he was going to spend the night in her room.

The excitement into which jealousy had thrown him, had been suddenly checked by the sight of Euphra's tears. The reaction, too, after his partial intoxication, had already begun to set in; to be accounted for partly by the fact that its source had been chiefly champagne, and partly by the other fact, that he had bound himself in honour, to dare a spectre in her own favourite haunt.

On the other hand, the sight of Euphra's emotion had given him a far better courage than jealousy or wine could afford. Yet, after ten minutes passed in the shadows of the Ghost's Walk, he would not have taken the bet at ten times its amount.

But to lose it now would have been a serious affair for him, the disgrace of failure unconsidered. If he could have lost a hundred guineas, it would have been comparatively a slight matter; but to lose a bet, and be utterly unable to pay it, would be disgraceful—no better than positive cheating. He had not thought of this at the time. Nor, even now, was it more than a passing thought; for he had not the smallest desire to recede. The ambition of proving his courage to Euphra, and, far more, the strength just afforded him by the sight of her tears, were quite sufficient to carry him on to the ordeal. Whether they would carry him through it with dignity, he did not ask himself.

And, after all, would the ghost appear? At the best, she might not come; at the very worst, she would be but a ghost; and he could say with Hamlet—

```
    "for my soul, what can it do to that,
 Being a thing as immortal as itself?"
```

But then, his jealousy having for the moment intermitted, Hugh was not able to say with Hamlet—

```
 "I do not set my life at a pin's fee;"
```

and that had much to do with Hamlet's courage in the affair of the ghost.

He walked up and down the avenue, till, beginning to feel the night chilly, he began to feel the avenue eerie; for cold is very antagonistic to physical courage. But what refuge would he find in the ghost's room?

He returned to the drawing—room. Von Funkelstein and Euphra were there alone, but in no proximity. Mr. Arnold soon entered.

"Shall I have the bed prepared for you, Mr. Sutherland?" said Euphra.

"Which of your maids will you persuade to that office?" said Mr. Arnold, with a facetious expression.

"I must do it myself," answered Euphra, "if Mr. Sutherland persists."

Hugh saw, or thought he saw, the Bohemian dart an angry glance at Euphra, who shrank under it. But before he could speak, Mr. Arnold rejoined:

"You can make a bed, then? That is the housemaid's phrase, is it not?"

"I can do anything another can, uncle."

"Bravo! Can you see the ghost?"

"Yes," she answered, with a low lingering on the sibilant; looking round, at the same time, with an expression that implied a hope that Hugh had heard it; as indeed he had.

"What! Euphra too?" said Mr. Arnold, in a tone of gentle contempt.

"Do not disturb the ghost's bed for me," said Hugh. "It would be a pity to disarrange it, after it has lain so for an age. Besides, I need not rouse the wrath of the poor spectre more than can't be helped. If I must sleep in her room, I need not sleep in her bed. I will lie on the old couch. Herr von Funkelstein, what proof shall I give you?"

"Your word, Mr. Sutherland," replied Funkelstein, with a bow.

David Elginbrod

"Thank you. At what hour must I be there."

"Oh! I don't know. By eleven I should think. Oh! any time before midnight. That's the ghost's own, is it not? It is now—let me see—almost ten."

"Then I will go at once," said Hugh, thinking it better to meet the gradual approach of the phantom-hour in the room itself, than to walk there through the desolate house, and enter the room just as the fear would be gathering thickest within it. Besides, he was afraid that his courage might have broken down a little by that time, and that he would not be able to conceal entirely the anticipative dread, whose inroad he had reason to apprehend.

"I have one good cup of tea yet, Mr. Sutherland," said Euphra. "Will you not strengthen your nerves with that, before we lead you to the tomb?"

"Then she will go with me," thought Hugh. "I will, thank you, Miss Cameron."

He approached the table at which she stood pouring out the cup of tea. She said, low and hurriedly, without raising her head:

"Don't go, dear Hugh. You don't know what may happen."

"I will go, Euphra. Not even you shall prevent me."

"I will pay the wager for you—lend you the money."

"Euphra!"—The tone implied many things.

Mr. Arnold approached. Other conversation followed. As half-past ten chimed from the clock on the chimney-piece, Hugh rose to go.

"I will just get a book from my room," he said; "and then perhaps Herr von Funkelstein will be kind enough to see me make a beginning at least."

"Certainly I will. And I advise you to let the book be Edgar Poe's Tales."

"No. I shall need all the courage I have, I assure you. I shall find you here?"

"Yes."

Hugh went to his room, and washed his face and hands. Before doing so, he pulled off his finger a ring of considerable value, which had belonged to his father. As he was leaving the room to return to the company, he remembered that he had left the ring on the washhand–stand. He generally left it there at night; but now he bethought himself that, as he was not going to sleep in the room, it might be as well to place it in the escritoire. He opened the secret place, and laid the diamond beside his poems and the crystal ring belonging to Mr. Arnold. This done, he took up his book again, and, returning to the drawing–room, found the whole party prepared to accompany him. Mr. Arnold had the keys. Von Funkelstein and he went first, and Hugh followed with Euphra.

"We will not contribute to your discomfiture by locking the doors on the way, Mr. Sutherland," said Mr. Arnold.

"That is, you will not compel me to win the wager in spite of my fears," said Hugh.

"But you will let the ghost loose on the household," said the Bohemian, laughing.

"I will be responsible for that," replied Mr. Arnold.

Euphra dropped a little behind with Hugh.

"Remember the secret passage," said she. "You can get out when you will, whether they lock the door, or not. Don't carry it too far, Hugh."

"The ghost you mean, Euphra.—I don't think I shall," said Hugh, laughing. But as he laughed, an involuntary shudder passed through him.

"Have I stepped over my own grave?" thought he.

They reached the room, and entered. Hugh would have begged them to lock him in, had he not felt that his knowledge of the secret door, would, although he intended no use of it, render such a proposal dishonourable. They gave him the key of the door, to lock it on the inside, and bade him good night. They were just leaving him, when Hugh on whom a new light had broken at last, in the gradual restoration of his faculties, said to the

266

Bohemian:

"One word with you, Herr von Funkelstein, if you please."

Funkelstein followed him into the room; when Hugh half–closing the door, said:

"I trust to your sympathy, as gentleman, not to misunderstand me. I wagered a hundred guineas with you in the heat of after–dinner talk. I am not at present worth a hundred shillings."

"Oh!" began Funkelstein, with a sneer, "if you wish to get off on that ground—"

"Herr von Funkelstein," interrupted Hugh, in a very decided tone, "I pointed to your sympathy as a gentleman, as the ground on which I had hoped to meet you now. If you have difficulty in finding that ground, another may be found to–morrow without much seeking."

Hugh paused for a moment after making this grand speech; but Funkelstein did not seem to understand him: he stood in a waiting attitude. Hugh therefore went on:

"Meantime, what I wanted to say is this:—I have just left a ring in my room, which, though in value considerably below the sum mentioned between us, may yet be a pledge of my good faith, in as far as it is of infinitely more value to me than can be reckoned in money. It was the property of one who by birth, and perhaps by social position as well, was Herr von Funkelstein's equal. The ring is a diamond, and belonged to my father."

Von Funkelstein merely replied:

"I beg your pardon, Mr. Sutherland, for misunderstanding you. The ring is quite an equivalent." And making him a respectful bow, he turned and left him.

CHAPTER XXIV. THE LADY EUPHRASIA.

The black jades of swart night trot foggy rings
'Bout heaven's brow. 'Tis now stark dead night.

David Elginbrod

As soon as Hugh was alone, his first action was to lock the door by which he had entered; his next to take the key from the lock, and put it in his pocket. He then looked if there were any other fastenings, and finding an old tarnished brass bolt as well, succeeded in making it do its duty for the first time that century, which required some persuasion, as may be supposed. He then turned towards the other door. As he crossed the room, he found four candles, a decanter of port, and some biscuits, on a table—placed there, no doubt, by the kind hands of Euphra. He vowed to himself that he would not touch the wine. "I have had enough of that for one night," said he. But he lighted the candles; and then saw that the couch was provided with plenty of wraps for the night. One of them—he recognised to his delight—was a Cameron tartan, often worn by Euphra. He buried his face in it for a moment, and drew from it fresh courage. He then went into the furthest recess, lifted the tapestry, and proceeded to fasten the concealed door. But, to his discomfiture, he could find no fastening upon it. "No doubt," thought he, "it does fasten, in some secret way or other." But he could discover none. There was no mark of bolt or socket to show whence one had been removed, nor sign of friction to indicate that the door had ever been made secure in such fashion. It closed with a spring.

"Then," said Hugh, apostrophising the door, "I must watch you."

As, however, it was not yet near the time when ghosts are to be expected, and as he felt very tired, he drank one glass of the wine, and throwing himself on the couch, drew Euphra's shawl over him, opened his book, and began to read. But the words soon vanished in a bewildering dance, and he slept.

He started awake in that agony of fear in which I suppose most people have awaked in the night, once or twice in their lives. He felt that he was not alone. But the feeling seemed, when he recalled it, to have been altogether different from that with which we recognise the presence of the most unwelcome bodily visitor. The whole of his nervous skeleton seemed to shudder and contract. Every sense was intensified to the acme of its acuteness; while the powers of volition were inoperative. He could not move a finger.

The moment in which he first saw the object I am about to describe, he could not recall. The impression made seemed to have been too strong for the object receiving it, destroying thus its own traces, as an overheated brand–iron would in dry timber. Or it

David Elginbrod

may be that, after such a pre−sensation, the cause of it could not surprise him.

He saw, a few paces off, bending as if looking down upon him, a face which, if described as he described it, would be pronounced as far past the most liberal boundary−line of art, as itself had passed beyond that degree of change at which a human countenance is fit for the upper world no longer, and must be hidden away out of sight. The lips were dark, and drawn back from the closed teeth, which were white as those of a skull. There were spots—in fact, the face corresponded exactly to the description given by Funkelstein of the reported ghost of Lady Euphrasia. The dress was point for point correspondent to that in the picture. Had the portrait of Lady Euphrasia been hanging on the wall above, instead of the portrait of the unknown nun, Hugh would have thought, as far as dress was concerned, that it had come alive, and stepped from its frame—except for one thing: there was no ring on the thumb.

It was wonderful to himself afterwards, that he should have observed all these particulars; but the fact was, that they rather burnt themselves in upon his brain, than were taken notice of by him. They returned upon him afterwards by degrees, as one becomes sensible of the pain of a wound.

But there was one sign of life. Though the eyes were closed, tears flowed from them; and seemed to have worn channels for their constant flow down this face of death, which ought to have been lying still in the grave, returning to its dust, and was weeping above ground instead. The figure stood for a moment, as one who would gaze, could she but open her heavy, death−rusted eyelids. Then, as if in hopeless defeat, she turned away. And then, to crown the horror literally as well as figuratively, Hugh saw that her hair sparkled and gleamed goldenly, as the hair of a saint might, if the aureole were combed down into it. She moved towards the door with a fettered pace, such as one might attribute to the dead if they walked;—to the dead body, I say, not to the living ghost; to that which has lain in the prison−hold, till the joints are decayed with the grave−damps, and the muscles are stiff with more than deathly cold. She dragged one limb after the other slowly and, to appearance, painfully, as she moved towards the door which Hugh had locked.

When she had gone half−way to the door, Hugh, lying as he was on a couch, could see her feet, for her dress did not reach the ground. They were bare, as the feet of the dead ought to be, which are about to tread softly in the realm of Hades, But how stained and

269

mouldy and iron—spotted, as if the rain had been soaking through the spongy coffin, did the dress show beside the pure whiteness of those exquisite feet! Not a sign of the tomb was upon them. Small, living, delicately formed, Hugh, could he have forgot the face they bore above, might have envied the floor which in their nakedness they seemed to caress, so lingeringly did they move from it in their noiseless progress.

She reached the door, put out her hand, and touched it. Hugh saw it open outwards and let her through. Nor did this strike him as in the smallest degree marvellous. It closed again behind her, noiseless as her footfalls.

The moment she vanished, the power of motion returned to him, and Hugh sprang to his feet. He leaped to the door. With trembling hand he inserted the key, and the lock creaked as he turned it.

In proof of his being in tolerable possession of his faculties at the moment, and that what he was relating to me actually occurred, he told me that he remembered at once that he had heard that peculiar creak, a few moments before Euphra and he discovered that they were left alone in this very chamber. He had never thought of it before.

Still the door would not open: it was bolted as well, and the bolt was very stiff to withdraw. But at length he succeeded.

When he reached the passage outside, he thought he saw the glimmer of a light, perhaps in the picture—gallery beyond. Towards this he groped his way.—He could never account for the fact, that he left the candles burning in the room behind him and went forward into the darkness, except by supposing that his wits had gone astray, in consequence of the shock the apparition had occasioned them.—When he reached the gallery, there was no light there; but somewhere in the distance he saw, or fancied, a faint shimmer.

The impulse to go towards it was too strong to be disputed with. He advanced with outstretched arms, groping. After a few steps, he had lost all idea of where he was, or how he ought to proceed in order to reach any known quarter. The light had vanished. He stood.—Was that a stealthy step he heard beside him in the dark? He had no time to speculate, for the next moment he fell senseless.

CHAPTER XXV. NEXT MORNING.

Darkness is fled: look, infant morn hath drawn
Bright silver curtains 'bout the couch of night;
And now Aurora's horse trots azure rings,
Breathing fair light about the firmament.
Stand; what's that?

JOHN MARSTON.—Second Part of Antonio and Mellida.

When he came to himself, it was with a slow flowing of the tide of consciousness. His head ached. Had he fallen down stairs?—or had he struck his head against some projection, and so stunned himself? The last he remembered was—standing quite still in the dark, and hearing something. Had he been knocked down? He could not tell.—Where was he? Could the ghost have been all a dream? and this headache be nature's revenge upon last night's wine?—For he lay on the couch in the haunted chamber, and on his bosom lay the book over which he had dropped asleep.

Mingled with all this doubt, there was another. For he remembered that, when consciousness first returned, he felt as if he had seen Euphra's face bending down close over his.—Could it be possible? Had Euphra herself come to see how he had fared?—The room lay in the grey light of the dawn, but Euphra was nowhere visible. Could she have vanished ashamed through the secret door? Or had she been only a phantasy, a projection outwards of the form that dwelt in his brain; a phenomenon often occurring when the last of sleeping and the first of waking are indistinguishably blended in a vague consciousness?

But if it was so, then the ghost?—what of it? Had not his brain, by the events of the preceding evening, been similarly prepared with regard to it? Was it not more likely, after all, that she too was the offspring of his own imagination—the power that makes images—especially when considered, that she exactly corresponded to the description given by the Bohemian?—But had he not observed many points at which the Count had not even hinted?—Still, it was as natural to expect that an excited imagination should supply the details of a wholly imaginary spectacle, as that, given the idea of Euphra's presence, it should present the detail of her countenance; for the creation of that which is not, belongs as much to the realm of the imagination, as the reproduction of that which is.

David Elginbrod

It seemed very strange to Hugh himself, that he should be able thus to theorize, before even he had raised himself from the couch on which, perhaps, after all, he had lain without moving, throughout that terrible night, swarming with the horrors of the dead that would not sleep. But the long unconsciousness, in which he had himself visited the regions of death, seemed to have restored him, in spite of his aching head, to perfect mental equilibrium. Or, at least, his brain was quiet enough to let his mind work. Still, he felt very ghastly within. He raised himself on his elbow, and looked into the room. Everything was the same as it had been the night before, only with an altered aspect in the dawn–light. The dawn has a peculiar terror of its own, sometimes perhaps even more real in character, but very different from the terrors of the night and of candle–light. The room looked as if no ghost could have passed through its still old musty atmosphere, so perfectly reposeful did it appear; and yet it seemed as if some umbra, some temporary and now cast–off body of the ghost, must be lying or lingering somewhere about it. He rose, and peeped into the recess where the cabinet stood. Nothing was there but the well remembered carving and blackness. Having once yielded to the impulse, he could not keep from peering every moment, now into one, and now into another of the many hidden corners. The next suggesting itself for examination, was always one he could not see from where he stood:—after all, even in the daylight, there might be some dead thing there—who could tell? But he remained manfully at his post till the sun rose; till bell after bell rang from the turret; till, in short, Funkelstein came to fetch him.

"Good morning, Mr. Sutherland," said he. "How have you slept?"

"Like a—somnambulist," answered Hugh, choosing the word for its intensity. "I slept so sound that I woke quite early."

"I am glad to hear it. But it is nearly time for breakfast, for which ceremony I am myself hardly in trim yet."

So saying, Funkelstein turned, and walked away with some precipitation. What occasioned Hugh a little surprise; was, that he did not ask him one question more as to how he had passed the night. He had, of course, slept in the house, seeing he presented himself in deshabille.

Hugh hastened to his own room, where, under the anti–ghostial influences of the bath, he made up his mind not to say a word about the apparition to any one.

David Elginbrod

"Well, Mr. Sutherland, how have you spent the night?" said Mr. Arnold, greeting him.

"I slept with profound stupidity," answered Hugh; "a stupidity, in fact, quite worthy of the folly of the preceding wager."

This was true, as relating to the time during which he had slept, but was, of course, false in the impression it gave.

"Bravo!" exclaimed Mr. Arnold, with an unwonted impulsiveness. "The best mood, I consider, in which to meet such creations of other people's brains! And you positively passed a pleasant night in the awful chamber? That is something to tell Euphra. But she is not down yet. You have restored the character of my house, Mr. Sutherland; and next to his own character, a man ought to care for that of his house. I am greatly in your debt, sir."

At this moment, Euphra's maid brought the message, that her mistress was sorry she was unable to appear at breakfast.

Mrs. Elton took her place.

"The day is so warm and still, Mr. Arnold, that I think Lady Emily might have a drive to-day. Perhaps Miss Cameron may be able to join us by that time."

"I cannot think what is the matter with Euphra," said Mr. Arnold. "She never used to be affected in this way."

"Should you not seek some medical opinion?" said Mrs. Elton. "These constant headaches must indicate something wrong."

The constant headache had occurred just once before, since Mrs. Elton had formed one of the family. After a pause, Mr. Arnold reverted to the former subject.

"You are most welcome to the carriage, Mrs. Elton. I am sorry I cannot accompany you myself; but I must go to town to-day. You can take Mr. Sutherland with you, if you like. He will take care of you."

"I shall be most happy," said Hugh.

"So shall we all," responded Mrs. Elton kindly. "Thank you, Mr. Arnold; though I am sorry you can't go with us."

"What hour shall I order the carriage?"

"About one, I think. Will Herr von Funkelstein favour us with his company?"

"I am sorry," replied Funkelstein; "but I too must leave for London to–day. Shall I have the pleasure of accompanying you, Mr. Arnold?"

"With all my heart, if you can leave so early. I must go at once to catch the express train."

"I shall be ready in ten minutes."

"Very well."

"Pray, Mrs. Elton, make my adieus to Miss Cameron. I am concerned to hear of her indisposition."

"With pleasure. I am going to her now. Good–bye."

As soon as Mrs. Elton left the breakfast–room, Mr. Arnold rose, saying:

"I will walk round to the stable, and order the carriage myself. I shall then be able, through your means, Mr. Sutherland, to put a stop to these absurd rumours in person. Not that I mean to say anything direct, as if I placed any importance upon it; but, the coachman being an old servant, I shall be able through him, to send the report of your courage and its result, all over the house."

This was a very gracious explanation of his measures. As he concluded it, he left the room, without allowing time for a reply.

Hugh had not expected such an immediate consequence of his policy, and felt rather uncomfortable; but he soon consoled himself by thinking, "At least it will do no harm."

While Mr. Arnold was speaking, Funkelstein had been writing at a side–table. He now handed Hugh a cheque on a London banking–house for a hundred guineas. Hugh, in his innocence, could not help feeling ashamed of gaining such a sum by such means; for betting, like tobacco–smoking, needs a special training before it can be carried out quite comfortably, especially by the winner, if he be at all of a generous nature. But he felt that to show the least reluctance would place him at great disadvantage with a man of the world like the count. He therefore thanked him slightly, and thrust the cheque into his trowsers–pocket, as if a greater sum of money than he had ever handled before were nothing more for him to win, than the count would choose it to be considered for him to lose. He thought with himself: "Ah! well, I need not make use of it;" and repaired to the school–room.

Here he found Harry waiting for him, looking tolerably well, and tolerably happy. This was a great relief to Hugh, for he had not seen him at the breakfast–table—Harry having risen early and breakfasted before; and he had felt very uneasy lest the boy should have missed him in the night (for they were still bed–fellows), and should in consequence have had one of his dreadful attacks of fear.—It was evident that this had not taken place.

CHAPTER XXVI. AN ACCIDENT.

```
There's a special providence in the fall of a sparrow.
```

```
Hamlet.
```

When Mrs. Elton left the breakfast table, she went straight to Miss Cameron's room to inquire after her, expecting to find her maid with her. But when she knocked at the door, there was no reply.

She went therefore to her own room, and sent her maid to find Euphra's maid.

She came.

"Is your mistress going to get up to–day, Jane?" asked Mrs. Elton.

"I don't know, ma'am. She has not rung yet."

David Elginbrod

"Have you not been to see how she is?"

"No, ma'am."

"How was it you brought that message at breakfast, then?"

Jane looked confused, and did not reply.

"Jane!" said Mrs. Elton, in a tone of objurgation.

"Well, ma'am, she told me to say so," answered Jane.

"How did she tell you?"

Jane paused again.

"Through the door, ma'am," she answered at length; and then muttered, that they would make her tell lies by asking her questions she couldn't answer; and she wished she was out of the house, that she did.

Mrs. Elton heard this, and, of course, felt considerably puzzled.

"Will you go now, please, and inquire after your mistress, with my compliments?"

"I daren't, ma'am."

"Daren't! What do you mean?"

"Well, ma'am, there is something about my mistress—" Here she stopped abruptly; but as Mrs. Elton stood expectant, she tried to go on. All she could add, however, was—"No, ma'am; I daren't."

"But there is no harm in going to her room."

"Oh, no, ma'am. I go to her room, summer and winter, at seven o'clock every morning," answered Jane, apparently glad to be able to say something.

David Elginbrod

"Why won't you go now, then?"

"Why—why—because she told me—" Here the girl stammered and turned pale. At length she forced out the words—"She won't let me tell you why," and burst into tears.

"Won't let you tell me?" repeated Mrs. Elton, beginning to think the girl must be out of her mind. Jane looked hurriedly over her shoulder, as if she expected to see her mistress standing behind her, and then said, almost defiantly:

"No, she won't; and I can't."

With these words, she hurried out of the room, while Mrs. Elton turned with baffled bewilderment to seek counsel from the face of Margaret. As to what all this meant, I am in doubt. I have recorded it as Margaret told it to Hugh afterwards—because it seems to indicate something. It shows evidently enough, that if Euphra had more than a usual influence over servants in general, she had a great deal more over this maid in particular. Was this in virtue of a power similar to that of Count Halkar over herself? And was this, or something very different, or both combined, the art which he had accused her of first exercising upon him? Might the fact that her defeat had resulted in such absolute subjection, be connected with her possession of a power similar to his, which she had matched with his in vain? Of course I only suggest these questions. I cannot answer them.

At one o'clock, the carriage came round to the door; and Hugh, in the hope of seeing Euphra alone, was the first in the hall. Mrs. Elton and Lady Emily presently came, and proceeded to take their places, without seeming to expect Miss Cameron. Hugh helped them into the carriage; but, instead of getting in, lingered, hoping that Euphra was yet going to make her appearance.

"I fear Miss Cameron is unable to join us," said Mrs. Elton, divining his delay.

"Shall I run up–stairs, and knock at her door?" said Hugh.

"Do," said Mrs. Elton, who, after the unsatisfactory conversation she had held with her maid, had felt both uneasy and curious, all the morning.

Hugh bounded up-stairs; but, just as he was going to knock, the door opened, and Euphra, appeared.

"Dear Euphra! how ill you look!" exclaimed Hugh.

She was pale as death, and dark under the eyes; and had evidently been weeping.

"Hush! hush!" she answered. "Never mind. It is only a bad headache. Don't take any notice of it."

"The carriage is at the door. Will you not come with us?"

"With whom?"

"Lady Emily and Mrs. Elton."

"I am sick of them."

"I am going, Euphra."

"Stay with me."

"I must go. I promised to take care of them."

"Oh, nonsense! What should happen to them? Stay with me."

"No. I am very sorry. I wish I could."

"Then I must go with you, I suppose." Yet her tone expressed annoyance.

"Oh! thank you," cried Hugh in delight. "Make haste. I will run down, and tell them to wait."

He bounded away, and told the ladies that Euphra would join them in a few minutes.

But Euphra was cool enough to inflict on them quite twenty minutes of waiting; by which time she was able to behave with tolerable propriety. When she did appear at last, she was closely veiled, and stepped into the carriage without once showing her face. But she made a very pretty apology for the delay she had occasioned; which was certainly due, seeing it had been perfectly intentional. She made room for Hugh; he took his place beside her; and away they drove.

Euphra scarcely spoke; but begged indulgence, on the ground of her headache. Lady Emily enjoyed the drive very much, and said a great many pleasant little nothings.

"Would you like a glass of milk?" said Mrs. Elton to her, as they passed a farm–house on the estate.

"I should—very much," answered Lady Emily.

The carriage was stopped, and the servant sent to beg a glass of milk. Euphra, who, from riding backward with a headache, had been feeling very uncomfortable for some time, wished to get out while the carriage was waiting. Hugh jumped out, and assisted her. She walked a little way, leaning on his arm, up to the house, where she had a glass of water; after which she said she felt better, and returned with him to the carriage. In getting in again, either from the carelessness or the weakness occasioned by suffering, her foot slipped from the step, and she fell with a cry of alarm. Hugh caught her as she fell; and she would not have been much injured, had not the horses started and sprung forward at the moment, so that the hind wheel of the carriage passed over her ankle. Hugh, raising her in his arms, found she was insensible.

He laid her down upon the grass by the roadside. Water was procured, but she showed no sign of recovering.—What was to be done? Mrs. Elton thought she had better be carried to the farm–house. Hugh judged it better to take her home at once. To this, after a little argument, Mrs. Elton agreed.

They lifted her into the carriage, and made what arrangements they best could to allow her to recline. Blood was flowing from her foot; and it was so much swollen that it was impossible to guess at the amount of the injury. The foot was already twice the size of the other, in which Hugh for the first time recognised such a delicacy of form, as, to his fastidious eye and already ensnared heart, would have been perfectly enchanting, but for the agony he suffered from the injury to the other. Yet he could not help the thought crossing his mind, that her habit of never lifting her dress was a very strange one, and that it must have had something to do with the present accident. I cannot account for this habit, but on one of two suppositions; that of an affected delicacy, or that of the desire that the beauty of her feet should have its full power, from being rarely seen. But it was dreadful to think how far the effects of this accident might permanently injure the beauty of one of them.

Hugh would have walked home that she might have more room, but he knew he could be useful when they arrived. He seated himself so as to support the injured foot, and prevent, in some measure, the torturing effects of the motion of the carriage. When they had gone about half—way, she opened her eyes feebly, glanced at him, and closed them again with a moan of pain.

He carried her in his arms up to her own room, and laid her on a couch. She thanked him by a pitiful attempt at a smile. He mounted his horse, and galloped for a surgeon.

The injury was a serious one; but until the swelling could be a little reduced, it was impossible to tell how serious. The surgeon, however, feared that some of the bones of the ankle might be crushed. The ankle seemed to be dislocated, and the suffering was frightful. She endured it well, however—so far as absolute silence constitutes endurance.

Hugh's misery was extreme. The surgeon had required his assistance; but a suitable nurse soon arrived, and there was no pretext for his further presence in the sick chamber. He wandered about the grounds. Harry haunted his steps like a spaniel. The poor boy felt it much; and the suffering abstraction of Hugh sealed up his chief well of comfort. At length he went to Mrs. Elton, who did her best to console him.

By the surgeon's express orders, every one but the nurse was excluded from Euphra's room.

CHAPTER XXVII. MORE TROUBLES.

```
    Come on and do your best
To fright me with your sprites: you're powerful at it.
```

David Elginbrod

```
You smell this business with a sense as cold
As is a dead man's nose.
```

```
A Winter's Tale.
```

When Mr. Arnold came home to dinner, and heard of the accident, his first feeling, as is the case with weak men, was one of mingled annoyance and anger. Hugh was the chief object of it; for had he not committed the ladies to his care? And the economy of his house being partially disarranged by it, had he not a good right to be angry? His second feeling was one of concern for his niece, which was greatly increased when he found that she was not in a state to see him. Still, nothing must interfere with the order of things; and when Hugh went into the drawing–room at the usual hour, he found Mr. Arnold standing there in tail coat and white neck–cloth, looking as if he had just arrived at a friend's house, to make one of a stupid party. And the party which sat down to dinner was certainly dreary enough, consisting only, besides the host himself, of Mrs. Elton, Hugh, and Harry. Lady Emily had had exertion enough for the day, and had besides shared in the shock of Euphra's misfortune.

Mr. Arnold was considerably out of humour, and ready to pounce upon any object of complaint. He would have attacked Hugh with a pompous speech on the subject of his carelessness, but he was rather afraid of his tutor now;—so certainly will the stronger get the upper hand in time. He did not even refer to the subject of the accident. Therefore, although it filled the minds of all at table, it was scarcely more than alluded to. But having nothing at hand to find fault with more suitable, he laid hold of the first wise remark volunteered by good Mrs. Elton; whereupon an amusing pas de deux immediately followed; for it could not be called a duel, inasmuch as each antagonist kept skipping harmlessly about the other, exploding theological crackers, firmly believed by the discharger to be no less than bomb–shells. At length Mrs. Elton withdrew.

"By the way, Mr. Sutherland," said Mr. Arnold, "have you succeeded in deciphering that curious inscription yet? I don't like the ring to remain long out of my own keeping. It is quite an heirloom, I assure you."

Hugh was forced to confess that he had never thought of it again.

"Shall I fetch it at once?" added he.

"Oh! no," replied Mr. Arnold. "I should really like to understand the inscription. To–morrow will do perfectly well."

They went to the drawing–room. Everything was wretched. However many ghosts might be in the house, it seemed to Hugh that there was no soul in it except in one room. The wind sighed fitfully, and the rain fell in slow, soundless showers. Mr. Arnold felt the vacant oppression as well as Hugh. Mrs Elton having gone to Lady Emily's room, he proposed back gammon; and on that surpassing game, the gentlemen expended the best part of two dreary hours. When Hugh reached his room he was too tired and spiritless for any intellectual effort; and, instead of trying to decipher the ring, went to bed, and slept as if there were never a ghost or a woman in the universe.

His first proceeding, after breakfast next day, was to get together his German books; and his next to take out the ring, which was to be subjected to their analytical influences. He went to his desk, and opened the secret place. There he stood fixed.—The ring was gone. His packet of papers was there, rather crumpled: the ring was nowhere. What had become of it? It was not long before a conclusion suggested itself. It flashed upon him all at once.

"The ghost has got it," he said, half aloud. "It is shining now on her dead finger. It was Lady Euphrasia. She was going for it then. It wasn't on her thumb when she went. She came back with it, shining through the dark—stepped over me, perhaps, as I lay on the floor in her way."

He shivered, like one in an ague–fit.

Again and again, with that frenzied, mechanical motion, which, like the eyes of a ghost, has "no speculation" in it, he searched the receptacle, although it freely confessed its emptiness to any asking eye. Then he stood gazing, and his heart seemed to stand still likewise.

But a new thought stung him, turning him almost sick with a sense of loss. Suddenly and frantically he dived his hand into the place yet again, useless as he knew the search to be. He took up his papers, and scattered them loose. It was all unavailing: his father's ring was gone as well.

He sank on a chair for a moment; but, instantly recovering, found himself, before he was quite aware of his own resolution, halfway down stairs, on his way to Mr. Arnold's room. It was empty. He rang for his servant. Mr. Arnold had gone away on horseback, and would not be home till dinner time. Counsel from Mrs. Elton was hopeless. Help from Euphra he could not ask. He returned to his own room. There he found Harry waiting for him. His neglected pupil was now his only comforter. Such are the revenges of divine goodness.

"Harry!" he said, "I have been robbed."

"Robbed!" cried Harry, starting up. "Never mind, Mr. Sutherland; my papa's a justice of the peace. He'll catch the thief for you."

"But it's your papa's ring that they've stolen. He lent it to me, and what if he should not believe me?"

"Not believe you, Mr. Sutherland? But he must believe you. I will tell him all about it; and he knows I never told him a lie in my life."

"But you don't know anything about it, Harry."

"But you will tell me, won't you?"

Hugh could not help smiling with pleasure at the confidence his pupil placed in him. He had not much fear about being believed, but, at the best, it was an unpleasant occurrence.

The loss of his own ring not only added to his vexation, but to his perplexity as well. What could she want with his ring? Could she have carried with her such a passion for jewels, as to come from the grave to appropriate those of others as well as to reclaim her own? Was this her comfort in Hades, 'poor ghost'?

Would it be better to tell Mr. Arnold of the loss of both rings, or should he mention the crystal only? He came to the conclusion that it would only exasperate him the more, and perhaps turn suspicion upon himself, if he communicated the fact that he too was a loser, and to such an extent; for Hugh's ring was worth twenty of the other, and was certainly as sacred as Mr. Arnold's, if not so ancient. He would bear it in silence. If the one could not be found, there could certainly be no hope of the other.

Punctual as the clock, Mr. Arnold returned. It did not prejudice him in favour of the reporter of bad tidings, that he begged a word with him before dinner, when that was on the point of being served. It was, indeed, exceeding impolitic; but Hugh would have felt like an impostor, had he sat down to the table before making his confession.

"Mr. Arnold, I am sorry to say I have been robbed, and in your house, too."

"In my house? Of what, pray, Mr. Sutherland?"

Mr. Arnold had taken the information as some weak men take any kind of information referring to themselves or their belongings—namely, as an insult. He drew himself up, and lowered portentously.

"Of your ring, Mr. Arnold."

"Of—my—ring?"

And he looked at his ring–finger, as if he could not understand the import of Hugh's words.

"Of the ring you lent me to decipher," explained Hugh.

"Do you suppose I do not understand you, Mr. Sutherland? A ring which has been in the family for two hundred years at least! Robbed of it? In my house? You must have been disgracefully careless, Mr. Sutherland. You have lost it."

"Mr. Arnold," said Hugh, with dignity, "I am above using such a subterfuge, even if it were not certain to throw suspicion where it was undeserved."

Mr. Arnold was a gentleman, as far as his self–importance allowed. He did not apologize for what he had said, but he changed his manner at once.

"I am quite bewildered, Mr. Sutherland. It is a very annoying piece of news—for many reasons."

David Elginbrod

"I can show you where I laid it—in the safest corner in my room, I assure you."

"Of course, of course. It is enough you say so. We must not keep the dinner waiting now. But after dinner I shall have all the servants up, and investigate the matter thoroughly."

"So," thought Hugh with himself, "some one will be made a felon of, because the cursed dead go stalking about this infernal house at midnight, gathering their own old baubles. No, that will not do. I must at least tell Mr. Arnold what I know of the doings of the night."

So Mr. Arnold must still wait for his dinner; or rather, which was really of more consequence in the eyes of Mr. Arnold, the dinner must be kept waiting for him. For order and custom were two of Mr. Arnold's divinities; and the economy of his whole nature was apt to be disturbed by any interruption of their laws, such as the postponement of dinner for ten minutes. He was walking towards the door, and turned with some additional annoyance when Hugh addressed him again:

"One moment, Mr. Arnold, if you please."

Mr. Arnold merely turned and waited.

"I fear I shall in some degree forfeit your good opinion by what I am about to say, but I must run the risk."

Mr. Arnold still waited.

"There is more about the disappearance of the ring than I can understand."

"Or I either, Mr. Sutherland."

"But I must tell you what happened to myself, the night that I kept watch in Lady Euphrasia's room."

"You said you slept soundly."

"So I did, part of the time."

"Then you kept back part of the truth?"

"I did."

"Was that worthy of you?"

"I thought it best: I doubted myself."

"What has caused you to change your mind now?"

"This event about the ring."

"What has that to do with it? How do you even know that it was taken on that night?"

"I do not know; for till this morning I had not opened the place where it lay: I only suspect."

"I am a magistrate, Mr. Sutherland: I would rather not be prejudiced by suspicions."

"The person to whom my suspicions refer, is beyond your jurisdiction, Mr. Arnold."

"I do not understand you."

"I will explain myself."

Hugh gave Mr. Arnold a hurried yet circumstantial sketch of the apparition he believed he had seen.

"What am I to judge from all this?" asked he, coldly, almost contemptuously.

"I have told you the facts; of course I must leave the conclusions to yourself, Mr. Arnold; but I confess, for my part, that any disbelief I had in apparitions is almost entirely removed since—"

"Since you dreamed you saw one?"

David Elginbrod

"Since the disappearance of the ring," said Hugh.

"Bah!" exclaimed Mr. Arnold, with indignation. "Can a ghost fetch and carry like a spaniel? Mr. Sutherland, I am ashamed to have such a reasoner for tutor to my son. Come to dinner, and do not let me hear another word of this folly. I beg you will not mention it to any one."

"I have been silent hitherto, Mr. Arnold; but circumstances, such as the commitment of any one on the charge of stealing the ring, might compel me to mention the matter. It would be for the jury to determine whether it was relevant or not."

It was evident that Mr. Arnold was more annoyed at the imputation against the nocturnal habits of his house, than at the loss of the ring, or even its possible theft by one of his servants. He looked at Hugh for a moment as if he would break into a furious rage; then his look gradually changed into one of suspicion, and, turning without another word, he led the way to the dining-room, followed by Hugh. To have a ghost held in his face in this fashion, one bred in his own house, too, when he had positively declared his absolute contempt for every legend of the sort, was more than man could bear. He sat down to dinner in gloomy silence, breaking it only as often as he was compelled to do the duties of a host, which he performed with a greater loftiness of ceremony than usual.

There was no summoning of the servants after dinner, however. Hugh's warning had been effectual. Nor was the subject once more alluded to in Hugh's hearing. No doubt Mr. Arnold felt that something ought to be done; but I presume he could never make up his mind what that something ought to be. Whether any reasons for not prosecuting the inquiry had occurred to him upon further reflection, I am unable to tell. One thing is certain; that from this time he ceased to behave to Hugh with that growing cordiality which he had shown him for weeks past. It was no great loss to Hugh; but he felt it; and all the more, because he could not help associating it with that look of suspicion, the remains of which were still discernible on Mr. Arnold's face. Although he could not determine the exact direction of Mr. Arnold's suspicions, he felt that they bore upon something associated with the crystal ring, and the story of the phantom lady. Consequently, there was little more of comfort for him at Arnstead.

Mr. Arnold, however, did not reveal his change of feeling so much by neglect as by ceremony, which, sooner than anything else, builds a wall of separation between those

287

who meet every day. For the oftener they meet, the thicker and the faster are the bricks and mortar of cold politeness, evidently avoided insults, and subjected manifestations of dislike, laid together.

CHAPTER XXVIII. A BIRD'S-EYE VIEW.

```
O, cocks are crowing a merry midnight,
  I wot the wild-fowls are boding day;
Give me my faith and troth again,
  And let me fare me on my way.

Sae painfully she clam the wa',
  She clam the wa' up after him;
Hosen nor shoon upon her feet,
  She hadna time to put them on.

Scotch Ballad.—Clerk Saunders.
```

Dreary days passed. The reports of Euphra were as favourable as the nature of the injury had left room to expect. Still they were but reports: Hugh could not see her, and the days passed drearily. He heard that the swelling was reduced, and that the ankle was found not to be dislocated, but that the bones were considerably injured, and that the final effect upon the use of the parts was doubtful. The pretty foot lay aching in Hugh's heart. When Harry went to bed, he used to walk out and loiter about the grounds, full of anxious fears and no less anxious hopes. If the night was at all obscure, he would pass, as often as he dared, under Euphra's window; for all he could have of her now was a few rays from the same light that lighted her chamber. Then he would steal away down the main avenue, and thence watch the same light, whose beams, in that strange play which the intellect will keep up in spite of—yet in association with—the heart, made a photo-materialist of him. For he would now no longer believe in the pulsations of an ethereal medium; but—that the very material rays which enlightened Euphra's face, whether she waked or slept, stole and filtered through the blind and the gathered shadows, and entered in bodily essence into the mysterious convolutions of his brain, where his soul and heart sought and found them.

When a week had passed, she was so far recovered as to be able to see Mr. Arnold; from whom Hugh heard, in a somewhat reproachful tone, that she was but the wreck of her former self. It was all that Hugh could do to restrain the natural outbreak of his feelings. A fortnight passed, and she saw Mrs. Elton and Lady Emily for a few moments. They would have left before, but had yielded to Mr. Arnold's entreaty, and were staying till Euphra should be at least able to be carried from her room.

One day, when the visitors were out with Mr. Arnold, Jane brought a message to Hugh, requesting him to walk into Miss Cameron's room, for she wanted to see him. Hugh felt his heart flutter as if doubting whether to stop at once, or to dash through its confining bars. He rose and followed the maid. He stood over Euphra pale and speechless. She lay before him wasted and wan; her eyes twice their former size, but with half their former light; her fingers long and transparent; and her voice low and feeble. She had just raised herself with difficulty to a sitting posture, and the effort had left her more weary.

"Hugh!" she said, kindly.

"Dear Euphra!" he answered, kissing the little hand he held in his.

She looked at him for a little while, and the tears rose in her eyes.

"Hugh, I am a cripple for life."

"God forbid, Euphra!" was all he could reply.

She shook her head mournfully. Then a strange, wild look came in her eyes, and grew till it seemed from them to overflow and cover her whole face with a troubled expression, which increased to a look of dull agony.

"What is the matter, dear Euphra?" said Hugh, in alarm. "Is your foot very painful?"

She made no answer. She was looking fixedly at his hand.

"Shall I call Jane?"

She shook her head.

"Can I do nothing for you?"

"No," she answered, almost angrily.

"Shall I go, Euphra?"

"Yes—yes. Go."

He left the room instantly. But a sharp though stifled cry of despair drew him back at a bound. Euphra had fainted.

He rang the bell for Jane; and lingered till he saw signs of returning consciousness.

What could this mean? He was more perplexed with her than ever he had been. Cunning love, however, soon found a way of explaining it—A way?—Twenty ways—not one of them the way.

Next day, Lady Emily brought him a message from Euphra—not to distress himself about her; it was not his fault.

This message the bearer of it understood to refer to the original accident, as the sender of it intended she should: the receiver interpreted it of the occurrence of the day before, as the sender likewise intended. It comforted him.

It had become almost a habit with Hugh, to ascend the oak tree in the evening, and sit alone, sometimes for hours, in the nest he had built for Harry. One time he took a book with him; another he went without; and now and then Harry accompanied him. But I have already said, that often after tea, when the house became oppressive to him from the longing to see Euphra, he would wander out alone; when, even in the shadows of the coming night, he would sometimes climb the nest, and there sit, hearing all that the leaves whispered about the sleeping birds, without listening to a word of it, or trying to interpret it by the kindred sounds of his own inner world, and the tree–talk that went on there in secret. For the divinity of that inner world had abandoned it for the present, in pursuit of an earthly maiden. So its birds were silent, and its trees trembled not.

An aging moon was feeling her path somewhere through the heavens; but a thin veil of cloud was spread like a tent under the hyaline dome where she walked; so that, instead of a white moon, there was a great white cloud to enlighten the earth,—a cloud soaked full of her pale rays. Hugh sat in the oak–nest. He knew not how long he had been there. Light after light was extinguished in the house, and still he sat there brooding, dreaming, in that state of mind in which to the good, good things come of themselves, and to the evil, evil things. The nearness of the Ghost's Walk did not trouble him, for he was too much concerned about Euphra to fear ghost or demon. His mind heeded them not, and so was beyond their influence.

But while he sat, he became aware of human voices. He looked out from his leafy screen, and saw once more, at the end of the Ghost's Walk, a form clothed in white. But there were voices of two. He sent his soul into his ears to listen. A horrible, incredible, impossible idea forced itself upon him—that the tones were those of Euphra and Funkelstein. The one voice was weak and complaining; the other firm and strong.

"It must be some horrible ghost that imitates her," he said to himself; for he was nearly crazy at the very suggestion.

He would see nearer, if only to get rid of that frightful insinuation of the tempter. He descended the tree noiselessly. He lost sight of the figure as he did so. He drew near the place where he had seen it. But there was no sound of voices now to guide him. As he came within sight of the spot, he saw the white figure in the arms of another, a man. Her head was lying on his shoulder. A moment after, she was lifted in those arms and borne towards the house,—down the Ghost's Avenue.

A burning agony to be satisfied of his doubts seized on Hugh. He fled like a deer to the house by another path; tried, in his suspicion, the library window; found it open, and was at Euphra's door in a moment. Here he hesitated. She must be inside. How dare he knock or enter?

If she was there, she would be asleep. He would not wake her. There was no time to lose. He would risk anything, to be rid of this horrible doubt.

He gently opened the door. The night–light was burning. He thought, at first, that Euphra was in the bed. He felt like a thief, but he stole nearer. She was not there. She was not on the couch. She was not in the room. Jane was fast asleep in the dressing–room. It was enough.

He withdrew. He would watch at his door to see her return, for she must pass his door to reach her own. He waited a time that seemed hours. At length—horrible, far more horrible to him than the vision of the ghost—Euphra crept past him, appearing in the darkness to crawl along the wall against which she supported herself, and scarcely suppressing her groans of pain. She reached her own room, and entering, closed the door.

Hugh was nearly mad. He rushed down the stair to the library, and out into the wood. Why or whither he knew not.

Suddenly he received a blow on the head. It did not stun him, but he staggered under it. Had he run against a tree? No. There was the dim bulk of a man disappearing through the boles. He darted after him. The man heard his footsteps, stopped, and waited in silence. As Hugh came up to him, he made a thrust at him with some weapon. He missed his aim. The weapon passed through his coat and under his arm. The next moment, Hugh had wrenched the sword–stick from him, thrown it away, and grappled with—Funkelstein. But strong as Hugh was, the Bohemian was as strong, and the contest was doubtful. Strange as it may seem—in the midst of it, while each held the other unable to move, the conviction flashed upon Hugh's mind, that, whoever might have taken Lady Euphrasia's ring, he was grappling with the thief of his father's.

"Give me my ring," gasped he.

An imprecation of a sufficiently emphatic character was the only reply. The Bohemian got one hand loose, and Hugh heard a sound like the breaking of glass. Before he could gain any advantage—for his antagonist seemed for the moment to have concentrated all his force in the other hand—a wet handkerchief was held firmly to his face. His fierceness died away; he was lapt in the vapour of dreams; and his senses departed.

CHAPTER XXIX. HUGH'S AWAKING.

```
But ah! believe me, there is more than so,
That works such wonders in the minds of men;
I, that have often proved, too well it know;
And whoso list the like assays to ken,
Shall find by trial, and confess it then,
That beauty is not, as fond men misdeem,
An outward show of things that only seem!
```

David Elginbrod

But ye, fair dames, the world's dear ornaments,
And lively images of heaven's light,
Let not your beams with such disparagements
De dimmed, and your bright glory darkened quite;
But, mindful still of your first country's sight,
Do still preserve your first informed grace,
Whose shadow yet shines in your beauteous face.

SPENSER.—Hymn in Honour of Beauty.

When Hugh came to himself, he was lying, in the first grey of the dawn, amidst the dews and vapours of the morning woods. He rose and looked around him. The Ghost's Walk lay in long silence before him. Here and there a little bird moved and peeped. The glory of a new day was climbing up the eastern coast of heaven. It would be a day of late summer, crowned with flame, and throbbing with ripening life. But for him the spirit was gone out of the world, and it was nought but a mass of blind, heartless forces.

Possibly, had he overheard the conversation, the motions only of which he had overseen the preceding night, he would, although equally perplexed, have thought more gently of Euphra; but, in the mood into which even then he must have been thrown, his deeper feelings towards her could hardly have been different from what they were now. Although he had often felt that Euphra was not very good, not a suspicion had crossed his mind as to what he would have called the purity of her nature. Like many youths, even of character inferior to his own, he had the loftiest notions of feminine grace, and unspottedness in thought and feeling, not to say action and aim. Now he found that he had loved a woman who would creep from her chamber, at the cost of great suffering, and almost at the risk of her life, to meet, in the night and the woods, a man no better than an assassin—probably a thief. Had he been more versed in the ways of women, or in the probabilities of things, he would have judged that the very extravagance of the action demanded a deeper explanation than what seemed to lie on the surface. Yet, although he judged Euphra very hardly upon those grounds, would he have judged her differently had he actually known all? About this I am left to conjecture alone.

But the effect on Hugh was different from what the ordinary reader of human nature might anticipate. Instead of being torn in pieces by storms of jealousy, all the summer growths of his love were chilled by an absolute frost of death. A kind of annihilation sank upon the image of Euphra. There had been no such Euphra. She had been but a creation of his own brain. It was not so much that he ceased to love, as that the being beloved—not died, but—ceased to exist. There were moments in which he seemed to love her still with a wild outcry of passion; but the frenzy soon vanished in the selfish feeling of his own loss. His love was not a high one—not such as thine, my Falconer. Thine was love indeed; though its tale is too good to tell, simply because it is too good to be believed; and we do men a wrong sometimes when we tell them more than they can receive.

Thought, Speculation, Suggestion, crowded upon each other, till at length his mind sank passive, and served only as the lists in which the antagonist thoughts fought a confused battle without herald or umpire.

But it is amazing to think how soon he began to look back upon his former fascination with a kind of wondering unbelief. This bespoke the strength of Hugh's ideal sense, as well as the weakness of his actual love. He could hardly even recall the feelings with which, on some well–remembered occasion, he had regarded her, and which then it had seemed impossible he should ever forget. Had he discovered the cloven foot of a demon under those trailing garments—he could hardly have ceased to love her more suddenly or entirely. But there is an aching that is worse to bear than pain.

I trust my reader will not judge very hardly of Hugh, because of the change which had thus suddenly passed upon his feelings. He felt now just as he had felt on waking in the morning and finding that he had been in love with a dream–lady all the night: it had been very delightful, and it was sad that it was all gone, and could come back no more. But the wonder to me is, not that some loves will not stand the test of absence, but that, their nature being what it is, they should outlast one week of familiar intercourse.

He mourned bitterly over the loss of those feelings, for they had been precious to him. But could he help it? Indeed he could not; for his love had been fascination; and the fascination having ceased, the love was gone.

I believe some of my readers will not need this apology for Hugh; but will rather admire the facility with which he rose above a misplaced passion, and dismissed its object. So do not I. It came of his having never loved. Had he really loved Euphra, herself, her own self, the living woman who looked at him out of those eyes, out of that face, such pity would have blended with the love as would have made it greater, and permitted no indignation to overwhelm it. As it was, he was utterly passive and helpless in the matter. The fault lay in the original weakness that submitted to be so fascinated; that gave in to it, notwithstanding the vague expostulations of his better nature, and the consciousness that he was neglecting his duty to Harry, in order to please Euphra and enjoy her society. Had he persisted in doing his duty, it would at least have kept his mind more healthy, lessened the absorption of his passion, and given him opportunities of reflection, and moments of true perception as to what he was about. But now the spell was broken at once, and the poor girl had lost a worshipper. The golden image with the feet of clay might arise in a prophet's dream, but it could never abide in such a lover's. Her glance was powerless now. Alas, for the withering of such a dream! Perhaps she deserved nothing else; but our deserts, when we get them, are sad enough sometimes.

All that day he walked as in a dream of loss. As for the person whom he had used to call Euphra, she was removed to a vast distance from him. An absolutely impassable gulf lay between them.

She sent for him. He went to her filled with a sense of insensibility. She was much worse, and suffering great pain. Hugh saw at once that she knew that all was over between them, and that he had seen her pass his door, or had been in her room, for he had left her door a little open, and she had left it shut. One pathetic, most pitiful glance of deprecating entreaty she fixed upon him, as after a few moments of speechless waiting, he turned to leave the room—which would have remained deathless in his heart, but that he interpreted it to mean: "Don't tell;" so he got rid of it at once by the grant of its supposed request. She made no effort to detain him. She turned her face away, and, hard-hearted, he heard her sob, not as if her heart would break—that is little—but like an immortal woman in immortal agony, and he did not turn to comfort her. Perhaps it was better—how could he comfort her? Some kinds of comfort—the only kinds which poor mortals sometimes have to give—are like the food on which the patient and the disease live together; and some griefs are soonest got rid of by letting them burn out. All the fire-engines in creation can only prolong the time, and increase the sense of burning. There is but one cure: the fellow-feeling of the human God, which converts the agony itself into the creative fire of a higher life.

As for Von Funkelstein, Hugh comforted himself with the conviction that they were destined to meet again.

David Elginbrod

The day went on, as days will go, unstayed, unhastened by the human souls, through which they glide silent and awful. After such lessons as he was able to get through with Harry,—who, feeling that his tutor did not want him, left the room as soon as they were over—he threw himself on the couch, and tried to think. But think he could not. Thoughts passed through him, but he did not think them. He was powerless in regard to them. They came and went of their own will: he could neither say come nor go. Tired at length of the couch, he got up and paced about the room for hours. When he came to himself a little, he found that the sun was nearly setting. Through the top of a beech–tree taller than the rest, it sent a golden light, full of the floating shadows of leaves and branches, upon the wall of his room. But there was no beauty for him in the going down of the sun; no glory in the golden light; no message from dream–land in the flitting and blending and parting, the constantly dissolving yet ever remaining play of the lovely and wonderful shadow–leaves. The sun sank below the beech–top, and was hidden behind a cloud of green leaves, thick as the wood was deep. A grey light instead of a golden filled the room. The change had no interest for him. The pain of a lost passion tormented him—the aching that came of the falling together of the ethereal walls of his soul, about the space where there had been and where there was no longer a world.

A young bird flew against the window, and fluttered its wings two or three times, vainly seeking to overcome the unseen obstacle which the glass presented to its flight. Hugh started and shuddered. Then first he knew, in the influence of the signs of the approaching darkness, how much his nerves had suffered from the change that had passed. He took refuge with Harry. His pupil was now to be his consoler; who in his turn would fare henceforth the better, for the decay of Hugh's pleasures. The poor boy was filled with delight at having his big brother all to himself again; and worked harder than ever to make the best of his privileges. For Hugh, it was wonderful how soon his peace of mind began to return after he gave himself to his duty, and how soon the clouds of disappointment descended below the far horizon, leaving the air clear above and around. Painful thoughts about Euphra would still present themselves; but instead of becoming more gentle and sorrowful as the days went on, they grew more and more severe and unjust and angry. He even entertained doubts whether she did not know all about the theft of both rings, for to her only had he discovered the secret place in the old desk. If she was capable of what he believed, why should she not be capable of anything else? It seemed to him most simple and credible. An impure woman might just as well be a thief too.—I am only describing Hugh's feelings.

But along with these feelings and thoughts, of mingled good and bad, came one feeling which he needed more than any—repentance. Seated alone upon a fallen tree one day, the face of poor Harry came back to him, as he saw it first, poring over Polexander in the library; and, full of the joy of life himself, notwithstanding his past troubles, strong as a sunrise, and hopeful as a Prometheus, the quivering perplexity of that sickly little face smote him with a pang. "What might I not have done for the boy! He, too, was in the hands of the enchantress, and, instead of freeing him, I became her slave to enchain him further." Yet, even in this, he did Euphra injustice; for he had come to the conclusion that she had laid her plans with the intention of keeping the boy a dwarf, by giving him only food for babes, and not good food either, withholding from him every stimulus to mental digestion and consequent hunger; and that she had objects of her own in doing so—one perhaps, to keep herself necessary to the boy as she was to the father, and so secure the future. But poor Euphra's own nature and true education had been sadly neglected. A fine knowledge of music and Italian, and the development of a sensuous sympathy with nature, could hardly be called education. It was not certainly such a development of her own nature as would enable her to sympathise with the necessities of a boy's nature. Perhaps the worst that could justly be said of her behaviour to Harry was, that, with a strong inclination to despotism, and some feeling of loneliness, she had exercised the one upon him in order to alleviate the other in herself. Upon him, therefore, she expended a certain, or rather an uncertain kind of affection, which, if it might have been more fittingly spent upon a lapdog, and was worth but little, might yet have become worth everything, had she been moderately good.

Hugh did not see Euphra again for more than a fortnight.

CHAPTER XXX. CHANGES.

Hey, and the rue grows bonny wi' thyme!
And the thyme it is withered, and rue is in prime.

Refrain of an old Scotch song, altered by BURNS.

  He hath wronged me; indeed he hath;—at a word, he hath;—believe me; Robert Shallow, Esquire, saith he is wronged.

Merry Wives of Windsor.

David Elginbrod

At length, one evening, entering the drawing–room before dinner, Hugh found Euphra there alone. He bowed with embarrassment, and uttered some commonplace congratulation on her recovery. She answered him gently and coldly. Her whole air and appearance were signs of acute suffering. She did not make the slightest approach to their former familiarity, but she spoke without any embarrassment, like one who had given herself up, and was, therefore, indifferent. Hugh could not help feeling as if she knew every thought that was passing in his mind, and, having withdrawn herself from him, was watching him with a cold, ghostly interest. She took his arm to go into the dining–room, and actually leaned upon it, as, indeed, she was compelled to do. Her uncle was delighted to see her once more. Mrs. Elton addressed her with kindness, and Lady Emily with sweet cordiality. She herself seemed to care for nobody and nothing. As soon as dinner was over, she sent for her maid, and withdrew to her own room. It was a great relief to Hugh to feel that he was no longer in danger of encountering her eyes.

Gradually she recovered strength, though it was again some days before she appeared at the dinner–table. The distance between Hugh and her seemed to increase instead of diminish, till at length he scarcely dared to offer her the smallest civility, lest she should despise him as a hypocrite. The further she removed herself from him, the more he felt inclined to respect her. By common consent they avoided, as much as before, any behaviour that might attract attention; though the effort was of a very different nature now. It was wretched enough, no doubt, for both of them.

The time drew near for Lady Emily's departure.

"What are your plans for the winter, Mrs. Elton?" said Mr. Arnold, one day.

"I intend spending the winter in London," she answered.

"Then you are not going with Lady Emily to Madeira?"

"No. Her father and one of her sisters are going with her."

"I have a great mind to spend the winter abroad myself; but the difficulty is what to do with Harry."

"Could you not leave him with Mr. Sutherland?"

David Elginbrod

"No. I do not choose to do that."

"Then let him come to me. I shall have all my little establishment up, and there will be plenty of room for Harry."

"A very kind offer. I may possibly avail myself of it."

"I fear we could hardly accommodate his tutor, though. But that will be very easily arranged. He could sleep out of the house, could he not?"

"Give yourself no trouble about that. I wish Harry to have masters for the various branches he will study. It will teach him more of men and the world generally, and prevent his being too much influenced by one style of thinking."

"But Mr. Sutherland is a very good tutor."

"Yes. Very."

To this there could be no reply but a question; and Mr. Arnold's manner not inviting one, the conversation was dropped.

Euphra gradually resumed her duties in the house, as far as great lameness would permit. She continued to show a quiet and dignified reserve towards Hugh. She made no attempts to fascinate him, and never avoided his look when it chanced to meet hers. But although there was no reproach any more than fascination in her eyes, Hugh's always fell before hers. She walked softly like Ahab, as if, now that Hugh knew, she, too, was ever conscious.

Her behaviour to Mrs. Elton and Lady Emily was likewise improved, but apparently only from an increase of indifference. When the time came, and they departed, she did not even appear to be much relieved.

Once she asked Hugh to help her with a passage of Dante, but betrayed no memory of the past. His pleased haste to assist her, showed that he at least, if fancy-free, was not memory-clear. She thanked him very gently and truly, took up her book like a school-girl, and limped away. Hugh was smitten to the heart. "If I could but do

299

something for her!" thought he; but there was nothing to be done. Although she had deserved it, somehow her behaviour made him feel as if he had wronged her in ceasing to love her.

One day, in the end of September, Mr. Arnold and Hugh were alone after breakfast. Mr. Arnold spoke:

"Mr. Sutherland, I have altered my plans with regard to Harry. I wish him to spend the winter in London."

Hugh listened and waited. Mr. Arnold went on, after a slight pause:

"There I wish him to reap such advantages as are to be gained in the metropolis. He has improved wonderfully under your instruction; and is now, I think, to be benefited principally by a variety of teachers. I therefore intend that he shall have masters for the different branches which it is desirable he should study. Consequently I shall be compelled to deny him your services, valuable as they have hitherto been."

"Very well, Mr. Arnold," said Mr. Sutherland, with the indifference of one who feels himself ill–used. "When shall I take my leave of him?"

"Not before the middle of the next month, at the earliest. But I will write you a cheque for your salary at once."

So saying, Mr. Arnold left the room for a moment, and returning, handed Hugh a cheque for a year's salary. Hugh glanced at it, and offering it again to Mr. Arnold, said:

"No, Mr. Arnold; I can claim scarcely more than half a year's salary."

"Mr. Sutherland, your engagement was at so much a year; and if I prevent you from fulfilling your part of it, I am bound to fulfil mine. Indeed, you might claim further provision."

"You are very kind, Mr. Arnold."

"Only just," rejoined Mr. Arnold, with conscious dignity. "I am under great obligation to you for the way in which you have devoted yourself to Harry."

Hugh's conscience gave him a pang. Is anything more painful than undeserved praise?

"I have hardly done my duty by him," said he.

"I can only say that the boy is wonderfully altered for the better, and I thank you. I am obliged to you: oblige me by putting the cheque in your pocket."

Hugh persisted no longer in his refusal; and indeed it had been far more a feeling of pride than of justice that made him decline accepting it at first. Nor was there any generosity in Mr. Arnold's cheque; for Hugh, as he admitted, might have claimed board and lodging as well. But Mr. Arnold was one of the ordinarily honourable, who, with perfect characters for uprightness, always contrive to err on the safe side of the purse, and the doubtful side of a severely interpreted obligation. Such people, in so doing, not unfrequently secure for themselves, at the same time, the reputation of generosity.

Hugh could not doubt that his dismissal was somehow or other connected with the loss of the ring; but he would not stoop to inquire into the matter. He hoped that time would set all right; and, in fact, felt considerable indifference to the opinion of Mr. Arnold, or of any one in the house, except Harry.

The boy burst into tears when informed of his father's decision with regard to his winter studies, and could only be consoled by the hope which Hugh held out to him—certainly upon a very slight foundation—that they might meet sometimes in London. For the little time that remained, Hugh devoted himself unceasingly to his pupil; not merely studying with him, but walking, riding, reading stories, and going through all sorts of exercises for the strengthening of his person and constitution. The best results followed both for Harry and his tutor.

CHAPTER XXXI. EXPLANATIONS.

```
I have done nothing good to win belief,
My life hath been so faithless; all the creatures
Made for heaven's honours, have their ends, and good ones;
```

David Elginbrod

```
All but...false women...When they die, like tales
Ill-told, and unbelieved, they pass away.

I will redeem one minute of my age,
Or, like another Niobe, I'll weep
Till I am water.

BEAUMONT AND FLETCHER.—The Maid's Tragedy.
```

The days passed quickly by; and the last evening that Hugh was to spend at Arnstead arrived. He wandered out alone. He had been with Harry all day, and now he wished for a few moments of solitude. It was a lovely autumn evening. He went into the woods behind the house. The leaves were still thick upon the trees, but most of them had changed to gold, and brown, and red; and the sweet faint odours of those that had fallen, and lay thick underfoot, ascended like a voice from the grave, saying: "Here dwelleth some sadness, but no despair." As he strolled about among them, the whole history of his past life arose before him. This often happens before any change in our history, and is surest to take place at the approach of the greatest change of all, when we are about to pass into the unknown, whence we came.

In this mood, it was natural that his sins should rise before him. They came as the shadows of his best pleasures. For now, in looking back, he could fix on no period of his history, around which the aureole, which glorifies the sacred things of the past, had gathered in so golden a hue, as around the memory of the holy cottage, the temple in which abode David, and Janet, and Margaret. All the story glided past, as the necromantic Will called up the sleeping dead in the mausoleum of the brain. And that solemn, kingly, gracious old man, who had been to him a father, he had forgotten; the homely tenderness which, from fear of its own force, concealed itself behind a humorous roughness of manner, he had—no, not despised—but forgotten, too; and if the dim pearly loveliness of the trustful, grateful maiden had not been quite forgotten, yet she too had been neglected, had died, as it were, and been buried in the churchyard of the past, where the grass grows long over the graves, and the moss soon begins to fill up the chiselled records. He was ungrateful. He dared not allow to himself that he was unloving; but he must confess himself ungrateful.

Musing sorrowfully and self-reproachfully, he came to the Ghost's Avenue. Up and down its aisle he walked, a fit place for remembering the past, and the sins of the present.

David Elginbrod

Yielding himself to what thoughts might arise, the strange sight he had seen here on that moonlit night, of two silent wandering figures—or could it be that they were one and the same, suddenly changed in hue?—returned upon him. This vision had been so speedily followed by the second and more alarming apparition of Lady Euphrasia, that he had hardly had time to speculate on what the former could have been. He was meditating upon all these strange events, and remarking to himself that, since his midnight encounter with Lady Euphrasia, the house had been as quiet as a church-yard at noon, when all suddenly, he saw before him, at some little distance, a dark figure approaching him. His heart seemed to bound into his throat and choke him, as he said to himself: "It is the nun again!" But the next moment he saw that it was Euphra. I do not know which he would have preferred not meeting alone, and in the deepening twilight: Euphra, too, had become like a ghost to him. His first impulse was to turn aside into the wood, but she had seen him, and was evidently going to address him. He therefore advanced to meet her. She spoke first, approaching him with painful steps.

"I have been looking for you, Mr. Sutherland. I wanted very much to have a little conversation with you before you go. Will you allow me?"

Hugh felt like a culprit directly. Euphra's manner was quite collected and kind; yet through it all a consciousness showed itself, that the relation which had once existed between them had passed away for ever. In her voice there was something like the tone of wind blowing through a ruin.

"I shall be most happy," said he.

She smiled sadly. A great change had passed upon her.

"I am going to be quite open with you," she said. "I am perfectly aware, as well as you are, that the boyish fancy you had for me is gone. Do not be offended. You are manly enough, but your love for me was boyish. Most first loves are childish, quite irrespective of age. I do not blame you in the least."

This seemed to Hugh rather a strange style to assume, if all was true that his own eyes had reported. She went on:

"Nor must you think it has cost me much to lose it."

David Elginbrod

Hugh felt hurt, at which no one who understands will be surprised.

"But I cannot afford to lose you, the only friend I have," she added.

Hugh turned towards her with a face full of manhood and truth.

"You shall not lose me, Euphra, if you will be honest to yourself and to me."

"Thank you. I can trust you. I will be honest."

At that moment, without the revival of a trace of his former feelings, Hugh felt nearer to her than he had ever felt before. Now there seemed to be truth between them, the only medium through which beings can unite.

"I fear I have wronged you much," she went on. "I do not mean some time ago." Here she hesitated.—"I fear I am the cause of your leaving Arnstead."

"You, Euphra? No. You must be mistaken."

"I think not. But I am compelled to make an unwilling disclosure of a secret—a sad secret about myself. Do not hate me quite—I am a somnambulist."

She hid her face in her hands, as if the night which had now closed around them did not hide her enough. Hugh did not reply. Absorbed in the interest which both herself and her confession aroused in him, he could only listen eagerly. She went on, after a moment's pause:

"I did not think at first that I had taken the ring. I thought another had. But last night, and not till then, I discovered that I was the culprit."

"How?"

"That requires explanation. I have no recollection of the events of the previous night when I have been walking in my sleep. Indeed, the utter absence of a sense of dreaming always makes me suspect that I have been wandering. But sometimes I have a vivid dream, which I know, though I can give no proof of it, to be a reproduction of some previous somnambulic experience. Do not ask me to recall the horrors I dreamed last night. I am sure I took the ring."

"Then you dreamed what you did with it?"

"Yes, I gave it to—"

Here her voice sank and ceased. Hugh would not urge her.

"Have you mentioned this to Mr. Arnold?"

"No. I do not think it would do any good. But I will, if you wish it," she added submissively.

"Not at all. Just as you think best."

"I could not tell him everything. I cannot tell you everything. If I did, Mr. Arnold would turn me out of the house. I am a very unhappy girl, Mr. Sutherland."

>From the tone of these words, Hugh could not for a moment suppose that Euphra had any remaining design of fascination in them.

"Perhaps he might want to keep you, if I told him all; but I do not think, after the way he has behaved to you, that you could stay with him, for he would never apologize. It is very selfish of me; but indeed I have not the courage to confess to him."

"I assure you nothing could make me remain now. But what can I do for you?"

"Only let me depend upon you, in case I should need your help; or—"

Here Euphra stopped suddenly, and caught hold of Hugh's left hand, which he had lifted to brush an insect from his face.

"Where is your ring?" she said, in a tone of suppressed anxiety.

"Gone, Euphra. My father's ring! It was lying beside Lady Euphrasia's."

Euphra's face was again hidden in her hands. She sobbed and moaned like one in despair. When she grew a little calmer, she said:

"I am sure I did not take your ring, dear Hugh—I am not a thief. I had a kind of right to the other, and he said it ought to have been his, for his real name was Count von Halkar—the same name as Lady Euphrasia's before she was married. He took it, I am sure."

"It was he that knocked me down in the dark that night then, Euphra."

"Did he? Oh! I shall have to tell you all.—That wretch has a terrible power over me. I loved him once. But I refused to take the ring from your desk, because I knew it would get you into trouble. He threw me into a somnambulic sleep, and sent me for the ring. But I should have remembered if I had taken yours. Even in my sleep, I don't think he could have made me do that. You may know I speak the truth, when I am telling my own disgrace. He promised to set me free if I would get the ring; but he has not done it; and he will not."

Sobs again interrupted her.

"I was afraid your ring was gone. I don't know why I thought so, except that you hadn't it on, when you came to see me. Or perhaps it was because I am sometimes forced to think what that wretch is thinking. He made me go to him that night you saw me, Hugh. But I was so ill, I don't think I should have been able, but that I could not rest till I had asked him about your ring. He said he knew nothing about it."

"I am sure be has it," said Hugh. And he related to Euphra the struggle he had had with Funkelstein and its result. She shuddered.

"I have been a devil to you, Hugh; I have betrayed you to him. You will never see your ring again. Here, take mine. It is not so good as yours, but for the sake of the old way you thought of me, take it."

"No, no, Euphra; Mr. Arnold would miss it. Besides, you know it would not be my father's ring, and it was not for the value of the diamond I cared most about it. And I am not sure that I shall not find it again. I am going up to London, where I shall fall in with

306

him, I hope."

"But do take care of yourself. He has no conscience. God knows, I have had little, but he has none."

"I know he has none; but a conscience is not a bad auxiliary, and there I shall have some advantage of him. But what could he want that ring of Lady Euphrasia's for?"

"I don't know. He never told me."

"It was not worth much."

"Next to nothing."

"I shall be surer to find that than my own. And I will find it, if I can, that Mr. Arnold may believe I was not to blame."

"Do. But be careful."

"Don't fear. I will be careful."

She held out her hand, as if to take leave of him, but withdrew it again with the sudden cry:

"What shall I do? I thought he had left me to myself, till that night in the library."

She held down her head in silence. Then she said, slowly, in a tone of agony:

"I am a slave, body and soul.—Hugh!" she added, passionately, and looking up in his face, "do you think there is a God?"

Her eyes glimmered with the faint reflex from gathered tears, that silently overflowed.

And now Hugh's own poverty struck him with grief and humiliation. Here was a soul seeking God, and he had no right to say that there was a God, for he knew nothing about him. He had been told so; but what could that far−off witness do for the need of a desolate heart? She had been told so a million of times. He could not say that he knew it. That was what she wanted and needed.

He was honest, and so replied:

"I do not know. I hope so."

He felt that she was already beyond him; for she had begun to cry into the vague, seemingly heartless void, and say:

"Is there a God somewhere to hear me when I cry?"

And with all the teaching he had had, he had no word of comfort to give. Yes, he had: he had known David Elginbrod.

Before he had shaped his thought, she said:

"I think, if there were a God, he would help me; for I am nothing but a poor slave now. I have hardly a will of my own."

The sigh she heaved told of a hopeless oppression.

"The best man, and the wisest, and the noblest I ever knew," said Hugh, "believed in God with his whole heart and soul and strength and mind. In fact, he cared for nothing but God; or rather, he cared for everything because it belonged to God. He was never afraid of anything, never vexed at anything, never troubled about anything. He was a good man."

Hugh was surprised at the light which broke upon the character of David, as he held it before his mind's eye, in order to describe it to Euphra. He seemed never to have understood him before.

"Ah! I wish I knew him. I would go to that man, and ask him to save me. Where does he live?"

"Alas! I do not know whether he is alive or dead—the more to my shame. But he lives, if he lives, far away in the north of Scotland."

She paused.

"No. I could not go there. I will write to him."

Hugh could not discourage her, though he doubted whether a real communication could be established between them.

"I will write down his address for you, when I go in," said he. "But what can he save you from?"

"From no God," she answered, solemnly. "If there is no God, then I am sure that there is a devil, and that he has got me in his power."

Hugh. felt her shudder, for she was leaning on his arm, she was still so lame. She continued:

"Oh! if I had a God, he would right me, I know."

Hugh could not reply. A pause followed.

"Good—bye. I feel pretty sure we shall meet again. My presentiments are generally true," said Euphra, at length.

Hugh kissed her hand with far more real devotion than he had ever kissed it with before.

She left him, and hastened to the house 'with feeble speed.' He was sorry she was gone. He walked up and down for some time, meditating on the strange girl and her strange words; till, hearing the dinner bell, he too must hasten in to dress.

Euphra met him at the dinner—table without any change of her late manner. Mr. Arnold wished him good night more kindly than usual. When he went up to his room, he found that Harry had already cried himself to sleep.

CHAPTER XXXII. DEPARTURE.

```
I fancy deemed fit guide to lead my way,
    And as I deemed I did pursue her track;
Wit lost his aim, and will was fancy's prey;
    The rebel won, the ruler went to wrack.
But now sith fancy did with folly end,
Wit, bought with loss—will, taught by wit, will mend.
```

SOUTHWELL.—David's Peccavi.

After dinner, Hugh wandered over the well–known places, to bid them good–bye. Then he went up to his room, and, with the vanity of a young author, took his poems out of the fatal old desk; wrote: "Take them, please, such as they are. Let me be your friend;" inclosed them with the writing, and addressed them to Euphra. By the time he saw them again, they were so much waste paper in his eyes.

But what were his plans for the future?

First of all, he would go to London. There he would do many things. He would try to find Funkelstein. He would write. He would make acquaintance with London life; for had he not plenty of money in his pocket? And who could live more thriftily than he?—During his last session at Aberdeen, he had given some private lessons, and so contrived to eke out his small means. These were wretchedly paid for, namely, not quite at the rate of sevenpence–halfpenny a lesson! but still that was something, where more could not be had.—Now he would try to do the same in London, where he would be much better paid. Or perhaps he might get a situation in a school for a short time, if he were driven to ultimate necessity. At all events, he would see London, and look about him for a little while, before he settled to anything definite.

With this hopeful prospect before him, he next morning bade adieu to Arnstead. I will not describe the parting with poor Harry. The boy seemed ready to break his heart, and Hugh himself had enough to do to refrain from tears. One of the grooms drove him to the railway in the dog–cart. As they came near the station, Hugh gave him half–a–crown. Enlivened by the gift, the man began to talk.

"He's a rum customer, that ere gemman with the foring name. The colour of his puss I couldn't swear to now. Never saw sixpence o' his'n. My opinion is, master had better look arter his spoons. And for missus—well, it's a pity! He's a rum un, as I say, anyhow."

The man here nodded several times, half compassionately, half importantly.

Hugh did not choose to inquire what he meant. They reached the station, and in a few minutes he was shooting along towards London, that social vortex, which draws everything towards its central tumult.

But there is a central repose beyond the motions of the world; and through the turmoil of London, Hugh was journeying towards that wide stillness—that silence of the soul, which is not desolate, but rich with unutterable harmonies.

END OF THE SECOND BOOK.

BOOK III. LONDON.

```
Art thou poor, yet hast thou golden slumbers?
    Oh, sweet content!
Art thou rich, yet is thy mind perplexed?
    Oh, punishment!
Dost thou laugh to see how fools are vexed
To add to golden numbers, golden numbers?
    Oh, sweet content!

Work apace, apace, apace, apace;
Honest labour bears a lovely face.
```

        Probably THOMAS DEKKER.—Comedy of Patient Grissell.

CHAPTER I. LODGINGS.

```
Heigh ho! sing heigh ho! unto the green holly:
Most friendship is feigning, most loving mere folly:
    Then, heigh ho! the holly!
    This life is most jolly.
```

311

David Elginbrod

Song in As You Like It.

Hugh felt rather dreary as, through Bermondsey, he drew nigh to the London Bridge Station. Fog, and drizzle, and smoke, and stench composed the atmosphere. He got out in a drift of human atoms. Leaving his luggage at the office, he set out on foot to explore—in fact, to go and look for his future, which, even when he met it, he would not be able to recognise with any certainty. The first form in which he was interested to find it embodied, was that of lodgings; but where even to look, he did not know. He had been in London for a few days in the spring on his way to Arnstead, so he was not utterly ignorant of the anatomy of the monster city; but his little knowledge could not be of much service to him now. And how different it was from the London of spring, which had lingered in his memory and imagination; when, transformed by the "heavenly alchemy" of the piercing sunbeams that slanted across the streets from chimney–tops to opposite basements, the dust and smoke showed great inclined planes of light, up whose steep slopes one longed to climb to the fountain glory whence they flowed! Now the streets, from garret to cellar, seemed like huge kennels of muddy, moist, filthy air, down through which settled the heavier particles of smoke and rain upon the miserable human beings who crawled below in the deposit, like shrimps in the tide, or whitebait at the bottom of the muddy Thames. He had to wade through deep thin mud even on the pavements. Everybody looked depressed, and hurried by with a cowed look; as if conscious that the rain and general misery were a plague drawn down on the city by his own individual crime. Nobody seemed to care for anybody or anything. "Good heavens!" thought Hugh; "what a place this must be for one without money!" It looked like a chaos of human monads. And yet, in reality, the whole mass was so bound together, interwoven, and matted, by the crossing and inter–twisting threads of interest, mutual help, and relationship of every kind, that Hugh soon found how hard it was to get within the mass at all, so as to be in any degree partaker of the benefits it shared within itself.

He did not wish to get lodgings in the outskirts, for he thought that would remove him from every centre of action or employment. But he saw no lodgings anywhere. Growing tired and hungry, he went at length into an eating–house, which he thought looked cheap; and proceeded to dine upon a cinder, which had been a steak. He tried to delude himself into the idea that it was a steak still, by withdrawing his attention from it, and fixing it upon a newspaper two days old. Finding nothing of interest, he dallied with the advertisements. He soon came upon a column from which single gentlemen appeared to be in request as lodgers. Looking over these advertisements, which had more interest for him at the moment than all home and foreign news, battles and murders included, he drew a map from his pocket, and began to try to find out some of the localities indicated. Most of them were in or towards the suburbs. At last he spied one in a certain square, which, after long and diligent search, and with the assistance of the girl who waited on him, he found on his map. It was in the neighbourhood of Holborn, and, from the place it occupied in the map, seemed central enough for his vague purposes. Above all, the terms were said to be moderate. But no description of the character of the lodgings was given, else Hugh would not have ventured to look at them. What he wanted was something of the same sort as he had had in Aberdeen—a single room, or a room and bed–room, for which he should have to pay only a few shillings a week.

Refreshed by his dinner, wretched as it was, he set out again. To his great joy, the rain was over, and an afternoon sun was trying, with some slight measure of success, to pierce the clouds of the London atmosphere: it had already succeeded with the clouds of the terrene. He soon found his way into Holborn, and thence into the square in question. It looked to him very attractive; for it was quietness itself, and had no thoroughfare, except across one of its corners. True, it was invaded by the universal roar—for what place in London is not?—but it contributed little or nothing of its own manufacture to the general production of sound in the metropolis. The centre was occupied by grass and trees, inclosed within an iron railing. All the leaves were withered, and many had dropped already on the pavement below. In the middle stood the statue of a queen, of days gone by. The tide of fashion had rolled away far to the west, and yielded a free passage to the inroads of commerce, and of the general struggle for ignoble existence, upon this once favoured island in its fluctuating waters. Old windows, flush with the external walls, whence had glanced fair eyes to which fashion was even dearer than beauty, now displayed Lodgings to Let between knitted curtains, from which all idea of drapery had been expelled by severe starching Amongst these he soon found the house he sought, and shrunk from its important size and bright equipments; but, summoning courage, thought it better to ring the bell. A withered old lady, in just the same stage of decay as the square, and adorned after the same fashion as the house, came to the door, cast a doubtful look at Hugh, and when he had stated his object, asked him, in a hard, keen, unmodulated voice, to walk in. He followed her, and found himself in a dining–room, which to him, judging by his purse, and not by what he had been used to of late, seemed sumptuous. He said at once:

"It is needless for me to trouble you further. I see your rooms will not suit me."

David Elginbrod

The old lady looked annoyed.

"Will you see the drawing–room apartments, then?" she said, crustily.

"No, thank you. It would be giving you quite unnecessary trouble."

"My apartments have always given satisfaction, I assure you, sir."

"Indeed, I have no reason to doubt it. I wish I could afford to take them," said Hugh, thinking it better to be open than to hurt her feelings. "I am sure I should be very comfortable. But a poor—"

He did not know what to call himself.

"O–oh!" said the landlady. Then, after a pause—"Well?" interrogatively.

"Well, I was a tutor last, but I don't know what I may be next."

She kept looking at him. Once or twice she looked at him from head to foot.

"You are respectable?"

"I hope so," said Hugh, laughing.

"Well!"—this time not interrogatively.

"How many rooms would you like?"

"The fewer the better. Half a one, if there were nobody in the other half."

"Well!—and you wouldn't give much trouble, I daresay."

"Only for coals and water to wash and drink."

"And you wouldn't dine at home?"

"No—nor anywhere else," said Hugh; but the second and larger clause was sotto voce.

"And you wouldn't smoke in–doors?"

"No."

"And you would wipe your boots clean before you went up–stairs?"

"Yes, certainly." Hugh was beginning to be exceedingly amused, but he kept his gravity wonderfully.

"Have you any money?"

"Yes; plenty for the meantime. But when I shall get more, I don't know, you see."

"Well, I've a room at the top of the house, which I'll make comfortable for you; and you may stay as long as you like to behave yourself."

"But what is the rent?"

"Four shillings a week—to you. Would you like to see it?"

"Yes, if you please."

She conducted him up to the third floor, and showed him a good–sized room, rather bare, but clean.

"This will do delightfully," said Hugh.

"I will make it a little more comfortable for you, you know."

"Thank you very much. Shall I pay you a month in advance?"

"No, no," she answered, with a grim smile. "I might want to get rid of you, you know. It must be a week's warning, no more."

"Very well. I have no objection. I will go and fetch my luggage. I suppose I may come in at once?"

"The sooner the better, young man, in a place like London. The sooner you come home the better pleased I shall be. There now!"

So saying, she walked solemnly down–stairs before him, and let him out. Hugh hurried away to fetch his luggage, delighted that he had so soon succeeded in finding just what he wanted. As he went, he speculated on the nature of his landlady, trying to account for her odd rough manner, and the real kindness of her rude words. He came to the conclusion that she was naturally kind to profusion, and that this kindness had, some time or other, perhaps repeatedly, been taken shameful advantage of; that at last she had come to the resolution to defend herself by means of a general misanthropy, and supposed that she had succeeded, when she had got no further than to have so often imitated the tone of her own behaviour when at its crossest, as to have made it habitual by repetition.

In all probability some unknown sympathy had drawn her to Hugh. She might have had a son about his age, who had run away thirty years ago. Or rather, for she seemed an old maid, she had been jilted some time by a youth about the same size as Hugh; and therefore she loved him the moment she saw him. Or, in short, a thousand things. Certainly seldom have lodgings been let so oddly or so cheaply. But some impulse or other of the whimsical old human heart, which will have its way, was satisfied therein.

When he returned in a couple of hours, with his boxes on the top of a cab, the door was opened, before he knocked, by a tidy maid, who, without being the least like her mistress, yet resembled her excessively. She helped him to carry his boxes up–stairs; and when he reached his room, he found a fire burning cheerily, a muffin down before it, a tea–kettle singing on the hob, and the tea–tray set upon a nice white cloth on a table right in front of the fire, with an old–fashioned high–backed easy–chair by its side—the very chair to go to sleep in over a novel. The old lady soon made her appearance, with the teapot in one hand, and a plate of butter in the other.

"Oh! thank you," said Hugh. "This is comfortable!"

She answered only by compressing her lips till her mouth vanished altogether, and nodding her head as much as to say: "I know it is. I intended it should be." She then poured water into the teapot, set it down by the fire, and vanished.

Hugh sat down in the easy–chair, and resolved to be comfortable, at least till he had had his tea; after which he would think what he was to do next. A knock at the door—and his landlady entered, laid a penny newspaper on the table, and went away. This was just what he wanted to complete his comfort. He took it up, and read while he consumed his bread and butter. When he had had enough of tea and newspaper, he said to himself:

"Now, what am I to do next?"

It is a happy thing for us that this is really all we have to concern ourselves about—what to do next. No man can do the second thing. He can do the first. If he omits it, the wheels of the social Juggernaut roll over him, and leave him more or less crushed behind. If he does it, he keeps in front, and finds room to do the next again; and so he is sure to arrive at something, for the onward march will carry him with it. There is no saying to what perfection of success a man may come, who begins with what he can do, and uses the means at his hand. He makes a vortex of action, however slight, towards which all the means instantly begin to gravitate. Let a man but lay hold of something—anything, and he is in the high road to success—though it may be very long before he can walk comfortably in it.—It is true the success may be measured out according to a standard very different from his.

But in Hugh's case, the difficulty was to grasp anything—to make a beginning anywhere. He knew nobody; and the globe of society seemed like a mass of adamant, on which he could not gain the slightest hold, or make the slightest impression. Who would introduce him to pupils? Nobody. He had the testimonials of his professors; but who would ask to see them?—His eye fell on the paper. He would advertise.

CHAPTER II. LETTERS FOR THE POST.

Nothing but drought and dearth, but bush and brake,
   Which way soe'er I look, I see.
Some may dream merrily, but when they wake,
   They dress themselves, and come to thee.

GEORGE HERBERT.—Home.

David Elginbrod

He got his writing materials, and wrote to the effect, that a graduate of a Scotch university was prepared to give private lessons in the classics and mathematics, or even in any of the inferior branches of education, This he would take to the Times next day.

As soon as he had done this, Duty lifted up her head, and called him. He obeyed, and wrote to his mother. Duty called again; and he wrote, though with much trepidation and humiliation, to David Elginbrod.

It was a good beginning. He had commenced his London life in doing what he knew he ought to do. His trepidation in writing to David, arose in part, it must be confessed, from the strange result of one of the experiments at Arnstead.

This was his letter. But he sat and meditated a long time before he began it.

"MY DEAR FRIEND,—If I did not think you would forgive me, I should feel, now that I have once allowed my mind to rest upon my conduct to you, as if I could never hold up my head again. After much occupation of thought and feeling with other things, a season of silence has come, and my sins look me in the face. First of them all is my neglect of you, to whom I owe more than to any man else, except, perhaps, my father. Forgive me, for forgiveness' sake. You know it takes a long time for a child to know its mother. It takes everything as a matter of course, till suddenly one day it lifts up its eyes, and knows that a face is looking at it. I have been like the child towards you; but I am beginning to feel what you have been to me. I want to be good. I am very lonely now in great noisy London. Write to me, if you please, and comfort me. I wish I were as good as you. Then everything would go right with me. Do not suppose that I am in great trouble of any kind. As yet I am very comfortable, as far as external circumstances go. But I have a kind of aching inside me. Something is not right, and I want your help. You will know what I mean. What am I to do? Please to remember me in the kindest, most grateful manner to Mrs. Elginbrod and Margaret. It is more than I deserve, but I hope they have not forgotten me as I have seemed to forget them.

"I am, my dear Mr. Elginbrod,

"Your old friend,

"HUGH SUTHERLAND."

David Elginbrod

I may as well insert here another letter, which arrived at Turriepuffit, likewise addressed to David, some six weeks after the foregoing. They were both taken to Janet, of course:

"SIR,—I have heard from one who knows you, that you believe—really believe in God. That is why I write to you. It may seem very strange in me to do so, but how can I help it? I am a very unhappy woman, for I am in the power of a bad man. I cannot explain it all to you, and I will not attempt it; for sometimes I almost think I am out of my mind, and that it is all a delusion. But, alas! delusion or not, it is a dreadful reality to me in all its consequences. It is of such a nature that no one can help me—but God, if there be a God; and if you can make me believe that there is a God, I shall not need to be persuaded that he will help me; for I will besiege him with prayers night and day to set me free. And even if I am out of my mind, who can help me but him? Ah! is it not when we are driven to despair, when there is no more help anywhere, that we look around for some power of good that can put right all that is wrong? Tell me, dear sir, what to do. Tell me that there certainly is a God; else I shall die raving. He said you knew about him better than anybody else.

"I am, honoured Sir,

"Your obedient servant,

"EUPHRASIA CAMERON.

"Arnstead, Surrey,

David's answer to this letter, would have been something worth having. But I think it would have been all summed up in one word: Try and see: call and listen.

But what could Janet do with such letters? She did the only thing she could: she sent them to Margaret.

Hugh found it no great hardship to go to bed in the same room in which he sat. The bed looked peculiarly inviting; for, strange to tell, it was actually hung with the same pattern of old-fashioned chintz, as the bed which had been his from his earliest recollection, till he left his father's house. How could he mistake the trees, growing with tufts to the ground, or the great birds which he used to think were crows, notwithstanding their red

319

and yellow plumage? It was all over red, brown, and yellow. He could remember, and reconstruct the very faces, distorted and awful, which, in the delirium of childish sicknesses, he used to discover in the foliage and stems of the trees. It made the whole place seem to him homely and kind. When he got tired, he knelt by his bedside, which he had not done for a long time, and then went to bed. Hardship! No. It was very pleasant to see the dying fire, and his books about and his papers; and to dream, half–asleep and half–awake, that the house–fairies were stealing out to gambol for a little in the fire–lighted silence of the room as he slept, and to vanish as the embers turned black. He had not been so happy for a long time as now. The writing of that letter had removed a load from his heart. True, we can never be at peace till we have performed the highest duty of all—till we have arisen, and gone to our Father; but the performance of smaller duties, yes, even of the smallest, will do more to give us temporary repose, will act more as healthful anodynes, than the greatest joys that can come to us from any other quarter. He soon fell asleep, and dreamed that he was a little child lost in a snow–storm; and that just as the snow had reached above his head, and he was beginning to be smothered, a great hand caught hold of him by the arm and lifted him out; and, lo! the storm had ceased, and the stars were sparkling overhead like diamonds that had been drinking the light of the sun all day; and he saw that it was David, as strong as ever, who had rescued him, the little child, and was leading him home to Janet. But he got sleepy and faint upon the way, which was long and cold; and then David lifted him up and carried him in his bosom, and he fell asleep. When he woke, and, opening his eyes, looked up to him who bore him, it was David no longer. The face was that which was marred more than any man's, because the soul within had loved more; it was the face of the Son of Man, and he was carrying him like a lamb in his bosom. He gazed more and more as they travelled through the cold night; and the joy of lying in the embrace of that man, grew and grew, till it became too strong for the bonds of sleep; and he awoke in the fog of a London morning.

CHAPTER III. ENDEAVOURS.

```
And, even should misfortunes come,
—I, here wha sit, hae met wi' some,
  An's thankfu' for them yet.
They gie the wit of age to youth;
  They let us ken oursel';
They mak' us see the naked truth,
  The real guid and ill.
```

David Elginbrod

Tho' losses, and crosses,
  Be lessons right severe,
There's wit there, ye'll get there,
Ye'll find nae other where.

BURNS.

Hugh took his advertisement to the Times office, and paid what seemed to him an awful amount for its insertion. Then he wandered about London till the middle of the day, when he went into a baker's shop, and bought two penny loaves, which he put in his pocket. Having found his way to the British Museum, he devoured them at his leisure as he walked through the Grecian and Roman saloons. "What is the use of good health," he said to himself, "if a man cannot live upon bread?" Porridge and oatmeal cakes would have pleased him as well; but that food for horses is not so easily procured in London, and costs more than the other. A cousin of his had lived in Edinburgh for six months upon eighteen–pence a week in that way, and had slept the greater part of the time upon the floor, training himself for the hardships of a soldier's life. And he could not forget the college youth whom his comrades had considered mean, till they learned that, out of his poor bursary of fourteen pounds a session, and what he could make besides by private teaching at the rate previously mentioned or even less, he helped his parents to educate a younger brother; and, in order to do so, lived himself upon oatmeal and potatoes. But they did not find this out till after he was dead, poor fellow! He could not stand it.

I ought at the same time to mention, that Hugh rarely made use of a crossing on a muddy day, without finding a half–penny somewhere about him for the sweeper. He would rather walk through oceans of mud, than cross at the natural place when he had no coppers—especially if he had patent leather boots on.

After he had eaten his bread, he went home to get some water. Then, as he had nothing else to do, he sat down in his room, and began to manufacture a story, thinking it just possible it might be accepted by one or other of the pseudo–literary publications with which London is inundated in hebdomadal floods. He found spinning almost as easy as if he had been a spider, for he had a ready invention, and a natural gift of speech; so that, in a few days, he had finished a story, quite as good as most of those that appear in the better sort of weekly publications. This, in his modesty, he sent to one of the inferior sort, and heard nothing more of it than if he had flung it into the sea. Possibly he flew too low. He tried again, but with no better success. His ambition grew with his disappointments, or perhaps rather with the exercise of his faculties. Before many days had passed he made up his mind to try a novel. For three months he worked at this six hours a day regularly. When material failed him, from the exhaustion consequent upon uninterrupted production, he would recreate himself by lying fallow for an hour or two, or walking out in a mood for merely passive observation. But this anticipates.

His advertisement did not produce a single inquiry, and he shrunk from spending more money in such an apparently unprofitable appliance. Day after day went by, and no voice reached him from the unknown world of labour. He went at last to several stationers' shops in the neighbourhood, bought some necessary articles, and took these opportunities of asking if they knew of any one in want of such assistance as he could give. But unpleasant as he felt it to make such inquiries, he soon found that to most people it was equally unpleasant to reply to them. There seemed to be something disreputable in having to answer such questions, to judge from the constrained, indifferent, and sometimes, though not often, surly answers which he received. "Can it be," thought Hugh, "as disgraceful to ask for work as to ask for bread?" If he had had a thousand a year, and had wanted a situation of another thousand, it would have been quite commendable; but to try to elude cold and hunger by inquiring after paltry shillings' worths of hard labour, was despicable.

So he placed the more hope upon his novel, and worked at that diligently. But he did not find it quite so easy as he had at first expected. No one finds anything either so easy or so difficult as, in opposite moods, he had expected to find it. Everything is possible; but without labour and failure nothing is achievable. The labour, however, comes naturally, and experience grows without agonizing transitions; while the failure generally points, in its detected cause, to the way of future success. He worked on.

He did not, however, forget the ring. Frequent were his meditations, in the pauses of his story, and when walking in the streets, as to the best means of recovering it. I should rather say any means than best; for it was not yet a question of choice and degrees. The count could not but have known that the ring was of no money value; therefore it was not likely that he had stolen it in order to part with it again. Consequently it would be of no use to advertise it, or to search for it in the pawnbrokers' or second-hand jewellers' shops. To find the crystal, it was clear as itself that he must first find the count.

But how?—He could think of no plan. Any alarm would place the count on the defensive, and the jewel at once beyond reach. Besides, he wished to keep the whole matter quiet, and gain his object without his or any other name coming before the public. Therefore he would not venture to apply to the police, though doubtless they would be able to discover the man, if he were anywhere in London. He surmised that in all probability they knew him already. But he could not come to any conclusion as to the object he must have had in view in securing such a trifle.

Hugh had all but forgotten the count's cheque for a hundred guineas; for, in the first place, he had never intended presenting it—the repugnance which some minds feel to using money which they have neither received by gift nor acquired by honest earning, being at least equal to the pleasure other minds feel in gaining it without the expense of either labour or obligation; and in the second place, since he knew more about the drawer, he had felt sure that it would be of no use to present it. To make this latter conviction a certainty, he did present it, and found that there were no effects.

CHAPTER IV. A LETTER FROM THE POST.

```
Hipolito.  Is your wife then departed?
 Orlando.  She's an old dweller in those high countries, yet not
from me: here, she's here; a good couple are seldom parted.—DEKKER.
```

What wonderful things letters are! In trembling and hope the fingers unclasp, and the folded sheet drops into—no, not the post–office letter–box—but into space.

I have read a story somewhere of a poor child that dropped a letter into the post–office, addressed to Jesus Christ in Heaven. And it reached him, and the child had her answer. For was it not Christ present in the good man or woman—I forget the particulars of the story—who sent the child the help she needed? There was no necessity for him to answer in person, as in the case of Abgarus, king of Edessa.

Out of space from somewhere comes the answer. Such letters as those given in a previous chapter, are each a spirit–cry sent out, like a Noah's dove, into the abyss; and the spirit turns its ear, where its mouth had been turned before, and leans listening for the spirit–echo—the echo with a soul in it—the answering voice which out of the abyss will enter by the gate now turned to receive it. Whose will be the voice? What will be the sense? What chords on the harp of life have been struck afar off by the arrow—words of the letter? What tones will they send back to the longing, hungering ear? The mouth hath spoken, that the fainting ear may be filled by the return of its words through the alembic of another soul.

One cause of great uneasiness to Hugh was, that, for some time after a reply might have been expected, he received no answer from David Elginbrod. At length, however, a letter arrived, upon the hand—writing of which he speculated in vain, perplexed with a resemblance in it to some writing that he knew; and when he opened it, he found the following answer to his own:

"DEAR MR. SUTHERLAND,—Your letter to my father has been sent to me by my mother, for what you will feel to be the sad reason, that he is no more in this world. But I cannot say it is so very sad to me to think that he is gone home, where my mother and I will soon join him. True love can wait well. Nor indeed, dear Mr. Sutherland, must you be too much troubled that your letter never reached him. My father was like God in this, that he always forgave anything the moment there was anything to forgive; for when else could there be such a good time?—although, of course, the person forgiven could not know it till he asked for forgiveness. But, dear Mr. Sutherland, if you could see me smiling as I write, and could yet see how earnest my heart is in writing it, I would venture to say that, in virtue of my knowing my father as I do—for I am sure I know his very soul, as near as human love could know it—I forgive you, in his name, for anything and everything with which you reproach yourself in regard to him. Ah! how much I owe you! And how much he used to say he owed you! We shall thank you one day, when we all meet.

"I am, dear Mr. Sutherland,

"Your grateful scholar,

"MARGARET ELGINBROD."

Hugh burst into tears on reading this letter,—with no overpowering sense of his own sin, for he felt that he was forgiven; but with a sudden insight into the beauty and grandeur of the man whom he had neglected, and the wondrous loveliness which he had transmitted from the feminine part of his nature to the wholly feminine and therefore delicately powerful nature of Margaret. The vision he had beheld in the library at Arnstead, about which, as well as about many other things that had happened to him there, he could form no theory capable of embracing all the facts—this vision returned to his mind's eye, and he felt that the glorified face he had beheld must surely have been Margaret's, whether he had seen it in the body or out of the body: such a face alone seemed to him worthy of the writer of this letter. Purposely or not, there was no address given in it; and to his surprise, when he examined the envelope with the utmost care, he could discover no postmark but the London one. The date–stamp likewise showed that it must have been posted in London.

"So," said he to himself, "in my quest of a devil, I may cross the track of an angel, who knows? But how can she be here?"

To this of course he had no answer at hand.

CHAPTER V. BEGINNINGS.

Since a man is bound no farther to himself than to do wisely, chance
is only to trouble them that stand upon chance.—SIR PHILIP
SIDNEY.—The Arcadia.

Meantime a feeble star, but sparkling some rays of comfort, began to shine upon Hugh's wintry prospects. The star arose in a grocer's shop. For one day his landlady, whose grim attentions had been increasing rather than diminishing, addressed him suddenly as she was removing his breakfast apparatus. This was a very extraordinary event, for she seldom addressed him it all; and replied, when he addressed her, only in the briefest manner possible.

"Have you got any pupils yet, Mr. Sutherland?"

"No—I am sorry to say. But how did you come to know I wanted any, Miss Talbot?"

"You shouldn't have secrets at home, Mr. Sutherland. I like to know what concerns my own family, and I generally find out."

"You saw my advertisement, perhaps?"

To this suggestion Miss Talbot made no other answer than the usual compression of her lips.

"You wouldn't be above teaching a tradesman's son to begin with?"

"Certainly not. I should be very happy. Do you know of such a pupil?"

"Well, I can't exactly say I do know or I don't know; but I happened to mention to my grocer round the corner that you wanted pupils. Don't suppose, Mr. Sutherland, that I'm in the way of talking about any young men of mine; but it—"

"Not for a moment," interrupted Hugh; and Miss Talbot resumed, evidently gratified.

"Well, if you wouldn't mind stepping round the corner, I shouldn't wonder if you might make an arrangement with Mr. Appleditch. He said you might call upon him if you liked."

Hugh jumped up, and got his hat at once; received the few necessary directions from Miss Talbot, and soon found the shop. There were a good many poor people in it, buying sugar, and soap, and one lady apparently giving a large order. A young man came to Hugh, and bent over the counter in a recipient position, like a live point of interrogation. Hugh answered—

"Mr. Appleditch."

"Mr. Appleditch will be disengaged in a few minutes. Will you take a seat?"

The grocer was occupied with the lady and her order; but as soon as she departed, he approached Hugh behind the rampart, and stood towards him in the usual retail attitude.

"My name is Sutherland."

"Sutherland?" said Mr. Appleditch; "I think I've 'eard the name somewheres, but I don't know the face."

"Miss Talbot mentioned me to you, I understand, Mr. Appleditch."

David Elginbrod

"Oh! ah! I remember. I beg your pardon. Will you step this way, Mr. Sutherland?"

Hugh followed him through a sort of draw–bridge which he lifted in the counter, into a little appendix at the back of the shop. Mr. Appleditch was a meek–looking man, with large eyes, plump pasty cheeks, and a thin little person.

"'Ow de do, Mr. Sutherland?" said he, holding out his hand, as soon as they had reached this retreat.

"Thank you—quite well;" answered Sutherland, shaking hands with him as well as he could, the contact not being altogether pleasant.

"So you want pupils, do you, sir?"

"Yes."

"Ah! well you see, sir, pupils is scarce at this season. They ain't to be bought in every shop—ha! ha!" (The laugh was very mild.) "But I think Mrs. Appleditch could find you one, if you could agree with her about the charge, you know, and all that."

"How old is he? A boy, I suppose?"

"Well, you're right, sir. It is a boy. Not very old, though. My Samuel is just ten, but a wonderful forward boy for his years—bless him!"

"And what would you wish him to learn?"

"Oh! Latin and Greek, and all that. We intend bringing him up for the ministry.—I hope your opinions are decided, sir?"

"On some points, they are. But I do not know to what you refer, exactly."

"I mean theological opinions, sir."

"But I shall not have to teach your little boy theology."

"Certainly not, sir. That department belongs to his mother and I. Unworthy vessels, sir; mere earthen vessels; but filled with the grace of God, I hope, sir."

The grocer parted his hands, which he had been rubbing together during this conversation, and lifted them upwards from the wrists, like the fins of a seal; then, dropping them, fell to rubbing them again.

"I hope so. Well—you know the best way will be for me—not knowing your opinions—to avoid everything of a religious kind."

"Ah! but it should be line upon line, you know; here a little, and there a little, sir. As the bow is bent, you know—the—hoop is made, you know, sir."

Here Mr. Appleditch stepped to the door suddenly, and peeped out, as if he feared he was wanted; but presently returning, he continued:

"But time's a precious gift, sir, and we must not waste it. So, if you'll do us the honour, sir, to dine with us next Lord's day—we may call it a work of necessity, you know—you will see the little Samuel, and—and—Mrs. Appleditch."

"I shall be very happy. What is your address, Mr. Appleditch?"

"You had better come to Salem Chapel, Dervish town, and we can go home together. Service commences at eleven. Mrs. Appleditch will be glad to see you. Ask for Mr. Appleditch's pew. Goo—ood morning, sir."

Hugh took his leave, half inclined to send an excuse before the day arrived, and decline the connection. But his principle was, to take whatever offered, and thus make way for the next thing. Besides, he thus avoided the responsibility of choice, from which he always shrunk.

He returned to his novel; but, alas! the inventive faculty point—blank refused to work under the weight of such a Sunday in prospect. He wandered out, quite dispirited; but, before long, to take his revenge upon circumstances, resolved at least to have a dinner out of them. So he went to a chop house, had a chop and a glass of ale, and was astonished to find how much he enjoyed them. In fact, abstinence gave his very plain dinner more than all the charms of a feast—a fact of which Hugh has not been the only discoverer. He studied Punch all the time he ate, and rose with his spirits perfectly restored.

"Now I am in for it," said he, "I will be extravagant for once." So he went and bought a cigar, which he spun out into three miles of smoke, as he wandered through Shoreditch, and Houndsditch, and Petticoat-lane, gazing at the faces of his brothers and sisters; which faces having been so many years wrapt in a fog both moral and physical, now looked out of it as if they were only the condensed nuclei of the same fog and filth.

As he was returning through Whitechapel, he passed a man on the pavement, whose appearance was so remarkable that he could not help looking back after him. When he reflected about it, he thought that it must have been a certain indescribable resemblance to David Elginbrod that had so attracted him. The man was very tall. Six-foot. Hugh felt dwarfed beside him; for he had to look right up, as he passed, to see his face. He was dressed in loose, shabby black. He had high and otherwise very marked features, and a dark complexion. A general carelessness of demeanour was strangely combined with an expression of reposeful strength and quiet concentration of will. At how much of this conclusion Hugh arrived after knowing more of him, I cannot tell; but such was the description he gave of him as he saw him first: and it was thoroughly correct. IIis countenance always seemed to me (for I knew him well) to represent a nature ever bent in one direction, but never in haste, because never in doubt.

To carry his extravagance and dissipation still further, Hugh now betook himself to the pit of the Olympic Theatre; and no one could have laughed more heartily, or cried more helplessly, that night, than he; for he gave himself wholly up to the influences of the ruler of the hour, the admirable Robson. But what was his surprise when, standing up at the close of the first act, and looking around and above him, he saw, unmistakeably, the same remarkable countenance looking down upon him from the front row of the gallery. He continued his circuit of observation, trying to discover the face of Funkelstein in the boxes or circles; but involuntarily he turned his gaze back to the strange countenance, which still seemed bent towards his. The curtain rose, and during the second act he forgot all about everything else. At its close he glanced up to the gallery again, and there was the face still, and still looking at him. At the close of the third act it had vanished, and he saw nothing more of it that evening. When the after-piece was over, for he sat it out, he walked quietly home, much refreshed. He had needed some relaxation, after many days of close and continuous labour.

But awfully solemn was the face of good Miss Talbot, as she opened the door for him at midnight. Hugh took especial pains with his boots and the door–mat, but it was of no use: the austerity of her countenance would not relax in the least. So he took his candle and walked up–stairs to his room, saying only as he went—being unable to think of anything else:

"Good night, Miss Talbot."

But no response proceeded from the offended divinity of the place.

He went to bed, somewhat distressed at the behaviour of Miss Talbot, for he had a weakness for being on good terms with everybody. But he resolved to have it out with her next morning; and so fell asleep and dreamed of the strange man who had watched him at the theatre.

He rose next morning at the usual time. But his breakfast was delayed half an hour; and when it came, the maid waited upon him, and not her mistress, as usual. When he had finished, and she returned to take away the ruins, he asked her to say to her mistress that he wanted to speak to her. She brought back a message, which she delivered with some difficulty, and evidently under compulsion—that if Mr. Sutherland wanted to speak to her, he would find her in the back parlour. Hugh went down instantly, and found Miss Talbot in a doubly frozen condition, her face absolutely blue with physical and mental cold combined. She waited for him to speak. Hugh began:

"Miss Talbot, it seems something is wrong between you and me."

"Yes, Mr. Sutherland."

"Is it because I was rather late last night."

"Rather late, Mr. Sutherland?"

Miss Talbot showed no excitement. With her, the thermometer, in place of rising under the influence of irritation, steadily sank.

"I cannot make myself a prisoner on parole, you know, Miss Talbot. You must leave me my liberty."

"Oh, yes, Mr. Sutherland. Take your liberty. You'll go the way of all the rest. It's no use trying to save any of you."

"But I'm not aware that I am in any particular want of saving, Miss Talbot."

"There it is!—Well, till a sinner is called and awakened, of course it's no use. So I'll just do the best I can for you. Who can tell when the Spirit may be poured from on high? But it's very sad to me, Mr. Sutherland, to see an amiable young man like you going the way of transgressors, which is hard. I am sorry for you, Mr. Sutherland."

Though the ice was not gone yet, it had begun to melt under the influences of Hugh's good–temper, and Miss Talbot's sympathy with his threatening fate. Conscience, too, had something to do with the change; for, much as one of her temperament must have disliked making such a confession, she ended by adding, after a pause:

"And very sorry, Mr. Sutherland, that I showed you any bad temper last night."

Poor Miss Talbot! Hugh saw that she was genuinely troubled about him, and resolved to offend but seldom, while he was under her roof.

"Perhaps, when you know me longer, you will find I am steadier than you think."

"Well, it may be. But steadiness won't make a Christian of you."

"It may make a tolerable lodger of me, though," answered Hugh; "and you wouldn't turn me into the street because I am steady and nothing more, would you?"

"I said I was sorry, Mr. Sutherland. Do you wish me to say more?"

"Bless your kind heart!" said Hugh. "I was only joking."

He held out his hand to Miss Talbot, and her eyes glistened as she took it. She pressed it kindly, and abandoned it instantly.

331

So all was right between them once more.

"Who knows," murmured Miss Talbot, "but the Lord may save him? He's surely not far from the kingdom of heaven. I'll do all I can to make him comfortable."

CHAPTER VI. A SUNDAY'S DINNER.

```
Some books are lies frae end to end,
And some great lies were never penned:
Even ministers, they hae been kenned,
     In holy rapture,
Great lies and nonsense baith to vend,
     And nail't wi' Scripture.

BURNS.
```

To the great discomposure of Hugh, Sunday was inevitable, and he had to set out for Salem Chapel. He found it a neat little Noah's Ark of a place, built in the shape of a cathedral, and consequently sharing in the general disadvantages to which dwarfs of all kinds are subjected, absurdity included. He was shown to Mr. Appleditch's pew. That worthy man received him in sleek black clothes, with white neck–cloth, and Sunday face composed of an absurd mixture of stupidity and sanctity. He stood up, and Mrs. Appleditch stood up, and Master Appleditch stood up, and Hugh saw that the ceremony of the place required that he should force his way between the front of the pew and the person of each of the human beings occupying it, till he reached the top, where there was room for him to sit down. No other recognition was taken till after service.

Meantime the minister ascended the pulpit stair, with all the solemnity of one of the self–elect, and a priest besides. He was just old enough for the intermittent attacks of self–importance to which all youth is exposed, to have in his case become chronic. He stood up and worshipped his creator aloud, after a manner which seemed to say in every tone: "Behold I am he that worshippeth Thee! How mighty art Thou!" Then he read the Bible in a quarrelsome sort of way, as if he were a bantam, and every verse were a crow of defiance to the sinner. Then they sang a hymn in a fashion which brought dear old Scotland to Hugh's mind, which has the sweetest songs in its cottages, and the worst singing in its churches, of any country in the world. But it was almost equalled here; the chief cause of its badness being the absence of a modest self–restraint, and consequent tempering of the tones, on the part of the singers; so that the result was what Hugh could describe only as scraichin.1

I was once present at the worship of some being who is supposed by negroes to love drums and cymbals, and all clangorous noises. The resemblance, according to Hugh's description, could not have been a very distant one. And yet I doubt not that some thoughts of worshipping love mingled with the noise; and perhaps the harmony of these with the spheric melodies, sounded the sweeter to the angels, from the earthly discord in which they were lapped.

Then came the sermon. The text was the story of the good Samaritan. Some idea, if not of the sermon, yet of the value of it, may be formed from the fact, that the first thing to be considered, or, in other words, the first head was, "The culpable imprudence of the man in going from Jerusalem to Jericho without an escort."

It was in truth a strange, grotesque, and somewhat awful medley—not unlike a dance of death, in which the painter has given here a lovely face, and there a beautiful arm or an exquisite foot, to the wild–prancing and exultant skeletons. But the parts of the sermon corresponding to the beautiful face or arm or foot, were but the fragments of Scripture, shining like gold amidst the worthless ore of the man's own production—worthless, save as gravel or chaff or husks have worth, in a world where dilution, and not always concentration, is necessary for healthfulness.

But there are Indians who eat clay, and thrive on it more or less, I suppose. The power of assimilation which a growing nature must possess is astonishing. It will find its food, its real Sunday dinner, in the midst of a whole cartload of refuse; and it will do the whole week's work on it. On no other supposition would it be possible to account for the earnest face of Miss Talbot, which Hugh espied turned up to the preacher, as if his face were the very star in the east, shining to guide the chosen kings. It was well for Hugh's power of endurance, that he had heard much the same thing in Scotland, and the same thing better dressed, and less grotesque, but more lifeless, and at heart as ill–mannered, in the church of Arnstead.

Just before concluding the service, the pastor made an announcement in the following terms: "After the close of the present service, I shall be found in the adjoining vestry by all persons desirous of communicating with me on the state of their souls, or of being admitted to the privileges of church–fellowship. Brethren, we have this treasure in earthen vessels, and so long as this vessel lasts"—here he struck his chest so that it resounded—"it shall be faithfully and liberally dispensed. Let us pray."

After the prayer, he spread abroad his arms and hands as if he would clasp the world in his embrace, and pronounced the benediction in a style of arrogance that the pope himself would have been ashamed of.

The service being thus concluded, the organ absolutely blasted the congregation out of the chapel, so did it storm and rave with a fervour anything but divine.

My readers must not suppose that I give this chapel as the type of orthodox dissenting chapels. I give it only as an approximate specimen of a large class of them. The religious life which these communities once possessed, still lingers in those of many country districts and small towns, but is, I fear, all but gone from those of the cities and larger towns. What of it remains in these, has its chief manifestation in the fungous growth of such chapels as the one I have described, the congregations themselves taking this for a sure indication of the prosperity of the body. How much even of the kind of prosperity which they ought to indicate, is in reality at the foundation of these appearances, I would recommend those to judge who are versed in the mysteries of chapel–building societies.

As to Hugh, whether it was that the whole was suggestive of Egyptian bondage, or that his own mood was, at the time, of the least comfortable sort, I will not pretend to determine; but he assured me that he felt all the time, as if, instead of being in a chapel built of bricks harmoniously arranged, as by the lyre of Amphion, he were wandering in the waste, wretched field whence these bricks had been dug, of all places on the earth's surface the most miserable, assailed by the nauseous odours, which have not character enough to be described, and only remind one of the colours on a snake's back.

When they reached the open air, Mr. Appleditch introduced Hugh to Mrs. Appleditch, on the steps in front of the chapel.

"This is Mr. Sutherland, Mrs. Appleditch."

Hugh lifted his hat, and Mrs. Appleditch made a courtesy. She was a very tall woman—a head beyond her husband, extremely thin, with sharp nose, hollow cheeks, and good eyes.

David Elginbrod

In fact, she was partly pretty, and might have been pleasant–looking, but for a large, thin–lipped, vampire–like mouth, and a general expression of greed and contempt. She was meant for a lady, and had made herself a money–maggot. She was richly and plainly dressed; and until she began to be at her ease, might have passed for an unpleasant lady. Master Appleditch, the future pastor, was a fat boy, dressed like a dwarf, in a frock coat and man's hat, with a face in which the meanness and keenness strove for mastery, and between them kept down the appearance of stupidity consequent on fatness. They walked home in silence, Mr. and Mrs. Appleditch apparently pondering either upon the spiritual food they had just received, or the corporeal food for which they were about to be thankful.

Their house was one of many in a crescent. Not content with his sign in town, the grocer had a large brass plate on his door, with Appleditch engraved upon it in capitals: it saved them always looking at the numbers. The boy ran on before, and assailed this door with a succession of explosive knocks.

As soon as it was opened, in he rushed, bawling:

"Peter, Peter, here's the new apprentice! Papa's brought him home to dinner, because he was at chapel this morning." Then in a lower tone—"I mean to have a ride on his back this afternoon."

The father and mother laughed. A solemn priggish little voice answered:

"Oh, no, Johnny. Don't you know what day this is? This is the Sabbath–day."

"The dear boy!" sighed his mother.

"That boy is too good to live," responded the father.

Hugh was shown into the dining–room, where the table was already laid for dinner. It was evident that the Appleditches were well–to–do people. The room was full of what is called handsome furniture, in a high state of polish. Over the chimney–piece hung the portrait of a preacher in gown and bands, the most prominent of whose features were his cheeks.

David Elginbrod

In a few minutes the host and hostess entered, followed by a pale–faced little boy, the owner of the voice of reproof.

"Come here, Peetie," said his mother, "and tell Mr. Sutherland what you have got." She referred to some toy—no, not toy, for it was the Sabbath—to some book, probably.

Peetie answered in a solemn voice, mouthing every vowel:

"I've got five bags of gold in the Bank of England."

"Poor child!" said his mother, with a scornful giggle. "You wouldn't have much to reckon on, if that were all."

Two or three gaily dressed riflemen passed the window. The poor fellows, unable to bear the look of their Sunday clothes, if they had any, after being used to their uniform, had come out in all its magnificence.

"Ah!" said Mr. Appleditch, "that's all very well in a state of nature; but when a man is once born into a state of grace, Mr. Sutherland—ah!"

"Really," responded Mrs. Appleditch, "the worldliness of the lower classes is quite awful. But they are spared for a day of wrath, poor things! I am sure that accident on the railway last Sabbath, might have been a warning to them all. After that they can't say there is not a God that ruleth in the earth, and taketh vengeance for his broken Sabbaths."

"Mr.—. I don't know your name," said Peter, whose age Hugh had just been trying in vain to conjecture.

"Mr. Sutherland," said the mother.

"Mr. Slubberman, are you a converted character?" resumed Peter.

"Why do you ask me that, Master Peter?" said Hugh, trying to smile.

"I think you look good, but mamma says she don't think you are, because you say Sunday instead of Sabbath, and she always finds people who do are worldly."

David Elginbrod

Mrs. Appleditch turned red—not blushed, and said, quickly:

"Peter shouldn't repeat everything he hears."

"No more I do, ma. I haven't told what you said about—" Here his mother caught him up, and carried him out of the room, saying:

"You naughty boy! You shall go to bed."

"Oh, no, I shan't!"

"Yes, you shall. Here, Jane, take this naughty boy to bed."

"I'll scream."

"Will you?"

"Yes, I will!"

> And such a yell was there
> Of sudden and portentous birth,
> As if...

ten cats were being cooked alive.

"Well! well! well! my Peetie! He shan't go to bed, if he'll be a good boy. Will he be good?"

"May I stay up to supper, then? May I?"

"Yes, yes; anything to stop such dreadful screaming. You are very naughty—very naughty indeed."

"No. I'm not naughty. I'll scream again."

"No, no. Go and get your pinafore on, and come down to dinner. Anything rather than a scream."

I am sick of all this, and doubt if it is worth printing; but it amused me very much one night as Hugh related it over a bottle of Chablis and a pipe.

He certainly did not represent Mrs. Appleditch in a very favourable light on the whole; but he took care to say that there was a certain liberality about the table, and a kind of heartiness in her way of pressing him to have more than he could possibly eat, which contrasted strangely with her behaviour afterwards in money matters. There are many people who can be liberal in almost anything but money. They seem to say, "Take anything but my purse." Miss Talbot told him afterwards, that this same lady was quite active amongst the poor of her district. She made it a rule never to give money, or at least never more than sixpence; but she turned scraps of victuals and cast-off clothes to the best account; and, if she did not make friends with the mammon of unrighteousness, she yet kept an eye on the eternal habitations in the distribution of the crumbs that fell from her table. Poor Mr. Appleditch, on the other hand, often embezzled a shilling or a half-crown from the till, for the use of a poor member of the same church—meaning by church, the individual community to which he belonged; but of this, Mrs. Appleditch was carefully kept ignorant.

After dinner was over, and the children had been sent away, which was effected without a greater amount of difficulty than, from the anticipative precautions adopted, appeared to be lawful and ordinary, Mr. Appleditch proceeded to business.

"Now, Mr. Sutherland, what do you think of Johnnie, sir?"

"It is impossible for me to say yet; but I am quite willing to teach him if you like."

"He's a forward boy," said his mother.

"Not a doubt of it," responded Hugh; for he remembered the boy asking him, across the table: "Isn't our Mr. Lixom"—(the pastor)—"a oner?"

"And very eager and retentive," said his father.

David Elginbrod

Hugh had seen the little glutton paint both cheeks to the eyes with damson tart, and render more than a quantity proportionate to the colouring, invisible.

"Yes, he is eager, and retentive, too, I daresay," he said; "but much will depend on whether he has a turn for study."

"Well, you will find that out to-morrow. I think you will be surprised, sir."

"At what hour would you like me to come?"

"Stop, Mr. Appleditch," interposed his wife. "You have said nothing yet about terms; and that is of some importance, considering the rent and taxes we pay."

"Well, my love, what do you feel inclined to give?"

"How much do you charge a lesson, Mr. Sutherland? Only let me remind you, sir, that he is a very little boy, although stout, and that you cannot expect to put much Greek and Latin into him for some time yet. Besides, we want you to come every day, which ought to be considered in the rate of charge."

"Of course it ought," said Hugh.

"How much do you say, then, sir?"

"I should be content with half-a-crown a lesson."

"I daresay you would!" replied the lady, with indignation.

"Half-a-crown! That's—six half-crowns is—fifteen shillings. Fifteen shillings a week for that mite of a boy! Mr. Sutherland, you ought to be ashamed of yourself, sir."

"You forget, Mrs. Appleditch, that it is as much trouble to me to teach one little boy—yes, a great deal more than to teach twenty grown men."

"You ought to be ashamed of yourself, sir. You a Christian man, and talk of trouble in teaching such a little cherub as that?"

David Elginbrod

"But do pray remember the distance I have to come, and that it will take nearly four hours of my time every day."

"Then you can get lodgings nearer."

"But I could not get any so cheap."

"Then you can the better afford to do it."

And she threw herself back in her chair, as if she had struck the decisive blow. Mr. Appleditch remarked, gently:

"It is good for your health to walk the distance, sir."

Mrs. Appleditch resumed:

"I won't give a farthing more than one shilling a lesson. There, now!"

"Very well," said Hugh, rising; "then I must wish you good day. We need not waste more time in talking about it."

"Surely you are not going to make any use of your time on a Sunday?" said the grocer, mildly. "Don't be in a hurry, Mr. Sutherland. We tradespeople like to make the best bargain we can."

"Mr. Appleditch, I am ashamed of you. You always will be vulgar. You always smell of the shop."

"Well, my dear, how can I help it? The sugar and soft–soap will smell, you know."

"Mr. Appleditch, you disgust me!"

"Dear! dear! I am sorry for that.—Suppose we say to Mr. Sutherland—"

"Now, you leave that to me. I'll tell you what, Mr. Sutherland—I'll give you eighteenpence a lesson, and your dinner on the Sabbath; that is, if you sit under Mr.

Lixom in our pew, and walk home with us."

"That I must decline" said Hugh. "I must have my Sundays for myself."

Mrs. Appleditch was disappointed. She had coveted the additional importance which the visible possession of a live tutor would secure her at "Salem."

"Ah! Mr. Sutherland," she said. "And I must trust my child, with an immortal soul in his inside, to one who wants the Lord's only day for himself!—for himself, Mr. Sutherland!"

Hugh made no answer, because he had none to make. Again Mrs. Appleditch resumed:

"Shall it be a bargain, Mr. Sutherland? Eighteen–pence a lesson—that's nine shillings a week—and begin to morrow?"

Hugh's heart sunk within him, not so much with disappointment as with disgust.

But to a man who is making nothing, the prospect of earning ever so little, is irresistibly attractive. Even on a shilling a day, he could keep hunger at arm's length. And a beginning is half the battle. He resolved.

"Let it be a bargain, then, Mrs. Appleditch."

The lady immediately brightened up, and at once put on her company–manners again, behaving to him with great politeness, and a sneer that would not be hid away under it. From this Hugh suspected that she had made a better bargain than she had hoped; but the discovery was now too late, even if he could have brought himself to take advantage of it. He hated bargain–making as heartily as the grocer's wife loved it.

He very soon rose to take his leave.

"Oh!" said Mrs. Appleditch to her husband, "but Mr. Sutherland has not seen the drawing–room!"

Hugh wondered what there could be remarkable about the drawing–room; but he soon found that it was the pride of Mrs. Appleditch's heart. She abstained from all use of it except upon great occasions—when parties of her friends came to drink tea with her. She made a point, however, of showing it to everybody who entered the house for the first time. So Hugh was led up–stairs, to undergo the operation of being shown the drawing–room, and being expected to be astonished at it.

I asked him what it was like. He answered: "It was just what it ought to be—rich and ugly. Mr. Appleditch, in his deacon's uniform, hung over the fire, and Mrs. Appleditch, in her wedding–dress, over the piano; for there was a piano, and she could play psalm–tunes on it with one finger. The round table in the middle of the room had books in gilded red and blue covers symmetrically arranged all round it. This is all I can recollect."

Having feasted his eyes on the magnificence thus discovered to him, he walked home, more depressed at the prospect of his new employment than he could have believed possible.

On his way he turned aside into the Regent's Park, where the sight of the people enjoying themselves—for it was a fine day for the season—partially dispelled the sense of living corruption and premature burial which he had experienced all day long. He kept as far off from the rank of open–air preachers as possible, and really was able to thank God that all the world did not keep Scotch Sabbath—a day neither Mosaic, nor Jewish, nor Christian: not Mosaic, inasmuch as it kills the very essence of the fourth commandment, which is Rest, transmuting it into what the chemists would call a mechanical mixture of service and inertia; not Jewish, inasmuch as it is ten times more severe, and formal, and full of negations, than that of the Sabbatarian Jews reproved by the Saviour for their idolatry of the day; and unchristian, inasmuch as it insists, beyond appeal, on the observance of times and seasons, abolished, as far as law is concerned, by the word of the chief of the apostles; and elevates into an especial test of piety a custom not even mentioned by the founders of christianity at all—that, namely, of accounting this day more holy than all the rest.

These last are but outside reasons for calling it unchristian. There are far deeper and more important ones, which cannot well be produced here.

It is not Hugh, however, who is to be considered accountable for all this, but the historian of his fortunes, between whom and the vision of a Lord's Day indeed, there arises too

342

often the nightmare–memory of a Scotch Saabbath—between which and its cousin, the English Sunday, there is too much of a family likeness. The grand men and women whom I have known in Scotland, seem to me, as I look back, to move about in the mists of a Scotch Sabbath, like a company of way–worn angels in the Limbo of Vanity, in which there is no air whereupon to smite their sounding wings, that they may rise into the sunlight of God's presence.

CHAPTER VII. SUNDAY EVENING.

```
Now resteth in my memory but this point, which indeed is the chief
to you of all others; which is the choice of what men you are to
direct yourself to; for it is certain no vessel can leave a worse
taste in the liquor it contains, than a wrong teacher infects an
unskilful hearer with that which hardly will ever out...But you may
say, "How shall I get excellent men to take pains to speak with me?"
Truly, in few words, either by much expense or much humbleness.

Letter of Sir Philip Sidney to his brother Robert.
```

How many things which, at the first moment, strike us as curious coincidences, afterwards become so operative on our lives, and so interwoven with the whole web of their histories, that instead of appearing any more as strange accidents, they assume the shape of unavoidable necessities, of homely, ordinary, lawful occurrences, as much in their own place as any shaft or pinion of a great machine!

It was dusk before Hugh turned his steps homeward. He wandered along, thinking of Euphra and the Count and the stolen rings. He greatly desired to clear himself to Mr. Arnold. He saw that the nature of the ring tended to justify Mr. Arnold's suspicions; for a man who would not steal for money's worth, might yet steal for value of another sort, addressing itself to some peculiar weakness; and Mr. Arnold might have met with instances of this nature in his position as magistrate. He greatly desired, likewise, for Euphra's sake, to have Funkelstein in his power. His own ring was beyond recovery; but if, by its means, he could hold such a lash over him as would terrify him from again exercising his villanous influences on her, he would he satisfied.

While plunged in this contemplation, he came upon two policemen talking together. He recognized one of them as a Scotchman, from his speech. It occurred to him at once to ask his advice, in a modified manner; and a moment's reflection convinced him that it would at least do no harm. He would do it. It was one of those resolutions at which one arrives by an arrow flight of the intellect.

"You are a countryman of mine, I think," said he, as soon as the two had parted.

"If ye're a Scotchman, sir—may be ay, may be no."

"Whaur come ye frae, man?"

"Ou, Aberdeen–awa."

"It's mine ain calf–country. An' what do they ca' ye?"

"They ca' me John MacPherson."

"My name's Sutherland."

"Eh, man! It's my ain mither's name. Gie's a grup o' yer han', Maister Sutherlan'.—Eh, man!" he repeated, shaking Hugh's hand with vehemence.

"I have no doubt," said Hugh, relapsing into English, "that we are some cousins or other. It's very lucky for me to find a relative, for I wanted some—advice."

He took care to say advice, which a Scotchman is generally prepared to bestow of his best. Had it been sixpence, the cousinship would have required elaborate proof, before the treaty could have made further progress.

"I'm fully at your service, sir."

"When will you be off duty?"

"At nine o'clock preceesely."

"Come to No. 13,—Square, and ask for me. It's not far."

David Elginbrod

"Wi' pleesir, sir, 'gin 'twar twise as far."

Hugh would not have ventured to ask him to his house on Sunday night, when no refreshments could be procured, had he not remembered a small pig (Anglicé stone bottle) of real mountain dew, which he had carried with him when he went to Arnstead, and which had lain unopened in one of his boxes.

Miss Talbot received her lodger with more show of pleasure than usual, for he came lapped in the odour of the deacon's sanctity. But she was considerably alarmed and beyond measure shocked when the policeman called and requested to see him. Sally had rushed in to her mistress in dismay.

"Please'm, there's a pleaceman wants Mr. Sutherland. Oh! lor'm!"

"Well, go and let Mr. Sutherland know, you stupid girl," answered her mistress, trembling.

"Oh! lor'm!" was all Sally's reply, as she vanished to bear the awful tidings to Hugh.

"He can't have been housebreaking already," said Miss Talbot to herself, as she confessed afterwards. "But it may be forgery or embezzlement. I told the poor deluded young man that the way of transgressors was hard."

"Please, sir, you're wanted, sir," said Sally, out of breath, and pale as her Sunday apron.

"Who wants me?" asked Hugh.

"Please, sir, the pleaceman, sir," answered Sally, and burst into tears.

Hugh was perfectly bewildered by the girl's behaviour, and said in a tone of surprise:

"Well, show him up, then."

"Ooh! sir," said Sally, with a Plutonic sigh, and began to undo the hooks of her dress; "if you wouldn't mind, sir, just put on my frock and apron, and take a jug in your hand, an' the pleaceman'll never look at you. I'll take care of everything till you come back, sir."

345

And again she burst into tears.

Sally was a great reader of the Family Herald, and knew that this was an orthodox plan of rescuing a prisoner. The kindness of her anxiety moderated the expression of Hugh's amusement; and having convinced her that he was in no danger, he easily prevailed upon her to bring the policeman upstairs.

Over a tumbler of toddy, the weaker ingredients of which were procured by Sally's glad connivance, with a lingering idea of propitiation, and a gentle hint that Missus mustn't know—the two Scotchmen, seated at opposite corners of the fire, had a long chat. They began about the old country, and the places and people they both knew, and both didn't know. If they had met on the shores of the central lake of Africa, they could scarcely have been more couthy together. At length Hugh referred to the object of his application to MacPherson.

"What plan would you have me pursue, John, to get hold of a man in London?"

"I could manage that for ye, sir. I ken maist the haill mengie o' the detaictives."

"But you see, unfortunately, I don't wish, for particular reasons, that the police should have anything to do with it."

"Ay! ay! Hm! Hm! I see brawly. Ye'll be efter a stray sheep, nae doot?"

Hugh did not reply; so leaving him to form any conclusion he pleased.

"Ye see," MacPherson continued, "it's no that easy to a body that's no up to the trade. Hae ye ony clue like, to set ye spierin' upo'?"

"Not the least."

The man pondered a while.

"I hae't," he exclaimed at last. "What a fule I was no to think o' that afore! Gin't be a puir bit yow–lammie like, 'at ye're efter, I'll tell ye what: there's ae man, a countryman o' our ain, an' a gentleman forbye, that'll do mair for ye in that way, nor a' the detaictives

346

thegither; an' that's Robert Falconer, Esquire.—I ken him weel."

"But I don't," said Hugh.

"But I'll introduce ye till 'im. He bides close at han' here; roun' twa corners jist. An' I'm thinkin' he'll be at hame the noo; for I saw him gaein that get, afore ye cam' up to me. An' the suner we gang, the better; for he's no aye to be gotten hand o'. Fegs! he may be in Shoreditch or this."

"But will he not consider it an intrusion?"

"Na, na; there's no fear o' that. He's ony man's an' ilka woman's freen—so be he can do them a guid turn; but he's no for drinkin' and daffin' an' that. Come awa', Maister Sutherlan', he's yer verra man."

Thus urged, Hugh rose and accompanied the policeman. He took him round rather more than two corners; but within five minutes they stood at Mr. Falconer's door. John rang. The door opened without visible service, and they ascended to the first floor, which was enclosed something after the Scotch fashion. Here a respectable looking woman awaited their ascent.

"Is Mr. Falconer at hom', mem?" said Hugh's guide.

"He is; but I think he's just going out again."

"Will ye tell him, mem, 'at hoo John MacPherson, the policeman, would like sair to see him?"

"I will," she answered; and went in, leaving them at the door.

She returned in a moment, and, inviting them to enter, ushered them into a large bare room, in which there was just light enough for Hugh to recognize, to his astonishment, the unmistakeable figure of the man whom he had met in Whitechapel, and whom he had afterwards seen apparently watching him from the gallery of the Olympic Theatre.

"How are you, MacPherson?" said a deep powerful voice, out of the gloom.

"Verra weel, I thank ye, Mr. Falconer. Hoo are ye yersel', sir?"

"Very well too, thank you. Who is with you?"

"It's a gentleman, sir, by the name o' Mr. Sutherlan', wha wants your help, sir, aboot somebody or ither 'at he's enteresstit in, wha's disappeared."

Falconer advanced, and, bowing to Hugh said, very graciously:

"I shall be most happy to serve Mr. Sutherland, if in my power. Our friend MacPherson has rather too exalted an idea of my capabilities, however."

"Weel, Maister Falconer, I only jist spier at yersel', whether or no ye was ever dung wi' onything ye took in han'."

Falconer made no reply to this. There was the story of a whole life in his silence—past and to come.

He merely said:

"You can leave the gentleman with me, then, John. I'll take care of him."

"No fear o' that, sir. Deil a bit! though a' the policemen i' Lonnon war efter 'im."

"I'm much obliged to you for bringing him."

"The obligation's mine sir—an' the gentleman's. Good nicht, sir. Good nicht, Mr. Sutherlan'. Ye'll ken whaur to fin' me gin ye want me. Yon's my beat for anither fortnicht."

"And you know my quarters," said Hugh, shaking him by the hand. "I am greatly obliged to you."

"Not a bit, sir. Or gin ye war, ye sud be hertily welcome."

David Elginbrod

"Bring candles, Mrs. Ashton," Falconer called from the door. Then, turning to Hugh, "Sit down, Mr. Sutherland," he said, "if you can find a chair that is not illegally occupied already. Perhaps we had better wait for the candles. What a pleasant day we have had!"

"Then you have been more pleasantly occupied than I have," thought Hugh, to whose mind returned the images of the Appleditch family and its drawing—room, followed by the anticipation of the distasteful duties of the morrow. But he only said:

"It has been a most pleasant day."

"I spent it strangely," said Falconer.

Here the candles were brought in.

The two men looked at each other full in the face. Hugh saw that he had not been in error. The same remarkable countenance was before him. Falconer smiled.

"We have met before," said he.

"We have," said Hugh.

"I had a conviction we should be better acquainted, but I did not expect it so soon."

"Are you a clairvoyant, then?"

"Not in the least."

"Or, perhaps, being a Scotchman, you have the second sight?"

"I am hardly Celt enough for that. But I am a sort of a seer, after all—from an instinct of the spiritual relations of things, I hope; not in the least from the nervo—material side."

"I think I understand you."

"Are you at leisure?"

David Elginbrod

"Entirely."

"Had we not better walk, then? I have to go as far as Somers Town—no great way; and we can talk as well walking as sitting."

"With pleasure," answered Hugh, rising.

"Will you take anything before you go? A glass of port? It is the only wine I happen to have."

"Not a drop, thank you. I seldom taste anything stronger than water."

"I like that. But I like a glass of port too. Come then."

And Falconer rose—and a great rising it was; for, as I have said, he was two or three inches taller than Hugh, and much broader across the shoulders; and Hugh was no stripling now. He could not help thinking again of his old friend, David Elginbrod, to whom he had to look up to find the living eyes of him, just as now he looked up to find Falconer's. But there was a great difference between those organs in the two men. David's had been of an ordinary size, pure keen blue, sparkling out of cerulean depths of peace and hope, full of lambent gleams when he was loving any one, and ever ready to be dimmed with the mists of rising emotion. All that Hugh could yet discover of Falconer's eyes was, that they were large, and black as night, and set so far back in his head, that each gleamed out of its caverned arch like the reversed torch of the Greek Genius of Death, just before going out in night. Either the frontal sinus was very large, or his observant faculties were peculiarly developed.

They went out, and walked for some distance in silence. Hugh ventured to say at length:

"You said you had spent the day strangely: may I ask how?"

"In a condemned cell in Newgate," answered Falconer. "I am not in the habit of going to such places, but the man wanted to see me, and I went."

As Falconer said no more, and as Hugh was afraid of showing anything like vulgar curiosity, this thread of conversation broke. Nothing worth recording passed until they entered a narrow court in Somers Town.

"Are you afraid of infection?" Falconer said.

"Not in the least, if there be any reason for exposing myself to it."

"That is right.—And I need not ask if you are in good health."

"I am in perfect health."

"Then I need not mind asking you to wait for me till I come out of this house. There is typhus in it."

"I will wait with pleasure. I will go with you if I can be of any use."

"There is no occasion. It is not your business this time."

So saying, Falconer opened the door, and walked in.

Said Hugh to himself: "I must tell this man the whole story; and with it all my own."

In a few minutes Falconer rejoined him, looking solemn, but with a kind of relieved expression on his face.

"The poor fellow is gone," said he.

"Ah!"

"What a thing it must be, Mr. Sutherland, for a man to break out of the choke–damp of a typhus fever into the clear air of the life beyond!"

"Yes," said Hugh; adding, after a slight hesitation, "if he be at all prepared for the change."

"Where a change belongs to the natural order of things," said Falconer, "and arrives inevitably at some hour, there must always be more or less preparedness for it. Besides, I

351

think a man is generally prepared for a breath of fresh air."

Hugh did not reply, for he felt that he did not fully comprehend his new acquaintance. But he had a strong suspicion that it was because he moved in a higher region than himself.

"If you will still accompany me," resumed Falconer, who had not yet adverted to Hugh's object in seeking his acquaintance, "you will, I think, be soon compelled to believe that, at whatever time death may arrive, or in whatever condition the man may be at the time, it comes as the best and only good that can at that moment reach him. We are, perhaps, too much in the habit of thinking of death as the culmination of disease, which, regarded only in itself, is an evil, and a terrible evil. But I think rather of death as the first pulse of the new strength, shaking itself free from the old mouldy remnants of earth–garments, that it may begin in freedom the new life that grows out of the old. The caterpillar dies into the butterfly. Who knows but disease may be the coming, the keener life, breaking into this, and beginning to destroy like fire the inferior modes or garments of the present? And then disease would be but the sign of the salvation of fire; of the agony of the greater life to lift us to itself, out of that wherein we are failing and sinning. And so we praise the consuming fire of life."

"But surely all cannot fare alike in the new life."

"Far from it. According to the condition. But what would be hell to one, will be quietness, and hope, and progress to another; because he has left worse behind him, and in this the life asserts itself, and is.—But perhaps you are not interested in such subjects, Mr. Sutherland, and I weary you."

"If I have not been interested in them hitherto, I am ready to become so now. Let me go with you."

"With pleasure."

As I have attempted to tell a great deal about Robert Falconer and his pursuits elsewhere, I will not here relate the particulars of their walk through some of the most wretched parts of London. Suffice it to say that, if Hugh, as he walked home, was not yet prepared to receive and understand the half of what Falconer had said about death, and had not yet that faith in God that gives as perfect a peace for the future of our brothers and sisters, who, alas! have as yet been fed with husks, as for that of ourselves, who have eaten bread of the finest of the wheat, and have been but a little thankful,—he yet felt at least that it was a blessed thing that these men and women would all die—must all die. That spectre from which men shrink, as if it would take from them the last shivering remnant of existence, he turned to for some consolation even for them. He was prepared to believe that they could not be going to worse in the end, though some of the rich and respectable and educated might have to receive their evil things first in the other world; and he was ready to understand that great saying of Schiller—full of a faith evident enough to him who can look far enough into the saying:

"Death cannot be an evil, for it is universal."

CHAPTER VIII. EUPHRA.

```
Samson.   O that torment should not be confined
          To the body's wounds and sores,

          But must secret passage find
          To the inmost mind.

          Dire inflammation, which no cooling herb
          Or medicinal liquor can asswage,
          Nor breath of vernal air from snowy Alp.
          Sleep hath forsook and given me o'er
          To death's benumming opium as my only cure,
          Thence faintings, swoonings of despair,
          And sense of heaven's desertion.

MILTON.—Samson Agonistes.
```

Hitherto I have chiefly followed the history of my hero, if hero in any sense he can yet be called. Now I must leave him for a while, and take up the story of the rest of the few persons concerned in my tale.

Lady Emily had gone to Madeira, and Mr. Arnold had followed. Mrs. Elton and Harry, and Margaret, of course, had gone to London. Euphra was left alone at Arnstead.

David Elginbrod

A great alteration had taken place in this strange girl. The servants were positively afraid of her now, from the butler down to the kitchen–maid. She used to go into violent fits of passion, in which the mere flash of her eyes was overpowering. These outbreaks would be followed almost instantaneously by seasons of the deepest dejection, in which she would confine herself to her room for hours, or, lame as she was, wander about the house and the Ghost's Walk, herself pale as a ghost, and looking meagre and wretched.

Also, she became subject to frequent fainting fits, the first of which took place the night before Hugh's departure, after she had returned to the house from her interview with him in the Ghost's Walk. She was evidently miserable.

For this misery we know that there were very sufficient reasons, without taking into account the fact that she had no one to fascinate now. Her continued lameness, which her restlessness aggravated, likewise gave her great cause for anxiety. But I presume that, even during the early part of her confinement, her mind had been thrown back upon itself, in that consciousness which often arises in loneliness and suffering; and that even then she had begun to feel that her own self was a worse tyrant than the count, and made her a more wretched slave than any exercise of his unlawful power could make her.

Some natures will endure an immense amount of misery before they feel compelled to look there for help, whence all help and healing comes. They cannot believe that there is verily an unseen mysterious power, till the world and all that is in it has vanished in the smoke of despair; till cause and effect is nothing to the intellect, and possible glories have faded from the imagination; then, deprived of all that made life pleasant or hopeful, the immortal essence, lonely and wretched and unable to cease, looks up with its now unfettered and wakened instinct, to the source of its own life—to the possible God who, notwithstanding all the improbabilities of his existence, may yet perhaps be, and may yet perhaps hear his wretched creature that calls. In this loneliness of despair, life must find The Life; for joy is gone, and life is all that is left: it is compelled to seek its source, its root, its eternal life. This alone remains as a possible thing. Strange condition of despair into which the Spirit of God drives a man—a condition in which the Best alone is the Possible!

Other simpler natures look up at once. Even before the first pang has passed away, as by a holy instinct of celestial childhood, they lift their eyes to the heavens whence cometh their aid. Of this class Euphra was not. She belonged to the former. And yet even she had begun to look upward, for the waters had closed above her head. She betook herself to the one man of whom she had heard as knowing about God. She wrote, but no answer came. Days and days passed away, and there was no reply.

"Ah! just so!" she said, in bitterness. "And if I cried to God for ever, I should hear no word of reply. If he be, he sits apart, and leaves the weak to be the prey of the bad. What cares he?"

Yet, as she spoke, she rose, and, by a sudden impulse, threw herself on the floor, and cried for the first time:

"O God, help me!"

Was there voice or hearing?

She rose at least with a little hope, and with the feeling that if she could cry to him, it might be that he could listen to her. It seemed natural to pray; it seemed to come of itself: that could not be except it was first natural for God to hear. The foundation of her own action must be in him who made her; for her call could be only a response after all.

The time passed wearily by. Dim, slow November days came on, with the fall of the last brown shred of those clouds of living green that had floated betwixt earth and heaven. Through the bare boughs of the overarching avenue of the Ghost's Walk, themselves living skeletons, she could now look straight up to the blue sky, which had been there all the time. And she had begun to look up to a higher heaven, through the bare skeleton shapes of life; for the foliage of joy had wholly vanished—shall we say in order that the children of the spring might come?—certainly in order first that the blue sky of a deeper peace might reflect itself in the hitherto darkened waters of her soul.

Perhaps some of my readers may think that she had enough to repent of to keep her from weariness. She had plenty to repent of, no doubt; but repentance, between the paroxysms of its bitterness, is a very dreary and November–like state of the spiritual weather. For its foggy mornings and cheerless noons cannot believe in the sun of spring, soon to ripen into the sun of summer; and its best time is the night, that shuts out the world and weeps its fill of slow tears. But she was not altogether so blameworthy as she may have appeared. Her affections had not been altogether false. She valued, and in a measure possessed, the feelings for which she sought credit. She had a genuine enjoyment of nature, though after a sensuous, Keats–like fashion, not a Wordsworthian. It was the body, rather than the soul, of nature that she loved—its beauty rather than its truth. Had her love of nature been of the deepest, she would have turned aside to conceal her emotions rather than have held them up as allurements in the eyes of her companion. But as no body and no beauty can exist without soul and truth, she who loves the former must at least be capable of loving the deeper essence to which they owe their very existence.

This view of her character is borne out by her love of music and her liking for Hugh. Both were genuine. Had the latter been either more or less genuine than it was, the task of fascination would have been more difficult, and its success less complete. Whether her own feelings became further involved than she had calculated upon, I cannot tell; but surely it says something for her, in any case, that she desired to retain Hugh as her friend, instead of hating him because he had been her lover.

How glad she would have been of Harry now! The days crawled one after the other like weary snakes. She tried to read the New Testament: it was to her like a mouldy chamber of worm–eaten parchments, whose windows had not been opened to the sun or the wind for centuries; and in which the dust of the decaying leaves choked the few beams that found their way through the age–blinded panes.

This state of things could not have lasted long; for Euphra would have died. It lasted, however, until she felt that she had been leading a false, worthless life; that she had been casting from her every day the few remaining fragments of truth and reality that yet kept her nature from falling in a heap of helpless ruin; that she had never been a true friend to any one; that she was of no value—fit for no one's admiration, no one's love. She must leave her former self, like a dead body, behind her, and rise into a purer air of life and reality, else she would perish with that everlasting death which is the disease and corruption of the soul itself.

To those who know anything of such experiences, it will not be surprising that such feelings as these should be alternated with fierce bursts of passion. The old self then started up with feverish energy, and writhed for life. Never any one tried to be better, without, for a time, seeming to himself, perhaps to others, to be worse. For the suffering of the spirit weakens the brain itself, and the whole physical nature groans under it; while the energy spent in the effort to awake, and arise from the dust, leaves the regions previously guarded by prudence naked to the wild inroads of the sudden destroying impulses born of suffering, self—sickness, and hatred. As in the delirious patient, they would dash to the earth whatever comes first within reach, as if the thing first perceived, and so (by perception alone) brought into contact with the suffering, were the cause of all the distress.

One day a letter arrived for her. She had had no letter from any one for weeks. Yet, when she saw the direction, she flung it from her. It was from Mrs. Elton, whom she disliked, because she found her utterly uninteresting and very stupid.

Poor Mrs. Elton laid no claim to the contraries of these epithets. But in proportion as she abjured thought, she claimed speech, both by word of mouth and by letter. Why not? There was nothing in it. She considered reason as an awful enemy to the soul, and obnoxious to God, especially when applied to find out what he means when he addresses us as reasonable creatures. But speech? There was no harm in that. Perhaps it was some latent conviction that this power of speech was the chief distinction between herself and the lower animals, that made her use it so freely, and at the same time open her purse so liberally to the Hospital for Orphan Dogs and Cats. Had it not been for her own dire necessity, the fact that Mrs. Elton was religious would have been enough to convince Euphra that there could not possibly be anything in religion.

The letter lay unopened till next day—a fact easy to account for, improbable as it may seem; for besides writing as largely as she talked, and less amusingly because more correctly, Mrs. Elton wrote such an indistinct though punctiliously neat hand, that the reading of a letter of hers involved no small amount of labour. But the sun shining out next morning, Euphra took courage to read it, while drinking her coffee, although she could not expect to make that ceremony more pleasant thereby. It contained an invitation to visit Mrs. Elton at her house in —— Street, Hyde Park, with the assurance that, now that everything was arranged, they had plenty of room for her. Mrs. Elton was sure she must be lonely at Arnstead; and Mrs. Horton could, no doubt, be trusted—and so on.

Had this letter arrived a few weeks earlier, Euphra would have infused into her answer a skilful concoction of delicate contempt; not for the amusement of knowing that Mrs. Elton would never discover a trace of it, but simply for a relief to her own dislike. Now she would have written a plain letter, containing as brief and as true an excuse as she could find, had it not been, that, inclosed in Mrs. Elton's note she found another, which ran thus:

"DEAR EUPHRA,—Do come and see us. I do not like London at all without you. There are no happy days here like those we had at Arnstead with Mr. Sutherland. Mrs. Elton and Margaret are very kind to me. But I wish you would come. Do, do, do. Please do.

"Your affectionate cousin,

"HARRY ARNOLD."

"The dear boy!" said Euphra, with a gush of pure and grateful affection; "I will go and see him."

Harry had begun to work with his masters, and was doing his best, which was very good. If his heart was not so much in it as when he was studying with his big brother, he gained a great benefit from the increase of exercise to his will, in the doing of what was less pleasant. Ever since Hugh had given his faculties a right direction, and aided him by healthful manly sympathy, he had been making up for the period during which childhood had been protracted into boyhood; and now he was making rapid progress.

When Euphra arrived, Harry rushed to the hall to meet her. She took him in her arms, and burst into tears. Her tears drew forth his. He stroked her pale face, and said:

"Dear Euphra, how ill you look!"

"I shall soon be better now, Harry."

"I was afraid you did not love me, Euphra; but now I am sure you do."

"Indeed I do. I am very sorry for everything that made you think I did not love you."

"No, no. It was all my fancy. Now we shall be very happy."

And so Harry was. And Euphra, through means of Harry, began to gain a little of what is better than most kinds of happiness, because it is nearest to the best happiness—I mean peace. This foretaste of rest came to her from the devotedness with which she now applied herself to aid the intellect, which she had unconsciously repressed and stunted before. She took Harry's books when he had gone to bed; and read over all his lessons, that she might be able to assist him in preparing them; venturing thus into some regions of labour into which ladies are too seldom conducted by those who instruct them. This produced in her quite new experiences. One of these was, that in proportion as she laboured for Harry, hope grew for herself. It was likewise of the greatest immediate benefit that the intervals of thought, instead of lying vacant to melancholy, or the vapours that sprung from the foregoing strife of the spiritual elements, should be occupied by healthy mental exercise.

Still, however, she was subject to great vicissitudes of feeling. A kind of peevishness, to which she had formerly been a stranger, was but too ready to appear, even when she was most anxious, in her converse with Harry, to behave well to him. But the pure forgiveness of the boy was wonderful. Instead of plaguing himself to find out the cause of her behaviour, or resenting it in the least, he only laboured, by increased attention and submission, to remove it; and seemed perfectly satisfied when it was followed by a kind word, which to him was repentance, apology, amends, and betterment, all in one. When he had thus driven away the evil spirit, there was Euphra her own self. So perfectly did she see, and so thoroughly appreciate this kindness and love of Harry, that he began to look to her like an angel of forgiveness come to live a boy's life, that he might do an angel's work.

Her health continued very poor. She suffered constantly from more or less headache, and at times from faintings. But she had not for some time discovered any signs of somnambulism.

Of this peculiarity her friends were entirely ignorant. The occasions, indeed, on which it had manifested itself to an excessive degree, had been but few.

CHAPTER IX. THE NEW PUPILS.

```
Think you a little din can daunt mine ears?
Have I not in my time heard lions roar?

And do you tell me of a woman's tongue,
That gives not half so great a blow to hear,
As will a chestnut in a farmer's fire?
```

David Elginbrod

Tush! tush! fear boys with bugs.

Taming of the Shrew.

During the whole of his first interview with Falconer, which lasted so long that he had been glad to make a bed of Falconer's sofa, Hugh never once referred to the object for which he had accepted MacPherson's proffered introduction; nor did Falconer ask him any questions. Hugh was too much interested and saddened by the scenes through which Falconer led him, not to shrink from speaking of anything less important; and with Falconer it was a rule, a principle almost, never to expedite utterance of any sort.

In the morning, feeling a little good–natured anxiety as to his landlady's reception of him, Hugh made some allusion to it, as he sat at his new friend's breakfast–table.

Falconer said:

"What is your landlady's name?"

"Miss Talbot."

"Oh! little Miss Talbot? You are in good quarters—too good to lose, I can tell you. Just say to Miss Talbot that you were with me."

"You know her, then?"

"Oh, yes."

"You seem to know everybody."

"If I have spoken to a person once, I never forget him."

"That seems to me very strange."

"It is simple enough. The secret of it is, that, as far as I can help it, I never have any merely business relations with any one. I try always not to forget that there is a deeper relation between us. I commonly succeed worst in a drawing–room; yet even there, for

360

the time we are together, I try to recognise the present humanity, however much distorted or concealed. The consequence is, I never forget anybody; and I generally find that others remember me—at least those with whom I have had any real relations, springing from my need or from theirs. The man who mends a broken chair for you, or a rent in your coat, renders you a human service; and, in virtue of that, comes nearer to your inner self, than nine–tenths of the ladies and gentlemen whom you meet only in what is called society, are likely to do."

"But do you not find it awkward sometimes?"

"Not in the least. I am never ashamed of knowing any one; and as I never assume a familiarity that does not exist, I never find it assumed towards me."

Hugh found the advantage of Falconer's sociology when he mentioned to Miss Talbot that he had been his guest that night.

"You should have sent us word, Mr. Sutherland," was all Miss Talbot's reply.

"I could not do so before you must have been all in bed. I was sorry, but I could hardly help it."

Miss Talbot turned away into the kitchen. The only other indication of her feeling in the matter was, that she sent him up a cup of delicious chocolate for his lunch, before he set out for Mr. Appleditch's, where she had heard at the shop that he was going.

My reader must not be left to fear that I am about to give a detailed account of Hugh's plans with these unpleasant little immortals, whose earthly nature sprang from a pair whose religion consisted chiefly in negations, and whose main duty seemed to be to make money in small sums, and spend it in smaller. When he arrived at Buccleuch Crescent, he was shown into the dining–room, into which the boys were separately dragged, to receive the first instalment of the mental legacy left them by their ancestors. But the legacy–duty was so heavy that they would gladly have declined paying it, even with the loss of the legacy itself; and Hugh was dismayed at the impossibility of interesting them in anything. He tried telling them stories even, without success. They stared at him, it is true; but whether there was more speculation in the open mouths, or in the fishy, overfed eyes, he found it impossible to determine. He could not help feeling the riddle of Providence in regard to the birth of these, much harder to read than that involved in the case of some of the little thieves whose acquaintance he had made, when with Falconer, the evening before. But he did his best; and before the time had expired—two hours, namely,—he had found out, to his satisfaction, that the elder had a turn for sums, and the younger for drawing. So he made use of these predilections to bribe them to the exercise of their intellect upon less-favoured branches of human accomplishment. He found the plan operate as well as it could have been expected to operate upon such material.

But one or two little incidents, relating to his intercourse with Mrs. Appleditch, I must not omit. Though a mother's love is more ready to purify itself than most other loves—yet there is a class of mothers, whose love is only an extended, scarcely an expanded, selfishness. Mrs. Appleditch did not in the least love her children because they were children, and children committed to her care by the Father of all children; but she loved them dearly because they were her children.

One day Hugh gave Master Appleditch a smart slap across the fingers, as the ultimate resource. The child screamed as he well knew how. His mother burst into the room.

"Johnny, hold your tongue!"

"Teacher's been and hurt me."

"Hold your tongue, I say. My head's like to split. Get out of the room, you little ruffian!"

She seized him by the shoulders, and turned him out, administering a box on his ear that made the room ring. Then turning to Hugh,

"Mr. Sutherland, how dare you strike my child?" she demanded.

"He required it, Mrs. Appleditch. I did him no harm. He will mind what I say another time."

"I will not have him touched. It's disgraceful. To strike a child!"

She belonged to that class of humane parents who consider it cruel to inflict any corporal suffering upon children, except they do it themselves, and in a passion. Johnnie behaved better after this, however; and the only revenge Mrs. Appleditch took for this interference with the dignity of her eldest born, and, consequently, with her own as his mother, was, that—with the view, probably, of impressing upon Hugh a due sense of the menial position he occupied in her family—she always paid him his fee of one shilling and sixpence every day before he left the house. Once or twice she contrived accidentally that the sixpence should be in coppers. Hugh was too much of a philosopher, however, to mind this from such a woman. I am afraid he rather enjoyed her spite; for he felt it did not touch him, seeing it could not be less honourable to be paid by the day than by the quarter or by the year. Certainly the coppers were an annoyance; but if the coppers could be carried, the annoyance could be borne. The real disgust in the affair was, that he had to meet and speak with a woman every day, for whom he could feel nothing but contempt and aversion. Hugh was not yet able to mingle with these feelings any of the leaven of that charity which they need most of all who are contemptible in the eye of their fellows. Contempt is murder committed by the intellect, as hatred is murder committed by the heart. Charity having life in itself, is the opposite and destroyer of contempt as well as of hatred.

After this, nothing went amiss for some time. But it was very dreary work to teach such boys—for the younger came in for the odd sixpence. Slow, stupid, resistance appeared to be the only principle of their behaviour towards him. They scorned the man whom their mother despised and valued for the self–same reason, namely, that he was cheap. They would have defied him had they dared, but he managed to establish an authority over them—and to increase it. Still, he could not rouse them to any real interest in their studies. Indeed, they were as near being little beasts as it was possible for children to be. Their eyes grew dull at a story–book, but greedily bright at the sight of bull's eyes or toffee. It was the same day after day, till he was sick of it. No doubt they made some progress, but it was scarcely perceptible to him. Through fog and fair, through frost and snow, through wind and rain, he trudged to that wretched house. No one minds the weather—no young Scotchman, at least—where any pleasure waits the close of the struggle: to fight his way to misery was more than he could well endure. But his deliverance was nearer than he expected. It was not to come just yet, however.

All went on with frightful sameness, till sundry doubtful symptoms of an alteration in the personal appearance of Hugh having accumulated at last into a mass of evidence, forced the conviction upon the mind of the grocer's wife, that her tutor was actually growing a beard. Could she believe her eyes? She said she could not. But she acted on their testimony notwithstanding; and one day suddenly addressing Hugh, said, in her usual cold, thin, cutting fashion of speech:

"Mr. Sutherland, I am astonished and grieved that you, a teacher of babes, who should set an example to them, should disguise yourself in such an outlandish figure."

"What do you mean, Mrs. Appleditch?" asked Hugh, who, though he had made up his mind to follow the example of Falconer, yet felt uncomfortable enough, during the transition period, to know quite well what she meant.

"What do I mean, sir? It is a shame for a man to let his beard grow like a monkey."

"But a monkey hasn't a beard," retorted Hugh, laughing. "Man is the only animal who has one."

This assertion, if not quite correct, was approximately so, and went much nearer the truth than Mrs. Appleditch's argument.

"It's no joking matter, Mr. Sutherland, with my two darlings growing up to be ministers of the gospel."

"What! both of them?" thought Hugh. "Good heavens!" But he said:

"Well, but you know, Mrs. Appleditch, the Apostles themselves wore beards."

"Yes, when they were Jews. But who would have believed them if they had preached the gospel like old clothesmen? No, no, Mr. Sutherland, I see through all that. My own uncle was a preacher of the word.—As soon as the Apostles became Christians, they shaved. It was the sign of Christianity. The Apostle Paul himself says that cleanliness is next to godliness."

Hugh restrained his laughter, and shifted his ground.

"But there is nothing dirty about them," he said.

"Not dirty? Now really, Mr. Sutherland, you provoke me. Nothing dirty in long hair all round your mouth, and going into it every spoonful you take?"

"But it can be kept properly trimmed, you know."

"But who's to trust you to do that? No, no, Mr. Sutherland; you must not make a guy of yourself."

Hugh laughed, and said nothing. Of course his beard would go on growing, for he could not help it.

So did Mrs. Appleditch's wrath.

CHAPTER X. CONSULTATIONS.

Wo keine Götter sind, walten Gespenster.

NOVALIS.— Christenheit.

Where gods are not, spectres rule.

Ein Charakter ist ein vollkommen gebildeter Wille.

NOVALIS.—Moralische Ansichten.

A character is a perfectly formed will.

It was not long before Hugh repeated his visit to Falconer. He was not at home. He went again and again, but still failed in finding him. The day after the third failure, however, he received a note from Falconer, mentioning an hour at which he would be at home on the following evening. Hugh went. Falconer was waiting for him.

"I am very sorry. I am out so much," said Falconer.

"I ought to have taken the opportunity when I had it," replied Hugh. "I want to ask your help. May I begin at the beginning, and tell you all the story? or must I epitomize and curtail it?"

David Elginbrod

"Be as diffuse as you please. I shall understand the thing the better."

So Hugh began, and told the whole of his history, in as far as it bore upon the story of the crystal. He ended with the words:

"I trust, Mr. Falconer, you will not think that it is from a love of talking that I have said so much about this affair."

"Certainly not. It is a remarkable story. I will think what can be done. Meantime I will keep my eyes and ears open. I may find the fellow. Tell me what he is like."

Hugh gave as minute a description of the count as he could.

"I think I see the man," said Falconer. "I am pretty sure I shall recognise him."

"Have you any idea what he could want with the ring?"

"It is one of the curious coincidences which are always happening," answered Falconer, "that a newspaper of this very day would have enabled me, without any previous knowledge of similar facts, to give a probably correct suggestion as to his object. But you can judge for yourself."

So saying, Falconer went to a side–table, heaped up with books and papers, maps, and instruments of various kinds, apparently in triumphant confusion. Without a moment's hesitation, notwithstanding, he selected the paper he wanted, and handed it to Hugh, who read in it a letter to the editor, of which the following is a portion:—

"I have for over thirty years been in the habit of investigating the question by means of crystals. And since 18—, I have possessed the celebrated crystal, once belonging to Lady Blessington, in which very many persons, both children and adults, have seen visions of the spirits of the deceased, or of beings claiming to be such, and of numerous angels and other beings of the spiritual world. These have in all cases supported the purest and most liberal Christianity. The faculty of seeing in the crystal I have found to exist in about one person in ten among adults, and in nearly nine in every ten among children; many of whom appear to lose the faculty as they grow to adult age, unless they practise it continually."

"Is it possible," said Hugh, pausing, "that this can be a veritable paper of to–day? Are there people to believe such things?"

"There are more fools in the world, Mr. Sutherland, than there are crystals in its mountains."

Hugh resumed his reading. He came at length to this passage:

"The spirits—which I feel certain they are—which appear, do not hesitate to inform us on all possible subjects which may tend to improve our morals, and confirm our faith in the Christian doctrines...The character they give of the class of spirits who are in the habit of communicating with mortals by rapping and such proceedings, is such that it behoves all Christian people to be on their guard against error and delusion through their means."

Hugh had read this passage aloud.

"Is not that a comfort, now, Mr. Sutherland?" said Falconer. "For in all the reports which I have seen of the religious instruction communicated in that highly articulate manner, Calvinism, high and low, has predominated. I strongly suspect the crystal phantoms of Arminianism, though. Fancy the old disputes of infant Christendom perpetuated amongst the paltry ghosts of another realm!"

"But," said Hugh, "I do not quite see how this is to help me, as to the count's object in securing the ring; for certainly, however deficient he may be in such knowledge, he is not likely to have committed the theft for the sake of instruction in the doctrines of the sects."

"No. But such a crystal might be put to other, not to say better, uses. Besides, Lady Blessington's crystal might be a pious crystal; and the other which belonged to Lady—"

"Lady Euphrasia."

"To Lady Euphrasia, might be a worldly crystal altogether. This might reveal demons and their counsels, while that was haunted by theological angels and evangelical ghosts."

"Ah! I see. I should have thought, however, that the count had been too much of a man of the world to believe such things."

"He might find his account in it, notwithstanding. But no amount of world—wisdom can set a man above the inroads of superstition. In fact, there is but one thing that can free a man from superstition, and that is belief. All history proves it. The most sceptical have ever been the most credulous. This is one of the best arguments for the existence of something to believe."

"You remind me of a passage in my story which I omitted, as irrelevant to the matter in hand."

"Do let me have it. It cannot fail to interest me."

Hugh gave a complete account of the experiments they had made with the careering plate. Now the writing of the name of David Elginbrod was the most remarkable phenomenon of the whole, and Hugh was compelled, in responding to the natural interest of Falconer, to give a description of David. This led to a sketch of his own sojourn at Turriepuffit; in which the character of David came out far more plainly than it could have come out in any description. When he had finished, Falconer broke out, as if he had been hitherto restraining his wrath with difficulty:

"And that was the man the creatures dared to personate! I hate the whole thing, Sutherland. It is full of impudence and irreverence. Perhaps the wretched beings may want another thousand years' damnation, because of the injury done to their character by the homage of men who ought to know better."

"I do not quite understand you."

"I mean, that you ought to believe as easily that such a man as you describe is laughing with the devil and his angels, as that he wrote a copy at the order of a charlatan, or worse."

"But it could hardly be deception."

"Not deception? A man like him could not get through them without being recognised."

"I don't understand you. By whom?"

368

David Elginbrod

"By swarms of low miserable creatures that so lament the loss of their beggarly bodies that they would brood upon them in the shape of flesh—flies, rather than forsake the putrifying remnants. After that, chair or table or anything that they can come into contact with, possesses quite sufficient organization for such. Don't you remember that once, rather than have no body to go into, they crept into the very swine? There was a fine passion for self—embodiment and sympathy! But the swine themselves could not stand it, and preferred drowning."

"Then you do think there was something supernatural in it?"

"Nothing in the least. It required no supernatural powers to be aware that a great man was dead, and that you had known him well. It annoys me, Sutherland, that able men, ay, and good men too, should consult with ghosts whose only possible superiority consists in their being out of the body. Why should they be the wiser for that? I should as soon expect to gain wisdom by taking off my clothes, and to lose it by getting into bed; or to rise into the seventh heaven of spirituality by having my hair cut. An impudent forgery of that good man's name! If I were you, Sutherland, I would have nothing to do with such a low set. They are the canaille of the other world. It's of no use to lay hold on their skirts, for they can't fly. They're just like the vultures—easy to catch, because they're full of garbage. I doubt if they have more intellect left than just enough to lie with.—I have been compelled to think a good deal about these things of late."

Falconer put a good many questions to Hugh, about Euphra and her relation to the count; and such was the confidence with which he had inspired him, that Hugh felt at perfect liberty to answer them all fully, not avoiding even the exposure of his own feelings, where that was involved by the story.

"Now," said Falconer, "I have material out of which to construct a theory. The count is at present like a law of nature concerning which a prudent question is the first half of the answer, as Lord Bacon says; and you can put no question without having first formed a theory, however slight or temporary; for otherwise no question will suggest itself. But, in the meantime, as I said before, I will make inquiry upon the theory that he is somewhere in London, although I doubt it."

"Then I will not occupy your time any longer at present," said Hugh. "Could you say, without fettering yourself in the least, when I might be able to see you again?"

369

"Let me see. I will make an appointment with you.—Next Sunday; here; at ten o'clock in the morning. Make a note of it."

"There is no fear of my forgetting it. My consolations are not so numerous that I can afford to forget my sole pleasure. You, I should think, have more need to make a note of it than I, though I am quite willing to be forgotten, if necessary."

"I never forget my engagements," said Falconer.

They parted, and Hugh went home to his novel.

CHAPTER XI. QUESTIONS AND DREAMS.

On a certain time the Lady St. Mary had commanded the Lord Jesus to fetch her some water out of the well. And when he had gone to fetch the water, the pitcher, when it was brought up full, brake. But Jesus, spreading his mantle, gathered up the water again, and brought it in that to his mother.—The First (apocryphal) Gospel of the INFANCY of JESUS CHRIST.

Mrs. Elton read prayers morning and evening;—very elaborate compositions, which would have instructed the apostles themselves in many things they had never anticipated. But, unfortunately, Mrs. Elton must likewise read certain remarks, in the form of a homily, intended to impress the scripture which preceded it upon the minds of the listeners. Between the mortar of the homilist's faith, and the dull blows of the pestle of his arrogance, the fair form of truth was ground into the powder of pious small talk. This result was not pleasant either to Harry or to Euphra. Euphra, with her life threatening to go to ruin about her, was crying out for him who made the soul of man, "who loved us into being,"2 and who alone can renew the life of his children; and in such words as those a scoffing demon seemed to mock at her needs. Harry had the natural dislike of all childlike natures to everything formal, exclusive, and unjust. But, having received nothing of what is commonly called a religious training, this advantage resulted from his new experiences in Mrs. Elton's family, that a good direction was given to his thoughts by the dislike which he felt to such utterances. More than this: a horror fell upon him lest these things should be true; lest the mighty All of nature should be only a mechanism, without expression and without beauty; lest the God who made us should be like us only in this, that he too was selfish and mean and proud; lest his ideas should resemble those that inhabit the brain of a retired money–maker, or of an arbitrary monarch claiming a divine right—instead of towering as the heavens over the earth, above the loftiest moods of highest poet, most generous child, or most devoted mother. I do not mean that these thoughts took these shapes in Harry's mind; but that his feelings were such as might have been condensed into such thoughts, had his intellect been more mature.

One morning, the passage of scripture which Mrs. Elton read was the story of the young man who came to Jesus, and went away sorrowful, because the Lord thought so well of him, and loved him so heartily, that he wanted to set him free from his riches. A great portion of the homily was occupied with proving that the evangelist could not possibly mean that Jesus loved the young man in any pregnant sense of the word; but merely meant that Jesus "felt kindly disposed towards him"—felt a poor little human interest in him, in fact, and did not love him divinely at all.

Harry's face was in a flame all the time she was reading. When the service was over—and a bond service it was for Euphra and him—they left the room together. As soon as the door was shut, he burst out:

"I say, Euphra! Wasn't that a shame? They would have Jesus as bad as themselves. We shall have somebody writing a book next to prove that after all Jesus was a Pharisee."

"Never mind," said the heart–sore, sceptical Euphra; "never mind, Harry; it's all nonsense."

"No, it's not all nonsense. Jesus did love the young man. I believe the story itself before all the Doctors of Divinity in the world. He loves all of us, he does—with all his heart, too."

"I hope so," was all she could reply; but she was comforted by Harry's vehement confession of faith.

Euphra was so far softened, or perhaps weakened, by suffering, that she yielded many things which would have seemed impossible before. One of these was that she went to church with Mrs. Elton, where that lady hoped she would get good to her soul. Harry of course was not left behind. The church she frequented was a fashionable one, with a vicar more fashionable still; for had he left that church, more than half his congregation, which consisted mostly of ladies, would have left it also, and followed him to the ends of London. He was a middle–aged man, with a rubicund countenance, and a gentle familiarity of manner, that was exceedingly pleasing to the fashionable sheep who, conscious that they had wandered from the fold, were waiting with exemplary patience for the barouches and mail–phaetons of the skies to carry them back without the trouble of walking. Alas for them! they have to learn that the chariots of heaven are chariots of fire.

The Sunday morning following the conversation I have just recorded, the clergyman's sermon was devoted to the illustration of the greatness and condescension of the Saviour. After a certain amount of tame excitement expended upon the consideration of his power and kingdom, one passage was wound up in this fashion:

"Yes, my friends, even her most gracious Majesty, Queen Victoria, the ruler over millions diverse in speech and in hue, to whom we all look up with humble submission, and whom we acknowledge as our sovereign lady—even she, great as she is, adds by her homage a jewel to his crown; and, hailing him as her Lord, bows and renders him worship! Yet this is he who comes down to visit, yea, dwells with his own elect, his chosen ones, whom he has led back to the fold of his grace."

For some reason, known to himself, Falconer had taken Hugh, who had gone to him according to appointment that morning, to this same church. As they came out, Hugh said:

"Mr.——is quite proud of the honour done his master by the queen."

"I do not think," answered Falconer, "that his master will think so much of it; for he once had his feet washed by a woman that was a sinner."

The homily which Mrs. Elton read at prayers that evening, bore upon the same subject nominally as the chapter that preceded it—that of election; a doctrine which in the Bible asserts the fact of God's choosing certain persons for the specific purpose of receiving first, and so communicating the gifts of his grace to the whole world; but which, in the homily referred to, was taken to mean the choice of certain persons for ultimate salvation, to the exclusion of the rest. They were sitting in silence after the close, when Harry started up suddenly, saying: "I don't want God to love me, if he does not love everybody;" and, bursting into tears, hurried out of the room. Mrs. Elton was awfully shocked at his wickedness. Euphra, hastened after him; but he would not return, and went supperless to bed. Euphra, however, carried him some supper. He sat up in bed and ate it with the tears in his eyes. She kissed him, and bade him good night; when, just as she was leaving the room, he broke out with:

"But only think, Euphra, if it should be true! I would rather not have been made."

"It is not true," said Euphra, in whom a faint glimmer of faith in God awoke for the sake of the boy whom she loved—awoke to comfort him, when it would not open its eyes for herself. "No, Harry dear, if there is a God at all, he is not like that."

"No, he can't be," said Harry, vehemently, and with the brightness of a sudden thought; "for if he were like that, he wouldn't be a God worth being; and that couldn't be, you know."

Euphra knelt by her bedside, and prayed more hopefully than for many days before. She prayed that God would let her know that he was not an idol of man's invention.

Till friendly sleep came, and untied the knot of care, both Euphra and Harry lay troubled with things too great for them. Even in their sleep, the care would gather again, and body itself into dreams. The first thought that visited Harry when he awoke, was the memory of his dream: that he died and went to heaven; that heaven was a great church just like the one Mrs. Elton went to, only larger; that the pews were filled with angels, so crowded together that they had to tuck up their wings very close indeed—and Harry could not help wondering what they wanted them for; that they were all singing psalms; that the pulpit by a little change had been converted into a throne, on which sat God the Father, looking very solemn and severe; that Jesus was seated in the reading–desk, looking very sad; and that the Holy Ghost sat on the clerk's desk, in the shape of a white dove; that a cherub, whose face reminded him very much of a policeman he knew, took him by the shoulder for trying to pluck a splendid green feather out of an archangel's wing, and led him up to the throne, where God shook his head at him in such a dreadful way, that he was terrified, and then stretched out his hand to lay hold on him; that he shrieked with fear; and that Jesus put out his hand and lifted him into the reading–desk, and hid him down below. And there Harry lay, feeling so safe, stroking and kissing the feet that had been weary and wounded for him, till, in the growing delight of the thought that he actually held those feet, he came awake and remembered it all. Truly it was a childish dream, but not without its own significance. For surely the only refuge from heathenish representations of God under Christian forms, the only refuge from man's blinding and paralysing theories, from the dead wooden shapes substituted for the living forms of human love and hope and aspiration, from the interpretations which render scripture as dry as a speech in Chancery—surely the one refuge from all these awful evils is the Son of man; for no misrepresentation and no misconception can destroy the beauty of that face which the marring of sorrow has elevated into the region of reality, beyond the marring of irreverent speculation and scholastic definition. >From the God of man's painting, we turn to the man of God's being, and he leads us to the true God, the radiation of whose glory we first see in him. Happy is that man who has a glimpse of this, even in a dream such as Harry's!—a dream in other respects childish and incongruous, but not more absurd than the instruction whence it sprung.

But the troubles returned with the day. Prayers revived them. He sought Euphra in her room.

"They say I must repent and be sorry for my sins," said he. "I have been trying very hard; but I can't think of any, except once that I gave Gog" (his Welsh pony) "such a beating because he would go where I didn't want him. But he's forgotten it long ago; and I gave him two feeds of corn after it, and so somehow I can't feel very sorry now. What shall I do?—But that's not what I mind most. It always seems to me it would be so much grander of God to say: 'Come along, never mind. I'll make you good. I can't wait till you are good; I love you so much.'"

His own words were too much for Harry, and he burst into tears at the thought of God being so kind. Euphra, instead of trying to comfort him, cried too. Thus they continued for some time, Harry with his head on her knees, and she kindly fondling it with her distressed hands. Harry was the first to recover; for his was the April time, when rain clears the heavens. All at once he sprung to his feet, and exclaimed:

"Only think, Euphra! What if, after all, I should find out that God is as kind as you are!"

How Euphra's heart smote her!

David Elginbrod

"Dear Harry," answered she, "God must be a great deal kinder than I am. I have not been kind to you at all."

"Don't say that, Euphra. I shall be quite content if God is as kind as you."

"Oh, Harry! I hope God is like what I dreamed about my mother last night."

"Tell me what you dreamed about her, dear Euphra."

"I dreamed that I was a little child—"

"Were you a little girl when your mother died?"

"Oh, yes; such a tiny! But I can just remember her."

"Tell me your dream, then."

"I dreamed that I was a little girl, out all alone on a wild mountain−moor, tripping and stumbling on my night−gown. And the wind was so cold! And, somehow or other, the wind was an enemy to me, and it followed and caught me, and whirled and tossed me about, and then ran away again. Then I hastened on, and the thorns went into my feet, and the stones cut them. And I heard the blood from them trickling down the hill−side as I walked."

"Then they would be like the feet I saw in my dream last night."

"Whose feet were they?"

"Jesus' feet."

"Tell me about it."

"You must finish yours first, please, Euphra."

So Euphra went on:

"I got dreadfully lame. And the wind ran after me, and caught me again, and took me in his great blue ghostly arms, and shook me about, and then dropped me again to go on. But it was very hard to go on, and I couldn't stop; and there was no use in stopping, for the wind was everywhere in a moment. Then suddenly I saw before me a great cataract, all in white, falling flash from a precipice; and I thought with myself, 'I will go into the cataract, and it will beat my life out, and then the wind will not get me any more.' So I hastened towards it, but the wind caught me many times before I got near it. At last I reached it, and threw myself down into the basin it had hollowed out of the rocks. But as I was falling, something caught me gently, and held me fast, and it was not the wind. I opened my eyes, and behold! I was in my mother's arms, and she was clasping me to her breast; for what I had taken for a cataract falling into a gulf, was only my mother, with her white grave–clothes floating all about her, standing up in her grave, to look after me. 'It was time you came home, my darling,' she said, and stooped down into her grave with me in her arms. And oh! I was so happy; and her bosom was not cold, or her arms hard, and she carried me just like a baby. And when she stooped down, then a door opened somewhere in the grave, I could not find out where exactly—and in a moment after, we were sitting together in a summer grove, with the tree–tops steeped in sunshine, and waving about in a quiet loving wind—oh, how different from the one that chased me home!—and we underneath in the shadow of the trees. And then I said, 'Mother, I've hurt my feet.'"

"Did you call her mother when you were a little girl?" interposed Harry.

"No," answered Euphra. "I called her mamma, like other children; but in my dreams I always call her mother."

"And what did she say?"

"She said—'Poor child!'—and held my feet to her bosom; and after that, when I looked at them, the bleeding was all gone, and I was not lame any more."

Euphra, paused with a sigh.

"Oh, Harry! I do not like to be lame."

"What more?" said Harry, intent only on the dream.

376

"Oh! then I was so happy, that I woke up directly."

"What a pity! But if it should come true?"

"How could it come true, dear Harry?"

"Why, this world is sometimes cold, and the road is hard—you know what I mean, Euphra."

"Yes, I do."

"I wish I could dream dreams like that! How clever you must be!"

"But you dream dreams, too, Harry. Tell me yours."

"Oh, no, I never dream dreams; the dreams dream me," answered Harry, with a smile.

Then he told his dream, to which Euphra listened with an interest uninjured by the grotesqueness of its fancy. Each interpreted the other's with reverence.

They ceased talking; and sat silent for a while. Then Harry, putting his arms round Euphra's neck, and his lips close to her ear, whispered:

"Perhaps God will say my darling to you some day, Euphra; just as your mother did in your dream."

She was silent. Harry looked round into her face, and saw that the tears were flowing fast.

At that instant, a gentle knock came to the door. Euphra could not reply to it. It was repeated. After another moment's delay, the door opened, and Margaret walked in.

CHAPTER XII. A SUNDAY WITH FALCONER.

```
How happy is he born and taught,
   That serveth not another's will;
Whose armour is his honest thought,
```

David Elginbrod

```
And simple truth his utmost skill.

This man is freed from servile bands
  Of hope to rise or fear to fall:
Lord of himself, though not of lands,
  And, having nothing, yet hath all.

SIR HENRY WOTTON.
```

It was not often that Falconer went to church; but he seemed to have some design in going oftener than usual at present. The Sunday after the one last mentioned, he went as well, though not to the same church, and calling for Hugh took him with him. What they found there, and the conversation following thereupon, I will try to relate, because, although they do not immediately affect my outward story, they greatly influenced Hugh's real history.

They heard the Morning Service and the Litany read in an ordinary manner, though somewhat more devoutly than usual. Then, from the communion–table, rose a voice vibrating with solemn emotion, like the voice of Abraham pleading for Sodom. It thrilled through Hugh's heart. The sermon which followed affected him no less, although, when he came out, he confessed to Falconer that he had only caught flying glimpses of its meaning, scope, and drift.

"I seldom go to church," said Falconer; "but when I do, I come here: and always feel that I am in the presence of one of the holy servants of God's great temple not made with hands. I heartily trust that man. He is what he seems to be."

"They say he is awfully heterodox."

"They do."

"How then can he remain in the church, if he is as honest as you say?"

"In this way, as I humbly venture to think," Falconer answered. "He looks upon the formulæ of the church as utterances of living truth—vital embodiments—to be regarded as one ought to regard human faces. In these human faces, others may see this or that inferior expression, may find out the mean and the small and the incomplete: he looks for

378

and finds the ideal; the grand, sacred, God–meant meaning; and by that he holds as the meaning of the human countenances, for it is the meaning of him who made them. So with the confession of the Church of England: he believes that not man only, but God also, and God first and chief, had to do with the making of it; and therefore he looks in it for the Eternal and the Divine, and he finds what he seeks. And as no words can avoid bearing in them the possibility of a variety of interpretations, he would exclude whatever the words might mean, or, regarded merely as words, do mean, in a narrow exposition: he thinks it would be dishonest to take the low meaning as the meaning. To return to the faces: he passes by moods and tempers, and beholds the main character—that on whose surface the temporal and transient floats. Both in faces and in formulæ he loves the divine substance, with his true, manly, brave heart; and as for the faults in both—for man, too, has his share in both—I believe he is ready to die by them, if only in so doing he might die for them.—I had a vision of him this morning as I sat and listened to his voice, which always seems to me to come immediately from his heart, as if his heart spoke with lips of its own. Shall I tell you my vision?—

"I saw a crowd—priests and laymen—speeding, hurrying, darting away, up a steep, crumbling height. Mitres, hoods, and hats rolled behind them to the bottom. Every one for himself, with hands and feet they scramble and flee, to save their souls from the fires of hell which come rolling in along the hollow below with the forward 'pointing spires' of billowy flame. But beneath, right in the course of the fire, stands one man upon a little rock which goes down to the centre of the great world, and faces the approaching flames. He stands bareheaded, his eyes bright with faith in God, and the mighty mouth that utters his truth, fixed in holy defiance. His denial comes from no fear, or weak dislike to that which is painful. On neither side will he tell lies for peace. He is ready to be lost for his fellow–men. In the name of God he rebukes the flames of hell. The fugitives pause on the top, look back, call him lying prophet, and shout evil opprobrious names at the man who counts not his own life dear to him, who has forgotten his own soul in his sacred devotion to men, who fills up what is left behind of the sufferings of Christ, for his body's sake—for the human race, of which he is the head. Be sure that, come what may of the rest, let the flames of hell ebb or flow, that man is safe, for he is delivered already from the only devil that can make hell itself a torture, the devil of selfishness—the only one that can possess a man and make himself his own living hell. He is out of all that region of things, and already dwelling in the secret place of the Almighty."

"Go on, go on."

David Elginbrod

"He trusts in God so absolutely, that he leaves his salvation to him—utterly, fearlessly; and, forgetting it, as being no concern of his, sets himself to do the work that God has given him to do, even as his Lord did before him, counting that alone worthy of his care. Let God's will be done, and all is well. If God's will be done, he cannot fare ill. To him, God is all in all. If it be possible to separate such things, it is the glory of God, even more than the salvation of men, that he seeks. He will not have it that his Father in heaven is not perfect. He believes entirely that God loves, yea, is love; and, therefore, that hell itself must be subservient to that love, and but an embodiment of it; that the grand work of Justice is to make way for a Love which will give to every man that which is right and ten times more, even if it should be by means of awful suffering—a suffering which the Love of the Father will not shun, either for himself or his children, but will eagerly meet for their sakes, that he may give them all that is in his heart."

"Surely you speak your own opinions in describing thus warmly the faith of the preacher."

"I do. He is accountable for nothing I say. All I assert is, that this is how I seem to myself to succeed in understanding him."

"How is it that so many good people call him heterodox?"

"I do not mind that. I am annoyed only when good–hearted people, with small natures and cultivated intellects, patronise him, and talk forgivingly of his warm heart and unsound judgment. To these, theology must be like a map—with plenty of lines in it. They cannot trust their house on the high table–land of his theology, because they cannot see the outlines bounding the said table–land. It is not small enough for them. They cannot take it in. Such can hardly be satisfied with the creation, one would think, seeing there is no line of division anywhere in it. They would take care there should be no mistake."

"Does God draw no lines, then?"

"When he does, they are pure lines, without breadth, and consequently invisible to mortal eyes; not Chinese walls of separation, such as these definers would construct. Such minds are à priori incapable of theorising upon his theories. Or, to alter the figure, they will discover a thousand faults in his drawing, but they can never behold the figure constructed by his lines, and containing the faults which they believe they discover."

"But can those theories in religion be correct which are so hard to see?"

"They are only hard to certain natures."

"But those natures are above the average."

"Yes, in intellect and its cultivation—nothing more."

"You have granted them heart."

"Not much; but what there is, good."

"That is allowing a great deal, though. Is it not hard then to say that such cannot understand him?"

"Why? They will get to heaven, which is all they want. And they will understand him one day, which is more than they pray for. Till they have done being anxious about their own salvation, we must forgive them that they can contemplate with calmness the damnation of a universe, and believe that God is yet more indifferent than they."

"But do they not bring the charges likewise against you, of being unable to understand them?"

"Yes. And so it must remain, till the Spirit of God decide the matter, which I presume must take place by slow degrees. For this decision can only consist in the enlightenment of souls to see the truth; and therefore has to do with individuals only. There is no triumph for the Truth but that. She knows no glorying over the vanquished, for in her victory the vanquished is already of the vanquishers. Till then, the Right must be content to be called the Wrong, and—which is far harder—to seem the Wrong. There is no spiritual victory gained by a verbal conquest; or by any kind of torture, even should the rack employed be that of the purest logic. Nay more: so long as the wicked themselves remain impenitent, there is mourning in heaven; and when there is no longer any hope over one last remaining sinner, heaven itself must confess its defeat, heap upon that sinner what plagues you will."

David Elginbrod

Hugh pondered, and continued pondering till they reached Falconer's chambers. At the door Hugh paused.

"Will you not come in?"

"I fear I shall become troublesome."

"No fear of that. I promise to get rid of you as soon as I find you so."

"Thank you. Just let me know when you have had enough of me."

They entered. Mrs. Ashton, who, unlike her class, was never missing when wanted, got them some bread and cheese; and Falconer's Fortunatus–purse of a cellar—the bottom of his cupboard—supplied its usual bottle of port; to which fare the friends sat down.

The conversation, like a bird descending in spirals, settled at last upon the subject which had more or less occupied Hugh's thoughts ever since his unsatisfactory conversation with Funkelstein, at their first meeting; and still more since he had learned that this man himself exercised an unlawful influence over Euphra. He begged Falconer, if he had any theory comprehending such things, to let him know what kind of a relation it was, in which Miss Cameron stood to Funkelstein, or Count von Halkar.

"I have had occasion to think a good deal about those things," said Falconer. "The first thing evident is, that Miss Cameron is peculiarly constituted, belonging to a class which is, however, larger than is commonly supposed, circumstances rarely combining to bring out its peculiarities. In those who constitute this class, the nervous element, either from preponderating, or from not being in healthy and harmonious combination with the more material element, manifests itself beyond its ordinary sphere of operation, and so occasions results unlike the usual phenomena of life, though, of course, in accordance with natural laws. To use a simile: it is, in such cases, as if all the nerves of the human body came crowding to the surface, and there exposed themselves to a thousand influences, from which they would otherwise be preserved. Of course I am not attempting to explain, only to suggest a conceivable hypothesis. Upon such constitutions, it would not be surprising that certain other constitutions, similar, yet differing, should exercise a peculiar influence. You are, I dare say, more or less familiar with the main features of mesmerism and its allies, among which is what is called biology. I presume it is on such constitutions as I have supposed, that those powers are chiefly operative. Miss Cameron has, at some time or other in her history, submitted herself to the influences of this Count Halkar; and he has thus gained a most dangerous authority over her, which he has exercised for his own ends."

"She more than implied as much in the last conversation I had with her."

"So his will became her law. There is in the world of mind a something corresponding to physical force in the material world.—I cannot avoid just touching upon a higher analogy. The kingdom of heaven is not come, even when God's will is our law: it is come when God's will is our will. While God's will is our law, we are but a kind of noble slaves; when his will is our will, we are free children. Nothing in nature is free enough to be a symbol for the state of those who act immediately from the essence of their hidden life, and the recognition of God's will as that essence. But, as I said, this belongs to a far higher region. I only wanted to touch on the relation of the freedoms—physical, mental, and spiritual. To return to the point in hand: I recognise in the story a clear evidence of strife and partial victory in the affair of the ring. The count—we will call him by the name he gives himself—had evidently been anxious for years to possess himself of this ring: the probable reasons we have already talked of. He had laid his injunctions on his slave to find it for him; and she, perhaps at first nothing loath, perhaps loving the man as well as submitting to him, had for a long time attempted to find it, but had failed. The count, probably doubting her sincerity, and hoping, at all events, to urge her search, followed her to Arnstead, where it is very likely he had been before, although he had avoided Mr. Arnold. Judging it advantageous to get into the house, in order to make observations, he employed his chance meeting with you to that result. But, before this, he had watched Miss Cameron's familiarity with you—was jealous and tyrannical. Hence the variations of her conduct to you; for when his power was upon her, she could not do as she pleased. But she must have had a real regard for you; for she evidently refused to get you into trouble by taking the ring from your custody. But my surprise is that the fellow limited himself to that one jewel."

"You may soon be relieved from that surprise," answered Hugh: "he took a valuable diamond of mine as well."

"The rascal! We may catch him, but you are not likely to find your diamond again. Still, there is some possibility."

383

David Elginbrod

"How do you know she was not willing to take it from me?"

"Because, by her own account, he had to destroy her power of volition entirely, before he could make her do it. He threw her into a mesmeric sleep."

"I should like to understand his power over her a little better. In such cases of biology—how they came to abuse the word, I should like to know—"

"Just as they call table–rapping, spiritualism."

"I suppose his relation to her must be classed amongst phenomena of that sort?"

"Certainly."

"Well, tell me, does the influence outlast the mesmeric condition?"

"If by mesmeric condition you mean any state evidently approaching to that of sleep—undoubtedly. It is, in many cases, quite independent of such a condition. Perhaps the degree of willing submission at first, may have something to do with it. But mesmeric influence, whatever it may mean, is entirely independent of sleep. That is an accident accompanying it, perhaps sometimes indicating its culmination."

"Does the person so influenced act with or against his will?"

"That is a most difficult question, involving others equally difficult. My own impression is, that the patient—for patient in a very serious sense he is—acts with his inclination, and often with his will; but in many cases with his inclination against his will. This is a very important distinction in morals, but often overlooked. When a man is acting with his inclination, his will is in abeyance. In our present imperfect condition, it seems to me that the absolute will has no opportunity of pure action, of operating entirely as itself, except when working in opposition to inclination. But to return: the power of the biologist appears to me to lie in this—he is able, by some mysterious sympathy, to produce in the mind of the patient such forceful impulses to do whatever he wills, that they are in fact irresistible to almost all who are obnoxious to his influence. The will requires an especial training and a distinct development, before it is capable of acting with any degree of freedom. The men who have undergone this are very few indeed; and no one whose will is not educated as will, can, if subjected to the influences of biology, resist the impulses roused in his passive brain by the active brain of the operator. This at least is my impression.

"Other things no doubt combined to increase the influence in the present case. She liked him, perhaps more than liked him once. She was partially committed to his schemes; and she was easily mesmerised. It would seem, besides, that she was naturally disposed to somnambulism. This is a remarkable co–existence of distinct developments of the same peculiarity. In this latter condition, even if in others she were able to resist him, she would be quite helpless; for all the thoughts that passed through her brain would owe their origin to his.—Imagine being forced to think another man's thoughts! That would be possession indeed! And this is not far removed from the old stories about the demons entering into a man.—He would be ruler over the whole intellectual life that passed in her during the time; and which to her, as far as the ideas suggested belonged to the outward world, would appear an outer life, passing all round her, not in her. She would, in fact, be a creature of his imagination for the time, as much as any character invented, and sent through varied circumstances, feelings, and actions, by the mind of the poet or novelist. Look at the facts. She warned you to beware of the count that night before you went into the haunted bed–chamber. Even when she entered it, by your own account—"

"Entered it? Then you do think it was Euphra who personated the ghost?"

"I am sure of it. She was sleep–walking."

"But so different—such a death–like look!"

"All that was easy enough to manage. She refused to obey him at first. He mesmerized her. It very likely went farther than he expected; and he succeeded too well. Experienced, no doubt, in disguises, he dressed her as like the dead Lady Euphrasia as he could, following her picture. Perhaps she possessed such a disguise, and had used it before. He thus protected her from suspicion, and himself from implication.—What was the colour of the hair in the picture?"

"Golden."

David Elginbrod

"Hence the sparkle of gold–dust in her hair. The count managed it all. He willed that she should go, and she went. Her disguise was certain safety, should she be seen. You would suspect the ghost and no one else if she appeared to you, and you lost the ring after. But even in this state she yielded against her better inclination, for she was weeping when you saw her. But she could not help it. While you lay on the couch in the haunted chamber, where he carried you, the awful death–ghost was busy in your room, was opening your desk, fingering your papers, and stealing your ring. It is rather a frightful idea."

"She did not take my ring, I am sure. He followed her, and took it.—But she could not have come in at either door—"

"Could not? Did she not go out at one of them? Besides, I do not doubt that such a room as that had private communication with the open air as well. I should much like to examine the place."

"But how could she have gone through the bolted door then?"

"That door may have been set in another, larger by half the frame or so, and opening with a spring and concealed hinges. There is no difficulty about that. There are such places to be found now and then in old houses. But, indeed, if you will excuse me, I do not consider your testimony, on every minute particular, quite satisfactory."

"Why?" asked Hugh, rather offended.

"First, because of the state of excitement you must have been in; and next, because I doubt the wine that was left in your room. The count no doubt knew enough of drugs to put a few ghostly horrors into the decanter. But poor Miss Cameron! The horrors he has put into her mind and life! It is a sad fate—all but a sentence of insanity."

Hugh sprang to his feet.

"By heaven!" he cried, "I will strangle the knave."

"Stop, stop!" said Falconer. "No revenge! Leave him to the sleeping divinity within him, which will awake one day, and complete the hell that he is now building for himself—for the very fire of hell is the divine in it. Your work is to set Euphra free. If you did strangle him, how do you know if that would free her from him?"

"Horrible!—Have you no news of him?"

"None whatever."

"What, then, can I do for her?"

"You must teach her to foil him."

"How am I to do that? Even if I knew how, I cannot see her, I cannot speak to her."

"I have a great faith in opportunity."

"But how should she foil him?"

"She must pray to God to redeem her fettered will—to strengthen her will to redeem herself. She must resist the count, should he again claim her submission (as, for her sake, I hope he will), as she would the devil himself. She must overcome. Then she will be free—not before. This will be very hard to do. His power has been excessive and peculiar, and her submission long and complete. Even if he left her alone, she would not therefore be free. She must defy him; break his bonds; oppose his will; assert her freedom; and defeat him utterly."

"Oh! who will help her? I have no power. Even if I were with her, I could not help her in such a struggle. I wish David were not dead. He was the man.—You could now, Mr. Falconer."

"No. Except I knew her, had known her for some time, and had a strong hold of all her nature, I could not, would not try to help her. If Providence brought this about, I would do my best; but otherwise I would not interfere. But if she pray to God, he will give her whatever help she needs, and in the best way, too."

"I think it would be some comfort to her if we could find the ring—the crystal, I mean."

"It would be more, I think, if we could find the diamond."

"How can we find either?"

"We must find the count first. I have not given that up, of course. I will tell you what I should like to do, if I knew the lady."

"What?"

"Get her to come to London, and make herself as public as possible: go to operas and balls, and theatres; be presented at court; take a stall at every bazaar, and sell charity puff–balls—get as much into the papers as possible. 'The lovely, accomplished, fascinating Miss Cameron,

"What do you mean?"

"I will tell you what I mean. The count has forsaken her now; but as soon as he heard that she was somebody, that she was followed and admired, his vanity would be roused, his old sense of property in her would revive, and he would begin once more to draw her into his toils. What the result would be, it is impossible to foretell; but it would at least give us a chance of catching him, and her a chance of resisting him."

"I don't think, however, that she would venture on that course herself. I should not dare to propose it to her."

"No, no. It was only an invention, to deceive myself with the fancy that I was doing something. There would be many objections to such a plan, even if it were practicable. I must still try to find him, and if fresh endeavours should fail, devise fresher still."

"Thank you a thousand times," said Hugh. "It is too good of you to take so much trouble."

"It is my business," answered Falconer. "Is there not a soul in trouble?"

Hugh went home, full of his new friend. With the clue he had given him, he was able to follow all the windings of Euphra's behaviour, and to account for almost everything that had taken place. It was quite painful to him to feel that he could be of no immediate service to her; but he could hardly doubt that, before long, Falconer would, in his wisdom and experience, excogitate some mode of procedure in which he might be able to take a part.

He sat down to his novel, which had been making but little progress for some time; for it is hard to write a novel when one is living in the midst of a romance. But the romance, at this time, was not very close to him. It had a past and a possible future, but no present. That same future, however, might at any moment dawn into the present.

In the meantime, teaching the Latin grammar and the English alphabet to young aspirants after the honours of the ministry, was not work inimical to invention, from either the exhaustion of its excitement or the absorption of its interest.

CHAPTER XIII. THE LADY'S-MAID.

```
Her yellow hair, beyond compare,
   Comes trinkling down her swan-white neck;
And her two eyes, like stars in skies,
   Would keep a sinking ship frae wreck.
Oh!  Mally's meek, Mally's sweet,
   Mally's modest and discreet;
Mally's rare, Mally's fair,
   Mally's every way complete.

BURNS.

What arms for innocence but innocence.

GILES FLETCHER.
```

Margaret had sought Euphra's room, with the intention of restoring to her the letter which she had written to David Elginbrod. Janet had let it lie for some time before she sent it to Margaret; and Euphra had given up all expectation of an answer.

Hopes of ministration filled Margaret's heart; but she expected, from what she knew of her, that anger would be Miss Cameron's first feeling. Therefore, when she heard no answer to her application for admission, and had concluded, in consequence, that Euphra was not in the room, she resolved to leave the letter where it would meet her eye, and thus prepare the way for a future conversation. When she saw Euphra and Harry, she would have retired immediately; but Euphra, annoyed by her entrance, was now quite able to speak.

"What do you want?" she said angrily.

"This is your letter, Miss Cameron, is it not?" said Margaret, advancing with it in her hand.

Euphra took it, glanced at the direction, pushed Harry away from her, started up in a passion, and let loose the whole gathered irritability of contempt, weariness, disappointment, and suffering, upon Margaret. Her dark eyes flashed with rage, and her sallow cheek glowed like a peach.

"What right have you, pray, to handle my letters? How did you get this? It has never been posted! And open, too. I declare! I suppose you have read it?"

Margaret was afraid of exciting more wrath before she had an opportunity of explaining; but Euphra gave her no time to think of a reply.

"You have read it, you shameless woman! Why don't you lie, like the rest of your tribe, and keep me from dying with indignation? Impudent prying! My maid never posted it, and you have found it and read it! Pray, did you hope to find a secret worth a bribe?"

She advanced on Margaret till within a foot of her.

"Why don't you answer, you hussy? I will go this instant to your mistress. You or I leave the house."

Margaret had stood all this time quietly, waiting for an opportunity to speak. Her face was very pale, but perfectly still, and her eyes did not quail. She had not in the least lost her self-possession. She would not say at once that she had read the letter, because that would instantly rouse the tornado again.

"You do not know my name, Miss Cameron; of course you could not."

"Your name! What is that to me?"

David Elginbrod

"That," said Margaret, pointing to the letter, "is my father's name."

Euphra looked at her own direction again, and then looked at Margaret. She was so bewildered, that if she had any thoughts, she did not know them. Margaret went on:

"My father is dead. My mother sent the letter to me."

"Then you have had the impertinence to read it!"

"It was my duty to read it."

"Duty! What business had you with it?"

Euphra felt ashamed of the letter as soon as she found that she had applied to a man whose daughter was a servant. Margaret answered:

"I could at least reply to it so far, that the writer should not think my father had neglected it. I did not know who it was from till I came to the end."

Euphra turned her back on her, with the words:

"You may go."

Margaret walked out of the room with an unconscious stately gentleness.

"Come back," cried Euphra.

Margaret obeyed.

"Of course you will tell all your fellow–servants the contents of this foolish letter."

Margaret's face flushed, and her eye flashed, at the first words of this speech; but the last words made her forget the first, and to them only she replied. Clasping. her hands, she said:

"Dear Miss Cameron, do not call it foolish. For God's sake, do not call it foolish."

391

David Elginbrod

"What is it to you? Do you think I am going to make a confidante of you?"

Margaret again left the room. Notwithstanding that she had made no answer to her insult, Euphra felt satisfied that her letter was safe from profanation.

No sooner was Margaret out of sight, than, with the reaction common to violent tempers, which in this case resulted the sooner, from the exhaustion produced in a worn frame by the violence of the outburst, Euphra sat down, in a hopeless, unresting way, upon the chair from which she had just risen, and began weeping more bitterly than before. She was not only exhausted, but ashamed; and to these feelings was added a far greater sense of disappointment than she could have believed possible, at the frustration of the hope of help from David Elginbrod. True, this hope had been small; but where there is only one hope, its death is equally bitter, whether it be a great or a little hope. And there is often no power of reaction, in a mind which has been gradually reduced to one little faint hope, when that hope goes out in darkness. There is a recoil which is very helpful, from the blow that kills a great hope.

All this time Harry had been looking on, in a kind of paralysed condition, pale with perplexity and distress. He now came up to Euphra, and, trying to pull her hand gently from her face, said:

"What is it all about, Euphra, dear?"

"Oh! I have been very naughty, Harry."

"But what is it all about? May I read the letter?"

"If you like," answered Euphra, listlessly.

Harry read the letter with quivering features. Then, laying it down on the table with a reverential slowness, went to Euphra, put his arms round her and kissed her.

"Dear, dear Euphra, I did not know you were so unhappy. I will find God for you. But first I will—what shall I do to the bad man? Who is it? I will—"

Harry finished the sentence by setting his teeth hard.

"Oh! you can't do anything for me, Harry, dear. Only mind you don't say anything about it to any one. Put the letter in the fire there for me."

"No—that I won't," said Harry, taking up the letter, and holding it tight. "It is a beautiful letter, and it does me good. Don't you think, though it is not sent to God himself, he may read it, and take it for a prayer?"

"I wish he would, Harry."

"But it was very wrong of you, Euphra, dear, to speak as you did to the daughter of such a good man."

"Yes, it was."

"But then, you see, you got angry before you knew who she was."

"But I shouldn't have got angry before I knew all about it"

"Well, you have only to say you are sorry, and Margaret won't think anything more about it. Oh, she is so good!"

Euphra recoiled from making confession of wrong to a lady's maid; and, perhaps, she was a little jealous of Harry's admiration of Margaret. For Euphra had not yet cast off all her old habits of mind, and one of them was the desire to be first with every one whom she cared for. She had got rid of a worse, which was, a necessity of being first in every company, whether she cared for the persons composing it, or not. Mental suffering had driven the latter far enough from her; though it would return worse than ever, if her mind were not filled with truth in the place of ambition. So she did not respond to what Harry said. Indeed, she did not speak again, except to beg him to leave her alone. She did not make her appearance again that day.

But at night, when the household was retiring, she rose from the bed on which she had been lying half-unconscious, and going to the door, opened it a little way, that she might hear when Margaret should pass from Mrs. Elton's room towards her own. She waited for some time; but judging, at length, that she must have passed without her knowledge, she went and knocked at her door. Margaret opened it a little, after a moment's delay,

393

half–undressed.

"May I come in, Margaret?"

"Pray, do, Miss Cameron," answered Margaret.

And she opened the door quite. Her cap was off, and her rich dark hair fell on her shoulders, and streamed thence to her waist. Her under–clothing was white as snow.

"What a lovely skin she has!" thought Euphra, comparing it with her own tawny complexion. She felt, for the first time, that Margaret was beautiful—yes, more: that whatever her gown might be, her form and her skin (give me a prettier word, kind reader, for a beautiful fact, and I will gladly use it) were those of one of nature's ladies. She was soon to find that her intellect and spirit were those of one of God's ladies.

"I am very sorry, Margaret, that I spoke to you as I did today."

"Never mind it, Miss Cameron. We cannot help being angry sometimes. And you had great provocation under the mistake you made. I was only sorry because I knew it would trouble you afterwards. Please don't think of it again."

"You are very kind, Margaret."

"I regretted my father's death, for the first time, after reading your letter, for I knew he could have helped you. But it was very foolish of me, for God is not dead."

Margaret smiled as she said this, looking full in Euphra's eyes. It was a smile of meaning unfathomable, and it quite overcame Euphra. She had never liked Margaret before; for, from not very obscure psychological causes, she had never felt comfortable in her presence, especially after she had encountered the nun in the Ghost's Walk, though she had had no suspicion that the nun was Margaret. A great many of our dislikes, both to persons and things, arise from a feeling of discomfort associated with them, perhaps only accidentally present in our minds the first time we met them. But this vanished entirely now.

"Do you, then, know God too, Margaret?"

David Elginbrod

"Yes," answered Margaret, simply and solemnly.

"Will you tell me about him?"

"I can at least tell you about my father, and what he taught me."

"Oh! thank you, thank you! Do tell me about him—now."

"Not now, dear Miss Cameron. It is late, and you are too unwell to stay up longer. Let me help you to bed to-night. I will be your maid."

As she spoke, Margaret proceeded to put on her dress again, that she might go with Euphra, who had no attendant. She had parted with Jane, and did not care, in her present mood, to have a woman about her, especially a new one.

"No, Margaret. You have enough to do without adding me to your troubles."

"Please, do let me, Miss Cameron. It will be a great pleasure to me. I have hardly anything to call work. You should see how I used to work when I was at home."

Euphra still objected, but Margaret's entreaty prevailed. She followed Euphra to her room. There she served her like a ministering angel; brushed her hair—oh, so gently! smoothing it out as if she loved it. There was health in the touch of her hands, because there was love. She undressed her; covered her in bed as if she had been a child; made up the fire to last as long as possible; bade her good night; and was leaving the room, when Euphra called her. Margaret returned to the bed-side.

"Kiss me, Margaret," she said.

Margaret stooped, kissed her forehead and her lips, and left her.

Euphra cried herself to sleep. They were the first tears she had ever shed that were not painful tears. She slept as she had not slept for months.

In order to understand this change in Euphrasia's behaviour to Margaret—in order, in fact, to represent it to our minds as at all credible—we must remember that she had been trying to do right for some time; that Margaret, as the daughter of David, seemed the only attainable source of the knowledge she sought; that long illness had greatly weakened her obstinacy; that her soul hungered, without knowing it, for love; and that she was naturally gifted with a strong will, the position in which she stood in relation to the count proving only that it was not strong enough, and not that it was weak. Such a character must, for any good, be ruled by itself, and not by circumstances. To have been overcome in the process of time by the persistent goodness of Margaret, might have been the blessed fate of a weaker and worse woman; but if Euphra did not overcome herself, there was no hope of further victory. If Margaret could even wither the power of her oppressor, it would be but to transfer the lordship from a bad man to a good woman; and that would not be enough. It would not be freedom. And indeed, the aid that Margaret had to give her, could only be bestowed on one who already had freedom enough to act in some degree from duty. She knew she ought to go and apologize to Margaret. She went.

In Margaret's presence, and in such a mood, she was subjected at once to the holy enchantment of her loving–kindness. She had never received any tenderness from a woman before. Perhaps she had never been in the right mood to profit by it if she had. Nor had she ever before seen what Margaret was. It was only when service—divine service—flowed from her in full outgoing, that she reached the height of her loveliness. Then her whole form was beautiful. So was it interpenetrated by, and respondent to, the uprising soul within, that it radiated thought and feeling as if it had been all spirit. This beauty rose to its best in her eyes. When she was ministering to any one in need, her eyes seemed to worship the object of her faithfulness, as if all the time she felt that she was doing it unto Him. Her deeds were devotion. She was the receiver and not the giver. Before this, Euphra had seen only the still waiting face; and, as I have said, she had been repelled by it. Once within the sphere of the radiation of her attraction, she was drawn towards her, as towards the haven of her peace: she loved her.

To this, it length, had her struggle with herself in the silence of her own room, and her meditations on her couch, conducted her. Shall we say that these alone had been and were leading her? Or that to all these there was a hidden root, and an informing spirit? Who would not rather believe that his thoughts come from an infinite, self–sphered, self–constituting thought, than that they rise somehow out of a blank abyss of darkness, and are only thought when he thinks them, which thinking he cannot pre–determine or even foresee?

David Elginbrod

When Euphra woke, her first breath was like a deep draught of spiritual water. She felt as if some sorrow had passed from her, and some gladness come in its stead. She thought and thought, and found that the gladness was Margaret. She had scarcely made the discovery, when the door gently opened, and Margaret peeped in to see if she were awake.

"May I come in?" she said.

"Yes, please, Margaret."

"How do you feel to–day?"

"Oh, so much better, dear Margaret! Your kindness will make me well."

"I am so glad! Do lie still awhile, and I will bring you some breakfast. Mrs. Elton will be so pleased to find you let me wait on you!"

"She asked me, Margaret, if you should; but I was too miserable—and too naughty, for I did not like you."

"I knew that; but I felt sure you would not dislike me always."

"Why?"

"Because I could not help loving you."

"Why did you love me?"

"I will tell you half the reason.—Because you looked unhappy."

"What was the other half?"

"That I cannot—I mean I will not tell you."

"Never?"

"Perhaps never. But I don't know.—Not now."

"Then I must not ask you?"

"No—please."

"Very well, I won't."

"Thank you. I will go and get your breakfast."

"What can she mean?" said Euphra to herself.

But she would never have found out.

CHAPTER XIV. DAVID ELGINBROD.

He being dead yet speaketh.

HEB., xi. 4.

    In all 'he' did
Some figure of the golden times was hid.

DR. DONNE.

From this time, Margaret waited upon Euphra, as if she had been her own maid. Nor had Mrs. Elton any cause of complaint, for Margaret was always at hand when she was wanted. Indeed, her mistress was full of her praises. Euphra said little.

Many and long were the conversations between the two girls, when all but themselves were asleep. Sometimes Harry made one of the company; but they could always send him away when they wished to be alone. And now the teaching for which Euphra had longed, sprang in a fountain at her own door. It had been nigh her long, and she had not known it, for its hour had not come. Now she drank as only the thirsty drink,—as they drink whose very souls are fainting within them for drought.

David Elginbrod

But how did Margaret embody her lessons?

The second night, she came to Euphra's room, and said:

"Shall I tell you about my father to−night? Are, you able?"

Euphra was delighted. It was what she had been hoping for all day.

"Do tell me. I long to hear about him."

So they sat down; and Margaret began to talk about her childhood; the cottage she lived in; the fir−wood all around it; the work she used to do;—her side, in short, of the story which, in the commencement of this book, I have partly related from Hugh's side. Summer and winter, spring−time and harvest, storm and sunshine, all came into the tale. Her mother came into it often; and often too, though not so often, the grand form of her father appeared, remained for a little while, and then passed away. Every time Euphra saw him thus in the mirror of Margaret's memory, she saw him more clearly than before: she felt as if, soon, she should know him quite well. Sometimes she asked a question or two; but generally she allowed Margaret's words to flow unchecked; for she painted her pictures better when the colours did not dry between. They talked on, or rather, Margaret talked and Euphra listened, far into the night. At length, Margaret stopped suddenly, for she became aware that a long time had passed. Looking at the clock on the chimney−piece, she said:

"I have done wrong to keep you up so late. Come—I must get you to bed. You are an invalid, you know, and I am your nurse as well as your maid."

"You will come to−morrow night, then?"

"Yes, I will."

"Then I will go to bed like a good child."

Margaret undressed her, and left her to the healing of sleep.

David Elginbrod

The next night she spoke again of her father, and what he taught her. Euphra had thought much about him; and at every fresh touch which the story gave to the portrait, she knew him better; till at last, even when circumstances not mentioned before came up, she seemed to have known them from the beginning.

"What was your father like, Margaret?"

Margaret described him very nearly as I have done, from Hugh's account, in the former part of the story. Euphra said:

"Ah! yes. That is almost exactly as I had fancied him. Is it not strange?"

"It is very natural, I think," answered Margaret.

"I seem now to have known him for years."

But what is most worthy of record is, that ever as the picture of David grew on the vision of Euphra, the idea of God was growing unawares upon her inward sight. She was learning more and more about God all the time. The sight of human excellence awoke a faint Ideal of the divine perfection. Faith came of itself, and abode, and grew; for it needs but a vision of the Divine, and faith in God is straightway born in the soul that beholds it. Thus, faith and sight are one. The being of her father in heaven was no more strange and far off from her, when she had seen such a father on earth as Margaret's was. It was not alone David's faith that begot hers, but the man himself was a faith–begetting presence. He was the evidence of God with them.—Thus he, being dead, yet spoke, and the departed man was a present power.

Euphra began to read the story of the Gospel. So did Harry. They found much on which to desire enlightenment; and they always applied to Margaret for the light they needed. It was long before she ventured to say I think. She always said:

"My father used to say—" or

"I think my father would have said—"

It was not until Euphra was in great trouble some time after this, and required the immediate consolation of personal testimony, that Margaret spoke as from herself; and then she spoke with positive assurance of faith. She did not then even say I think, but, I am sure; I know; I have seen.

Many interviews of this sort did not take place between them before Euphra, in her turn, began to confide her history to Margaret.

It was a strangely different one—full of outward event and physical trouble; but, till it approached the last stages, wonderfully barren as to inward production or development. It was a history of Euphra's circumstances and peculiarities, not of Euphra herself. Till of late, she had scarcely had any history. Margaret's, on the contrary, was a true history; for, with much of the monotonous in circumstance, it described individual growth, and the change of progress. Where there is no change there can be no history; and as all change is either growth or decay, all history must describe progress or retrogression. The former had now begun for Euphra as well; and it was one proof of it that she told Margaret all I have already recorded for my readers, at least as far as it bore against herself. How much more she told her I am unable to say; but after she had told it, Euphra was still more humble towards Margaret, and Margaret more tender, more full of service, if possible, and more devoted to Euphra.

CHAPTER XV. MARGARET'S SECRET.

```
     Love is not love
Which alters when it alteration finds,
Or bends with the remover to remove.
```

SHAKSPERE.—Sonnet cxvi.

Margaret could not proceed very far in the story of her life, without making some reference to Hugh Sutherland. But she carefully avoided mentioning his name. Perhaps no one less calm, and free from the operation of excitement, could have been so successful in suppressing it.

"Ah!" said Euphra, one day, "your history is a little like mine there; a tutor comes into them both. Did you not fall dreadfully in love with him?"

"I loved him very much."

"Where is he now?"

"In London, I believe."

"Do you never see him?"

"No."

"Have you never seen him since he left your home—with the curious name?"

"Yes; but not spoken to him."

"Where?"

Margaret was silent. Euphra knew her well enough now not to repeat the question.

"I should have been in love with him, I know."

Margaret only smiled.

Another day, Euphra said:

"What a good boy that Harry is! And so clever too. Ah! Margaret, I have behaved like the devil to that boy. I wanted to have him all to myself, and so kept him a child. Need I confess all my ugliest sins?"

"Not to me, certainly, dear Miss Cameron. Tell God to look into your heart, and take them all out of it."

"I will. I do.—I even enticed Mr. Sutherland away from him to me, when he was the only real friend he had, that I might have them both."

"But you have done your best to make up for it since."

"I have tried a little. I cannot say I have done my best. I have been so peevish and irritable."

"You could not quite help that."

"How kind you are to excuse me so! It makes me so much stronger to try again."

"My father used to say that God was always finding every excuse for us that could be found; every true one, you know; not one false one."

"That does comfort one."

After a pause, Euphra resumed:

"Mr. Sutherland did me some good, Margaret."

"I do not wonder at that."

"He made me think less about Count Halkar; and that was something, for he haunted me. I did not know then how very wicked he was. I did love him once. Oh, how I hate him now!"

And she started up and paced the room like a tigress in its cage.

Margaret did not judge this the occasion to read her a lecture on the duty of forgiveness. She had enough to do to keep from hating the man herself, I suspect. But she tried to turn her thoughts into another channel.

"Mr. Sutherland loved you very much, Miss Cameron."

"He loved me once," said poor Euphra, with a sigh.

"I saw he did. That was why I began to love you too."

Margaret had at last unwittingly opened the door of her secret. She had told the other reason for loving Euphra. But, naturally enough, Euphra could not understand what she

403

meant. Perhaps some of my readers, understanding Margaret's words perfectly, and their reference too, may be so far from understanding Margaret herself, as to turn upon me and say:

"Impossible! You cannot have understood her or any other woman."

Well!

"What do you mean, Margaret?"

Margaret both blushed and laughed outright.

"I must confess it," said she, at once; "it cannot hurt him now: my tutor and yours are the same."

"Impossible!"

"True."

"And you never spoke all the time you were both at Arnstead?"

"Not once. He never knew I was in the house."

"How strange! And you saw he loved me?"

"Yes."

"And you were not jealous?"

"I did not say that. But I soon found that the only way to escape from my jealousy, if the feeling I had was jealousy, was to love you too. I did."

"You beautiful creature! But you could not have loved him much."

"I loved him enough to love you for his sake. But why did he stop loving you? I fear I shall not be able to love him so much now."

"He could not help it, Margaret. I deserved it."

Euphra hid her face in her hands.

"He could not have really loved you, then?"

"Which is better to believe, Margaret," said Euphra, uncovering her face, which two tears were lingering down, and looking up at her—"that he never loved me, or that he stopped loving me?"

"For his sake, the first."

"And for my sake, the second?"

"That depends."

"So it does. He must have found plenty of faults in me. But I was not so bad as he thought me when he stopped loving me."

Margaret's answer was one of her loving smiles, in which her eyes had more share than her lips.

It would have been unendurable to Euphra, a little while before, to find that she had a rival in a servant. Now she scarcely regarded that aspect of her position. But she looked doubtfully at Margaret, and then said:

"How is it that you take it so quietly?—for your love must have been very different from mine. Indeed, I am not sure that I loved him at all; and after I had made up my mind to it quite, it did not hurt me so very much. But you must have loved him dreadfully."

"Perhaps I did. But I had no anxiety about it."

"But that you could not leave to a father such as yours even to settle."

"No. But I could to God. I could trust God with what I could not speak to my father about. He is my father's father, you know; and so, more to him and me than we could be to each other. The more we love God, the more we love each other; for we find he makes the very love which sometimes we foolishly fear to do injustice to, by loving him most. I love my father ten times more because he loves God, and because God has secrets with him."

"I wish God were a father to me as he is to you, Margaret."

"But he is your father, whether you wish it or not. He cannot be more your father than he is. You may be more his child than you are, but not more than he meant you to be, nor more than he made you for. You are infinitely more his child than you have grown to yet. He made you altogether his child, but you have not given in to it yet."

"Oh! yes; I know what you mean. I feel it is true."

"The Prodigal Son was his father's child. He knew it, and gave in to it. He did not say: 'I wish my father loved me enough to treat me like a child again.' He did not say that, but—I will arise and go to my father."

Euphra made no answer, but wept, Margaret said no more.

Euphra was the first to resume.

"Mr. Sutherland was very kind, Margaret. He promised—and I know he will keep his promise—to do all he could to help me. I hope he is finding out where that wicked count is."

"Write to him, and ask him to come and see you. He does not know where you are."

"But I don't know where he is."

"I do."

"Do you?" rejoined Euphra with some surprise.

"But he does not know where I am. I will give you his address, if you like."

Euphra pondered a little. She would have liked very much to see him, for she was anxious to know of his success. The love she had felt for him was a very small obstacle to their meeting now; for her thoughts had been occupied with affairs, before the interest of which the poor love she had then been capable of, had melted away and vanished—vanished, that is, in all that was restrictive and engrossing in its character. But now that she knew the relation that had existed between Margaret and him, she shrunk from doing anything that might seem to Margaret to give Euphra an opportunity of regaining his preference. Not that she had herself the smallest hope, even had she had the smallest desire of doing so; but she would not even suggest the idea of being Margaret's rival. At length she answered:

"No, thank you, Margaret. As soon as he has anything to report, he will write to Arnstead, and Mrs. Horton will forward me the letter. No—it is quite unnecessary."

Euphra's health was improving a little, though still she was far from strong.

CHAPTER XVI. FOREBODINGS.

```
Faust.        If heaven was made for man, 'twas made for me.
Good Angel.   Faustus, repent; yet heaven will pity thee.
Bad Angel.    Thou art a spirit, God cannot pity thee.
Faust.        Be I a devil, yet God may pity me.
Bad Angel.    Too late.
Good Angel.   Never too late if Faustus will repent.
Bad Angel.    If thou repent, devils will tear thee in pieces.

Old Man.      I see an angel hover o'er thy head,
              And with a vial full of precious grace,
              Offers to pour the same into thy soul.
```

MARLOWE.—Doctor Faustus.

Mr. Appleditch had had some business-misfortunes, not of a heavy nature, but sufficient to cast a gloom over the house in Dervish Town, and especially over the face of his spouse, who had set her heart on a new carpet for her drawing-room, and feared she ought not to procure it now. It is wonderful how conscientious some people are towards their balance at the banker's. How the drawing-room, however, could come to want a new carpet is something mysterious, except there is a peculiar power of decay inherent in things deprived of use. These influences operating, however, she began to think that the two scions of grocery were not drawing nine shillings' worth a week of the sap of divinity. This she hinted to Mr. Appleditch. It was resolved to give Hugh warning.

As it would involve some awkwardness to state reasons, Mrs. Appleditch resolved to quarrel with him, as the easiest way of prefacing his discharge. It was the way she took with her maids–of–all–work; for it was grand in itself, and always left her with a comfortable feeling of injured dignity.

As a preliminary course, she began to treat him with still less politeness than before. Hugh was so careless of her behaviour, that this made no impression upon him. But he came to understand it all afterwards, from putting together the remarks of the children, and the partial communications of Mr. Appleditch to Miss Talbot, which that good lady innocently imparted to her lodger.

At length, one day, she came into the room where Hugh was more busy in teaching than his pupils were in learning, and seated herself by the fire to watch for an opportunity. This was soon found. For the boys, rendered still more inattentive by the presence of their mother, could not be induced to fix the least thought upon the matter in hand; so that Hugh was compelled to go over the same thing again and again, without success. At last he said:

"I am afraid, Mrs. Appleditch, I must ask you to interfere, for I cannot get any attention from the boys to–day."

"And how could it be otherwise, Mr. Sutherland, when you keep wearing them out with going over and over the same thing, till they are sick of it? Why don't you go on?"

"How can I go on when they have not learned the thing they are at? That would be to build the chimneys before the walls."

"It is very easy to be witty, sir; but I beg you will behave more respectfully to me in the presence of my children, innocent lambs!"

Looking round at the moment, Hugh caught in his face what the elder lamb had intended for his back, a grimace hideous enough to have procured him instant promotion in the kingdom of apes. The mother saw it too, and added:

"You see you cannot make them respect you. Really, Mr. Sutherland!"

Hugh was about to reply, to the effect that it was useless, in such circumstances, to attempt teaching them at all, some utterance of which sort was watched for as the occasion for his instant dismission; but at that very moment a carriage and pair pulled sharply up at the door, with more than the usual amount of quadrupedation, and mother and sons darted simultaneously to the window.

"My!" cried Johnnie, "what a rum go! Isn't that a jolly carriage, Peetie?"

"Papa's bought a carriage!" shouted Peetie.

"Be quiet, children," said their mother, as she saw a footman get down and approach the door.

"Look at that buffer," said Johnnie. "Do come and see this grand footman, Mr. Sutherland. He's such a gentleman!"

A box on the ear from his mother silenced him. The servant entering with some perturbation a moment after, addressed her mistress, for she dared not address any one else while she was in the room:

"Please 'm, the carriage is astin' after Mr. Sutherland."

"Mr. Sutherland?"

"Yes 'm."

The lady turned to Mr. Sutherland, who, although surprised as well, was not inclined to show his surprise to Mrs. Appleditch.

"I did not know you had carriage-friends, Mr. Sutherland," said she, with a toss of her head.

"Neither did I," answered Hugh. "But I will go and see who it is."

When he reached the street, he found Harry on the pavement, who having got out of the carriage, and not having been asked into the house, was unable to stand still for impatience. As soon as he saw his tutor, he bounded to him, and threw his arms round his neck, standing as they were in the open street. Tears of delight filled his eyes.

"Come, come, come," said Harry; "we all want you."

"Who wants me?"

"Mrs. Elton and Euphra and me. Come, get in."

"And he pulled Hugh towards the carriage.

"I cannot go with you now. I have pupils here."

Harry's face fell.

"When will you come?"

"In half–an–hour."

"Hurrah! I shall be back exactly in half–an–hour then. Do be ready, please, Mr. Sutherland."

"I will."

Harry jumped into the carriage, telling the coachman to drive where he pleased, and be back at the same place in half–an–hour. Hugh returned into the house.

As may be supposed, Margaret was the means of this happy meeting. Although she saw plainly enough that Euphra would like to see Hugh, she did not for some time make up her mind to send for him. The circumstances which made her resolve to do so were these.

David Elginbrod

For some days Euphra seemed to be gradually regaining her health and composure of mind. One evening, after a longer talk than usual, Margaret had left her in bed, and had gone to her own room. She was just preparing to get into bed herself, when a knock at her door startled her, and going to it, she saw Euphra standing there, pale as death, with nothing on but her nightgown, notwithstanding the bitter cold of an early and severe frost. She thought at first she must be walking in her sleep, but the scared intelligence of her open eyes, soon satisfied her that it was not so.

"What is the matter, dear Miss Cameron?" she said, as calmly as she could.

"He is coming. He wants me. If he calls me, I must go."

"No, you shall not go," rejoined Margaret, firmly.

"I must, I must," answered Euphra, wringing her hands.

"Do come in," said Margaret, "you must not stand there in the cold."

"Let me get into your bed."

"Better let me go with you to yours. That will be more comfortable for you."

"Oh! yes; please do."

Margaret threw a shawl round Euphra, and went back with her to her room.

"He wants me. He wants me. He will call me soon," said Euphra, in an agonised whisper, as soon as the door was shut. "What shall I do!"

"Come to bed first, and we will talk about it there."

As soon as they were in bed, Margaret put her arm round Euphra, who was trembling with cold and fear, and said:

"Has this man any right to call you?"

411

"No, no," answered Euphra, vehemently.

"Then don't go."

"But I am afraid of him."

"Defy him in God's name."

"But besides the fear, there is something that I can't describe, that always keeps telling me—no, not telling me, pushing me—no, drawing me, as if I could not rest a moment till I go. I cannot describe it. I hate to go, and yet I feel that if I were cold in my grave, I must rise and go if he called me. I wish I could tell you what it is like. It is as if some demon were shaking my soul till I yielded and went. Oh! don't despise me. I can't help it."

"My darling, I don't, I can't despise you. You shall not go to him."

"But I must," answered she, with a despairing faintness more convincing than any vehemence; and then began to weep with a slow, hopeless weeping, like the rain of a November eve.

Margaret got out of bed. Euphra thought she was offended. Starting up, she clasped her hands, and said:

"Oh Margaret! I won't cry. Don't leave me. Don't leave me."

She entreated like a chidden child.

"No, no, I didn't mean to leave you for a moment. Lie down again, dear, and cry as much as you like. I am going to read a little bit out of the New Testament to you."

"I am afraid I can't listen to it."

"Never mind. Don't try. I want to read it."

Margaret got a New Testament, and read part of that chapter of St. John's Gospel which speaks about human labour and the bread of life. She stopped at these words:

David Elginbrod

"For I came down from heaven, not to do mine own will, but the will of him that sent me."

Euphra's tears had ceased. The sound of Margaret's voice, which, if it lost in sweetness by becoming more Scotch when she read the Gospel, yet gained thereby in pathos, and the power of the blessed words themselves, had soothed the troubled spirit a little, and she lay quiet.

"The count is not a good man, Miss Cameron?"

"You know he is not, Margaret. He is the worst man alive."

"Then it cannot be God's will that you should go to him."

"But one does many things that are not God's will."

"But it is God's will that you should not go to him."

Euphra lay silent for a few moments. Suddenly she exclaimed:

"Then I must not go to him,"—got out of bed, threw herself on her knees by the bedside, and holding up her clasped hands, said, in low tones that sounded as if forced from her by agony:

"I won't! I won't! O God, I will not. Help me, help me!"

Margaret knelt beside her, and put her arm round her. Euphra spoke no more, but remained kneeling, with her extended arms and clasped hands lying on the bed, and her head laid between them. At length Margaret grew alarmed, and looked at her. But she found that she was in a sweet sleep. She gently disengaged herself, and covering her up soft and warm, left her to sleep out her God–sent sleep undisturbed, while she sat beside, and watched for her waking.

She slept thus for an hour. Then lifting her head, and seeing Margaret, she rose quietly, as if from her prayers, and said with a smile:

David Elginbrod

"Margaret, I was dreaming that I had a mother."

"So you have, somewhere."

"Yes, so I have, somewhere," she repeated, and crept into bed like a child, lay down, and was asleep again in a moment.

Margaret watched her for another hour, and then seeing no signs of restlessness, but that on the contrary her sleep was profound, lay down beside her, and soon shared in that repose which to weary women and men is God's best gift.

She rose at her usual hour the next day, and was dressed before Euphra awoke. It was a cold grey December morning, with the hoar–frost lying thick on the roofs of the houses. Euphra opened her eyes while Margaret was busy lighting the fire. Seeing that she was there, she closed them again, and fell once more fast asleep. Before she woke again, Margaret had some tea ready for her; after taking which, she felt able to get up. She rose looking more bright and hopeful than Margaret had seen her before.

But Margaret, who watched her intently through the day, saw a change come over her cheer. Her face grew pale and troubled. Now and then her eyes were fixed on vacancy; and again she would look at Margaret with a woebegone expression of countenance; but presently, as if recollecting herself, would smile and look cheerful for a moment. Margaret saw that the conflict was coming on, if not already begun—that at least its shadow was upon her; and thinking that if she could have a talk with Hugh about what he had been doing, it would comfort her a little, and divert her thoughts from herself, even if no farther or more pleasantly than to the count, she let Harry know Hugh's address, as given in the letter to her father. She was certain that, if Harry succeeded in finding him, nothing more was necessary to insure his being brought to Mrs. Elton's. As we have seen, Harry had traced him to Buccleuch Terrace.

Hugh re–entered the house in the same mind in which he had gone out; namely, that after Mrs. Appleditch's behaviour to him before his pupils, he could not remain their tutor any longer, however great his need might be of the pittance he received for his services.

But although Mrs. Appleditch's first feeling had been jealousy of Hugh's acquaintance with "carriage–people," the toadyism which is so essential an element of such jealousy,

414

had by this time revived; and when Hugh was proceeding to finish the lesson he had begun, intending it to be his last, she said:

"Why didn't you ask your friend into the drawing room, Mr. Sutherland?"

"Good gracious! The drawing–room!" thought Hugh—but answered: "He will fetch me when the lesson is over."

"I am sure, sir, any friends of yours that like to call upon you here, will be very welcome. It will be more agreeable to you to receive them here, of course; for your accommodation at poor Miss Talbot's is hardly suitable for such visitors."

"I am sorry to say, however," answered Hugh, "that after the way you have spoken to me to–day, in the presence of my pupils, I cannot continue my relation to them any longer."

"Ho! ho!" resnorted the lady, indignation and scorn mingling with mortification; "our grand visitors have set our backs up. Very well, Mr. Sutherland, you will oblige me by leaving the house at once. Don't trouble yourself, pray, to finish the lesson. I will pay you for it all the same. Anything to get rid of a man who insults me before the very faces of my innocent lambs! And please to remember," she added, as she pulled out her purse, while Hugh was collecting some books he had lent the boys, "that when you were starving, my husband and I took you in and gave you employment out of charity—pure charity, Mr. Sutherland. Here is your money."

"Good morning, Mrs. Appleditch," said Hugh; and walked out with his books under his arm, leaving her with the money in her hand.

He had to knock his feet on the pavement in front of the house, to keep them from freezing, for half–an–hour, before the carriage arrived to take him away. As soon as it came up, he jumped into it, and was carried off in triumph by Harry.

Mrs. Elton received him kindly. Euphra held out her hand with a slight blush, and the quiet familiarity of an old friend. Hugh could almost have fallen in love with her again, from compassion for her pale, worn face, and subdued expression.

David Elginbrod

Mrs. Elton went out in the carriage almost directly, and Euphra begged Harry to leave them alone, as she had something to talk to Mr. Sutherland about.

"Have you found any trace of Count Halkar, Hugh?" she said, the moment they were by themselves.

"I am very sorry to say I have not. I have done my best."

"I am quite sure of that.—I just wanted to tell you, that, from certain indications which no one could understand so well as myself, I think you will have more chance of finding him now."

"I am delighted to hear it," responded Hugh. "If I only had him!"

Euphra sighed, paused, and then said:

"But I am not sure of it. I think he is in London; but he may be in Bohemia, for anything I know. I shall, however, in all probability, know more about him within a few days."

Hugh resolved to go at once to Falconer, and communicate to him what Euphra had told him. But he said nothing to her as to the means by which he had tried to discover the count; for although he felt sure that he had done right in telling Falconer all about it, he was afraid lest Euphra, not knowing what sort of a man he was, might not like it. Euphra, on her part, did not mention Margaret's name; for she had begged her not to do so.

"You will tell me when you know yourself?"

"Perhaps.—I will, if I can. I do wish you could get the ring. I have a painful feeling that it gives him power over me."

"That can only be a nervous fancy, surely," Hugh ventured to say.

"Perhaps it is. I don't know. But, still, without that, there are plenty of reasons for wishing to recover it. He will put it to a bad use, if he can. But for your sake, especially, I wish we could get it."

"Thank you. You were always kind."

"No," she replied, without lifting her eyes; "I brought it all upon you."

"But you could not help it."

"Not at the moment. But all that led to it was my fault."

She paused; then suddenly resumed:

"I will confess.—Do you know what gave rise to the reports of the house being haunted?"

"No."

"It was me wandering about it at night, looking for that very ring, to give to the count. It was shameful. But I did. Those reports prevented me from being found out. But I hope not many ghosts are so miserable as I was.—You remember my speaking to you of Mr. Arnold's jewels?"

"Yes, perfectly."

"I wanted to find out, through you, where the ring was. But I had no intention of involving you."

"I am sure you had not."

"Don't be too sure of anything about me. I don't know what I might have been led to do. But I am very sorry. Do forgive me."

"I cannot allow that I have anything to forgive. But tell me, Euphra, were you the creature, in white that I saw in the Ghost's Walk one night? I don't mean the last time."

"Very likely," she answered, bending her head yet lower, with a sigh.

"Then who was the creature in black that met you? And what became of you then?"

"Did you see her?" rejoined Euphra, turning paler still. "I fainted at sight of her. I took her for the nun that hangs in that horrid room."

"So did I," said Hugh. "But you could not have lain long; for I went up to the spot where you vanished, and found nothing."

"I suppose I got into the shrubbery before I fell. Or the count dragged me in.—But was that really a ghost? I feel now as if it was a good messenger, whether ghost or not, come to warn me, if I had had the courage to listen. I wish I had taken the warning."

They talked about these and other things, till Mrs. Elton, who had made Hugh promise to stay to lunch, returned. When they were seated at table, the kind–hearted woman said:

"Now, Mr. Sutherland, when will you begin again with Harry?"

"I do not quite understand you," answered Hugh.

"Of course you will come and give him lessons, poor boy. He will be broken–hearted if you don't."

"I wish I could. But I cannot—at least yet; for I know his father was dissatisfied with me. That was one of the reasons that made him send Harry to London."

Harry looked wretchedly disappointed, but said nothing.

"I never heard him say anything of the sort."

"I am sure of it, though. I am very sorry he has mistaken me; but he will know me better some day."

"I will take all the responsibility," persisted Mrs. Elton.

"But unfortunately the responsibility sticks too fast for you to take it. I cannot get rid of my share if I would."

"You are too particular. I am sure Mr. Arnold never could have meant that. This is my house too."

"But Harry is his boy. If you will let me come and see him sometimes, I shall be very thankful, though. I may be useful to him without giving him lessons."

"Thank you," said Harry with delight.

"Well, well! I suppose you are so much in request in London that you won't miss him for a pupil."

"On the contrary, I have not a single engagement. If you could find me one, I should be exceedingly obliged to you."

"Dear! dear! dear!" said Mrs. Elton. "Then you shall have Harry."

"Oh! yes; please take me," said Harry, beseechingly.

"No, I cannot. I must not."

Mrs. Elton rang the bell.

"James, tell the coachman I want the carriage in an hour."

Mrs. Elton was as submissive to her coachman as ladies who have carriages generally are, and would not have dreamed of ordering the horses out so soon again for herself; but she forgot everything else when a friend was in need of help, and became perfectly pachydermatous to the offended looks or indignant hints of that important functionary.

Within a few minutes after Hugh took his leave, Mrs. Elton was on her way to repeat a visit she had already paid the same morning, and to make several other calls, with the express object of finding pupils for Hugh. But in this she was not so successful as she had expected. In fact, no one whom she could think of, wanted such services at present. She returned home quite down—hearted, and all but convinced that nothing could be done before the approach of the London season.

CHAPTER XVII. STRIFE.

```
They'll turn me in your arms, Janet,
   An adder and a snake;
But haud me fast, let me not pass,
   Gin ye would be my maik.

They'll turn me in your arms, Janet,
   An adder and an aske;
They'll turn me in your arms, Janet,
   A bale that burns fast.

They'll shape me in your arms, Janet,
   A dove, but and a swan;
And last, they'll shape me in your arms
   A mother-naked man:
Cast your green mantle over me—
   And sae shall I be wan.

Scotch Ballad: Tamlane.
```

As soon as Hugh had left the house, Margaret hastened to Euphra. She found her in her own room, a little more cheerful, but still strangely depressed. This appearance increased towards the evening, till her looks became quite haggard, revealing an inward conflict of growing agony. Margaret remained with her.

Just before dinner, the upstairs bell, whose summons Margaret was accustomed to obey, rang, and she went down. Mrs. Elton detained her for a few minutes. The moment she was at liberty, she flew to Euphra's room by the back staircase. But, as she ascended, she was horrified to meet Euphra, in a cloak and thick veil, creeping down the stairs like a thief. Without saying a word, the strong girl lifted her in her arms as if she had been a child, and carried her back to her room. Euphra neither struggled nor spoke. Margaret laid her on her couch, and sat down beside her. She lay without moving, and, although wide awake, gave no other sign of existence than an occasional low moan, that seemed to come from a heart pressed almost to death.

Having lain thus for an hour, she broke the silence.

"Margaret, do you despise me dreadfully?"

David Elginbrod

"No, not in the least."

"Yet you found me going to do what I knew was wrong."

"You had not made yourself strong by thinking about the will of God. Had you, dear?"

"No. I will tell you how it was. I had been tormented with the inclination to go to him, and had been resisting it till I was worn out, and could hardly bear it more. Suddenly all grew calm within me, and I seemed to hate Count Halkar no longer. I thought with myself how easy it would be to put a stop to this dreadful torment, just by yielding to it—only this once. I thought I should then be stronger to resist the next time; for this was wearing me out so, that I must yield the next time, if I persisted now. But what seemed to justify me, was the thought that so I should find out where he was, and be able to tell Hugh; and then he would get the ring for me, and, perhaps that would deliver me. But it was very wrong of me. I forgot all about the will of God. I will not go again, Margaret. Do you think I may try again to fight him?"

"That is just what you must do. All that God requires of you is, to try again. God's child must be free. Do try, dear Miss Cameron."

"I think I could, if you would call me Euphra. You are so strong, and pure, and good, Margaret! I wish I had never had any thoughts but such as you have, you beautiful creature! Oh, how glad I am that you found me! Do watch me always."

"I will call you Euphra. I will be your sister–servant—anything you like, if you will only try again."

"Thank you, with all my troubled heart, dear Margaret. I will indeed try again."

She sprang from the couch in a sudden agony, and grasping Margaret by the arm, looked at her with such a terror–stricken face, that she began to fear she was losing her reason.

"Margaret," she said, as if with the voice as of one just raised from the dead, speaking with all the charnel damps in her throat, "could it be that I am in love with him still?"

Margaret shuddered, but did not lose her self–possession.

"No, no, Euphra, darling. You were haunted with him, and so tired that you were not able to hate him any longer. Then you began to give way to him. That was all. There was no love in that."

Euphra's grasp relaxed.

"Do you think so?"

"Yes."

A pause followed.

"Do you think God cares to have me do his will? Is it anything to him?"

"I am sure of it. Why did he make you else? But it is not for the sake of being obeyed that he cares for it, but for the sake of serving you and making you blessed with his blessedness. He does not think about himself, but about you."

"Oh, dear! oh, dear! I must not go."

"Let me read to you again, Eupra."

"Yes, please do, Margaret."

She read the fortieth chapter of Isaiah, one of her father's favourite chapters, where all the strength and knowledge of God are urged to a height, that they may fall in overwhelming profusion upon the wants and fears and unbelief of his children. How should he that calleth the stars by their names forget his people?

While she read, the cloud melted away from Euphra's face; a sweet sleep followed; and the paroxysm was over for the time.

Was Euphra insane? and were these the first accesses of daily fits of madness, which had been growing and approaching for who could tell how long?

Even if she were mad, or going mad, was not this the right way to treat her? I wonder how often the spiritual cure of faith in the Son of Man, the Great Healer, has been tried on those possessed with our modern demons. Is it proved that insanity has its origin in the physical disorder which, it is now said, can be shown to accompany it invariably? Let it be so: it yet appears to me that if the physician would, like the Son of Man himself, descend as it were into the disorganized world in which the consciousness of his patient exists, and receiving as fact all that he reveals to him of its condition—for fact it is, of a very real sort—introduce, by all the means that sympathy can suggest, the one central cure for evil, spiritual and material, namely, the truth of the Son of Man, the vision of the perfect friend and helper, with the revelation of the promised liberty of obedience—if he did this, it seems to me that cures might still be wrought as marvellous as those of the ancient time.

It seems to me, too, that that can be but an imperfect religion, as it would be a poor salvation, from which one corner of darkness may hide us; from whose blessed health and freedom a disordered brain may snatch us; making us hopeless outcasts, till first the physician, the student of physical laws, shall interfere and restore us to a sound mind, or the great God's–angel Death crumble the soul–oppressing brain, with its thousand phantoms of pain and fear and horror, into a film of dust in the hollow of the deserted skull.

Hugh repaired immediately to Falconer's chambers, where he was more likely to find him during the day than in the evening. He was at home. He told him of his interview with Euphra, and her feeling that the count was not far off.

"Do you think there can be anything in it?" asked he, when he had finished his relation.

"I think very likely," answered his friend. "I will be more on the outlook than ever. It may, after all, be through the lady herself that we shall find the villain. If she were to fall into one of her trances, now, I think it almost certain she would go to him. She ought to be carefully watched and followed, if that should take place. Let me know all that you learn about her. Go and see her again to–morrow, that we may be kept informed of her experiences, so far as she thinks proper to tell them."

"I will," said Hugh, and took his leave.

But Margaret, who knew Euphra's condition, both spiritual and physical, better than any other, had far different objects for her, through means of the unholy attraction which the count exercised over her, than the discovery of the stolen ring. She was determined that neither sleeping nor waking should she follow his call, or dance to his piping. She should resist to the last, in the name of God, and so redeem her lost will from the power of this devil, to whom she had foolishly sold it.

The next day, the struggle evidently continued; and it had such an effect on Euphra, that Margaret could not help feeling very anxious about the result as regarded her health, even if she should be victorious in the contest. But not for one moment did Margaret quail; for she felt convinced, come of it what might, that the only hope for Euphra lay in resistance. Death, to her mind, was simply nothing in the balance with slavery of such a sort.

Once—but evidently in a fit of absence—Euphra rose, went to the door, and opened it. But she instantly dashed it to again, and walking slowly back, resumed her seat on the couch. Margaret came to her from the other side of the bed, where she had been working by the window, for the last quarter of an hour, for the sake of the waning light.

"What is it, dear?" she said.

"Oh, Margaret! are you there? I did not know you were in the room. I found myself at the door before I knew what I was doing."

"But you came back of yourself this time."

"Yes I did. But I still feel inclined to go."

"There is no sin in that, so long as you do not encourage the feeling, or yield to it."

"I hate it."

"You will soon be free from it. Keep on courageously, dear sister. You will be in liberty and joy soon."

"God grant it."

David Elginbrod

"He will, Euphra. I am sure he will."

"I am sure you know, or you would not say it."

A knock came to the street door. Euphra started, and sat in the attitude of a fearful listener. A message was presently brought her, that Mr. Sutherland was in the drawing–room, and wished to see her.

Euphra rose immediately, and went to him. Margaret, who did not quite feel that she could be trusted yet, removed to a room behind the drawing–room, whence she could see Euphra if she passed to go down stairs.

Hugh asked her if she could tell him anything more about Count Halkar.

"Only," she answered, "that I am still surer of his being near me."

"How do you know it?"

"I need not mind telling you, for I have told you before that he has a kind of supernatural power over me. I know it by his drawing me towards him. It is true I might feel it just the same whether he was in America or in London; but I do not think he would care to do it, if he were so far off. I know him well enough to know that he would not wish for me except for some immediate advantage to himself."

"But what is the use of his doing so, when you don't know where he is to be found."

"I should go straight to him, without knowing where I was going."

Hugh rose in haste.

"Put on your bonnet and cloak, and come with me. I will take care of you. Lead me to him, and the ring shall soon be in your hands again."

Euphra hesitated, half rose, but sat down immediately.

"No, no! Not for worlds," she said. "Do not tempt me. I must not—I dare not—I will not go."

"But I shall be with you. I will take care of you. Don't you think I am able, Euphra?"

"Oh, yes! quite able. But I must not go anywhere at that man's bidding."

"But it won't be at his bidding: it will be at mine."

"Ah! that alters the case rather, does it not? I wonder what Margaret would say."

"Margaret! What Margaret?" said Hugh.

"Oh! my new maid," answered Euphra, recollecting herself.

"Not being well at present, she is my nurse."

"We shall take a cab as soon as we get to the corner."

"I don't think the count would be able to guide the horse," said Euphra, with a smile. "I must walk. But I should like to go. I will. It would be such a victory to catch him in his own toils."

She rose and ran up stairs. In a few minutes she came down again, cloaked and veiled. But Margaret met her as she descended, and leading her into the back drawing-room, said:

"Are you going, Euphra?"

"Yes; but I am going with Mr. Sutherland," answered Euphra, in a defensive tone. "It is to please him, and not to obey the count."

"Are you sure it is all to please Mr. Sutherland? If it were, I don't think you would be able to guide him right. Is it not to get rid of your suffering by yielding to temptation, Euphra? At all events, if you go, even should Mr. Sutherland be successful with him, you will never feel that you have overcome him, or he, that he has lost you. He will still hold you fast. Don't go. I am sure you are deceiving yourself."

Euphra stood for a moment and pouted like a naughty child. Then suddenly throwing her arms about Margaret's neck, she kissed her, and said:

"I won't go, Margaret. Here, take my things up stairs for me."

She threw off her bonnet and cloak, and rejoined Hugh in the drawing–room.

"I can't go," she said. "I must not go. I should be yielding to him, and it would make a slave of me all my life."

"It is our only chance for the ring," said Hugh.

Again Euphra hesitated and wavered; but again she conquered.

"I cannot help it," she said. "I would rather not have the ring than go—if you will forgive me."

"Oh, Euphra!" replied Hugh. "You know it is not for myself."

"I do know it. You won't mind then if I don't go?"

"Certainly not, if you have made up your mind. You must have a good reason for it."

"Indeed I have." And even already she felt that resistance brought its own reward.

Hugh went almost immediately, in order to make his report to Falconer, with whom he had an appointment for the purpose.

"She is quite right," said Falconer. "I do not think, in the relation in which she stands to him, that she could safely do otherwise. But it seems to me very likely that this will turn out well for our plans, too. Let her persist, and in all probability he will not only have to resign her perforce, but will so far make himself subject to her in turn, as to seek her who will not go to him. He will pull upon his own rope till he is drawn to the spot where he has fixed it. What remains for you and me to do, is to keep a close watch on the house

427

and neighbourhood. Most likely we shall find the villain before long."

"Do you really think so?"

"The whole affair is mysterious, and has to do with laws with which we are most imperfectly acquainted; but this seems to me a presumption worth acting upon. Is there no one in the house on whom you could depend for assistance—for information, at least?"

"Yes. There is the same old servant that Mrs. Elton had with her at Arnstead. He is a steady old fellow, and has been very friendly with me."

"Well, what I would advise is, that you should find yourself quarters as near the spot as possible; and, besides keeping as much of a personal guard upon the house as you can, engage the servant you mention to let you know, the moment the count makes his appearance. It will probably be towards night when he calls, for such a man may have reasons as well as instincts to make him love the darkness rather than the light. You had better go at once; and when you have found a place, leave or send the address here to me, and towards night–fall I will join you. But we may have to watch for several days. We must not be too sanguine."

Almost without a word, Hugh went to do as Falconer said. The only place he could find suitable, was a public–house at the corner of a back street, where the men–servants of the neighbourhood used to resort. He succeeded in securing a private room in it, for a week, and immediately sent Falconer word of his locality. He then called a second time at Mrs. Elton's, and asked to see the butler. When he came:

"Irwan," said he, "has Herr von Funkelstein called here to–day?"

"No, sir, he has not."

"You would know him, would you not?"

"Yes, sir; perfectly."

"Well, if he should call to–night, or to–morrow, or any time within the next few days, let me know the moment he is in the house. You will find me at the Golden Staff, round the corner. It is of the utmost importance that I should see him at once. But do not let him know that any one wants to see him. You shall not repent helping me in this affair. I know I can trust you."

Hugh had fixed him with his eyes, before he began to explain his wishes. He had found out that this was the best way of securing attention from inferior natures, and that it was especially necessary with London servants; for their superciliousness is cowed by it, and the superior will brought to bear upon theirs. It is the only way a man without a carriage has to command attention from such. Irwan was not one of this sort. He was a country servant, for one difference. But Hugh made his address as impressive as possible.

"I will with pleasure, sir," answered Irwan, and Hugh felt tolerably sure of him.

Falconer came. They ordered some supper, and sat till eleven o'clock. There being then no chance of a summons, they went out together. Passing the house, they saw light in one upper window only. That light would burn there all night, for it was in Euphra's room. They went on, Hugh accompanying Falconer in one of his midnight walks through London, as he had done repeatedly before. >From such companionship and the scenes to which Falconer introduced him, he had gathered this fruit, that he began to believe in God for the sake of the wretched men and women he saw in the world. At first it was his own pain at the sight of such misery that drove him, for consolation, to hope in God; so, at first, it was for his own sake. But as he saw more of them, and grew to love them more, he felt that the only hope for them lay in the love of God; and he hoped in God for them. He saw too that a God not both humanly and absolutely divine, a God less than that God shadowed forth in the Redeemer of men, would not do. But thinking about God thus, and hoping in him for his brothers and sisters, he began to love God. Then, last of all, that he might see in him one to whom he could abandon everything, that he might see him perfect and all in all and as he must be—for the sake of God himself, he believed in him as the Saviour of these his sinful and suffering kin.

As early as was at all excusable, the following morning, he called on Euphra. The butler said that she had not come down yet, but he would send up his name. A message was brought back that Miss Cameron was sorry not to see him, but she had had a bad night, and was quite unable to get up. Irwan replied to his inquiry, that the count had not called.

David Elginbrod

Hugh withdrew to the Golden Staff.

A bad night it had been indeed. As Euphra slept well the first part of it, and had no attack such as she had had upon both the preceding nights, Margaret had hoped the worst was over. Still she laid herself only within the threshold of sleep ready to wake at the least motion.

In the middle of the night she felt Euphra move. She lay still to see what she would do. Euphra slipped out of bed, and partly dressed herself; then went to her wardrobe, and put on a cloak with a large hood, which she drew over her head. Margaret lay with a dreadful aching at her heart. Euphra went towards the door. Margaret called her, but she made no answer. Margaret flew to the door, and reached it before her. Then, to her intense delight, she saw that Euphra's eyes were closed. Just as she laid her hand on the door, Margaret took her gently in her arms.

"Let me go, let me go!" Euphra almost screamed. Then suddenly opening her eyes, she stared at Margaret in a bewildered fashion, like one waking from the dead.

"Euphra! dear Euphra!" said Margaret.

"Oh, Margaret! is it really you?" exclaimed Euphra, flinging her arms about her. "Oh, I am glad. Ah! you see what I must have been about. I suppose I knew when I was doing it, but I don't know now. I have forgotten all about it. Oh dear! oh dear! I thought it would come to this."

"Come to bed, dear. You couldn't help it. It was not yourself. There is not more than half of you awake, when you walk in your sleep."

They went to bed. Euphra crept close to Margaret, and cried herself asleep again. The next day she had a bad head–ache. This with her always followed somnambulation. She did not get up all that day. When Hugh called again in the evening, he heard she was better, but still in bed.

Falconer joined Hugh at the Golden Staff, at night; but they had no better success than before. Falconer went out alone, for Hugh wanted to keep himself fresh. Though very strong, he was younger and less hardened than Falconer, who could stand an incredible amount of labour and lack of sleep. Hugh would have given way under the half.

CHAPTER XVIII. VICTORY

```
O my admired mistress, quench not out
The holy fires within you, though temptations
Shower down upon you: clasp thine armour on;
Fight well, and thou shalt see, after these wars,
Thy head wear sunbeams, and thy feet touch stars.

MASSINGER.—The Virgin Martyr.
```

But Hugh could sleep no more than if he had been out with Falconer. He was as restless as a wild beast in a cage. Something would not let him be at peace. So he rose, dressed, and went out. As soon as he turned the corner, he could see Mrs. Elton's house. It was visible both by intermittent moonlight above, and by flickering gaslight below, for the wind blew rather strong. There was snow in the air, he knew. The light they had observed last night, was burning now. A moment served to make these observations; and then Hugh's eyes were arrested by the sight of something else—a man walking up and down the pavement in front of Mrs. Elton's house. He instantly stepped into the shadow of a porch to watch him. The figure might be the count's; it might not; he could not be sure. Every now and then the man looked up to the windows. At length he stopped right under the lighted one, and looked up. Hugh was on the point of gliding out, that he might get as near him as possible before rushing on him, when, at the moment, to his great mortification, a policeman emerged from some mysterious corner, and the figure instantly vanished in another. Hugh did not pursue him; because it would be to set all on a single chance, and that a poor one; for if the count, should it be he, succeeded in escaping, he would not return to a spot which he knew to be watched. Hugh, therefore, withdrew once more under a porch, and waited. But, whatever might be the cause, the man made his appearance no more. Hugh contrived to keep watch for two hours, in spite of suspicious policemen. He slept late into the following morning.

Calling at Mrs. Elton's, he learned that the count had not been there; that Miss Cameron had been very ill all night; but that she was rather better since the morning.

That night, as the preceding, Margaret had awaked suddenly. Euphra was not in the bed beside her. She started up in an agony of terror; but it was soon allayed, though not

431

removed. She saw Euphra on her knees at the foot of the bed, an old—fashioned four—post one. She had her arms twined round one of the bed—posts, and her head thrown back, as if some one were pulling her backwards by her hair, which fell over her night—dress to the floor in thick, black masses. Her eyes were closed; her face was death—like, almost livid; and the cold dews of torture were rolling down from brow to chin. Her lips were moving convulsively, with now and then the appearance of an attempt at articulation, as if they were set in motion by an agony of inward prayer. Margaret, unable to move, watched her with anxious sympathy and fearful expectation. How long this lasted she could not tell, but it seemed a long time. At length Margaret rose, and longing to have some share in the struggle, however small, went softly, and stood behind her, shadowing her from a feeble ray of moonlight which, through a wind—rent cloud, had stolen into the room, and lay upon her upturned face. There she lifted up her heart in prayer. In a moment after the tension of Euphra's countenance relaxed a little; composure slowly followed; her head gradually rose, so that Margaret could see her face no longer; then, as gradually, drooped forward. Next her arms untwined themselves from the bed—post, and her hands clasped themselves together. She looked like one praying in the intense silence of absorbing devotion. Margaret stood still as a statue.

In speaking about it afterwards to Hugh, Margaret told him that she distinctly remembered hearing, while she stood, the measured steps of a policeman pass the house on the pavement below.

In a few minutes Euphra bowed her head yet lower, and then rose to her feet. She turned round towards Margaret, as if she knew she was there. To Margaret's astonishment, her eyes were wide open. She smiled a most child—like, peaceful, happy smile, and said:

"It is over, Margaret, all over at last. Thank you, with my whole heart. God has helped me."

At that moment, the moon shone out full, and her face appeared in its light like the face of an angel. Margaret looked on her with awe. Fear, distress, and doubt had vanished, and she was already beautiful like the blessed. Margaret got a handkerchief, and wiped the cold damps from her face. Then she helped her into bed, where she fell asleep almost instantly, and slept like a child. Now and then she moaned; but when Margaret looked at her, she saw the smile still upon her countenance.

David Elginbrod

She woke weak and worn, but happy.

"I shall not trouble you to–day, Margaret, dear," said she. "I shall not get up yet, but you will not need to watch me. A great change has passed upon me. I am free. I have overcome him. He may do as he pleases now. I do not care. I defy him. I got up last night in my sleep, but I remember all about it; and, although I was asleep, and felt powerless like a corpse, I resisted him, even when I thought he was dragging me away by bodily force. And I resisted him, till he left me alone. Thank God!"

It had been a terrible struggle, but she had overcome. Nor was this all: she would no more lead two lives, the waking and the sleeping. Her waking will and conscience had asserted themselves in her sleeping acts; and the memory of the somnambulist lived still in the waking woman. Hence her two lives were blended into one life; and she was no more two, but one. This indicated a mighty growth of individual being.

"I woke without terror," she went on to say. "I always used to wake from such a sleep in an agony of unknown fear. I do not think I shall ever walk in my sleep again."

Is not salvation the uniting of all our nature into one harmonious whole—God first in us, ourselves last, and all in due order between? Something very much analogous to the change in Euphra takes place in a man when he first learns that his beliefs must become acts; that his religious life and his human life are one; that he must do the thing that he admires. The Ideal is the only absolute Real; and it must become the Real in the individual life as well, however impossible they may count it who never try it, or who do not trust in God to effect it, when they find themselves baffled in the attempt.

In the afternoon, Euphra fell asleep, and when she woke, seemed better. She said to Margaret:

"Can it be that it was all a dream, Margaret? I mean my association with that dreadful man. I feel as if it were only some horrid dream, and that I could never have had anything to do with him. I may have been out of my mind, you know, and have told you things which I believed firmly enough then, but which never really took place. It could not have been me, Margaret, could it?"

"Not your real, true, best self, dear."

433

"I have been a dreadful creature, Margaret. But I feel that all that has melted away from me, and gone behind the sunset, which will for ever stand, in all its glory and loveliness, between me and it, an impassable rampart of defence."

Her words sounded strange and excited, but her eye and her pulse were calm.

"How could he ever have had that hateful power over me?"

"Don't think any more about him, dear, but enjoy the rest God has given you."

"I will, I will."

At that moment, a maid came to the door, with Funkelstein's card for Miss Cameron.

"Very well," said Margaret; "ask him to wait. I will tell Miss Cameron. She may wish to send him a message. You may go."

She told Euphra that the count was in the house. Euphra showed no surprise, no fear, no annoyance.

"Will you see him for me, Margaret, if you don't mind; and tell him from me, that I defy him; that I do not hate him, only because I despise and forget him; that I challenge him to do his worst."

She had forgotten all about the ring. But Margaret had not.

"I will," said she, and left the room.

On her way down, she went into the drawing–room, and rang the bell.

"Send Mr. Irwan to me here, please. It is for Miss Cameron."

The man went, but presently returned, saying that the butler had just stepped out.

"Very well. You will do just as well. When the gentleman leaves who is calling now, you must follow him. Take a cab, if necessary, and follow him everywhere, till you find where he stops for the night. Watch the place, and send me word where you are. But don't let him know. Put on plain clothes, please, as fast as you can."

"Yes, Miss, directly."

The servants all called Margaret, Miss.

She lingered yet a little, to give the man time. She was not at all satisfied with her plan, but she could think of nothing better. Happily, it was not necessary. Irwan had run as fast as his old legs would carry him to the Golden Staff. Hugh received the news with delight. His heart seemed to leap into his throat, and he felt just as he did, when, deer—stalking for the first time, he tried to take aim at a great red stag.

"I shall wait for him outside the door. We must have no noise in the house. He is a thief, or worse, Irwan."

"Good gracious! And there's the plate all laid out for dinner on the sideboard!" exclaimed Irwan, and hurried off faster than he had come.

But Hugh was standing at the door long before Irwan got up to it. Had Margaret known who was watching outside, it would have been a wonderful relief to her.

She entered the dining—room, where the count stood impatient. He advanced quickly, acting on his expectation of Euphra, but seeing his mistake, stopped, and bowed politely. Margaret told him that Miss Cameron was ill, and gave him her message, word for word. The count turned pale with mortification and rage. He bit his lip, made no reply, and walked out into the hall, where Irwan stood with the handle of the door in his hand, impatient to open it. No sooner was he out of the house, than Hugh sprang upon him; but the count, who had been perfectly upon his guard, eluded him, and darted off down the street. Hugh pursued at full speed, mortified at his escape. He had no fear at first of overtaking him, for he had found few men his equals in speed and endurance; but he soon saw, to his dismay, that the count was increasing the distance between them, and feared that, by a sudden turn into some labyrinth, he might escape him altogether. They passed the Golden Staff at full speed, and at the next corner Hugh discovered what gave the count the advantage: it was his agility and recklessness in turning corners. But, like the sorcerer's impunity, they failed him at last; for, at the next turn, he ran full upon Falconer,

435

who staggered back, while the count reeled and fell. Hugh was upon him in a moment. "Help!" roared the count, for a last chance from the sympathies of a gathering crowd.

"I've got him!" cried Hugh.

"Let the man alone," growled a burly fellow in the crowd, with his fists clenched in his trowser–pockets.

"Let me have a look at him," said Falconer, stooping over him. "Ah! I don't know him. That's as well for him. Let him up, Sutherland."

The bystanders took Falconer for a detective, and did not seem inclined to interfere, all except the carman before mentioned. He came up, pushing the crowd right and left.

"Let the man alone," said he, in a very offensive tone.

"I assure you," said Falconer, "he's not worth your trouble; for—"

"None o' your cursed jaw!" said the fellow, in a louder and deeper growl, approaching Falconer with a threatening mien.

"Well, I can't help it," said Falconer, as if to himself.

"Sutherland, look after the count."

"That I will," said Hugh, confidently.

Falconer turned on the carman, who was just on the point of closing with him, preferring that mode of fighting; and saying only: "Defend yourself," retreated a step. The man was good at his fists too, and, having failed in his first attempt, made the best use of them he could. But he had no chance with Falconer, whose coolness equalled his skill.

Meantime, the Bohemian had been watching his chance; and although the contest certainly did not last longer than one minute, found opportunity, in the middle of it, to wrench himself free from Hugh, trip him up, and dart off. The crowd gave way before him. He vanished so suddenly and completely, that it was evident he must have studied the neighbourhood from the retreat side of the question. With rat–like instinct, he had consulted the holes and corners in anticipation of the necessity of applying to them. Hugh got up, and, directed, or possibly misdirected by the bystanders, sped away in pursuit; but he could hear or see nothing of the fugitive.

At the end of the minute, the carman lay in the road.

"Look after him, somebody," said Falconer.

"No fear of him, sir; he's used to it," answered one of the bystanders, with the respect which Falconer's prowess claimed.

Falconer walked after Hugh, who soon returned, looking excessively mortified, and feeling very small indeed.

"Never mind, Sutherland," said he. "The fellow is up to a trick or two; but we shall catch him yet. If it hadn't been for that big fool there—but he's punished enough."

"But what can we do next? He will not come here again."

"Very likely not. Still he may not give up his attempts upon Miss Cameron. I almost wonder, seeing she is so impressible, that she can give no account of his whereabouts. But I presume clairvoyance depends on the presence of other qualifications as well. I should like to mesmerize her myself, and see whether she could not help us then."

"Well, why not, if you have the power?"

"Because I have made up my mind not to superinduce any condition of whose laws I am so very partially informed. Besides, I consider it a condition of disease in which, as by sleeplessness for instance, the senses of the soul, if you will allow the expression, are, for its present state, rendered unnaturally acute. To induce such a condition, I dare not exercise a power which itself I do not understand."

CHAPTER XIX. MARGARET.

```
For though that ever virtuous was she,
   She was increased in such excellence,
Of thewes good, yset in high bounté,
   And so discreet and fair of eloquence,
   So benign, and so digne of reverence,
And couthé so the poeple's hert embrace,
That each her loveth that looketh in her face.
```

CHAUCER.—The Clerk's Tale.

Hugh returned to Mrs. Elton's, and, in the dining—room, wrote a note to Euphra, to express his disappointment, and shame that, after all, the count had foiled him; but, at the same time, his determination not to abandon the quest, till there was no room for hope left. He sent this up to her, and waited, thinking that she might be on the sofa, and might send for him. A little weary from the reaction of the excitement he had just gone through, he sat down in the corner farthest from the door. The large room was dimly lighted by one untrimmed lamp.

He sat for some time, thinking that Euphra was writing him a note, or perhaps preparing herself to see him in her room. Involuntarily he looked up, and a sudden pang, as at the vision of the disembodied, shot through his heart. A dim form stood in the middle of the room, gazing earnestly at him. He saw the same face which he had seen for a moment in the library at Arnstead—the glorified face of Margaret Elginbrod, shimmering faintly in the dull light. Instinctively he pressed his hands together, palm to palm, as if he had been about to kneel before Madonna herself. Delight, mingled with hope, and tempered by shame, flushed his face. Ghost or none, she brought no fear with her, only awe.

She stood still.

"Margaret!" he said, with trembling voice.

"Mr. Sutherland!" she responded, sweetly.

"Are you a ghost, Margaret?"

She smiled as if she were all spirit, and, advancing slowly, took his joined hands in both of hers.

"Forgive me, Margaret," sighed he, as if with his last breath, and burst into an agony of tears.

She waited motionless, till his passion should subside, still holding his hands. He felt that her hands were so good.

"He is dead!" said Hugh, at last, with all effort, followed by a fresh outburst of weeping.

"Yes, he is dead," rejoined Margaret, calmly. "You would not weep so if you had seen him die as I did—die with a smile like a summer sunset. Indeed, it was the sunset to me; but the moon has been up for a long time now."

She sighed a gentle, painless sigh, and smiled again like a saint. She spoke nearly as Scotch as ever in tone, though the words and pronunciation were almost pure English.—This lapse into so much of the old form, or rather garment, of speech, constantly recurred, as often as her feelings were moved, and especially when she talked to children.

"Forgive me," said Hugh, once more.

"We are the same as in the old days," answered Margaret; and Hugh was satisfied.

"How do you come to be here?" said Hugh, at last, after a silence.

"I will tell you all about that another time. Now I must give you Miss Cameron's message. She is very sorry she cannot see you, but she is quite unable. Indeed, she is not out of bed. But if you could call to-morrow morning, she hopes to be better and to be able to see you. She says she can never thank you enough."

The lamp burned yet fainter. Margaret went, and proceeded to trim it. The virgins that arose must have looked very lovely, trimming their lamps. It is a deed very fair and womanly—the best for a woman—to make the lamp burn. The light shone up in her face, and the hands removing the globe handled it delicately. He saw that the good hands were very beautiful hands; not small, but admirably shaped, and very pure. As she replaced the globe,—

"That man," she said, "will not trouble her any more."

"I hope not," said Hugh; "but you speak confidently: why?"

"Because she has behaved gloriously. She has fought and conquered him on his own ground; and she is a free, beautiful, and good creature of God for ever."

"You delight me," rejoined Hugh "Another time, perhaps, you will be able to tell me all about it."

"I hope so. I think she will not mind my telling you."

They bade each other good night; and Hugh went away with a strange feeling, which he had never experienced before. To compare great things with small, it was something like what he had once felt in a dream, in which, digging in his father's garden, he had found a perfect marble statue, young as life, and yet old as the hills. To think of the girl he had first seen in the drawing–room at Turriepuffit, idealizing herself into such a creature as that, so grand, and yet so womanly! so lofty, and yet so lovely; so strong, and yet so graceful!

Would that every woman believed in the ideal of herself, and hoped for it as the will of God, not merely as the goal of her own purest ambition! But even if the lower development of the hope were all she possessed, it would yet be well; for its inevitable failure would soon develope the higher and triumphant hope.

He thought about her till he fell asleep, and dreamed about her till he woke. Not for a moment, however, did he fancy he was in love with her: the feeling was different from any he had hitherto recognized as embodying that passion. It was the recognition and consequent admiration of a beauty which everyone who beheld it must recognize and admire; but mingled, in his case, with old and precious memories, doubly dear now in the increased earnestness of his nature and aspirations, and with a deep personal interest from the fact that, however little, he had yet contributed a portion of the vital food whereby the gracious creature had become what she was.

David Elginbrod

In the so–called morning he went to Mrs. Elton's. Euphra was expecting his visit, and he was shown up into her room, where she was lying on a couch by the fire. She received him with the warmth of gratitude added to that of friendship. Her face was pale and thin, but her eyes were brilliant. She did not appear at first sight to be very ill: but the depth and reality of her sickness grew upon him. Behind her couch stood Margaret, like a guardian angel. Margaret could bear the day, for she belonged to it; and therefore she looked more beautiful still than by the lamp–light. Euphra held out a pale little hand to Hugh, and before she withdrew it, led Hugh's towards Margaret. Their hands joined. How different to Hugh was the touch of the two hands! Life, strength, persistency in the one: languor, feebleness, and fading in the other.

"I can never thank you enough," said Euphra; "therefore I will not try. It is no bondage to remain your debtor."

"That would be thanks indeed, if I had done anything."

"I have found out another mystery," Euphra resumed, after a pause.

"I am sorry to hear it," answered he. "I fear there will be no mysteries left by–and–by."

"No fear of that," she rejoined, "so long as the angels come down to men." And she turned towards Margaret as she spoke.

Margaret smiled. In the compliment she felt only the kindness.

Hugh looked at her. She turned away, and found something to do at the other side of the room.

"What mystery, then, have you destroyed?"

"Not destroyed it; for the mystery of courage remains. I was the wicked ghost that night in the Ghost's Walk, you know—the white one: there is the good ghost, the nun, the black one."

"Who? Margaret?"

441

"Yes, indeed. She has just been confessing it to me. I had my two angels, as one whose fate was undetermined; my evil angel in the count—my good angel in Margaret. Little did I think then that the holy powers were watching me in her. I knew the evil one; I knew nothing of the good. I suppose it is so with a great many people."

Hugh sat silent in astonishment. Margaret, then, had been at Arnstead with Mrs. Elton all the time. It was herself he had seen in the study.

"Did you suspect me, Margaret?" resumed Euphra, turning towards her where she sat at the window.

"Not in the least. I only knew that something was wrong about the house; that some being was terrifying the servants, and poor Harry; and I resolved to do my best to meet it, especially if it should be anything of a ghostly kind."

"Then you do believe in such appearances?" said Hugh.

"I have never met anything of the sort yet. I don't know."

"And you were not afraid?"

"Not much. I am never really afraid of anything. Why should I be?"

No justification of fear was suggested either by Hugh or by Euphra. They felt the dignity of nature that lifted Margaret above the region of fear.

"Come and see me again soon," said Euphra, as Hugh rose to go.

He promised.

Next day he dined by invitation with Mrs. Elton and Harry. Euphra was unable to see him, but sent a kind message by Margaret as he was taking his leave. He had been fearing that he should not see Margaret; and when she did appear he was the more delighted; but the interview was necessarily short.

He called the next day, and saw neither Euphra nor Margaret. She was no better. Mrs. Elton said the physicians could discover no definite disease either of the lungs or of any other organ. Yet life seemed sinking. Margaret thought that the conflict which she had passed through, had exhausted her vitality; that, had she yielded, she might have lived a slave; but that now, perhaps, she must die a free woman.

Her continued illness made Hugh still more anxious to find the ring, for he knew it would please her much. Falconer would have applied to the police, but he feared that the man would vanish from London, upon the least suspicion that he was watched. They held many consultations on the subject.

CHAPTER XX. A NEW GUIDE.

Das Denken ist nur ein Traum des Fühlens, ein erstorbenes Fühlen, ein blass-graues, schwaches Leben.

Thinking is only a dream of feeling; a dead feeling; a pale-grey, feeble life.

NOVALIS.—Die Lehrlinge zu Sais.

For where's no courage, there's no ruth nor mone.

Faerie Queene: vi. 7, 18.

One morning, as soon as she waked, Euphra said:

"Have I been still all the night, Margaret?"

"Quite still. Why do you ask?"

"Because I have had such a strange and vivid dream, that I feel as if I must have been to the place. It was a foolish question, though; because, of course, you would not have let me go."

"I hope it did not trouble you much."

"No, not much; for though I was with the count, I did not seem to be there in the body at all, only somehow near him, and seeing him. I can recall the place perfectly."

"Do you think it really was the place he was in at the time?"

"I should not wonder. But now I feel so free, so far beyond him and all his power, that I don't mind where or when I see him. He cannot hurt me now."

"Could you describe the place to Mr. Sutherland? It might help him to find the count."

"That's a good idea. Will you send for him?"

"Yes, certainly. May I tell him for what?"

"By all means."

Margaret wrote to Hugh at once, and sent the note by hand. He was at home when it arrived. He hurriedly answered it, and went to find Falconer. To his delight he was at home—not out of bed, in fact.

"Read that."

"Who is it from?"

"Miss Cameron's maid."

"It does not look like a maid's production."

"It is though. Will you come with me? You know London ten thousand times better than I do. I don't think we ought to lose a chance."

"Certainly not. I will go with you. But perhaps she will not see me."

"Oh! yes, she will, when I have told her about you."

"It will be rather a trial to see a stranger."

David Elginbrod

"A man cannot be a stranger with you ten minutes, if he only looks at you;—still less a woman."

Falconer looked pleased, and smiled.

"I am glad you think so. Let us go."

When they arrived, Margaret came to them. Hugh told her that Falconer was his best friend, and one who knew London perhaps better than any other man in it. Margaret looked at him full in the face for a moment. Falconer smiled at the intensity of her still gaze. Margaret returned the smile, and said:

"I will ask Miss Cameron to see yet."

"Thank you," was all Falconer's reply; but the tone was more than speech.

After a little while, they were shown up to Euphra's room. She had wanted to sit up, but Margaret would not let her; so she was lying on her couch. When Falconer was presented to her, he took her hand, and held it for a moment. A kind of indescribable beam broke over his face, as if his spirit smiled and the smile shone through without moving one of his features as it passed. The tears stood in his eyes. To understand all this look, one would need to know his history as I do. He laid her hand gently on her bosom, and said: "God bless you!"

Euphra felt that God did bless her in the very words. She had been looking at Falconer all the time. It was only fifteen seconds or so; but the outcome of a life was crowded into Falconer's side of it; and the confidence of Euphra rose to meet the faithfulness of a man of God.—What words those are!—A man of God! Have I not written a revelation? Yes—to him who can read it—yes.

"I know enough of your story, Miss Cameron," he said, "to understand without any preface what you choose to tell me."

Euphra began at once:

David Elginbrod

"I dreamed last night that I found myself outside the street door. I did not know where I was going; but my feet seemed to know. They carried me, round two or three corners, into a wide, long street, which I think was Oxford-street. They carried me on into London, far beyond any quarter I knew. All I can tell further is, that I turned to the left beside a church, on the steeple of which stood what I took for a wandering ghost just lighted there;—only I ought to tell you, that frequently in my dreams—always in my peculiar dreams—the more material and solid and ordinary things are, the more thin and ghostly they appear to me. Then I went on and on, turning left and right too many times for me to remember, till at last I came to a little, old-fashioned court, with two or three trees in it. I had to go up a few steps to enter it. I was not afraid, because I knew I was dreaming, and that my body was not there. It is a great relief to feel that sometimes; for it is often very much in the way. I opened a door, upon which the moon shone very bright, and walked up two flights of stairs into a back room. And there I found him, doing something at a table by candlelight. He had a sheet of paper before him; but what he was doing with it, I could not see. I tried hard; but it was of no use. The dream suddenly faded, and I awoke, and found Margaret.—Then I knew I was safe," she added, with a loving glance at her maid.

Falconer rose.

"I know the place you mean perfectly," he said. "It is too peculiar to be mistaken. Last night, let me see, how did the moon shine?—Yes. I shall be able to tell the very door, I think, or almost."

"How kind of you not to laugh at me!"

"I might make a fool of myself if I laughed at any one. So I generally avoid it. We may as well get the good out of what we do not understand—or at least try if there be any in it. Will you come, Sutherland?"

Hugh rose, and took his leave with Falconer.

"How pleased she seemed with you, Falconer!" said he, as they left the house.

"Yes, she touched me."

446

David Elginbrod

"Won't you go and see her again?"

"No; there is no need, except she sends for me."

"It would please her—comfort her, I am sure."

"She has got one of God's angels beside her, Sutherland. She doesn't want me."

"What do you mean?"

"I mean that maid of hers."

A pang—of jealousy, was it?—shot through Hugh's heart. How could he see—what right had he to see anything in Margaret?

Hugh might have kept himself at peace, even if he had loved Margaret as much as she deserved, which would have been about ten times as much as he did. Is a man not to recognize an angel when he sees her, and to call her by her name? Had Hugh seen into the core of that grand heart—what form sat there, and how—he would have been at peace—would almost have fallen down to do the man homage. He was silent.

"My dear fellow!" said Falconer, as if he divined his feeling—for Falconer's power over men and women came all from sympathy with their spirits, and not their nerves—"if you have any hold of that woman, do not lose it; for as sure as there's a sun in heaven, she is one of the winged ones. Don't I know a woman when I see her!"

He sighed with a kind of involuntary sigh, which yet did not seek to hide itself from Hugh.

"My dear boy," he added, laying a stress on the word, "—I am nearly twice your age—don't be jealous of me."

"Mr. Falconer," said Hugh humbly, "forgive me. The feeling was involuntary; and if you have detected in it more than I was aware of, you are at least as likely to be right as I am. But you cannot think more highly of Margaret than I do."

David Elginbrod

And yet Hugh did not know half the good of her then, that the reader does now.

"Well, we had better part now, and meet again at night."

"What time shall I come to you?"

"Oh! about nine I think will do."

So Hugh went home, and tried to turn his thoughts to his story; but Euphra, Falconer, Funkelstein, and Margaret persisted in sitting to him, the one after the other, instead of the heroes and heroines of his tale. He was compelled to lay it aside, and betake himself to a stroll and a pipe.

As he went down stairs, he met Miss Talbot.

"You're soon tired of home, Mr. Sutherland. You haven't been in above half an hour, and you're out again already."

"Why, you see, Miss Talbot, I want a pipe very much."

"Well, you ain't going to the public house to smoke it, are you?"

"No," answered Hugh laughing. "But you know, Miss Talbot, you made it part of the agreement that I shouldn't smoke indoors. So I'm going to smoke in the street."

"Now, think of being taken that way!" retorted Miss Talbot, with an injured air. "Why, that was before I knew anything about you. Go up stairs directly, and smoke your pipe; and when the room can't hold any more, you can open the windows. Your smoke won't do any harm, Mr. Sutherland. But I'm very sorry you quarrelled with Mrs. Appleditch. She's a hard woman, and over fond of her money and her drawing–room; and for those boys of hers—the Lord have mercy on them, for she has none! But she's a true Christian for all that, and does a power of good among the poor people."

"What does she give them, Miss Talbot?"

David Elginbrod

"Oh!—she gives them—hm–m—tracts and things. You know," she added, perceiving the weakness of her position, "people's souls should come first. And poor Mrs. Appleditch—you see—some folks is made stickier than others, and their money sticks to them, somehow, that they can't part with it   poor woman!"

To this Hugh had no answer at hand; for though Miss Talbot's logic was more than questionable, her charity was perfectly sound; and Hugh felt that he had not been forbearing enough with the mother of the future pastors. So he went back to his room, lighted his pipe, and smoked till he fell asleep over a small volume of morbid modern divinity, which Miss Talbot had lent him. I do not mention the name of the book, lest some of my acquaintance should abuse me, and others it, more than either deserves. Hugh, however, found the best refuge from the diseased self–consciousness which it endeavoured to rouse, and which is a kind of spiritual somnambulism, in an hour of God's good sleep, into a means of which the book was temporarily elevated. When he woke he found himself greatly refreshed by the influence it had exercised upon him.

It was now the hour for the daily pretence of going to dine. So he went out. But all he had was some bread, which he ate as he walked about. Loitering here, and trifling there, passing five minutes over a volume on every bookstall in Holborn, and comparing the shapes of the meerschaums in every tobacconist's window, time ambled gently along with him; and it struck nine just as he found himself at Falconer's door.

"You are ready, then?" said Falconer.

"Quite."

"Will you take anything before you go? I think we had better have some supper first. It is early for our project."

This was a welcome proposal to Hugh. Cold meat and ale were excellent preparatives for what might be required of him; for a tendency to collapse in a certain region, called by courtesy the chest, is not favourable to deeds of valour. By the time he had spent ten minutes in the discharge of the agreeable duty suggested, he felt himself ready for anything that might fall to his lot.

David Elginbrod

The friends set out together; and, under the guidance of the two foremost bumps upon Falconer's forehead, soon arrived at the place he judged to be that indicated by Euphra. It was very different from the place Hugh had pictured to himself. Yet in everything it corresponded to her description.

"Are we not great fools, Sutherland, to set out on such a chase, with the dream of a sick girl for our only guide?"

"I am sure you don't think so, else you would not have gone."

"I think we can afford the small risk to our reputation involved in the chase of this same wild—goose. There is enough of strange testimony about things of the sort to justify us in attending to the hint. Besides, if we neglected it, it would be mortifying to find out some day, perhaps a hundred years after this, that it was a true hint. It is altogether different from giving ourselves up to the pursuit of such things.—But this ought to be the house," he added, going up to one that had a rather more respectable look than the rest.

He knocked at the door. An elderly woman half opened it and looked at them suspiciously.

"Will you take my card to the foreign gentleman who is lodging with you, and say I am happy to wait upon him?" said Falconer.

She glanced at him again, and turned inwards, hesitating whether to leave the door half—open or not. Falconer stood so close to it, however, that she was afraid to shut it in his face.

"Now, Sutherland, follow me," whispered Falconer, as soon as the woman had disappeared on the stair.

Hugh followed behind the moving tower of his friend, who strode with long, noiseless strides till he reached the stair. That he took three steps at a time. They went up two flights, and reached the top just as the woman was laying her hand on the lock of the back—room door. She turned and faced them.

"Speak one word," said Falconer, in a hissing whisper, "and—"

David Elginbrod

He completed the sentence by an awfully threatening gesture. She drew back in terror, and yielded her place at the door.

"Come in," bawled some one, in second answer to the knock she had already given.

"It is he!" said Hugh, trembling with excitement.

"Hush!" said Falconer, and went in.

Hugh followed. He know the back of the count at once. He was seated at a table, apparently writing; but, going nearer, they saw that he was drawing. A single closer glance showed them the portrait of Euphra growing under his hand. In order to intensify his will and concentrate it upon her, he was drawing her portrait from memory. But at the moment they caught sight of it, the wretch, aware of a hostile presence, sprang to his feet, and reached the chimney−piece at one bound, whence he caught up a sword.

"Take care, Falconer," cried Hugh; "that weapon is poisoned. He is no every−day villain you have to deal with."

He remembered the cat.

Funkelstein made a sudden lunge at Hugh, his face pale with hatred and anger. But a blow from Falconer's huge fist, travelling faster than the point of his weapon, stretched him on the floor. Such was Falconer's impetus, that it hurled both him and the table across the fallen villain. Falconer was up in a moment. Not so Funkelstein. There was plenty of time for Hugh to secure the rapier, and for Falconer to secure its owner, before he came to himself.

"Where's my ring?" said Hugh, the moment he opened his eyes.

"Gentlemen, I protest," began Funkelstein, in a voice upon which the cord that bound his wrists had an evident influence.

"No chaff!" said Falconer. "We've got all our feathers. Hand over the two rings, or be the security for them yourself."

"What witness have you against me?"

"The best of witnesses—Miss Cameron."

"And me," added Hugh.

"Gentlemen, I am very sorry. I yielded to temptation. I meant to restore the diamond after the joke had been played out, but I was forced to part with it."

"The joke is played out, you see," said Falconer. "So you had better produce the other bauble you stole at the same time."

"I have not got it."

"Come, come, that's too much. Nobody would give you more than five shillings for it. And you knew what it was worth when you took it. Sutherland, you stand over him while I search the room. This portrait may as well be put out of the way first."

As he spoke, Falconer tore the portrait and threw it into the fire. He then turned to a cupboard in the room. Whether it was that Funkelstein feared further revelations, I do not know, but he quailed.

"I have not got it," he repeated, however.

"You lie," answered Falconer.

"I would give it you if I could."

"You shall."

The Bohemian looked contemptible enough now, despite the handsomeness of his features. It needed freedom, and the absence of any urgency, to enable him to personate a gentleman. Given those conditions, he succeeded. But as soon as he was disturbed, the gloss vanished, and the true nature came out, that of a ruffian and a sneak. He quite quivered at the look with which Falconer turned again to the cupboard.

David Elginbrod

"Stop," he cried; "here it is."

And muttering what sounded like curses, he pulled out of his bosom the ring, suspended from his neck

"Sutherland," said Falconer, taking the ring, "secure that rapier, and be careful with it. We will have its point tested. Meantime,"—here he turned again to his prisoner—"I give you warning that the moment I leave this house, I go to Scotland Yard.—Do you know the place? I there recommend the police to look after you, and they will mind what I say. If you leave London, a message will be sent, wherever you go, that you had better be watched. My advice to you is, to stay where you are as long as you can. I shall meet you again."

They left him on the floor, to the care of his landlady, whom they found outside the room, speechless with terror.

As soon as they were in the square, on which the moon was now shining, as it had shone in Euphra's dream the night before, Falconer gave the ring to Hugh.

"Take it to a jeweller's, Sutherland, and get it cleaned, before you give it to Miss Cameron."

"I will," answered Hugh, and added, "I don't know how to thank you."

"Then don't," said Falconer, with a smile.

When they reached the end of the street, he turned, and bade Hugh good night.

"Take care of that cowardly thing. It may be as you say."

Hugh turned towards home. Falconer dived into a court, and was out of sight in a moment.

CHAPTER XXI. THE LAST GROAT.

```
    Thou hast been
As one, in suffering all, that suffers nothing;
A man that fortune's buffets and rewards
Hast ta'en with equal thanks; and blessed are those
Whose blood and judgment are so well commingled
That they are not a pipe for fortune's finger
To sound what stop she please.

Hamlet.


Most friends befriend themselves with friendship's show.

SOUTHWELL.
```

Hugh took the ring to Mrs. Elton's, and gave it into Margaret's hand. She brought him back a message of warmest thanks from Euphra. She had asked for writing materials at once, and was now communicating the good news to Mr. Arnold, in Madeira.

"I have never seen her look so happy," added Margaret. "She hopes to be able to see you in the evening, if you would not mind calling again."

Hugh did call, and saw her. She received him most kindly. He was distressed to see how altered she was. The fire of one life seemed dying out—flowing away and spending from her eyes, which it illuminated with too much light as it passed out. But the fire of another life, the immortal life, which lies in thought and feeling, in truth and love divine, which death cannot touch, because it is not of his kind, was growing as fast. He sat with her for an hour, and then went.

This chapter of his own history concluded, Hugh returned with fresh energy to his novel, and worked at it as his invention gave him scope. There was the more necessity that he should make progress, from the fact that, having sent his mother the greater part of the salary he had received from Mr. Arnold, he was now reduced to his last sovereign. Poverty looks rather ugly when she comes so close as this. But she had not yet accosted him; and with a sovereign in his pocket, and last week's rent paid, a bachelor is certainly not poverty–stricken, at least when he is as independent, not only of other people, but of himself, as Hugh was. Still, without more money than that a man walks in fetters, and is ready to forget that the various restraints he is under are not incompatible with most honourable freedom. So Hugh worked as hard as he could to finish his novel, and succeeded within a week. Then the real anxiety began. He carried it, with much doubtful hope, to one of the principal publishing houses. Had he been more selfishly wise, he would have put it into the hands of Falconer to negotiate for him. But he thought he had given him quite trouble enough already. So he went without an introduction even. The manuscript was received politely, and attention was promised. But a week passed, and another, and another. A human soul was in commotion about the meat that perisheth—and the manuscript lay all the time unread,—forgotten in a drawer.

At length he reached his last coin. He had had no meat for several days, except once that he dined at Mrs. Elton's. But he would not borrow till absolutely compelled, and sixpence would keep him alive another day. In the morning he had some breakfast (for he knew his books were worth enough to pay all he owed Miss Talbot), and then he wandered out. Through the streets he paced and paced, looking in at all the silversmiths' and printsellers' windows, and solacing his poverty with a favourite amusement of his in uneasy circumstances, an amusement cheap enough for a Scotchman reduced to his last sixpence—castle-building. This is not altogether a bad employment where hope has laid the foundation; but it is rather a heartless one where the imagination has to draw the ground plan as well as the elevations. The latter, however, was not quite Hugh's condition yet.—He returned at night, carefully avoiding the cook-shops and their kindred snares, with a silver groat in his pocket still. But he crawled up stairs rather feebly, it must be confessed, for a youth with limbs moulded in the fashion of his.

He found a letter waiting him, from a friend of his mother, informing him that she was dangerously ill, and urging him to set off immediately for home. This was like the blast of fiery breath from the dragon's maw, which overthrew the Red-cross knight—but into the well of life, where all his wounds were healed, and—and—well—board and lodging provided him gratis.

When he had read the letter, he fell on his knees, and said to his father in heaven: "What am I to do?"

There was no lake with golden pieces in its bottom, whence a fish might bring him a coin. Nor in all the wide London lay there one he could claim as his, but the groat in his pocket.

He rose with the simple resolution to go and tell Falconer. He went. He was not at home. Emboldened by necessity, Hugh left his card, with the words on it: "Come to me; I need you." He then returned, packed a few necessaries, and sat down to wait. But he had not sat five minutes before Falconer entered.

"What's the matter, Sutherland, my dear fellow? You haven't pricked yourself with that skewer, have you?"

Hugh handed him the letter with one hand; and when he had read it, held out the fourpenny piece in the other hand, to be read likewise. Falconer understood at once.

"Sutherland," he said, in a tone of reproof, "it is a shame of you to forget that men are brothers. Are not two who come out of the heart of God, as closely related as if they had lain in the womb of one mother? Why did you not tell me? You have suffered—I am sure you have."

"I have—a little," Hugh confessed. "I am getting rather low in fact. I haven't had quite enough to eat."

He said this to excuse the tears which Falconer's kindness—not hunger—compelled from their cells.

"But," he added, "I would have come to you as soon as the fourpence was gone; or at least, if I hadn't got another before I was very hungry again."

"Good heavens!" exclaimed Falconer, half angrily. Then pulling out his watch, "We have two hours," said he, "before a train starts for the north. Come to my place."

Hugh rose and obeyed. Falconer's attendant soon brought them a plentiful supper from a neighbouring shop; after which Falconer got out one of his bottles of port, well known to his more intimate friends; and Hugh thought no more about money than if he had had his purse full. If it had not been for anxiety about his mother, he would have been happier than he had ever been in his life before. For, crossing in the night the wavering, heaving morass of the world, had he not set his foot upon one spot which did not shake; the summit, indeed, of a mighty Plutonic rock, that went down widening away to the very centre of the earth? As he sped along in the railway that night, the prophecy of thousands of years came back: "A man shall be a hiding–place from the wind, a covert from the tempest, the shadow of a great rock in a weary land." And he thought it would be a blessed time indeed, when this was just what a man was. And then he thought of the Son of Man, who, by being such first, was enabling all his friends to be such too. Of him Falconer had already learned this "truth in the inward parts"; and had found, in the process of learning it, that this was the true nature which God had made his from the first, no new thing superinduced upon it. He had had but to clear away the rubbish of worldliness, which more or less buries the best natures for a time, and so to find himself.

After Hugh had eaten and drunk, and thus once more experienced the divinity that lay in food and wine, he went to take leave of his friends at Mrs. Elton's. Like most invalids, Euphra was better in the evening: she requested to see him. He found her in bed, and much wasted since he saw her last. He could not keep the tears from filling his eyes, for all the events of that day had brought them near the surface.

"Do not cry, dear friend," she said sweetly. "There is no room for me here any more, and I am sent for."

Hugh could not reply. She went on:

"I have written to Mr. Arnold about the ring, and all you did to get it. Do you know he is going to marry Lady Emily?"

Still Hugh could not answer.

Margaret stood on the other side of the bed, the graceful embodiment of holy health, and in his sorrow, he could not help feeling the beauty of her presence. Her lovely hands were the servants of Euphra, and her light, firm feet moved only in ministration. He felt that Euphra had room in the world while Margaret waited on her. It is not house, and fire, and plenty of servants, and all the things that money can procure, that make a home—not father or mother or friends; but one heart which will not be weary of helping, will not be offended with the petulance of sickness, nor the ministrations needful to weakness: this "entire affection hating nicer hands" will make a home of a cave in a rock, or a gipsy's tent. This Euphra had in Margaret, and Hugh saw it.

David Elginbrod

"I trust you will find your mother better, Hugh" said Euphra.

"I fear not," answered he.

"Well, Margaret has been teaching me, and I think I have learned it, that death is not at all such a dreadful thing as it looks. I said to her: 'It is easy for you, Margaret, who are so far from death's door.' But she told me that she had been all but dead once, and that you had saved her life almost with your own. Oh, Hugh! she is such a dear!"

Euphra smiled with ten times the fascination of any of her old smiles; for the soul of the smile was love.

"I shall never see you again, I daresay," she went on. "My heart thanks you, from its very depths, for your goodness to me. It has been a thousand times more than I deserve."

Hugh kissed in silence the wasted hand held out to him in adieu, and departed. And the world itself was a sad wandering star.

Falconer had called for him. They drove to Miss Talbot's, where Hugh got his 'bag of needments,' and bade his landlady good—bye for a time. Falconer then accompanied him to the railway.

Having left him for a moment, Falconer rejoined him, saying: "I have your ticket;" and put him into a first—class carriage.

Hugh remonstrated. Falconer replied:

"I find this hulk of mine worth taking care of. You will be twice the good to your mother, if you reach her tolerably fresh."

He stood by the carriage door talking to him, till the train started; walked alongside till it was fairly in motion; then, bidding him good—bye, left in his hand a little packet, which Hugh, opening it by the light of the lamp, found to consist of a few sovereigns and a few shillings folded up in a twenty—pound—note.

David Elginbrod

I ought to tell one other little fact, however. Just before the engine whistled, Falconer said to Hugh:

"Give me that fourpenny piece, you brave old fellow!"

"There it is," said Hugh. "What do you want it for?"

"I am going to make a wedding–present of it to your wife, whoever she may happen to be. I hope she will be worthy of it."

Hugh instantly thought within himself:

"What a wife Margaret would make to Falconer!"

The thought was followed by a pang, keen and clear.

Those who are in the habit of regarding the real and the ideal as essentially and therefore irreconcileably opposed, will remark that I cannot have drawn the representation of Falconer faithfully. Perhaps the difficulty they will experience in recognizing its truthfulness, may spring from the fact that they themselves are un–ideal enough to belong to the not small class of strong–minded friends whose chief care, in performing the part of the rock in the weary land, is—not to shelter you imprudently. They are afraid of weakening your constitution by it, especially if it is not strong to begin with; so if they do just take off the edge of the tempest with the sharp corners of their sheltering rock for a moment, the next, they will thrust you out into the rain, to get hardy and self–denying, by being wet to the skin and well blown about.

The rich easily learn the wisdom of Solomon, but are unapt scholars of him who is greater than Solomon. It is, on the other hand, so easy for the poor to help each other, that they have little merit in it: it is no virtue—only a beauty. But there are a few rich, who, rivalling the poor in their own peculiar excellences, enter into the kingdom of heaven in spite of their riches; and then find that by means of their riches they are made rulers over many cities. She to whose memory this book is dedicated, is—I will not say was—one of the noblest of such.

There are two ways of accounting for the difficulty which a reader may find in believing in such a character: either that, not being poor, he has never needed such a friend; or that, being rich, he has never been such a friend.

Or if it be that, being poor, he has never found such a friend; his difficulty is easy to remove:—I have.

CHAPTER XXII. DEATH.

```
Think then, my soul, that death is but a groom
Which brings a taper to the outward room,
Whence thou spy'st first a little glimmering light;
And after brings it nearer to thy sight:
For such approaches doth heaven make in death.

DR. DONNE.
```

Hugh found his mother even worse than he had expected; but she rallied a little after his arrival.

In the evening, he wandered out in the bright moonlit snow.

How strange it was to see all the old forms with his heart so full of new things! The same hills rose about him, with all the lines of their shapes unchanged in seeming. Yet they were changing as surely as himself; nay, he continued more the same than they; for in him the old forms were folded up in the new. In the eyes of Him who creates time, there is no rest, but a living sacred change, a journeying towards rest. He alone rests; and he alone, in virtue of his rest, creates change.

He thought with sadness, how all the haunts of his childhood would pass to others, who would feel no love or reverence for them; that the house would be the same, but sounding with new steps, and ringing with new laughter. A little further thought, however, soon satisfied him that places die as well as their dwellers; that, by slow degrees, their forms are wiped out; that the new tastes obliterate the old fashions; and that ere long the very shape of the house and farm would be lapped, as it were, about the tomb of him who had been the soul of the shape, and would vanish from the face of the earth.

David Elginbrod

All the old things at home looked sad. The look came from this, that, though he could sympathize with them and their story, they could not sympathize with him, and he suffused them with his own sadness. He could find no refuge in the past; he must go on into the future.

His mother lingered for some time without any evident change. He sat by her bedside the most of the day. All she wanted was to have him within reach of her feeble voice, that she might, when she pleased, draw him within touch of her feeble hand. Once she said:

"My boy, I am going to your father."

"Yes, mother, I think you are," Hugh replied. "How glad he will be to see you!"

"But I shall leave you alone."

"Mother, I love God."

The mother looked at him, as only a mother can look, smiled sweetly, closed her eyes as with the weight of her contentment, fell asleep holding his hand, and slept for hours.

Meanwhile, in London, Margaret was watching Euphra. She was dying, and Margaret was the angel of life watching over her.

"I shall get rid of my lameness there, Margaret, shall I not?" said Euphra, one day, half playfully.

"Yes, dear."

"It will be delightful to walk again without pain."

"Perhaps you will not get rid of it all at once, though."

"Why do you think so?" asked Euphra, with some appearance of uneasiness.

"Because, if it is taken from you before you are quite willing to have it as long as God pleases, by and by you will not be able to rest, till you have asked for it back again, that you may bear it for his sake."

"I am willing, Margaret, I am willing. Only one can't like it, you know."

"I know that," answered Margaret.

She spoke no more, and Margaret heard her weeping gently. Half an hour had passed away, when she looked up, and said:

"Margaret, dear, I begin to like my lameness, I think."

"Why, dear?"

"Why, just because God made it, and bade me bear it. May I not think it is a mark on me from his hand?"

"Yes, I think so."

"Why do you think it came on me?"

"To walk back to Him with, dear."

"Yes, yes; I see it all."

Until now, Margaret had not known to what a degree the lameness of Euphra had troubled her. That her pretty ancle should be deformed, and her light foot able only to limp, had been a source of real distress to her, even in the midst of far deeper.

The days passed on, and every day she grew weaker. She did not suffer much, but nothing seemed to do her good. Mrs. Elton was kindness itself. Harry was in dreadful distress. He haunted her room, creeping in whenever he had a chance, and sitting in corners out of the way. Euphra liked to have him near her. She seldom spoke to him, or to any one but Margaret, for Margaret alone could hear with ease what she said. But now and then she would motion him to her bedside, and say—it was always the same—

"Harry, dear, be good."

"I will; indeed I will, dear Euphra," was still Harry's reply.

Once, expressing to Margaret her regret that she should be such a trouble to her, she said:

"You have to do so much for me, that I am ashamed."

"Do let me wash the feet of one of his disciples;" Margaret replied, gently expostulating; after which, Euphra never grumbled at her own demands upon her.

Again, one day, she said:

"I am not right at all to-day, Margaret. God can't love me, I am so hateful."

"Don't measure God's mind by your own, Euphra. It would be a poor love that depended not on itself, but on the feelings of the person loved. A crying baby turns away from its mother's breast, but she does not put it away till it stops crying. She holds it closer. For my part, in the worst mood I am ever in, when I don't feel I love God at all, I just look up to his love. I say to him: 'Look at me. See what state I am in. Help me!" Ah! you would wonder how that makes peace. And the love comes of itself; sometimes so strong, it nearly breaks my heart."

"But there is a text I don't like."

"Take another, then."

"But it will keep coming."

"Give it back to God, and never mind it."

"But would that be right?"

"One day, when I was a little girl, so high, I couldn't eat my porridge, and sat looking at it. 'Eat your porridge,' said my mother. 'I don't want it,' I answered. 'There's nothing else for you,' said my mother—for she had not learned so much from my father then, as she did before he died. 'Hoots!' said my father—I cannot, dear Euphra, make his words into English."

"No, no, don't," said Euphra; "I shall understand them perfectly."

"'Hoots! Janet, my woman!' said my father. 'Gie the bairn a dish o' tay. Wadna ye like some tay, Maggy, my doo?' 'Ay wad I,' said I. 'The parritch is guid eneuch," said my mother. 'Nae doot aboot the parritch, woman; it's the bairn's stamack, it's no the parritch.' My mother said no more, but made me a cup of such nice tea; for whenever she gave in, she gave in quite. I drank it; and, half from anxiety to please my mother, half from reviving hunger, attacked the porridge next, and ate it up. 'Leuk at that!' said my father. 'Janet, my woman, gie a body the guid that they can tak', an' they'll sune tak' the guid that they canna. Ye're better noo, Maggy, my doo?' I never told him that I had taken the porridge too soon after all, and had to creep into the wood, and be sick. But it is all the same for the story."

Euphra laughed a feeble but delighted laugh, and applied the story for herself.

So the winter days passed on.

"I wish I could live till the spring," said Euphra. "I should like to see a snowdrop and a primrose again."

"Perhaps you will, dear; but you are going into a better spring. I could almost envy you, Euphra."

"But shall we have spring there?"

"I think so."

"And spring–flowers?"

"I think we shall—better than here."

"But they will not mean so much."

"Then they won't be so good. But I should think they would mean ever so much more, and be ever so much more spring–like. They will be the spring–flowers to all winters in one, I think."

464

Folded in the love of this woman, anointed for her death by her wisdom, baptized for the new life by her sympathy and its tears, Euphra died in the arms of Margaret.

Margaret wept, fell on her knees, and gave God thanks. Mrs. Elton was so distressed, that, as soon as the funeral was over, she broke up her London household, sending some of the servants home to the country, and taking some to her favourite watering place, to which Harry also accompanied her.

She hoped that, now the affair of the ring was cleared up, she might, as soon as Hugh returned, succeed in persuading him to follow them to Devonshire, and resume his tutorship. This would satisfy her anxiety about Hugh and Harry both.

Hugh's mother died too, and was buried. When he returned from the grave which now held both father and mother, he found a short note from Margaret, telling him that Euphra was gone. Sorrow is easier to bear when it comes upon sorrow; but he could not help feeling a keen additional pang, when he learned that she was dead whom he had loved once, and now loved better. Margaret's note informed him likewise that Euphra had left a written request, that her diamond ring should be given to him to wear for her sake.

He prepared to leave the home whence all the homeness had now vanished, except what indeed lingered in the presence of an old nurse, who had remained faithful to his mother to the last. The body itself is of little value after the spirit, the love, is out of it: so the house and all the old things are little enough, after the loved ones are gone who kept it alive and made it home.

All that Hugh could do for this old nurse was to furnish a cottage for her out of his mother's furniture, giving her everything she liked best. Then he gathered the little household treasures, the few books, the few portraits and ornaments, his father's sword, and his mother's wedding—ring; destroyed with sacred fire all written papers; sold the remainder of the furniture, which he would gladly have burnt too, and so proceeded to take his last departure from the home of his childhood.

CHAPTER XXIII. NATURE AND HER LADY.

Die Frauen sind ein liebliches Geheimniss, nur verhüllt, nicht verschlossen.—NOVALIS.—Moralische Ansichten.

David Elginbrod

Women are a lovely mystery—veiled, however, not shut up.

Her twilights were more clear than our mid-day;
She dreamt devoutlier than most used to pray.

DR. DONNE.

Perhaps the greatest benefit that resulted to Hugh from being thus made a pilgrim and a stranger in the earth, was, that Nature herself saw him, and took him in, Hitherto, as I have already said, Hugh's acquaintance with Nature had been chiefly a second–hand one—he knew friends of hers. Nature in poetry—not in the form of Thomsonian or Cowperian descriptions, good as they are, but closely interwoven with and expository of human thought and feeling—had long been dear to him. In this form he had believed that he knew her so well, as to be able to reproduce the lineaments of her beloved face. But now she herself appeared to him—the grand, pure, tender mother, ancient in years, yet ever young; appeared to him, not in the mirror of a man's words, but bending over him from the fathomless bosom of the sky, from the outspread arms of the forest–trees, from the silent judgment of the everlasting hills. She spoke to him from the depths of air, from the winds that harp upon the boughs, and trumpet upon the great caverns, and from the streams that sing as they go to be lost in rest. She would have shone upon him out of the eyes of her infants, the flowers, but they had their faces turned to her breast now, hiding from the pale blue eyes and the freezing breath of old Winter, who was looking for them with his face bent close to their refuge. And he felt that she had a power to heal and to instruct; yea, that she was a power of life, and could speak to the heart and conscience mighty words about God and Truth and Love.

For he did not forsake his dead home in haste. He lingered over it, and roamed about its neighbourhood. Regarding all about him with quiet, almost passive spirit, he was astonished to find how his eyes opened to see nature in the mass. Before, he had beheld only portions and beauties. When or how the change passed upon him he could not tell. But he no longer looked for a pretty eyebrow or a lovely lip on the face of nature: the soul of nature looked out upon him from the harmony of all, guiding him unsought to the discovery of a thousand separate delights; while from the expanded vision new meanings flashed upon him every day. He beheld in the great All the expression of the thoughts and feelings of the maker of the heavens and the earth and the sea and the fountains of water. The powers of the world to come, that is, the world of unseen truth and ideal reality, were

466

upon him in the presence of the world that now is. For the first time in his life, he felt at home with nature; and while he could moan with the wintry wind, he no longer sighed in the wintry sunshine, that foretold, like the far-off flutter of a herald's banner, the approach of victorious lady-spring.

With the sorrow and loneliness of loss within him, and Nature around him seeming to sigh for a fuller expression of the thought that throbbed within her, it is no wonder that the form of Margaret, the gathering of the thousand forms of nature into one intensity and harmony of loveliness, should rise again upon the world of his imagination, to set no more. Father and mother were gone. Margaret remained behind. Nature lay around him like a shining disk, that needed a visible centre of intensest light—a shield of silver, that needed but a diamond boss: Margaret alone could be that centre—that diamond light-giver; for she alone, of all the women he knew, seemed so to drink of the sun-rays of God, as to radiate them forth, for very fulness, upon the clouded world.

She had dawned on him like a sweet crescent moon, hanging far-off in a cold and low horizon: now, lifting his eyes, he saw that same moon nearly at the full, and high overhead, yet leaning down towards him through the deep blue air, that overflowed with her calm triumph of light. He knew that he loved her now. He knew that every place he went through, caught a glimmer of romance the moment he thought of her; that every most trifling event that happened to himself, looked like a piece of a story-book the moment he thought of telling it to her. But the growth of these feelings had been gradual—so slow and gradual, that when he recognized them, it seemed to him as if he had felt them from the first. The fact was, that as soon as he began to be capable of loving Margaret, he had begun to love her. He had never been able to understand her till he was driven into the desert. But now that Nature revealed herself to him full of Life, yea, of the Life of Life, namely, of God himself, it was natural that he should honour and love that 'lady of her own'; that he should recognize Margaret as greater than himself, as nearer to the heart of Nature—yea, of God the father of all. She had been one with Nature from childhood, and when he began to be one with nature too, he must become one with her.

And now, in absence, he began to study the character of her whom, in presence, he had thought he knew perfectly. He soon found that it was a Manoa, a golden city in a land of Paradise—too good to be believed in, except by him who was blessed with the beholding of it. He knew now that she had always understood what he was only just waking to recognize. And he felt that the scholar had been very patient with the stupidity of the master, and had drawn from his lessons a nourishment of which he had known nothing himself.

But dared he think of marrying her, a creature inspired with a presence of the Spirit of God which none but the saints enjoy, and thence clothed with a garment of beauty, which her spirit wove out of its own loveliness? She was a being to glorify any man merely by granting him her habitual presence: what, then, if she gave her love! She would bring with her the presence of God himself, for she walked ever in his light, and that light clung to her and radiated from her. True, many young maidens must be walking in the sunshine of God, else whence the light and loveliness and bloom, the smile and the laugh of their youth? But Margaret not only walked in this light: she knew it and whence it came. She looked up to its source, and it illuminated her face.

The silent girl of old days, whose countenance wore the stillness of an unsunned pool, as she listened with reverence to his lessons, had blossomed into the calm, stately woman, before whose presence he felt rebuked he knew not why, upon whose face lay slumbering thought, ever ready to wake into life and motion. Dared he love her? Dared he tell her that he loved her? Dared he, so poor, so worthless, seek for himself such a world's treasure?—He might have known that worth does not need honour; that its lowliness is content with ascribing it.

Some of my readers may be inclined to think that I hide, for the sake of my hero—poor little hero, one of God's children, learning to walk—an inevitable struggle between his love and his pride; inasmuch as, being but a tutor, he might be expected to think the more of his good family, and the possibility of his one day coming to honour without the drawback of having done anything to merit it, a title being almost within his grasp; while Margaret was a ploughman's daughter, and a lady's maid. But, although I know more of Hugh's faults than I have thought it at all necessary to bring out in my story, I protest that, had he been capable of giving the name of love to a feeling in whose presence pride dared to speak, I should have considered him unworthy of my poor pen. In plain language, I doubt if I should have cared to write his story at all.

He gathered together, as I have said, the few memorials of the old ship gone down in the quiet ocean of time; paid one visit of sorrowful gladness to his parent's grave, over which he raised no futile stone—leaving it, like the forms within it, in the hands of holy decay; and took his road—whither? To Margaret's home—to see old Janet; and to go once to the grave of his second father. Then he would return to the toil and hunger and hope of London.

What made Hugh go to Turriepuffit? His love to Margaret? No. A better motive even than that:—Repentance. Better I mean for Hugh as to the individual occasion; not in itself; for love is deeper than repentance, seeing that without love there can be no repentance. He had repented before; but now that he haunted in silence the regions of the past, the whole of his history in connection with David returned on him clear and vivid, as if passing once again before his eyes and through his heart; and he repented more deeply still. Perhaps he was not quite so much to blame as he thought himself. Perhaps only now was it possible for the seeds of truth, which David had sown in his heart, to show themselves above the soil of lower, yet ministering cares. They had needed to lie a winter long in the earth. Now the keen blasts and griding frosts had done their work, and they began to grow in the tearful prime. Sorrow for loss brought in her train sorrow for wrong—a sister more solemn still, and with a deeper blessing in the voice of her loving farewell.—It is a great mistake to suppose that sorrow is a part of repentance. It is far too good a grace to come so easily. A man may repent, that is, think better of it, and change his way, and be very much of a Pharisee—I do not say a hypocrite—for a long time after: it needs a saint to be sorrowful. Yet repentance is generally the road to this sorrow.—And now that in the gracious time of grief, his eyesight purified by tears, he entered one after another all the chambers of the past, he humbly renewed once more his friendship with the noble dead, and with the homely, heartful living. The grey–headed man who walked with God like a child, and with his fellow–men like an elder brother who was always forgetting his birthright and serving the younger; the woman who believed where she could not see, and loved where she could not understand; and the maiden who was still and lustreless, because she ever absorbed and seldom reflected the light—all came to him, as if to comfort him once more in his loneliness, when his heart had room for them, and need of them yet again. David now became, after his departure, yet more of a father to him than before, for that spirit, which is the true soul of all this body of things, had begun to recall to his mind the words of David, and so teach him the things that David knew, the everlasting realities of God. And it seemed to him the while, that he heard David himself uttering, in his homely, kingly voice, whatever truth returned to him from the echo–cave of the past. Even when a quite new thought arose within him, it came to him in the voice of David, or at least with the solemn music of his tones clinging about it as the murmur about the river's course. Experience had now brought him up to the point where he could begin to profit by David's communion; he needed the things which David could teach him; and David began forthwith to give them to him.

That birth of nature in his soul, which enabled him to understand and love Margaret, helped him likewise to contemplate with admiration and awe, the towering peaks of David's hopes, trusts, and aspirations. He had taught the ploughman mathematics, but that ploughman had possessed in himself all the essential elements of the grandeur of the old prophets, glorified by the faith which the Son of Man did not find in the earth, but left behind him to grow in it, and which had grown to a noble growth of beauty and strength in this peasant, simple and patriarchal in the midst of a self–conceited age. And, oh! how good he had been to him! He had built a house that he might take him in from the cold, and make life pleasant to him, as in the presence of God. He had given him his heart every time he gave him his great manly hand. And this man, this friend, this presence of Christ, Hugh had forsaken, neglected, all but forgotten. He could not go, and, like the prodigal, fall down before him, and say, "Father, I have sinned against heaven and thee," for that heaven had taken him up out of his sight. He could only weep instead, and bitterly repent. Yes; there was one thing more he could do. Janet still lived. He would go to her, and confess his sin, and beg her forgiveness. Receiving it, he would be at peace. He knew David forgave him, whether he confessed or not; and that, if he were alive, David would seek his confession only as the casting away of the separation from his heart, as the banishment of the worldly spirit, and as the natural sign by which he might know that Hugh was one with him yet.

Janet was David's representative on earth: he would go to her.

So he returned, rich and great; rich in knowing that he was the child of Him to whom all the gold mines belong; and great in that humility which alone recognizes greatness, and in the beginnings of that meekness which shall inherit the earth. No more would he stunt his spiritual growth by self–satisfaction. No more would he lay aside, in the cellars of his mind, poor withered bulbs of opinions, which, but for the evil ministrations of that self–satisfaction, seeking to preserve them by drying and salting, might have been already bursting into blossoms of truth, of infinite loveliness.

He knew that Margaret thought far too well of him—honoured him greatly beyond his deserts. He would not allow her to be any longer thus deceived. He would tell her what a poor creature he was. But he would say, too, that he hoped one day to be worthy of her praise, that he hoped to grow to what she thought him. If he should fail in convincing her, he would receive all the honour she gave him humbly, as paid, not to him, but to what he ought to be. God grant it might be as to his future self!

In this mood he went to Janet

CHAPTER XXIV. THE FIR–WOOD AGAIN.

```
Er stand vor der himmlischen Jungfrau.  Da hob er den leichten,
glänzenden Schleir, und—Rosenblüthchen sank in seine
Arme.—Novalis.—Die Lehrlinge zu Sais.

He stood before the heavenly Virgin (Isis, the Goddess of Nature).
Then lifted he the light, shining veil, and—Rosebud (his old love)
sank into his arms.

So womanly, so benigne, and so meek.

CHAUCER.—Prol. to Leg. of Good Women.
```

It was with a mingling of strange emotions, that Hugh approached the scene of those not very old, and yet, to his feeling, quite early memories. The dusk was beginning to gather. The hoar–frost lay thick on the ground. The pine–trees stood up in the cold, looking, in their garment of spikes, as if the frost had made them. The rime on the gate was unfriendly, and chilled his hand. He turned into the footpath. He say the room David had built for him. Its thatch was one mass of mosses, whose colours were hidden now in the cuckoo–fruit of the frost. Alas! how Death had cast his deeper frost over all; for the man was gone from the hearth! But neither old Winter nor skeleton Death can withhold the feet of the little child Spring. She is stronger than both. Love shall conquer hate; and God will overcome sin.

He drew night to the door, trembling. It seemed strange to him that his nerves only, and not his mind, should feel.—In moments of unusual excitement, it sometimes happens that the only consciousness a strong man has of emotion, lies in an unwonted physical vibration, the mind itself refusing to be disturbed. It is, however, but a seeming: the emotion is so deep, that consciousness can lay hold of its physical result only.—The cottage looked the same as ever, only the peat–stack outside was smaller. In the shadowiness of the firs, the glimmer of a fire was just discernible on the kitchen window.

471

David Elginbrod

He trembled so much that he could not enter. He would go into the fir–wood first, and see Margaret's tree, as he always called it in his thoughts and dreams.

Very poor and stunted and meagre looked the fir–trees of Turriepuffit, after the beeches and elms of Arnstead. The evening wind whistled keen and cold through their dry needles, and made them moan, as if because they were fettered, and must endure the winter in helpless patience. Here and there amongst them, rose the Titans of the little forest—the huge, old, contorted, wizard–like, yet benevolent beings—the Scotch firs. Towards one of these he bent his way. It was the one under which he had seen Margaret, when he met her first in the wood, with her whole soul lost in the waving of its wind–swung, sun–lighted top, floating about in the sea of air like a golden nest for some silvery bird of heaven. To think that the young girl to whom he had given the primrose he had just found, the then first–born of the Spring, should now be the queen of his heart! Her childish dream of the angel haunting the wood had been true, only she was the angel herself. He drew near the place. How well he knew it! He seated himself, cold as it was in the February of Scotland, at the foot of the blessed tree. He did not know that it was cold.

While he sat with his eyes fixed on the ground, a light rustle in the fallen leaves made him raise them suddenly. It was all winter and fallen leaves about him; but he lifted his eyes, and in his soul it was summer: Margaret stood before him. He was not in the least surprised. For how can one wonder to see before his eyes, the form of which his soul is full?—there is no shock. She stood a little way off, looking—as if she wanted to be sure before she moved a step. She was dressed in a grey winsey gown, close to her throat and wrists. She had neither shawl nor bonnet. Her fine health kept her warm, even in a winter wood at sun–down. She looked just the same;—at home everywhere; most at home in Nature's secret chamber. Like the genius of the place, she made the winter–wood look homely. What were the oaks and beeches of Arnstead now? Homeliness and glory are Heaven.

She came nearer.

"Margaret!" he murmured, and would have risen.

"No, no; sit still," she rejoined, in a pleading tone. "I thought it was the angel in the picture. Now I know it. Sit still, dear Mr. Sutherland, one moment more."

David Elginbrod

Humbled by his sense of unworthiness, and a little distressed that she could so quietly reveal the depth of her feeling towards him, he said:

"Ah, Margaret! I wish you would not praise one so little deserving it."

"Praise?" she repeated, with an accent of wonder. "I praise you! No, Mr. Sutherland; that I am not guilty of. Next to my father, you made me know and feel. And as I walked here, I was thinking of the old times, and older times still; and all at once I saw the very picture out of the old Bible."

She came close to him now. He rose, trembling, but held out no hand, uttered no greeting.

"Margaret, dare I love you?" he faltered.

She looked at him with wide–open eyes.

"Me?" she said; and her eyes did not move from his. A slight rose–flush bloomed out on her motionless face.

"Will you be my wife?" he said, trembling yet more.

She made no answer, but looked at him still, with parted lips, motionless.

"I am very poor, Margaret. I could not marry now."

It was a stupid speech, but he made it.

"I don't care," she answered, with a voice like thinking, "if you never marry me."

He misunderstood her, and turned cold to the very heart. He misunderstood her stillness. Her heart lay so deep, that it took a long time for its feelings to reach and agitate the surface. He said no more, but turned away with a sigh.

"Come home to my mother," she said.

David Elginbrod

He obeyed mechanically, and walked in silence by her side. They reached the cottage and entered. Margaret said: "Here he is, mother;" and disappeared.

Janet was seated—in her widow's mutch, with the plain black ribbon down both sides, and round the back—in the arm-chair by the fire, pondering on the past, or gently dreaming of him that was gone. She turned her head. Sorrow had baptized her face with a new gentleness. The tender expression which had been but occasional while her husband lived, was almost constant now. She did not recognize Hugh. He saw it, and it added weight to his despair. He was left outside.

"Mother!" he said, involuntarily.

She started to her feet, cried: "My bairn! my bairn!" threw her arms around him, and laid her head on his bosom. Hugh sobbed as if his heart would break. Janet wept, but her weeping was quiet as a summer rain. He led her to her chair, knelt by her side, and hiding his face in her lap like a child, faltered out, interrupted by convulsive sobs:

"Forgive me; forgive me. I don't deserve it, but forgive me."

"Hoot awa! my bairn! my bonny man! Dinna greet that gait. The Lord preserve's! what are ye greetin' for? Are na ye come hame to yer ain? Didna Dawvid aye say—'Gie the lad time, woman. It's unco chaip, for the Lord's aye makin't. The best things is aye the maist plentifu'. Gie the lad time, my bonny woman!'—didna he say that? Ay, he ca'd me his bonny woman, ill as I deserved it at his han'. An' it's no for me to say ae word agen you, Maister Sutherlan', gin ye had been a hantle waur nor a young thochtless lad cudna weel help bein'. An' noo ye're come hame, an' nothing cud glaidden my heart mair, 'cep', maybe, the Maister himsel' was to say to my man: 'Dawvid! come furth.'"

Hugh could make no reply. He got hold of Margaret's creepie, which stood in its usual place, and sat down upon it, at the old woman's feet. She gazed in his face for a while, and then, putting her arm round his neck, drew his head to her bosom, and fondled him as if he had been her own first-born.

"But eh! yer bonnie face is sharp an' sma' to what it used to be, Maister Sutherlan'. I doot ye hae come through a heap o' trouble."

David Elginbrod

"I'll tell you all about it," said Hugh.

"Na, na; bide still a wee. I ken a' aboot it frae Maggy. An' guid preserve's! ye're clean perished wi' cauld. Lat me up, my bairn."

Janet rose, and made up the fire, which soon cast a joyful glow throughout the room. The peat–fire in the little cottage was a good symbol of the heart of its mistress: it gave far more heat than light. And for my part, dear as light is, I like heat better. She then put on the kettle,—or the boiler I think she called it—saying:

"I'm jist gaein' to mak' ye a cup o' tay, Mr. Sutherlan'. It's the handiest thing, ye ken. An' I doot ye're muckle in want o' something. Wad ye no tak' a drappy oot o' the bottle, i' the mane time?"

"No, thank you," said Hugh, who longed to be alone, for his heart was cold as ice; "I would rather wait for the tea; but I should be glad to have a good wash, after my journey."

"Come yer wa's, than, ben the hoose. I'll jist gang an' get a drappy o' het water in a decanter. Bide ye still by the fire."

Hugh stood, and gazed into the peat–fire. But he saw nothing in it. A light step passed him several times, but he did not heed it. The loveliest eyes looked earnestly towards him as they passed, but his were not lifted to meet their gaze.

"Noo, Maister Sutherlan', come this way."

Hugh was left alone at length, in the room where David had slept, where David had used to pray. He fell on his knees, and rose comforted by the will of God. A few things of Margaret's were about the room. The dress he had seen her in at Mrs. Elton's, was hanging by the bed. He kissed the folds of the garment, and said: "God's will be done." He had just finished a hasty ablution when Janet called him.

"Come awa', Maister Sutherlan'; come ben to yer ain chaumer," said she, leading the way to the room she still called the study. Margaret was there. The room was just as he had left it. A bright fire was on the hearth. Tea was on the table, with eggs, and oatcakes, and flour–scons in abundance; for Janet had the best she could get for Margaret, who was only her guest for a little while. But Hugh could not eat. Janet looked distressed, and Margaret glanced at him uneasily.

"Do eat something, Mr. Sutherland," said Margaret.

Hugh looked at her involuntarily. She did not understand his look, and it alarmed her. His countenance was changed.

"What is the matter, dear—Hugh?" she said, rising, and laying her hand on his shoulder.

"Hoots! lassie," broke in her mother; "are ye makin' love till a man, a gentleman, afore my verra een?"

"He did it first, mother," answered Margaret, with a smile.

A pang of hope shot through Hugh's heart.

"Ow! that's the gait o't, is't? The bairn's gane dementit! Ye're no efter merryin' a gentleman, Maggy? Na, na, lass!"

So saying, the old lady, rather crossly, and very imprudently, left the room to fill the teapot in the kitchen.

"Do you remember this?" said Margaret,—who felt that Hugh must have misunderstood something or other,—taking from her pocket a little book, and from the book a withered flower.

Hugh saw that it was like a primrose, and hoped against hope that it was the one which he had given to her, on the spring morning in the fir–wood. Still, a feeling very different from his might have made her preserve it. He must know all about it.

"Why did you keep that?" he said.

"Because I loved you."

476

David Elginbrod

"Loved me?"

"Yes. Didn't you know?"

"Why did you say, then, that you didn't care if—if—?"

"Because love is enough, Hugh.—That was why."

THE END.

1 ch guttural. The land–rail is a corn–scraich.

2 Goldsmith; twice, in the Citizen of the World.

Note from John Bechard, creator of this Electronic text.

The following is a list of Scottish words which are found in George MacDonald's "David Elginbrod". I have compiled this list myself and worked out the definitions from context with the help of Margaret West, from Leven in Fife, Scotland, and also by referring to a word list found in a collection of poems by Robert Burns. There are about 6 words which we could not work out definitions for and would welcome any feedback on those words or any others in the list which may be wrong (my e–mail address is JaBBechard@aol.com). This was never meant to be a comprehensive list of the National Scottish Language, but rather an aid to understanding some of Mr MacDonald's conversations which are carried out in the Broad Scots. I do apologise for any mistakes or omissions. I aimed for my list to be very comprehensive, and it often repeats the same word in a plural or diminutive form. As well, it includes words that are quite obvious to native English speakers.

There is a web site under construction which will feature the Scottish language; and the National Scottish Dictionary can be consulted if you have access to one.

This list is a compressed form that consists of three columns for 'word', 'definition', and 'additional notes'. It is set up with a comma between each item and a hard return at the end of each definition. This means that this section could easily be cut and pasted into its own text file and imported into a database or spreadsheet as a comma separated variable file (.csv file). Failing that, you could do a search and replace for commas in this section (I have not used any commas in my words, definitions or notes) and replace the commas with spaces or tabs.

```
Word,Definition,Notes
a',all,also have
a' thing,everything; anything,
aboon,above; up; over,
aboot,about,
aboot and aboot,all about,
abune,above; up,
abusin',abusing,
accordin',according,
actin',acting,
admirin',admiring,
ae,one,
aff,off; away,
afore,before; in front of,
agen,against,
ahin',behind,
ahint,behind,
Ahmen,Amen,
Ahva!,At all!,exclamation
aiblins,perhaps,
ailin',ailing; sick,
ain,own; one,
airgument,argument,
airguments,arguments,
airm,arm,
airms,arms,
aither,either,
alane,alone,
alang,along,
alicht,alight,
Almichty,Almighty; God,
a'maist,almost,
amang,among,
amo',among,
amo't,among it,
an',and,
an aucht days,?,possibly an old reference to a week?
ance,once,
ane,one,
```

David Elginbrod

aneath, beneath,
aneath't, beneath it,
aneth, beneath,
aneuch, enough,
anithor, another,
appintment, appointment,
appintments, appointments,
appruved, approved,
aske, asp,
as'll, as will,
'at, that,
at ane mair, all agog,
a'thegither, all together,
a'thing, everything; anything,
atween, between,
aucht, eight,
auld, old,
auld-fashioned, old-fashioned,
ava, at all; of all,
awa', away,
awfu', awful,
awthegither, all together,
aye, yes; indeed,
baain', baaing,
backbane, backbone,
bairn, child,
bairnie, child, diminutive
bairnies, children, diminutive
bairns, children,
baith, both,
ballant, ballad,
ballants, ballads,
banes, bones,
bauchles, old pair of Sunday shoes,
bauks, supporting timbers; bulk heads, as in ship building
bawbees, half pennies,
beastie, beast; animal, diminutive
beginnin', beginning,
begude, began,
bein', being,
ben, room; indoors; into; within; inwards,
ben the hoose, inside; to the back of the house,
beowty, beauty,
beuk, book, also the Bible

David Elginbrod

```
beukie,little book,diminutive
beuks,books,
beuky,little book,diminutive
beurds,boards,
biddin',bidding,
bide,endure; bear; remain; live,also stay for;
bield,protection; shelter; cover,
bien,cosy; comfortable; well-stocked,
big,build,
bin',bind,
bin'in',binding,
binna,be not,
birdie,little bird,diminutive
birdies,little birds,diminutive
bit,but; bit,also little-diminutive
bitties,little bits,diminutive
blastit,blasted,
bleck,black,also nonplus; perplex
bluid,blood,
boddom,bottom,
body,person; fellow,
boiler,kettle,
bonnie,good; beautiful; pretty; handsome,
bonny,good; beautiful; pretty; handsome,
boo,bow,
bossie,large wooden bowl,serving bowl
boun',bound,
bout,swath,
bouts,swaths,
brakfast,breakfast,
braw,beautiful; good; fine,also-lovely (girl); handsome (boy)
brawly,admirably; very; very much; well,
bringin',bringing,
brither-men,fellowmen; brethren,
brocht,brought,
brods,boards; (book covers),
broos,eyebrows,
bud,intended; meant to,
bude,would prefer to,
buik,book,
buiks,books,
burdie,little bird,diminutive
burnin',burning,
burnside,along the side of a stream,
```

```
butt,main room in a croft; front room,includes kitchen and storage
butt the hoose,into the house; into the front room,
by ordinar',out of the ordinary; supernatural,
byke,hive; swarm; crowd,
ca',call; name,
ca'd,called,
calf-country,country or place where one grew up,
caller,fresh; refreshing; cool,
cam,came,
cam',came,
canna,cannot,
carefu',careful,
cart-fu's,cartloads,
ca's,calls,
ca't,call it,
cauld,cold,
caup,small wooden bowl,
'cause,because,
causin',causing,
'cep',except,
chaip,blow; stroke,also fellow; chap
chaumer,chamber; room,
chield,child; young person; lad,used when expressing sympathy
chields,children; lads; young people,used when expressing sympathy
chimla,fireside; hearth,
chimla-lug,side wall of chimney recess,also chimney corner
chow,chew,
clam,climbed,
clappit,clapped (on the shoulder); praised,
clavers,idle talk; chatter,smarmy compliments; buttering up
clean,quite; utterly,also comely; shapely; empty
cleed,clothe,
clippin',clipping; shearing,
clyack,harvest,
colliginer,college boy,
Come butt the hoose.,'Come on in!',colloquial and familiar
Come yer wa's butt.,'Come on in!',colloquial and familiar
Come yer wa's.,'Come on in!',colloquial and familiar
comin',coming,
comparateevely,comparatively,
consistin',consisting,
contradickin',contradicting,
coorse,coarse,also course
corn-scraich,land-rail,type of bird
```

David Elginbrod

```
corp,corpse,
corps,bodies; corpses,
cot,cottage,
couples,joining pieces; cross beams,
couthy,loving; kind; buddy-buddy,
coverin',covering,
craig,throat; neck; gullet,
crater,creature,
craytur,creature,
crayturs,creatures,
creater,creature,
creaters,creatures,
creatur',creature,
creepie,three legged stool,
creepin',creeping,
crookit,crooked,
croonin',crooning; moaning; whining,
cud,could,
cudna,could not,
cuiticans,leather gaiters,
cuttin',cutting,
dacent,decent,
daffin',dallying; fooling; frolic; flirtation,
darin',daring,
daunder,casual stroll,
daured,dared,
daursay,dare say,
dawtie,darling; pet,term of endearment
Dawvid,David,
daylicht,daylight,
deed,died,also deed; indeed
deeth,death,
deevilich,devilish,
deid,dead,
deid-stane,gravestone; tombstone,
deil,devil,
Deil a bit!,Not at all!  Not a bit!,
deit,died,
deith,death,
dementit,demented; mad,
denner-time,dinner time,
depen',depend,
detaictives,detectives,
devallt,intermission; a break,
```

didna,did not,
dinna,do not,
direckly,directly; immediately,
dischairgin',discharging,
disjaskit,worn out; fatigued,
disturbin',disturbing,
dochter,daughter,
doin',doing,
doitit,out of the mind; muddled,also in a whirl with worry
doo,dove,term of endearment
doon,down,
doonsettin',setting down,
doonsittin',place to sit down or rest,
door-cheek,door jamb,
doot,doubt,also know
dootless,doubtless,
do't,do it,
douce,sensible; sober; prudent,
doun,down,
dout,doubt,also know
dowie,sad; lonely; depressing; dismal,
downa,dare not; can not,
drappy,drop; a little (liquor),diminutive
dreed,dread; fear,
dreid,dread,
driftin',drifting,snow driven by the wind
drinkin',drinking,
driv't,drive it,
duin',doing,
dune,done,
dune't,done it,
dung,beaten; overcome; worn out,
ear',early,
'ee,eye,
een,eyes,
e'en,even; just; simply,also eyes
eesicht,eye sight; by all appearances,
efter,after; afterwards,
eident,evident,
ellwan',ell-wand; ruler; yardstick,1 ell = 37 inches or 94 cm
'en,end,
en',end,
ends-errand,went on purpose; specifically to,
eneuch,enough,

```
enlichtened,enlightened,
enteresstit,interested,
ettle,reach; try to climb; purpose; aim,
ettlin',seeking (to understand); aiming,
evenin',putting on the same level; comparing,
exackly,exactly,
excep,except,
exerceese,exercise,
expec,expect,
expeck,expect,
expeckin',expecting,
eynds,ends,
eyther,either,
fa',fall; befall,
fac,fact,
fair-oot,far out,
fand,found,
fardins,farthings,
fegs,golly,exclamation
fell,very; potent; keen; harsh,more emphasis
feow,few,
fillin',filling,
fin',find,
firin',firing; heating,
fir-taps,tops of the fir trees,
fit,foot; base,also fit
flatterin',flattering,
flauchterin',fluttering,
fleein',flying,
flutterin',fluttering,
flytin',telling off; scolding,flaying with the tongue
followin',following,
forbear,ancestor,
forbears,ancestors,
forby,as well; as well as; besides,
forbye,as well; as well as; besides,
forenichts,fore-nights; early evenings,
forfochten,overcome; done for,
forgetfu'ness,forgetfulness,
forgie,forgive,
for's,for his,
for't,for it,
fortnicht,fortnight; two weeks,
fower,four,
```

David Elginbrod

```
fowk,folk,
fowth,plenty; abundance; full measure,
frae,from,
frae the tae side to the tither,from one side to the other,
freen,friend,
frien',friend,
friens,friends,
frien's,friends,
fu',full; very; quite,
fule,fool,
furth,forth,
gae,gave,
gaed,went,
gaein,going,
gaein',going,
gaeing,going,
gaen,going,
gait,way,
gane,gone,
gane up the stairs,gone to heaven,
gane wull,lost its way,
gang,go; goes; depart; walk,
gangs,goes,
gar,cause; make; compel,
garrin',making; causing; compelling,
gars,causes; makes,
gart,caused; made; compelled,
gat,got,
get,way,also get
gettin',getting,
gey,very,
gie,give,
gie a lift,give a helping hand,
giein',giving,
gie's,gives,
gin,if; as if; then; whether,
gin',if; as if; then; whether,
gin't,if it,
glaid,glad,
glaidden,gladden,
glamour,spell; charm; enchantment,
glass,magnifying glass,
gleed,?,
gleg,quick; lively; smart; quick-witted,
```

David Elginbrod

```
gleg 'ee,quick or sharp eye to notice things,
gloamin',twilight; dusk,
God-fearin',God-fearing,
got grips,got a hold of; grasped; understood,
gowd,gold,
gowpenfu's,enough,enough (to cause one to stare)
gran',grand,
gran'father,grandfather,
grat,cried; wept,
gravestane,gravestone; tombstone; headstone,
greet,cry; weep,
greetin',crying; weeping,
grip,grasp; understand,
grips,grasp; understanding,
growin',growing,
grup,grip; grab,
gude,good; God,
guid,good; God,
guidit,guided; managed,
ha',have,also hall
hadna,had not,
hae,have,
ha'e,have,
haein',having,
haena,have not,
hae't,have it,
haill,whole,
hairst-rig,harvest crew,
halesome,wholesome; pure,
hame,home,
hamely,homely; familiar; friendly; common,
hame-ower,homely; simple and straightforward,
han',hand,
han'fu',handful,
han's,hands,
hantle,much; far,
hap,cover; wrap; shield,
happin,covering; wrapping,
hasna',has not; hasn't,
haud,hold; keep,
haud the hert in her,hold the heart in her,also keep her spirits up
haudin',holding; keeping,
hauds,holds; keeps,
haven,heaven,
```

David Elginbrod

```
haverin',blethering; talking rubbish,
havers,blether; (verbal) rubbish,
heap,lot; heap,
hearin',hearing,
hearken,hear; have a listen,
hech!,Oh! strange!,a sighing exclamation
heeds,heads,
heid,head; heading,
herdin',herding; shepherding,
hert,heart,
hertily,heartily,
herts,hearts,
het,hot; burning,
hev',have,
hicht,height,
hidin',hiding,
hill-moss,mountain-moor,'moss' is a swamp or peat bog
himsel,himself,
himsel',himself,
hindmost,last; final,
hingin',hanging,
hit,it,'h' gives emphasis
hither-come,ancestry; past history,
hizzie,hussy; silly girl,
hizzy,hussy; silly girl,
hom',home,
hoo,how,
hoose,house,
hoosehold,household,
hoose-room,living space,
hoot,no meaning,exclamation
hootoot,see hootoots,
hootoots,-no meaning-,exclamation
hoots,no meaning,exclamation
hosen,stockings; socks,
hostin',coughing,
houp,hope,
houpit,hoped,
howkin',digging; delving,
hunner,hundred,
huz,us,
i',in; into,
I canna min',I can not think or remember,
I doot,I don't doubt it; I know,
```

David Elginbrod

```
I wat,I see; I declare; I know,
I wot,I see; I declare,
idlin',idling,
ilka,every; each,
ill,bad; evil,
'ill,will,
ill-faured,ill-favoured,
ill-min'ins,ill meanings; ill intent,
'im,him,
imaigins,imagines,
immedantly,immediately,
impairts,imparts,
imputit,imputed,
in sma',in short,
ingle-neuk,chimney corner or recess,
in's,in his,
instruck,instruct,
in't,in it,
intellec,intellect,
interferin',interfering,
intill,into,
intill't,into it,
I'se,I shall,
is't,is it,
ither,other; another; further,
itherwise,otherwise,
itsel,itself,
itsel',itself,
itsel's,itself is,
jeedgement,judgement,
jeedgment,judgement,
jist,just,
judgin',judging,
justifeed,justified,
keepit,kept,
keepit his thoom...ellwan,to short change someone,a short measure
ken,know; be aware of,
kenna,do not know,
kenned,known; knew,
kens,knows,
kent,known; knew,
kep,keep; catch,
killin',killing,
kin',kind; agreeable,
```

```
kin'ness,kindness,
kintra-side,countryside,
kirk,church,
kirkyard,churchyard,
kirn,churn,
knittin',knitting,
kye,cattle; cows,
lad,boy,
laddies,boys,diminutive
lads,boys,
laird,landed proprietor; squire,
lammie,little lamb,diminutive; term of endearment
lan',land; country,
lane,lone; alone,
lanes,lone; alone,
lang,long,
langer,longer,
lass,girl,
lass-bairn,girl child,
lassie,girl,diminutive
lat,let,
lats,lets,
lat's,lets,
lattin,letting,
lauch,laugh,
lave,rest; leave; remainder,
laverocks,larks (type of bird),
layin',laying,
lea',leave,
learnin',learning; teaching,
learnt,learned; taught,
leein',lying,
lees,lies,
leevin',living,
leisur',leisure,
len',lend; give; grant,
lenth,length,
letten,let; allowed,
leuk,look; watch; appearance,
leukin',looking; watching,
leukit,looked; watched,
licht,light,
lichtlyin',belittling; making light of,
lichts,lights,
```

David Elginbrod

```
lifelang,lifelong,
lift,load; boost; helping hand,also sky; heavens
likit,liked,
lik'ly,likely,
lippen,trust; depend on,
'll,will,
loe,love,
lo'e,love,
lo'ed,loved,
Lonnon,London,
loot,let; allowed,
lovin'kindness,lovingkindness,
luckie-daddy,fondly regarded forefather,also a revered forefather
lug,ear,also shallow wooden dish
luik,look,
luikin',looking,
luikit,looked,
lum,chimney,
lyin',lying,
maijesty,majesty,
maik,?,mate?
mair,more; greater,
maist,most; almost,
maister,master; mister,
maistly,mostly,
maitter,matter,
mak,make; do,
mak',make; do,
mak' shifts,making do with false things,
mak' ups,covering up (of truth),
makin',making,
makin't,making it; doing it,
maks,makes; does,
mane,mean,
maukin,hare,reference to a poem by Burns
maun,must; have to,
maunna,must not; may not,
meanin',meaning,
measur',measure,
meesery,misery,
meetin',meeting,
mem,Mam; Miss; Madam,
mend,amend; cure; heal,as in 'mend your ways'
mengie,menagerie; lot; crowd,
```

David Elginbrod

```
merchan',merchant,
mercifu',merciful,
merryin',marrying,
micht,might,
michtna,might not,
michty,mighty; God,
mids,midst,
min',mind; recollection,also recollect; remember
minit,minute,
minny,mother; mommy,
mint,aimed; intended to,
min't,mind it; remember it,
misbelievin',not believing,
mischeef,mischief,
mista'en,mistaken,
misunderstandin',misunderstanding,
mither,mother,
mony,many,
mornin',morning,
mornin's,mornings,
mou's,mouths,
muckle,huge; enormous; big; great; much,
munsie,fool,
muntain-side,mountainside,
mutch,cap with protruding frill,worn under the bonnet
muved,moved; affected,
My certie!,?,My goodness!?
my lane,on my own,
mysel,myself,
mysel',myself,
na,not; by no means,
na',not; by no means,
nae,no,
naething,nothing,
naewise,nowise; in no way,
nain,own,
nane,none,
nater,nature,
nateral,natural,
natur',nature,
near-han',nearly; almost,
neebor,neighbour,
neebours,neighbours,
needna,do not need; need not,
```

David Elginbrod

```
neep,turnip,
neep-seed,turnip seed,
ne'er,never,
ne'er-do-well,never do well; troublemaker,
negleckin',neglecting,
neglecks,neglects,
neist,next,
neives,fists,
nicht,night,
nichtly,nightly; at night,
nigh,nearly,
nigher,nearer; closer,
no,not,
no that ill to win at,not that difficult to get at,
noo,now,
noo-a-days,nowadays,
nor,nor; than,
not,needed,also not
o',of; on,
obleeged,obliged,
ohn,without,Scottish uses past participle not present prog.
on's,on his,
ony,any,
onything,anything,
ook,week,
ooman,woman,
oor,our,
oors,ours,
oorsels,ourselves,
oot,out,
ootside,outside,
opingan,opinion,
opingans,opinions,
or,before; ere; by,also or
orderin',ordering,
ordinar',ordinary; natural,
o's,of us,
o't,of it,
oucht,ought; all,
our lanes,on our own,
oursel',ourselves,
oursel's,ourselves,
ower,over; too,
owse,ox,
```

David Elginbrod

```
pairt,part,
pairtrick,partridge,
pairts,parts,
parritch,porridge,
passin',passing,
pat,put; made,
peint,point,
perfeck,perfect,
persâudit,persuaded,
picter,picture,
pig,stone bottle,
pint,point,
pinted,pointed,
pit,put; make,
pitawta,potato,
pits,puts; makes,
pitten,put; made,
pittin',putting; making,
playin',playing,
pleesir,pleasure,
pleesur,pleasure,
plentifu',plentiful,
pleuch,?,stall?
ploo,plough,
poapies,poppies,
poopit,pulpit,
Popp,Pope,
praisin',praising,
preceesely,precisely,
preevilege,privilege,
prenciple,principle,
prentit,printed,
presence-chaumer,presence chamber of a king,
prood,proud,
prospeck,prospect,
puir,poor,
puirest,poorest,
quean,queen; young girl; hussy,
quo',swore; said,
raither,rather,
rax,overdo it; stretch,
readin',reading,
reasonin's,reasonings,
reestlin',rustling,
```

David Elginbrod

```
refeese,refuse,
reid-coatit,red-coated,
reid-heedit,red-headed,
remin'in',reminding,
repentit,repented,
reprocht,reproached,
respeck,respect; consider worthy,
respecks,respects; considers worthy,
richt,right; correct,
richteousness,righteousness,
richtly,rightly,
richts,rights,
rizzon,reason,
roomie,little room,diminutive
roose,rouse; stir up; agitate,
rouch,rough,
roun',around; round,
routin',lowing,
rue't,rue it; feel sorry for it,
rumgumption,common sense,
's,us; his; as; is,
sae,so,
sae's,so is,
saft,soft; silly,
sair,sore; sorely; sad; hard,also serve
sairpent,serpent,
saitisfeed,satisfied,
sall,shall,
sanctifee,sanctify,
sanctificaition,sanctification,
sang,song,
sangs,songs,
sanna,shall not,
Sant,saint,
saplin's,saplings,
sat,set,
sattle,settle,
sattles,settles,
sauld,sold,
sawin',sowing,
sayin',saying,
scabbit,scabby; scaly,
schraichin,screaming,
scomfisht,confiscated; destroyed,
```

David Elginbrod

Scotlan', Scotland,
scoug, stunted bush,
scunner, disgust; disgusting; revolting,
seein', seeing,
seemilies, similes,
see't, see it,
sel, self,
sel', self,
self-forgettin', self-forgetting,
sels, selves,
sempathy, sympathy,
semple, simple,
settisfaction, satisfaction,
settle, sofa,
shanna, shall not,
shavin', shaving; cutting,
shinin', shining,
shiverin', shivering,
shoon, shoes,
shouldna, should not,
sic, such,
sicht, sight,
sichts, sights,
siller, silver; money; wealth,
siller-bag, silver-bag; purse,
simmer, Summer,
sin', since,
sinfu', sinful,
singin', singing,
sinset, sunset,
sittin', sitting,
skelf, shelf, also splinter of wood
skelp-doup, lit. slap on the backside, derogatory term
sklet, (school) slate, also roofing slate
sma', small; little; slight; narrow,
sma'est, smallest; littlest; slightest; narrowest,
smoored, caught in; covered by; trapped in, also smothered
smorin', smothering; entrapping,
smut, dirt,
snaw, snow,
snaw-ba's, snowballs,
snaw-vraith, snow-wreath; snowdrift,
snaw-wreaths, snowdrifts,
somehoo, somehow,

David Elginbrod

```
soun',sound,
soundet,sounded,
souns,sounds,
soun's,sounds,
sowl,soul,
spak,spoke,
spak',spoke,
speakin',speaking,
speikin',speaking,
speyk,speak,
spier,ask; question; inquire,
spierin',asking; questioning; inquiring,
stamack,stomach,
stan',stand; stop,
stane,stone; measure of weight,1 stone = 14 pounds
stanes,stones,
stan'in',standing,
stappit,stopped; plugged,also stepped
starnies,little stars,diminutive
starns,stars,
steek,shut; close,also stitch (as in clothing)
steekit,shut; closed,
steekit neives,clenched fists,
stew,?,stew?
stour,dust,
strae,straw,
strang,strong; violent,
straucht,straighten,
straucht-foret,straightforward,
stravaguin',wandering; meandering,
streekit,stretched,
sud,should,
sune,soon; early,
suner,sooner,
supposin',supposing,
suspeecion,suspicion,
sut,?,suet?
syne,time; since; then,in (good) time
't,it,
tae,toe,also one
taen,taken; seized,
ta'en,taken; seized,
tak',take; seize,
tak' tent,look out; pay attention,
```

```
takin',taking,
taks,takes; seizes,
talans,talents,
tap,top,
tauld,told,
tay,tea,
te,to,
ted,fellow,
tee,'to ye' i.e. to you; also too,also tea
tellin',telling; relating,
tellt,told; related,
tent,attention,
thae,those,
thankfu',thankful,
that'll,that will,
the day,today,
the morn,tomorrow,
the nicht,tonight,
the noo,right now,
thegither,together,
themsels,themselves,
themsels',themselves,
thenk,think,
theroot,outside; out there,
thinkin',thinking,
this day week,in a week's time; a week from now,
thocht,thought,
thochtless,thoughtless,
thochts,thoughts,
thoom,thumb,
thrang,full; well filled; busy; crowd,
through't,through it,
throw't,through it,
till,to; till; until; about; towards,
till's,to his; to us,
till't,to it,
timmer,timber; wood,
tither,other,
tocher,dowry,
toddlin',toddling; walking unsteadily,
toot-moot,loud mouthed bantering,
tow,rope; string,
troth,truth; indeed,also used as an exclamation
trowth,truth; indeed,
```

David Elginbrod

```
truff,wood; material,
tummelin',tumbling,
turnin',turning,
twa,two,
'twar,it were,
'twas,it was,
'twere,it were; it was,
twise,twice,
tyauve,strive; struggle,
t'ye,to you,
unco,odd; strange; very,
understan',understand,
unnerstan',understand,
uphaud,uphold; maintain,
uphaudin',upholding; maintaining,
upo',upon,
upo't,upon it,
upricht,upright,
uptak,uptake; understanding,
veesible,visible,
veesits,visits,
verra,very; true; real,
vratch,wretch,
vrite,write,
wad,would,
wadna,would not,
waggin',wagging; nodding,
waggin' his heid,nodding his head (while preaching),
waitin',waiting,
wan,reached; gained; got,
want,want; lack; without; be in want of,
war,were,
wark,work; labour,
wark-hours,working hours,
warl',world,
warld,world,
warldly,worldly,
warna,were not,
warran',warrant; guarantee,
warst,worst,
warstle,wrestle,
wa's,walls,
wasna,was not,
was't,was it,
```

wastry,waste; extravagance,
wat,wet,see also 'I wat.'
waur,worse,
waurd,word,
we maun bide a wee,we need to wait a bit,
wean,child; infant,
weans,children; infants,
wee,small; little; bit,
weel,well; fine,
weel-faured,well favoured,
weicht,weight,
well-ee,well; pit; deep shaft,
we'se,we shall,
weyds,weeds,
wha,who,
wha',who,
wham,whom,
whan,when,
wha's,who is,
Wha's that o't?,Who is that?,
whase,whose,
What for no?,Why not?,
What for?,Why?,
whaur,where,
wheen,baby; little (adj.),
wheyt,wheat,
whiles,sometimes; at times,
wi,with,
wi',with,
wilfu',wilful,
willin',willing,
win,reach; gain; get,
win',wind,
winlestrae,straw dried on its root,weak willed; easily lead astray
winna,will not,
winnock,window,
wintin',wanting; without,
wi'out,without,
wis',wish,
wi't,with it,
wonner,wonder; marvel,
wonnerfu',wonderful,
wonnerfully,wonderfully,
woo',wool,

David Elginbrod

```
woosh,washed,
wrang,wrong,
wrang-duins,wrongdoings; misdeeds,
wud,wood; forest,adj.-enraged; angry; also would
wull,will; desire; pleasure; Will(iam),also astray; stray; wild
wull hizzie,wild hussy,
wuman,woman,
wumman,woman,
ye,you,
ye'll,you will,
yer,your,
ye'r,you are,
ye're,you are,
yersel,yourself,
yersel',yourself,
ye'se,you shall,
yestreen,yesterday (evening),
ye've,you have,
yon's,yonder is; that (thing) there is,
yow-lammie,ewe lamb; runaway,diminutive
```

Printed in the United States
40950LVS00005B/10